TEAM OF STEVES

TEAM OF STEVES

Scott R. Weinstein

Copyright © 2019 Scott R. Weinstein
All rights reserved
ISBN 978-1-7336771-0-3

PRAISE FOR *TEAM OF STEVES*

"*Team of Steves* is both every teenagers worst nightmare and dream come true. An adventure full of shocks, excitement and crushing embarrassment. Join the Steve Team!"
- Judd Winick
Hilo Graphic Novels

"*Team of Steves* takes many of my favorite things -- teen comedies, inter-dimensional travel, dudes named Steve -- and whisks them into a smart, surprising and sincere page-turner. Somewhere, in a parallel universe, another version of me is reading this book for the first time and loving every second of it."
- Whitney Matheson
USA Today's "Pop Candy"

"*Team of Steves* is wonderfully fun and exceedingly clever. It's a well-crafted story that goes in unexpected directions, subverts expectations and is still completely rewarding. I want more, please."
- Thom Zahler
Love and Capes, Warning Label

"In *Team of Steves*, Scott Weinstein not only recreates the angst, joy, and madness of being a teen, but deftly juggles four somewhat similar yet very different main characters, as all four learn about each other... but maybe more about themselves... along the way."
- Todd Dezago
Spider-Man, Tellos, The Perhapanauts

"It's human nature to fantasize about lives we might have lived, especially when we're hormonal, awkward teenagers. Scott has put a clever and unique twist on a story of self-discovery with *Team of Steves*. A refreshing blend of sci-fi, humor, heart... and Steves."
- Joe Kelly
I Kill Giants, Ben 10, Spider-Man/Deadpool

To Abby,

For listening to me talk about this book for WAY longer than anyone should ever have to.

Chapter 1

"In what universe do you think that would work?" Mr. White laughed.

Steve Buchmann ran his fingers through his red, shaggy hair, puffing it out another five inches. This was exactly why he didn't raise his hand in physics anymore. That vindictive man never wasted a single opportunity to humiliate him.

Mr. White leaned against the dry-erase board, getting fresh marker all over the back of his short-sleeve button-down shirt. "The equation Mr. Buchmann used was all wrong. We're trying to determine momentum. Mr. Buchmann's solution would have failed miserably." He chuckled again to emphasize how wrong Steve was.

It had taken Steve since the moment class had started that morning to work up the courage to raise his hand. Before that, he hadn't said anything in class for weeks, not since just after the fall semester had started. Steve loved science. This physics class was his dream. But Mr. White seemed determined to ruin it for him. From the second he had first walked into the classroom, Steve found himself in Mr. White's crosshairs. This was solely because of his last name.

What made this whole situation worse was that Steve's equation *did* work. Steve discovered that the night before, while doing the problem set. It was a simpler solution than what Mr. White wanted them to use, and it was far more accurate. Steve had stayed up until one testing his theory on a dozen other equations. Each time, he got the correct answer. It was a very exciting night for the fifteen-year-old high school sophomore.

It really was. Nights like that were what he loved about science. Making connections that had eluded others and opening up a new way of seeing the world was thrilling. With the right formulas and instruments, Steve could one day explain all the mysteries of the universe.

"Let's look at another problem. We have two people..." Mr. White turned back to the board to draw two crude versions of humans falling from the sky. Even with arms fully extended, the diminutive Mr. White could only reach a third of the way up the board. "One weighs seventy kilograms. The other weighs one hundred kilograms. But, this time, cut by half the height at which the fall starts. How does that change the formula?"

It meant they would never reach terminal velocity. Steve knew that immediately, then readjusted the formula in his head to compensate. As he had realized last night, his method easily accounted for the change. Without scribbling anything in the open notebook in front of him, he had revised the numbers before anyone else in the class raised their hand. No matter how confident he was in his math, Steve was not about to make the same mistake twice and challenge Mr. White with his modified formula.

This frustrated Steve even more. He didn't doubt he was right. His work backed it up. He was just too scared to confront Mr. White. Now Steve was getting mad. Five minutes ago he was ready to turn things around for himself in class. Now he was back where he started, afraid of Mr. White. In the time Steve had spent berating himself, no one else had raised their hand. They were all facedown in their notebooks, furiously scribbling out equations. This only made Steve feel worse for his cowardice.

Then out of the corner of his eye, Steve saw one hand go up. He risked a glance to his left. It was Becky Anderson, her arm was locked straight up, fingers pointing to the ceiling. It remained there, alone. Mr. White's gaze drifted to his right, them immediately shot back to the other side of the room, avoiding Becky completely.

Becky was very smart. In the other classes Steve had with her, she never failed to impress him with her scientific understanding. But she was wasting her time now. Mr. White never called on the girls in class. No matter how many of them raised their hands, he just ignored them. It didn't matter if they were asking a question, volunteering to solve a problem, or asking to go to the bathroom, he appeared to have no use for their presence.

Another minute went by and no more hands were raised. Mr. White let his head hang in frustration, still careful to not look in Becky's direction. "Really? Not one of you knows? That's pathetic. I thought only Mr. Buchmann would disappoint me today."

Steve tensed, wanting to scream out the answer he knew was right. Instead he looked away and saw Becky's fingers straining for Mr. White's attention. Steve wouldn't take a chance, and here was Becky not giving up, no matter how futile it was.

"Someone must at least have a guess." Mr. White laughed at how ridiculous that proposal would be.

"Becky does." Ice water ran through Steve's veins when he

realized he had muttered that out loud. The shock of what he said was reflected on the faces of everyone in the class, especially Becky's.

The only person more surprised by Steve's outburst was Mr. White. "What was that?"

Steve froze.

Justin Bloomfield, who sat in front of Steve, straightened up his lanky beanpole body in his seat. He looked back at Steve when he offered Mr. White his recap. "Steve said that Big Beck knows the answer."

Mr. White did not correct the cruel nickname that haunted the overweight Becky. "Is that so, Mr. Buchmann? Do you think I am unaware of what is happening in my classroom? Who are you to presume to tell *me* how to teach physics?"

"I... um..." Steve searched for some way to explain himself that didn't involve calling Mr. White a chauvinist.

"Why are you so concerned about Becky? She can speak for herself. You are being very protective. Is she your girlfriend?"

Steve just shook his head.

A cruel smile crossed Mr. White's face. "No? Is Becky not good enough to be your girlfriend? I think someone like you would be lucky to date a girl as sweet as Becky."

Any power of speech Steve had left vanished. He looked at Becky. Her hand was down now and covering her very red face. Steve had dragged her down to a new level of humiliation. Before it could get any worse, the bell sounded. Becky was out of her seat and through the door before the electronic chime ended.

The rest of the class was not as quick in leaving. "The problem set for this weekend's homework is posted. Upload your answers to my page by nine A.M. Monday." Mr. White was always able to get out the homework assignment before anyone could leave the room. "And, Mr. Buchmann, I need you to stay behind for a few minutes."

Steve sat in his chair as the rest of the class filed out, like a prisoner on display. It would have been the perfect humiliation cherry on top of his day if Madison Parker hadn't stopped in front of his desk. She leaned forward and her hand lightly touched his forearm. Blood rushed so loudly through Steve's body, he could barely hear when she whispered, "Thank you for trying." As quickly as she appeared before him, she whipped her long brunette ponytail around and walked out of class. A whiff of her strawberry-scented perfume lingered.

THWACK!

Justin's hand landed dead center on the back of Steve's head. "Toolbox!" Justin shouted at Steve as he barreled into the hallway. That was fun while it lasted. Steve managed to hold off rubbing his head until everyone was out of the room. The whole time, the ghost of Justin's long, stringy fingers haunted his scalp.

Mr. White, pulling up his forever-drooping pants, sauntered over to Steve. Even still seated, Steve, who was stuck at five-foot-five, waiting for a long-promised growth spurt, was eye to eye with Mr. White. Pushing his glasses back up the bridge of his nose, Mr. White said, "I'll get right to the point. You should consider transferring."

Steve flinched. "Transfer out of this class?"

"No. This school. Clearly you're not up to par with the others. That was more than obvious today. This is a demanding program. I would normally not say anything, but I am concerned about past mistakes being repeated."

He was referring to mistakes made by Steve's mom, Melissa. The investigation had placed the blame for the accident at Stepstone Labs on her. That was certainly easy to do, since she had died in the explosion and couldn't defend herself. Regardless, the accident had cost many people their jobs, including Mr. White.

"If you want to stay, that's fine," Mr. White continued, "but don't expect me to keep coddling you."

That had been coddling? Steve hadn't broken the C barrier all year. Every homework assignment and test was torn apart by Mr. White's red pen. He had found a way to deduct points for everything, even when Steve had the right answer. Forget participating in any class discussion. Mr. White relished publicly decimating Steve.

"So now you have nothing to say?" Mr. White shook his head.

The blood pounding in Steve's brain made it hard to think. He had plenty to say. None of it would have helped, and some may have gotten him expelled. Fortunately, he was saved when the bell rang again.

Mr. White pointed to the door. "You should get going. You're late for your next class."

"I don't know why you don't just tell that guy off." Noah Evans straightened out the collar on his paint-covered blazer, which contrasted nicely with his vintage baggy skater jeans and his pajama top that he was wearing as a shirt. "You're already smarter than him."

"It's not that bad. Besides, that would just make things way worse." Steve unloaded his overstuffed backpack into his locker, then began carefully sorting his books into their proper places.

"How? By standing up for yourself?"

"Noah, it's not like an Art Sider class. I can't argue the aesthetic value of a formula." Steve stood on his tiptoes so he could study the spines of the books he needed for the afternoon. These lockers were not designed for a sophomore still cursed with the body of a middle schooler. "Besides, what if I say something wrong? I don't want to risk that."

"So what? You're wrong. Big deal. White's an ass!" Noah adjusted the piece of duct tape that was holding his left shoe together.

"Shh!" Steve pointed to the row of students at their lockers. Each, like Steve, was wearing a variation of the Sci Sider's unofficial dress code: a button-down shirt and nice pants or a skirt. Noah's Art Side attire was a hot, flashing radioactive warning sign in a sea of beige conformity.

That difference was at the very heart of the Sinatra Edison Magnet School for the Arts and Sciences. New Jersey's premier high school was a happy accident born out of a budget crisis. In richer days, the state had plans for two magnificent magnet schools in the heart of Longview: one for the arts and one for the sciences. Then the money went away. All that was left was an overcrowded school where two completely opposite types of people separated themselves with a strict, self-imposed, figurative Berlin Wall. Students on the Art Side and students on the Sci Side refused to mingle. They insisted that their classes be either one hundred percent Art Sider or Sci Sider—no tourists allowed. Extracurricular activities were even more strictly divided. No one on either side was willing to incur the wrath of the school by crossing over... except for Noah.

As Noah continued to look down the row of highly focused Sci Siders, Steve realized Noah had completely missed his point about being in enemy territory. Noah's gaze was focused on a junior opening her locker at the end of the hall. He then buttoned his massive blazer. That past summer he had dragged Steve to a big and tall outlet store, specifically to rummage through their discontinued bin for the biggest jacket

Noah could find. He told Steve he loved how it made him look like he'd recently lost two hundred pounds.

"I'll be right back." Noah patted Steve on the shoulder and headed toward the girl.

Steve grabbed Noah's jacket and pulled him back. "Whoa! Hold on a second. What was your promise?"

Noah sighed. "That I'd run my plans by you first."

"Right. So what were you going to say to Kayla?"

"Her name's Kayla? I can work with that." Noah nodded to himself. "I was going to ask to take a picture of her hair."

"You just want to photograph her hair?"

"Yeah! It's genius. I tell her I'm working on a painting and her hair is the exact right color I've been looking for. So I need a picture of it for reference. Here's the brilliant part: I actually paint something using the color and show her. Then I have her eating out of the palm of my hand."

As promised, Steve considered Noah's proposal for a full ten seconds. "That would have an 89.4 percent chance of failure."

"Come on! I've never tried that before."

"I'm extrapolating from previous attempts."

"Really?"

"Yes." Steve began an imaginary PowerPoint presentation showing his thought process. "The four times that you've told a girl that something about her inspired you, they all called you a creep and stormed off."

"All four times?"

"Yeah, and that's before I factor in the ones who completely ignored you."

Steve watched Noah's face drop. His swagger and excitement dimmed as the harsh reality of his romantic prospects sunk in. Doing some quick calculations, Steve smiled and grabbed Noah by the shoulders. "*But*, here's the good news. I also did a detailed response analysis of the five times you've presented a girl with artwork, one of those girls said—and I'm quoting directly—'That's awesome.' Aaannnd she *hugged* you!"

Noah's eyes lit up as he remembered that glorious moment. "Oh yeah! Dana Ashford... Why didn't she ever go out with me?"

"You wouldn't let go when she stopped hugging you."

"Oh, right..."

Before Noah's hopes crashed again, Steve continued. "So, according to my calculations, you have a 22.6 percent chance of success if you give her a sketch. The odds increase by 4.3 percent if the sketch is not of her but of a neutral subject. Maybe one of the view from the overlook in Mountainside. Then... I don't know... ask her to take a walk there with you."

"That's a great idea!" Noah looked off as he considered the details of Steve's proposal. "But... *screw that*! Keep your math numbers. I'm sticking with my original plan."

As the bell sounded, signaling the start of lunch, Noah smoothed out his jacket. "I want you to pay attention. I'm doing this to inspire you. You're too scared of following your heart and taking chances." Noah marched toward Kayla.

"A stalker! She called me a *stalker*! Sci Sider women have no sense of whimsy." Noah dragged his feet as he followed Steve through the Sinatra Edison lunchroom.

Steve had been worried that Noah's attempt would eat into their twenty minute lunch period. Fortunately, it was over and done with moments after it started, leaving him plenty of time to eat. He just needed to get to his table before Noah launched into a full-fledged anti-Sci Sider tirade.

The traditional high school social divisions didn't plague the lunchroom at Sinatra Edison. There were no separate jock, nerd, pretty people tables to be found. Here, there was only one distinction: Sci Side and Art Side. In fact, the distribution of tables literally divided the lunchroom in half. There was no actual line on the floor, but it could be easily plotted by the way the tables were laid out. Each side played their roles as expected. The Sci Side was orderly and respectful. Students sat in their seats, having quiet conversations the whole time. At the end of the meal, all tables were cleared. Not on the Art Side. It was a constant mass of people intermingling, jumping around, and randomly breaking into song.

This presented a problem for Steve and Noah. They had been friends since long before they went to Sinatra Edison. Just two years after Steve lost his mom, Noah's dad died of a massive heart attack. At the time they were both in seventh grade at Longview Middle School. While the twelve year-old boys had all the same classes, they had never hung out at all. The news about Noah's dad had spread quickly through the school. For Steve it brought back fresh memories of the loneliness he felt when his mom had died. When he saw Noah sitting alone at lunch one day, Steve joined him. The two bonded over their mutual loss, even though neither actually talked about it. From there, their friendship solidified. The two were so inseparable that when Steve got accepted into Sinatra Edison's science program, Noah applied to the magnet school's art program. Once there, neither was ready to let the school's divide truly push them apart... no matter how strictly the separate sides were maintained.

While people mixed and matched which tables they sat at every day, being on the wrong side of the cafeteria was never tolerated. Enforcers like Justin were happy to drag any ignorant freshman Art Sider across the cafeteria to help them learn their place. So rather than cause a scene to sit with his friend, Steve came up with a solution. Two tables at the end of the cafeteria were next to each other, but still on opposite sides of the border. Steve sat at one, Noah at the other. Next to each other, but separate... and separated from everyone else.

"Look at them." Noah gestured to the tables full of Sci Siders on Steve's half of the cafeteria. Steve was grateful that Noah had managed to hold in his monologue this long, but Noah was quite capable of projecting his voice. Hoping to avoid attracting more attention, Steve lifted his chair before sliding it away from the table. Noah let his chair scrape against the floor, which was slightly less noisy than beating a metal trash can with a hammer.

"The problem is Sci Siders are cold. They have no compassion." Noah dropped down into his chair and hung his head over the back in Steve's general direction.

"Not all of them." Steve corrected Noah as he took his lunch out of his backpack. "Madison was really nice to me today."

"Wait a second! Madison as in *Madison Parker* Madison?" Noah stood and pointed over Steve's shoulder into the Sci Sider half of the cafeteria toward Madison's table.

"Sit down." Steve jumped up, crossed the Sci Sider/Art Sider line, pulled down Noah's arm and pushed him back into his chair. Hoping Madison didn't notice, Steve dashed back to his side and started unwrapping his turkey sandwich.

"What did she do?" Noah had clearly forgotten about his recent failure with Kayla.

"She thanked me for standing up for Becky." Steve couldn't help but smile.

"Hold on! She thanked you for something you didn't even do for *her*?" Once again Noah was on his feet scanning the Sci Sider half of the room.

Steve dropped his sandwich and scrambled back to Noah's table, pulling him back into his seat. "Stop that. What's wrong with you?"

"What's wrong with you? Madison's totally into you?"

"Because she was being polite? You're the only person I know who'd think that was a declaration of love." Steve's heart was pounding from dashing back and forth between tables. He pulled a water bottle out of his backpack and took a sip.

"Love isn't some logical equation to be solved with an abacus, you cold-blooded nerd!"

Steve spat out his water, laughing.

Despite knowing better than to listen to Noah's advice on romance, he glanced over at Madison. She was sitting three tables away, surrounded by her friends. As opposed to Steve, who was sitting alone on the edge of the Sci Side/Art Side neutral zone.

"What am I supposed to do? Ask her out after she said one thing to me? What if she says no?" Steve took a bite of his turkey sandwich.

"I have a better idea," Noah declared as he turned around in his chair to face Steve's back.

"No thanks."

"Hold on. This is a great one... Try out for the play." Noah waited for a "That's brilliant!" that wasn't coming.

Steve took another bite of his turkey sandwich rather than answering Noah.

"Oh, come on. You know it's a good idea. You love acting. And you're awesome at it."

"Are you talking about our Iron Man fan film from eighth grade?"

"Yeah. You were a better Tony Stark than Robert Downey Jr. But I'm also talking about last year when we saw the spring play. You were so excited about coming here and getting a chance to be in a show."

He had been. Everyone on that stage looked like they were having an amazing time. Steve hadn't dreamed that he could follow his passion during the day, then do something as cool as acting after school as well. That lasted until his first day at Sinatra Edison. "Then I found out Sci Siders can't audition," Steve said through a mouthful of sandwich. He noticed Noah had not taken out a lunch bag. It was the second time this week he had forgotten to pack it.

"They *can*. There's no official school policy against it. They just don't."

"Right... that's why there are so many Art Siders on the Mathletes." Steve reached back across the divide to hand Noah the untouched half of his sandwich. "I'm not going to finish this."

"Thanks. Dude, no one wants to join the Mathletes. Math is boring." Noah pressed the entire half of the sandwich into his mouth.

"No, it's not—" Steve tried to protest.

"I know for a fact that there's another Sci Sider who's been talking about trying out for the play. A certain brown-eyed girl..."

"Madison?" Steve shook his head.

"Not yet. But I heard Sherri talking to Tina about it. They said she wants to but she's scared of the whole Sci Sider boycott." Noah leaned back in his chair to get closer to Steve. "Here's a scenario. You're all brave and cross the lines to try out. Clear the way for her. Then it's just two Sci Siders all alone in the scary Art Sider world. Think about it."

It was all Steve could think about.

Chapter 2

"There's no place left for you to run, you pathetic traitor!"

Steve could feel the blade of the sword digging further into his back. There wasn't much room to maneuver in here. Diving left or right would put him face-first into a wall. Behind him lay certain death. The only solution was up. Leaping straight into the air, he burst through the roof of the structure. His assailant was stunned long enough for Steve to grab the enchanted sword out of his hands. Flinging it to the side, he grabbed the armor-clad enemy and spun him in a circle. The assailant squealed with delight.

"That's not fair, Steve! You can't do that!" Josh was laughing as Steve dropped him on the remnants of the pillow fort.

"I totally can. I activated the enlargement nanobots that live in my bloodstream," Steve informed his little brother.

"Stop making stuff up." As Josh struggled to stand up, Steve pushed him back onto the pillows. This led to another explosion of laughter.

"Nanobots are real," Steve explained. "In fact, they're the

future of medicine. Imagine only needing one shot your entire life and you would never have to—"

"Who cares? Nanotechnology isn't in the Echelon books." For a ten-year-old, Josh had a remarkably annoying sense of official canon.

"Well, I'm bigger than you and I say I can use them." Steve lifted Josh into the air again. Josh was not having it this time.

"I'm serious. Rebuild the fort. I had you cornered," Josh demanded as his brother set him back on the floor.

"Belay that order." Daniel Buchmann struck a heroic pose in the doorway of the living room. "The mission on Rigel 18 is over. You have new orders, Mr. Buchmann. Time to pack up."

"Dad! There are so many things wrong with what you just said." Josh freed himself from Steve's grip.

"Unless all those things are about how you're already packed and ready to go, I don't want to hear it. Aunt Leslie will be here in ten minutes." This weekend their dad was going away to the Poconos with his girlfriend, Nicole. Since Steve and Josh were not invited, Josh was spending the weekend with Aunt Leslie. At fifteen, Steve was allowed to stay at home by himself.

Their dad snatched up two pillows from the ruins of the fort. At just over six feet tall, Daniel Buchmann was the only hope Steve had that he would possibly one day actually have that long-promised growth spurt. There was no grunting sigh from the nearly fifty-year-old man as he squatted down to clean up the floor. Even as a jaded teen, Steve was able to appreciate how in-shape his dad was. All of this would have given Steve hope for his physical future if he hadn't looked exactly like his mother.

On the other hand, Josh and his father were the same person, separated by forty years. For every angular, sharp feature that Steve and his mother had shared, Josh and their dad were rounder and softer. They weren't overweight—at least, Dad certainly wasn't. It was just a little hard to tell if Josh had ever lost his baby fat. Family gatherings were a nightmare for Josh's cheeks.

"Ha! The joke's on you. I packed already." Josh pulled a small rolling suitcase over from the corner of the room.

"Wait. You packed your own bag?" Dad was floored.

Steve stumbled over the pillows to the suitcase. "Without anyone having to tell you what to bring?"

"Yeah. I'm ten. What's so hard to believe about that?" Josh was getting irritated.

"You still make Dad tuck you in at night," Steve noted.

"You can't remember our phone number," their father pointed out.

"You won't go into the basement alone," Steve piled on.

"You forget to flush the toilet... even when it's number two."

Steve smiled, ready for his killer blow. "You make us—"

"Did you put my bag in the car already?" a cold voice interrupted Steve, ending their game. Her tight jeans hugged her hips and her cleavage bounced in a low-cut tank top as she entered the living room. This kind of display would normally have grabbed Steve's attention, except these revealing curves belonged to Nicole, his dad's girlfriend.

"Not yet. It's still in the bedroom." Dad's voice got more grave. The time for fun was over.

"What are you guys doing?" Nicole asked, clearly forcing a smile. Steve set down the suitcase and started putting the couch back together. She was a reporter at the station where Dad was a producer. The trip was to celebrate her latest story that exposed two researchers at Tarp Scientific, who had falsified the results of their tests on a new synthetic material they had developed.

"I was just making sure Josh was packed and ready when Leslie picks him up." Dad pulled Nicole over to him and kissed her on the forehead. "Then we can start our road trip."

Steve punched the last pillow into place on the couch.

"And I told you, I'm packed," Josh insisted.

"Then you won't mind if I check your bag?" Dad opened Josh's suitcase, and his head slumped. "This is just full of action figures. There are no clothes in here. We'll be gone for three days. You at least need a change of underwear."

"Why?" Josh asked.

"You know you can't wear the same clothes every day, right?" Nicole's question had the same tone as if she were asking a mechanic about ripping off a customer.

Josh was silent.

"You *do* know that?" Now Dad was concerned.

"They do it in cartoons all the time. I'll be fine." Josh closed his suitcase.

Steve could tell by the smile on Dad's face that rather than lay down the law with Josh, he was choosing the faster and easier route of bribery. "I figured you'd be a little nicer to me today. Considering what I did for you guys."

Steve froze with a couch cushion still in his hand. Josh looked at his brother. The same smile was forming on both of their faces.

"You got them?" Steve blurted.

"Yup." His father nodded proudly.

Josh leapt into Steve's arms and they spun around the living room. Dad smiled. He had given his boys Christmas early this year. Nicole stepped back to the edge of the room to avoid the maelstrom of joy.

"What's the matter with them?" she asked Daniel.

"*Reflex!*" Josh screamed. "We're going to see *Reflex*."

"The movie?" Nicole tried to clarify.

"Yeah!" Josh screeched.

Nicole covered her ears. "Of course you are. Everyone is going to see it. It's tracking to the be the biggest blockbuster of the year."

Dad rested his hands on her shoulders and kissed her cheek. "I got them into that advanced press screening. They're going to see it two weeks before it opens."

For over twenty years, Dad had been a producer with New Jersey Channel 14, the state's number one channel for all things New Jersey. It was also the only channel for all things New Jersey.

"That's... nice," Nicole offered.

"It's amazing!" Steve corrected. "I've been waiting to see this movie since I was a kid."

A frozen smile creaked across Nicole's face as she gave a slight nod of acknowledgement.

"So." Daniel pointed to Josh. "Please pack some clothes."

Josh may have said yes, but it was lost in a blur as he dashed up the stairs. Daniel looked to Nicole. "Would you mind helping him? His manic energy doesn't give me much faith that he'll actually pack the right clothes."

Nicole looked up the stairs, listening to Josh's excited yelps about *Reflex* coming from his room. "I should really finish putting on my makeup." She left the room before Steve's dad could respond.

Steve and his father looked at each other. Dad took a breath, like he was ready to explain something he wasn't sure he needed to explain. Before that could happen, Steve returned to reassembling the couch.

"You'll be OK?" Dad asked.

Steve abandoned his task and faced his dad. "Yeah. I can stay by myself for a weekend."

"No. I know." Steve's dad watched him. "I'm talking about

next month. I want to make sure that you... *like* Nicole and are really OK with her moving in."

"Sure. She's nice. It'll be great." Steve looked his dad in the eye and nodded cheerily.

"Hello?" Aunt Leslie yelled from the front hallway.

"In the living room," Dad yelled back.

"*In the living room*," Aunt Leslie replied in her best impression of Daniel. "Hiiii, Stevie." Fifteen years old and she still kissed him all over his face like he was an adorable infant.

Calling her an "aunt" wasn't accurate. Well, she was an aunt, just not theirs. When Steve was first born, his mom used to push him in his stroller up and down the mountain every day. Leslie lived at the bottom of their street. One day she stopped Melissa to see the block's newest resident. They talked for five hours straight. From that day forward, she was a permanent part of their lives, whether they wanted her or not.

"Where is the monster child you're abandoning?" Aunt Leslie asked, as she dashed around the living room looking for Josh. This was a remarkable feat for a woman her age, though Steve could never figure out exactly how old she was. Her hair was auburn with not a single speck of grey. But her skin was so wrinkly that her wrinkles had wrinkles. She looked like a giant balloon that had deflated. Whenever he asked her age, she would only say, "Too old to have to answer that question." Based on empirical evidence that he had gathered about Aunt Leslie, including historical references she had made, the length of time she had lived in Longview, and how much her body seemed to have shrunk, he estimated her age to be around infinity years old.

A rushing pair of feet and a heavy bouncing suitcase heralded Josh's return. He flew through the room, dropped his bag, and barreled into Aunt Leslie's arms. "Did you charge your camera?" Josh blurted.

Aunt Leslie grunted as she lifted Josh in a bear hug. "Daniel, what are you feeding this kid?"

"If we clear out a work space in your basement tonight, we can start right away in the morning on the Battle of Harold's Hall." Josh had apparently started this conversation in his head a few minutes ago and felt no need to bring anyone else up to speed.

The baffled looks from everyone else prompted Steve. "From the Echelons of War books," he said. "Echelon," as fans called it, was *Game of Thrones* for tweens. It had all the palace intrigue, dragons, and war and none of the sex, incest, or torture.

That didn't clear anything up for them, but Josh continued explaining his plan anyway. "I think I know how Keepstone's forces could have countered Stockcar's charge and won the battle."

"You sure you don't want to join us?" Aunt Leslie pleaded with Steve.

Before Steve could reply, Nicole rejoined them with her rolling suitcase. "We should go before traffic gets too heavy. All that stopping and starting makes me carsick."

Steve sighed and slipped past Nicole into the hall. He was headed for the back room den behind the kitchen, where he wouldn't have to listen to Nicole.

Chapter 3

Kieron Gill leaned forward, one hand holding his studio headphones in place as he spoke into his mic. "So how long exactly did you have to suffer through the 'Nicole Era'?"

"It felt like a billion cosmic years." Steve chuckled at his reference. "But I guess it's been a little over a year."

"What did your dad see in her?" Kieron stroked his beard.

"I have no idea. Maybe it has something to do with their jobs. She's a reporter at his station. Other than that—"

HONK!

Steve snapped out of his fantasy conversation. A car on the street next to him had blared its horn just before one of Steve's neighbors almost backed her minivan down the driveway into them. The car on the street screeched off as soon as the minivan completely stopped. It took Steve the rest of the block to remember where he was in his imaginary interview.

Steve resumed. "Nicole is the coldest, most uninteresting person I have ever met. She never gets any of my dad's jokes. I know he's corny. But he's still a funny guy. And the worst part is she pretends to laugh with the fakest smile I've ever seen."

Inertia, Kieron Gill's top-rated podcast, was Steve's fantasy interview of choice. It was his dream to one day be an actual guest on the show. Any scientist of any note in the country had been a guest on *Inertia*. They would spend a little time talking about their discoveries, but the real draw of the show was Kieron's ability to get his guests to open up and reveal their innermost feelings. Steve loved the podcast and had listened to every second of each episode. Anytime he walked somewhere, he liked to pretend he was a guest on the show. It was his own version of therapy.

"If she was so wrong for him, why didn't you say something to your dad?"

Steve leaned back in his seat. "A couple of years ago, Dad was dating this woman Diane he met on an app. It only lasted a month or so. I think she was like twenty-five years old."

"Sounds a little young for your father."

"No kidding. Aunt Leslie thought the same thing. One day she told Dad she'd watch Diane for him if he needed a babysitter. He got so mad at Aunt Leslie that he threw her out of the house. It was three weeks before he apologized to her. That also happened to be when he finally broke up with Diane."

"You think your dad would do the same thing to you if you told him how you feel about Nicole?"

"Maybe not that bad. But he seems happy. He's been alone since Mom died. I don't want to upset him. I can pretend to be happy. It won't be that hard. College is only... three years away."

Ten minutes after his dad and Nicole had left, Steve set out for Mountainside Park. Any time he spent with Nicole made him tense, and sitting around the house that she was soon going to invade did not help. He had only gone a few blocks from his house and was already feeling more relaxed.

"Enough about your dad's love life. You, my friend, have scored yourself a bona fide hottie."

"Yup. Madison. It all started when I stood up for Becky. That really impressed her."

Steve smiled in his fantasy and in his real life. The interview trailed off as the image of Madison and her lips popped into his head. Then as he replayed her whispering "Thank you" to him, his thoughts drifted from her face to the rest of her body.

That delightful fantasy was shattered by a very panicked voice calling Steve's name. He looked around, realizing that he was in front of Dr. Edward Hicks's house. Steve had been walking for ten minutes, just long enough for him to completely zone out in his imaginary role as podcast guest. One block past Hicks's house was the entrance to Mountainside Park. Dr. Hicks's pickup truck was parked in the driveway, next to his back door. Standing behind the truck, Dr. Hicks looked more like a homeless man than a brilliant physicist. He was actually a few years younger than Steve's dad, but his scraggily gray hair and thin, brittle frame made him seem much older. Dr. Hicks was trying to unload a massive crate that was hanging over the edge of the flatbed. He had pulled it that far before it started tipping toward him. Now it was sliding out of the truck, seconds away from crushing him to death.

Steve leapt up into the flatbed, grabbed one of the crate's handles, and pulled it back toward him. Though all that Steve's 120-pound body managed to do was slow the crate's decent. "Uh... Dr. Hicks..." Steve tried to swallow his panic.

After years of being in similar situations, Dr. Hicks's reaction was one of puzzlement more than fright. This was just another physics equation that happened to involve real world conditions and potential crushed legs. "Grab the crate by the bottom," Dr. Hicks instructed Steve.

"Won't that leave it—"

"I know. It's fine."

Steve lifted up the bottom of the crate, bracing for Dr. Hicks's anguished scream. Instead, the crate began a controlled rotation. Using the edge of the truck as a fulcrum, Hicks eased his end onto the ground.

"Is it OK that it's upside down?" Steve looked at the THIS END UP arrow that was pointing toward the ground.

"Uh... probably." Dr. Hicks knocked on the side of the crate as if that could really determine how well the contents were packaged.

Now that the massive crate was settled on the ground, Steve had a second to process what the two of them had tried to wrangle and wondered just how Dr. Hicks, who was a head shorter than Steve, thought he would do this by himself. For more than a decade, Dr. Hicks had worked for Steve's mother at Stepstone. She had always talked about how dedicated he was. Although Steve wondered what kind of dedication would make Dr. Hicks try to move a massive box on his own.

As Steve studied the crate, another label caught his attention. "Is this a generator?"

"Um... yes." Dr. Hicks was now studying the distance from the crate to his back door.

"Are you testing it soon?" Steve asked, following Dr. Hicks's gaze to the door that led to his basement lab. As quickly as the excitement came, Steve felt it fading from his face.

For a brief time, Steve had been an assistant to Dr. Hicks, who had set out on a mission to prove that Melissa Buchmann's design for a Wireless Energy Transmitter would have worked. Steve had never believed the accident was his mother's fault. Helping Dr. Hicks had been his chance to help prove she wasn't responsible. Without any funding, or any job of any kind, Dr. Hicks's work moved slowly. Steve did mostly grunt work, recording measurements, fetching tools, and occasionally soldering a circuit board or two. It had been exhilarating for Steve to be doing the work his mother had started. But it wouldn't last more than a few months. When Steve came home with one too many set of cuts and bruises due to Dr. Hicks's lax safety standards, his dad banned him from working with Dr. Hicks again.

"Possibly. There are still several settings I need to adjust." Dr. Hicks was wheeling a dolly over when he noticed Steve's expression. "I was planning to inform you. I was just—"

"That's OK." Steve forced a smile. "I totally understand. I can wait until you're ready."

As Dr. Hicks worked to edge the crate onto the dolly by himself, Steve rushed over. "Here. Let me help."

"That's not necessary." Dr. Hicks wheeled the crate toward the back door, leaving Steve alone by the truck.

"I guess I'll talk to you later."

Those words seeped through the haze of Dr. Hicks's focus. "Yes... of course." He let go of the crate and turned to Steve. "Has school started yet?"

"Like three months ago."

"Do you have Timothy White for any of your classes?"

"Yeah, for physics."

"He used to work for us at Stepstone. If he ever gives you any trouble, let me know."

"That would be awesome! Thanks." Steve laughed, mainly because he couldn't imagine a worse idea.

They looked at each other in silence. Steve watched Dr. Hicks wait a socially acceptable amount of time before he returned to his task. With a sigh, Steve continued on his walk. It had been over six months since he had last worked with Dr. Hicks. In that time, school, Mr. White, Madison, and Nicole had come to dominate his life. Steve was hit with a shocking amount of guilt over how quickly he had forgotten about redeeming his mother.

A couple of tourists were huffing their way up the long, snaking path that led into Mountainside Park. Steve sprinted past them. When he got to the abandoned information booth at the gate, he looked back down at the tourists as they struggled to catch their breath. They stared up at him in awe. But there was nothing special about Steve. Any Longview local could make the steep walk up to the park without getting winded. The whole town was built on the side of a mountain in the Watchung range, and walking uphill everywhere was a fact of life.

Mountainside Park covered the very top of the mountain overlooking Longview, which was spread out on the slope beneath it. The centerpiece of the park and Steve's destination that afternoon was the Essex County Aqueduct. It was a fifty-mile-long engineering marvel that was designed to transport water from a lake in New York State to Northern New Jersey. Art Deco arches supported a massive concrete-enclosed pipe thirty feet off the ground. Each set of legs was spaced a football field apart and contained more pipes that fed water to other towns it passed through. It would have worked flawlessly, except for an interstate fight over who actually owned the water in the lake. As a result, the aqueduct never delivered a single drop of water anywhere.

Whenever Steve needed to escape his troubles, he went straight to the park. His family had a favorite getaway at the northernmost edge of the park, where the mountain ridge dropped away and the aqueduct soared over a hidden valley protected from the busy hiking trails. In the shade of the massive structure, the pale Buchmanns could spend hours undisturbed.

This was also where Steve first fell in love with science. One Sunday, their mom sent him and Josh to either end of the valley, where they waited by the main body of the aqueduct. She plugged a portable speaker into her phone and placed it flat against the support leg at the bottom of the valley. Since no water had ever been pumped through the aqueduct's massive pipe system, it was just a giant echo chamber.

Eight-year-old Steve was fascinated by that demonstration. When his mother explained sound waves, his mind exploded. A new world had opened up to him, and he was hooked. From that point on, every picnic involved Mom explaining a new scientific principle. It was a tradition that they continued until the week she died.

As Steve sat down against one of the aqueduct supports, he watched as pitch-black clouds gathered in the distance. They had appeared suddenly. It wasn't supposed to rain that afternoon. He watched the giant shadows they cast overtake downtown Longview. Only the high school seemed to still be bathed in light, reminding him of his disappointment. Steve wanted to be a physicist, like his mother. That was his whole reason for going to Sinatra Edison. Graduates from there had a free pass to the best science colleges in the country. That wasn't the case for students barely passing their most important classes. Mr. White was determined to not let Steve leave his physics class with anything above a D.

The weekend had officially begun and Steve didn't want to start it wallowing in that drama.

"What made you first think about trying out for the play?" Kieron asked.

"Noah suggested it. Getting cast would be amazing. Sinatra Edison plays are so cool. Usually they do some recent Broadway hit. It's the best."

"So what's stopping you from signing up?"

"Sci Siders are never in the plays." Steve sighed. *"If I got cast, it would change everything. But there is no way— What if I actually was able to cross the lines and sign up, but I didn't get cast? That would be so embarrassing. I can't even imagine what Madison would—"*

And that thought put an end to his attempted retreat from the world. Steve stood up, dusted off his pants, and checked his phone. Sometime during his hike, he had missed a message from Noah telling him that he was stopping by for a video game bacchanal to help him recover from his latest rejection. Leaning against the aqueduct support, Steve started typing his reply.

THOOOM!!!

His phone dropped out of his hand as he grabbed the support to steady himself. Everything in his line of sight seemed to vibrate, but nothing was shaking. It felt like pure bass.

THOOOM!!!

This time Steve's heart felt like it had skipped a beat. A massive vibration trembled through the support. Rather than shaking Steve free, his hand was locked to the structure like it had become magnetized. He felt like he could feel all fifty miles of the aqueduct through his fingers.

THOOOM!!!

Everything went black. Not gradually—immediately, there was no light. It may have lasted a second or a year. All existence stopped and started inside of this darkness. Then the dot appeared. A tiny pinprick of light bore a hole through all of reality.

THOOOM!!!

Light and dark inversed. The view of the valley was back. In place of the point of light there was now a black dot hovering between the two legs of the aqueduct supports.

All Steve could look at was the dot. It was so small it

should have been easily overlooked. Instead, this dot dominated the valley with its decisive position.

THOOOM!!!

All the air around the dot shifted to the left or the right, like two transparencies of the same image being slid over the top of one another. Everything was a blur. Then the images realigned. Three figures now stood in between the supports.

The vibrations stopped and released Steve from their hold. He crumpled to the ground. All he wanted to do was pass out. It was the voices that kept him conscious. They were panicked and angry and scared. They all sounded very, very familiar.

Steve rolled onto his side to face the figures. The blurred effect must not have gone away. Standing in front of Steve were three other versions of himself

Chapter 4

It would have been totally acceptable for Steve to pass out in that situation. He was experiencing déjà vu, nausea, and hallucinations all at the same time. The three other Steves also seemed to be struggling with at least one of those sensations.

A cacophony of chaotic voices exploded in the valley.

"Where did you come from?"

"How did you get in here?"

"What the hell is going on?"

"WHY DO ALL OF YOU LOOK LIKE ME???"

They all asked their questions at exactly the same time.

All four stumbled backwards when they heard their voices coming out of the others' bodies. Except, that is, for the higher-pitched voice coming out of the Steve with boobs. Boobs? That Steve was a girl. A second grade chant echoed through Steve's head: *Steve is a girl! Steve is a girl!*

"Nobody move," one Steve growled.

Steve never saw himself as intimidating, but this Steve looked like a badass. His eyes focused on each of the others like a sniper's. His buzz-cut red hair and the veins bulging in his arms only added to his intensity. As he turned his body, looking at all the Steves in the valley, his gray, short-sleeve T-shirt rode up and Steve caught sight of a six-pack. Steve was about a thousand sit-ups shy of his stomach looking like that.

"This is fascinating. Each of you appeared before me simultaneously." The second of the new Steves was hunched over, making him appear shorter than the others. He scratched his bowl-cut red hair as he considered their situation. "Although it's entirely possible that I am the one who appeared in front of you."

"Is this what I'd look like as a boy?" Girl Steve looked at the others in disgust. "I thought I'd be taller."

Steve studied her. His initial discomfort as seeing himself as a girl faded some. People had always said that he looked like his mother. Now he understood. Her red hair was even pulled back in a ponytail over her left shoulder, just like his mom used to wear it.

"The landscape has remained the same; however, this version of the aqueduct is in serious disrepair. I appear to not be on my world anymore. This is some impoverished incarnation of my dimension." The bowl-cut Steve nodded to himself.

"We're not poor. It's just Jersey," Steve muttered as he began to process what was happening. "Is this some kind of dimensional shift?"

"A dimensional shift?" The bowl-cut one's eyes darted back and forth as if he were trying to remember something. Then his expression grew irritated. "Proposing random theories will not help this situation." Steve looked down, embarrassed at his amateur scientific method.

"Everyone shut up! I know what's going on. This is textbook psychological warfare." The badass Steve moved from under the aqueduct structure and positioned himself in front of the other Steves. "The costumes and makeup are convincing, but you're not getting any information out of me."

"Yeah, guys. He's really serious. He's got his *GRRR* face on." The girl Steve laughed.

"Don't laugh at me—"

"The question remains... if I am no longer on my world, on whose world am I?" The bowl-cut Steve began pacing the valley. The way he walked with his head down made it seem as if he were walking much faster than he was.

"It must be mine." The girl Steve stepped into the center of the group. "You are all clearly alternate versions of me."

"This is insane. None of this is possible." The badass Steve punched the aqueduct support next to him to emphasize his point.

"Actually, it kinda is." Steve eyed the bowl-cut Steve, waiting to see if he would be shot down again. "There's this theory called quantum mult—"

"Yes. Yes. The quantum multiverse theory," bowl-cut Steve interjected.

A massive wind gust tore suddenly through the valley. A second gust followed immediately. Clouds above the group rolled in like waves.

"Whatever world we're on, we're about to get drenched," the girl Steve informed the others.

"We should go back to my—I guess, our house," Steve suggested.

The badass Steve hung back and watched the rest of the group start walking out of the valley. "No way. You can't think I'm that stupid to just follow you into your trap."

Steve looked back at him. What little light remained from the setting sun had been swallowed by the blackening sky. Any storm moving this fast would be incredibly violent.

"I don't know what's going on either," Steve said. "But I

promise this isn't a trap."

The only response from the badass Steve was him narrowing his eyes at Steve.

"If you can't trust yourself, who can you trust, right?" Steve smiled, hoping badass Steve had a similar sense of humor.

He didn't. "You lead. I'll be right behind you. Do anything suspicious and I will snap your neck."

The rain arrived in one huge splash, turning the path into an instant Slip 'N Slide. As hard as it was to make their way down the mountain in the mud and growing darkness, Steve found it that much harder to move under the threat of being murdered by himself.

"Do not call me Steve," the Steve with the bowl-cut hair whined as he took a towel from Steve.

"Your name isn't Steve?" This bizarre waking nightmare was about to get much more confusing. Being back in his house with them as the storm raged outside had only made it weirder.

"Unless I am demoted to the Dregs, I insist on being addressed by my full given name."

"Sure thing, Stephen." Steve crossed the room and handed another towel to the badass version of him. "Here you go... uh... Stephen?"

"Buck." He ran the towel over his buzz cut. "Everyone outside of my family calls me Buck."

"Why?" Steve wondered.

"Just a nickname the guys in my unit gave me. I guess they thought Buchmann was too long to say all the time."

"OK." Steve turned to his girl version. "What's your name?"

She glared at him. "Stephanie. That should have gone without saying."

Steve shrugged. "Not necessarily. Mom said that if I had been a girl she wanted to name me Natalie."

"What the hell?" Stephanie pointed across the Buchmanns' living room. "I've never seen that bookshelf before in my life."

"We've had it as long as I can remember." Steve handed her a towel as she stormed over to the bookshelf, scanning it carefully.

"So it seems there is a strong probability that we have been transported to your world," Stephen said as he closed his eyes to process this new information.

"Yeah, that's what I have been say—"

From across the room, Buck gasped. He was standing in front of Daniel's DVD collection and turned to present one of the cases to the room. "What is this?"

"It appears to be an antiquated digital video disk," Stephen answered. "Do they not have those on your world?"

"Yeah. No, I mean the cover." He showed them the *Raiders of the Lost Ark* box.

"That's Indiana Jones." Steve answered. "You've never seen that one before?"

"They don't make movies on my world anymore."

"I haven't seen this in forever! Mom threw ours out years ago." Stephanie had flipped open the game chest next to the TV and was pulling out Clue. "This was the *best* game!"

"Mom threw out your games?" Steve asked.

Stephanie nodded. "She always said they were wastes of time for the simpleminded."

"That's weird." Steve shrugged. "My mom loved games."

"Mine too." Buck sat on the floor next to Stephanie.

She suddenly upended the box. "What the hell is going on?" The contents of the Clue game set scattered. One card remained in her hand. "Colonel Mustard? There's no Colonel Mustard in Clue. All the other people: Mrs. White, Mr. Green, Mrs. Peacock... I know them. There's no Colonel Mustard! It's Lieutenant Lemon!"

"Really? Colonel Mustard is the man!" Steve insisted. "Look at his eyes. Mustard saw some serious action in World War One. He's the real deal."

From a ledge by the stairs, Stephen picked up a picture frame. He studied it before he spoke. It was just above a whisper. "Who is this child?"

Steve came over. "That's Josh. My—our?—brother."

"Josh is here!" Stephanie jumped up and grabbed the picture.

"Where is he?" A voice growled next to Steve. Buck moved him aside to study the picture.

"Spending the weekend at Aunt Leslie's house," Steve said.

"That traitor? How could you trust him with her?" Buck snapped. "Someone explain what's going on. Right now!"

Pacing the floor, Stephen began talking through the situation—although mostly to himself. "An unexplained anomaly triggered a dimensional shift..."

"Now he agrees with me," Steve complained under his breath.

Stephen continued, apparently having not heard Steve. "... taking us out of our various realities and bringing us here to this alternate one."

"Alternate to you," Steve mumbled.

"According to the quantum multiverse theory, every possible observation contains a probable universe corresponding to a variation of the root condition." Stephen looked back at the others. Buck and Stephanie waited for Stephen to elaborate. To Steve, that explanation sounded like a memorized Wikipedia definition.

When Stephen did not offer to explain himself any further, Steve took a chance and jumped in. "The idea of the multiverse theory is that every time you are faced with a choice, a new universe is created for each option. If you see an apple, you have two choices: eat it or not. If you eat it, that creates one reality. If you don't, that creates another. Every millisecond of every single day of existence has created an infinite number of alternate universes."

Buck exhaled. "I... uh... I need to sit down."

Stephanie stormed over to Stephen. "How do we get back?"

"That's simple, really. We reverse the process that brought us here." Stephen nodded to himself, approving of his own answer.

"Great! What was that process?" Stephanie asked.

Stephen curled further into himself. "I am uncertain of that."

"Vibrations," Steve said. When no one cut him off, he continued. "The aqueduct was vibrating."

Stephanie looked at Stephen. "Is that helpful?"

Steve started to protest, but stopped himself when he saw how the others waited for Stephen's answer.

"Possibly." He looked away, considering the options. "Something brought us here. That same unknown entity should be able to return us to our dimensions of origin."

"OK! Now we're talking." Stephanie tossed her towel on the couch and moved to the center of the living room. "In the meantime, there can't be four versions of the same person walking around."

"We... You can stay here for a while," Steve offered. "Our... well, *my* dad won't be home until Sunday night. No one will be here. You'll be—"

DING-DONG.

All the Steves looked toward the door, then to Steve. Switching gears from his *Twilight Zone* nightmare back to real life had stalled his brain. He could not imagine who would be at the door.

"Stay here. I'll handle this." Buck picked up an iron poker from the fireplace and moved toward the door.

"Wait—hold on." Steve raced to stop him.

In one motion, Buck opened the door and yelled, "What do you want?"

Noah jumped back onto the porch. His best friend was holding a weapon and screaming at him. Then a second Steve ran up beside the first one yelling, "Don't! That's just Noah." Following the horrifying look in Noah's eyes, Steve turned, realizing that Noah was also seeing yet another Steve and a girl, who looked like the sister Steve never had. Later on, Noah would admit that even he was surprised that his reaction to the multiple Steves was to burst into tears.

Chapter 5

How many Steves does it take to bring a catatonic best friend in from the rain?

Four.

Two to carry him. One to cover his mouth so the neighbors don't hear him blubbering. And one to hold the door open, shaking her head in disgust.

Steve and Buck dragged Noah into the living room and set him down on the couch. Maybe all of them ganging up on him wasn't the best way to calm him down. Letting someone wave an iron rod in his face was an even worse idea. "We've been compromised. We need to get rid of him," Buck determined.

"Whoa!" Steve pushed him away from Noah. "It's OK. He's my best friend. He won't compromise us... or whatever."

From beneath Stephen's hand, Noah began a muffled scream of protest. Steve pulled the hand away. "I know this is really weird. But you have to calm down."

"Steve! Is he going to kill me?" Noah heaved through sobs.

"No one's going to kill you," promised Steve.

"That hasn't been decided yet," Buck snapped.

"Steve!" Noah was starting to hyperventilate.

"Just give us a second." Steve edged the others back into the living room.

"There are four of you." Noah could not look away from Steve's doppelgängers. "There are four of you! Four Steves. Four. What? What? WHAT! WHAT?"

"That's pretty much what we've been doing for the past hour." Steve sat down next to Noah.

"If I'm dreaming, you have to tell me, right? Like that thing with undercover cops."

"This is definitely not a dream."

"What the hell is going on?" Noah asked.

"We're not really sure." Steve shrugged.

"Yes, we are," Stephen corrected Steve. "Dimensional shift. We've already reached that conclusion."

"You have to pay better attention." Stephanie readjusted her ponytail as she glared at Steve.

Noah froze. His eyes locked on her.

"Is that a *girl* you?" Noah asked.

"This is going to take forever if he can't grasp the basics," Stephanie snapped.

"Dude, you are really hot as a girl!" Noah smiled.

"Noah! That's my—that's me? Argghh! Just stop. It's confusing." Organizing that thought had disturbed Steve.

He helped Noah to his feet and joined the others in the living room. Stephen had occupied the recliner, hunched forward with his head resting in his hands. Buck and Stephanie were on the couch. She sat with her legs crossed, tapping her foot on the coffee table. "What's our first step?"

"Find a safer location." Buck folded his arms in front of his chest and glared at Noah.

That attempt at intimidating Noah did exactly the opposite. "Ha ha ha!" Noah said to Steve. "That Steve does the same thing you do when you're trying to act tough."

"His name isn't Steve," Steve corrected him. "He calls himself Buck."

"Like Buck Rogers?" Noah stared at Buck. "Is he a future you?"

"He is not from the future," snapped Stephen.

Noah turned to face Stephen. "Fine. Whatever, Steve."

"He's Stephen," Steve explained.

"That's what I said."

"No. He goes by my full name."

"Your name's Stephen?" Noah was genuinely surprised. "Since when?"

"Can we please get back to the matter at hand?" demanded Stephen.

"Jeez! Is everyone this serious in the future?" Noah asked.

"None of us are from the future, you simpleton!" Stephen yelled. The outburst shocked everyone. A tension filled the room as Stephen's face flushed red.

Steve laughed. "It's OK. He's an Art Sider. What can you do?" When that didn't loosen anyone up, Steve provided another option. "Anyone hungry? We can order some pizzas."

Buck sat up straight. All his suspicion and anger was gone. "You can get pizza here?"

Three pizza boxes were stacked by the door, waiting to be taken out to recycling. The fourth rested beside Buck, who refused to share any from his box. He had slowed down some on his previous slice, but now he was determined to finish every last bite. If they went back home soon, who knew when he would have pizza again? Buck had explained that pizza had been banned on his world after protesters had used them to plaster the windshields of Everlast Security vehicles to blind the drivers.

"So, your world never had Vietnam or Korea?" Steve asked Stephen.

"No. We have those countries on my world." Stephen spoke slowly so Steve would understand.

"I think what he means is that after World War Two, there were no wars in those countries," Stephanie clarified.

"I see the misunderstanding." Stephen leaned back as he again explained the history of his world. "After the conclusion of the Second World War, a global government was instituted. Wars between countries became obsolete. Korea and Vietnam going to war with one another would be like Virginia fighting New York."

"They didn't fight each other. The US fought two separate wars in those countries," Steve explained.

"Your United States was involved in two entire wars after the conclusion of World War Two?" Stephen was baffled.

"Well, there were actually a few more than that."

"The amount of money your government wastes on military costs is staggering. No wonder your education is so substandard." Stephen poured himself a huge glass of orange soda, which apparently didn't exist in his dimension.

"Yeah. It's pretty un-good," Steve whispered to Noah.

Through a mouthful of pizza, Buck added, "My world doesn't have wars either. Just oppression. This world doesn't have any watchtowers or checkpoints on the streets. People can move about freely. You can get something this wonderful..." Buck grabbed the final slice in his box. ". . . in twenty minutes. If you ask me, I'd take this world with all its conflict over one that imposes peace through unrelenting control."

"OK. He comes from a hell world." Noah turned to

Stephanie. "What about your world? Is everyone there the opposite sex? Is there a Noah-ina who's your best friend?"

"Absolutely not!" Even though she was sitting on the couch across the room from Noah, she scooted back. "I think my world is pretty much like this one. The biggest difference seems to be that you live with your dad and I live with my mom."

Steve and Buck turned to her in shock. "Is your dad dead?" Steve asked.

"No. They got divorced."

"Really?" Buck was too stunned to finish his last slice. "That doesn't make sense. Mom and Dad are absolutely devoted to each other. Unquestionably."

"Well, there's a big difference." Stephanie shook her head. "My dad wasn't quite as devoted as yours."

"Do you ever see him at all?" Steve couldn't imagine that life.

"All the time. He lives in a condo downtown. Do you see your mom much?"

"No. She died five years ago."

Buck and Stephanie went silent. Normally, when Steve told someone that his mother had died, the other person muttered their condolences. This news seemed to hit Buck and Stephanie harder. Sharing the same mother must have made the prospect of losing her all the more immediate and jarring for them.

Not so much for Stephen, who didn't appear to be moved at all by what he heard. "Those are painful stories. But that is what results from illogical anachronistic institutions such as marriage. Completely inefficient. Couples should be paired by the Reproduction Department based on genetic compatibility. It's only logical."

"I don't know how we can be the same person if you

oppose free will!" Buck jumped to his feet and stormed over to Stephen. "My Dad and Josh are rotting in some Everlast detention center because Dad stood up for our freedom. How could you possibly be OK with some government overlord telling you who you can and can't have sex with?"

Stephen stared back at Buck, not backing away. "I believe you have overlooked the fact that it is just that free will that you seek that has resulted in your family's imprisonment."

Buck's arm flew down to his side, searching for his iron poker. Before he could do anything worse with his fist, Stephanie jumped up from her chair and grabbed his hand. "OK. That's enough." There was none of the usual force to her voice. There was just comfort as she put her arm around him.

"Dude!" Noah jumped up. "You moved faster than Reflex. That was sick."

Confusion replaced all the anger Buck was feeling. "You know about Reflex?"

"Yeah." Steve stood up, unsure if that answer was a good thing or bad. "I've got the whole run in the garage. You have the comic on your world?"

Buck responded by taking off his shirt. "He's my inspiration. My whole unit got these." He turned his right shoulder to Steve and Noah, revealing a tattoo of Reflex's R logo.

"That's badass!" Noah blurted.

"You have a tattoo?" Steve ran his finger over the symbol, knowing that the same design on his far-less-muscular arm would not have the same effect.

"Then you're going to flip when the movie comes out," Noah informed him.

"They made a Reflex movie?!" Instantly, Buck was ten years old.

"It'll be out in a month!" Steve replied. Buck's excitement had infected him.

"Hopefully we won't still be here in a month." Stephanie walked over to Stephen. "This is great fun, but how do we get home?

Stephen looked down and slumped further into himself.

Over the course of the night, the Steves had spread throughout the house. Buck had been concerned about the lack of weapons. He began to inventory everyday items that could be useful in a fight, but was distracted by the Buchmanns' DVD collection. By the time he finally fell asleep, he had made it halfway through *Indiana Jones and the Temple of Doom*.

Stephanie started organizing their efforts to get home. Since Stephen sounded like he had the best grasp on the situation, she sat with him to flesh out what had brought them there. Steve wasn't about to miss out on a front row seat to a physics lesson taught by a version of himself from a super advanced science dimension.

Most of the theories Stephen was mentioning were beyond anything Steve had heard of. But Stephen was also only offering the simplest of explanations of these theories. Every time Steve asked him to elaborate, Stephen snapped at him, saying he couldn't concentrate. Even with the sketchiest of details, Steve was able to combine his knowledge of physics with these new theories and extrapolate some understanding. The three of them were starting to flesh out some sort of a picture. Unfortunately, it wasn't enough to overcome the exhaustion they felt.

Steve told Stephanie to take his dad's room and he sent

Stephen to Josh's. Buck was asleep on the couch in front of the TV. Steve was scared of what would happen if he woke that ball of tension. Early in the night, Noah had broken out his sketch pad and gone up to Steve's room. As Steve had expected, Noah was passed out on the bed. Steve was too tired to fight and fell asleep on the floor of his own room.

Halfway through a nightmare about taking a test in Buck's hell world high school, there was a jarring crash that woke Steve. The glare of the sun through the window made it hard for him to focus. Slowly, his mind processed two facts. It was morning. And the front door had just slammed shut.

"Dad's home!" Steve gasped.

Chapter 6

Every vacation Steve's dad had taken them on ended the same way—with his father crashing through the door carrying all the suitcases they brought. It didn't matter if it was a few small overnighters or a bunch of massive bags from a three-week getaway. Dad refused to make more than one trip from the garage to the house.

This time, Dad was also apparently trying to impress his girlfriend. From the top of the stairs where he was out of view, Steve watched, frozen, as his dad struggled through the door. He knew he had to hide all of his doubles. But if he went down now and Buck, who was on the couch somehow still sleeping, woke up, it would be all over. Nicole clearly had no idea about Dad's obsession, so she tried to help by holding the door open from the inside of the house. Standing in his way made the dance into the house far more chaotic than usual. Bags slammed into doors and crunched fingers. But not one curse word slipped from Dad's mouth.

As soon as both feet were in the house, he let the pile of luggage drop. Technically, his streak remained unbroken.

Nicole stared at the pile as Dad climbed over it to get into the hall bathroom. Without saying a word to her, he shut the door. A fresh wave of panic washed over Steve as he watched helplessly as Nicole took out her phone and plopped down on the couch, landing on a pair of feet.

Buck, the owner of the feet, rolled onto the floor, landing in a crouch ready for a fight.

Nicole's scream brought Dad running out of the bathroom... pants thankfully pulled up. "What happened?" he yelled.

To Steve everything now seemed to be moving in horrifying slow motion.

"Oh my God! Oh my God! That scared me so badly. I didn't see him there," Nicole said to Daniel.

"What'd you fall asleep watching TV?" Dad asked the ball of tension as it slowly rose to its feet.

Buck seemed to loosen up some. If Steve would normally be disoriented when his father woke him up, he couldn't imagine what Buck was going through. In fact Buck could only manage one word: "Dad."

"We decided to cut the trip short," Dad informed him.

"It was the hotel. I just couldn't sleep there. You could hear everything," Nicole offered.

Buck ignored Nicole. Steve remembered what Buck had told him about his father on his world. All he seemed able to do was stare at this man who both was and wasn't his father.

"All right. We obviously woke you. Go on up to bed." Dad patted the boy, who he thought was his son, on his back and kissed his forehead. "Did you get a haircut? Looks good." Dad ran his hand through Buck's buzz cut before heading to the kitchen.

Nicole lingered, smiling at Buck, who just stared past her into the kitchen. After neither of them said anything for another minute, Nicole nodded and followed Steve's dad into the kitchen. Buck ran his hand through his buzz-cut hair.

"What the hell are you doing?" Steve whisper-yelled from the stairs.

"I haven't seen Dad in six months," Buck said.

"What was that, boychick?" Dad called out from the kitchen.

"Nothing!" Steve shouted as he dashed into the living room and pulled Buck to the floor to hide behind the couch. The kitchen was separated from the living room by a wall and an open doorway that provided an unobstructed view into each room. "Go out to the room above the garage. I'll send the others out in a few minutes," Steve whispered to Buck.

"Why?"

"Dad can't see any of you." Steve kept his voice as soft as possible.

"What would happen if he did?" Buck was not bothering to keep quiet.

"It's not Dad I'm worried about." Steve tried to hide the rising panic in his voice. "Please just go."

To end the conversation, Steve stood up and walked toward the kitchen. "Dad, are you making breakfast?" As he said the words, he passed a mirror hanging next to the entrance to the kitchen. Steve caught sight of his ruffled bed-head hair in the reflection. A frantic few seconds passed while his father's back was still turned away, and Steve scanned around him. On the hook by the front door was his Sinatra Edison baseball cap. He sprinted over to grab it. Dad and Nicole had both turned around when they heard Steve running. A second later, a slightly out-of-breath Steve walked into the kitchen, now wearing the hat.

"What were you running like that for?" his father asked him.

"Sorry." Steve struggled for an excuse.

"When did you change your shirt?" Nicole asked.

Steve froze. His eyes darted to the couch as his mind raced to remember what shirt Buck had been wearing. Did he own the same shirt? Had she realized that he didn't own a shirt like that? How long had Steve been standing here silently thinking?

"Uh..." Steve offered.

"Do you need a few more minutes to think about it? Mornings aren't your best time." Dad handed a container to Steve. "Open this for Nicole."

"What's *quinoa flour*?" Steve asked as he twisted open the jar and handed it back to his father.

"I'm making gluten-free pancakes with a fruit compote, tofu bacon, and vegan scrambled eggs. I interviewed this SoHo chef once who gave me all these amazing recipes." Nicole held out her hand, waiting for Daniel to hand her the flour.

"This is going to be really good." Dad locked eyes with Steve, making it clear to him that this would be the official Buchmann stance on this meal. "But you don't have to do all this. I can make some omelets."

"Oh God, no." Nicole reeled back as if she had been presented with rancid meat. "I need something healthy. That's the first thing we're going to change when I move in." She poured the flour into a mixing bowl. Steve winced when he saw how thick the batter was getting.

"Healthy" and "Dad's cooking" were never uttered in the same breath. Butter. Sugar. Oil. More butter. That was how Dad cooked. One time, Mom bought sugar-free cookies. Dad called them a "crime against nature."

"Why don't you take our bags upstairs?" Dad suggested to Steve. "I think you can handle menial labor—"

BA-LOOSH!

There was something unique about the positioning of the

upstairs hall bathroom in the Buchmann house. It didn't matter if the door was opened or closed, when the toilet was flushed it could be heard in every single part of the house. Even worse, the walls of the house enriched the sound like a Roman amphitheater. The farther away a person was from the bathroom, the louder it was. Anyone who visited their house quickly learned to use the normal-volume downstairs toilet, unless they were comfortable with everyone knowing their bathroom habits.

Dad looked at Steve. "Who's upstairs?"

"Uh..." Steve froze.

As his dad marched to the steps, Steve considered tackling him. He would have looked insane. But he couldn't let him find out about the three doppelgängers.

"I..." Steve's brain was not helping him at all.

"Ugh. You were right. Pineapple and peppers were a bad topping combo. That pizza sailed right through me." Noah came galloping down the stairs. At just the right second, he ducked his head to avoid slamming it into the doorframe. He stuck out his hand, grabbing Dad's in a jovial handshake.

"Hey, Mr. Buchmann! Hi, Ms. Davies!" Noah's feigned surprised was pretty convincing for such an awful actor.

"Steve didn't tell me you were spending the night," Daniel said.

"Wasn't planning on it, but Call of Duty wasn't going to play itself." Noah spun over to the kitchen and swiped a finger into the pancake batter. "Mmm. Pancakes."

"Don't—" Nicole was appalled, but Noah was too fast.

"You're welcome to stay for breakfast," Dad offered as he watched Noah taste the batter.

Noah's face twisted in disgust. "Ugh! That's definitely a no." He wiped the remaining batter on his finger onto his jeans. "I have to get home."

Steve mouthed a "You saved my ass" to Noah while he walked him to the door. Noah's mouthed response was too complicated for Steve to make out, but he got the gist: "You're welcome."

After he shut the front door, Steve turned back, and his heart stopped. Buck was still lying behind the couch. Checking the kitchen, he saw that his dad and Nicole were busy scraping something off the griddle.

"What are you still doing here?" Steve whispered to Buck.

"You don't understand. I haven't heard Dad's voice for months." At least now Buck was showing some restraint and being quiet.

"You should have gone already. Nicole's going to be done with her vegan cakes or whatever soon. Just stay here. I have an idea."

Steve dragged a suitcase to the stairs. "Well, I guess I should go upstairs," he yelled up the steps. "By myself." His stiff announcement was met with an "Uh-huh" from Dad, who was struggling with rapidly hardening faux pancake batter.

In the upstairs hallway, Steve saw Stephanie standing outside the door to Dad's room. Next to her was Stephen, whose face was flushed red. Steve led them back into his bedroom. He slowly shut the door before turning to his others. "You *have* to be quiet. Dad's home. Who flushed the toilet?"

"Was I supposed to die from septic shock to maintain this farce?" Stephen snapped.

Steve studied the group. There was no way he would be able to sneak them all out of the house without his dad noticing.

"Are we supposed to remain hidden here until your father leaves again?" Stephen insisted.

"No, there's a room above the garage. He never goes up there."

"Why are you hiding us?" Stephanie asked. "Your dad may be able to help."

"He can't know about you." Steve tried to slow himself down, so he could explain this as rationally as possible. "Really it's his girlfriend. She can't find out about what's happening. She's a reporter. This is the story of the century. There's no way she would ignore this. And when everyone finds out about you... who knows what will happen. But you definitely won't be able to get home. So, they can't see you."

"OK. Then why don't we just wait here until the coast is clear?" Stephanie asked.

"If Dad's home now, Josh will be here soon," Steve pointed out as he took off his shirt and opened the door. "Stay here. I'll be right back."

The balled-up shirt sailed down the stairs and landed on the floor a few yards out of Buck's reach. He army-crawled over to it, staying out of Daniel and Nicole's line of sight. As soon as he had Steve's shirt on, he stood up.

"If I'm going to let you stay home alone, you have to take responsibility for the house." Dad barked as he moved trash from last night's snack and pizza binge-fest to the side in the overflowing can to make room for the charred remains of the first failed batch of pancakes.

From the top of the stairs, Steve watched as Buck froze. His well-defined shoulders filled out Steve's shirt, taking it from schlubby to nicely fitted in seconds. Buck stared at Steve's father as he took the full bag out of the can and replaced it with a fresh one. It was the most mundane, suburban action possible and it looked to Steve like it was pushing Buck to the brink of tears. Before him was a version of the man who, on Buck's world, was taken from their home by the government.

"Would you take this out?" When Daniel handed him the bag, Buck hugged him. It wasn't actually his father, but it didn't matter to him.

"Easy," Dad shook free. "You're crushing me." He rested his hand on Buck's shoulder. "Have you been working out?"

"Yeah." Buck's voice caught, as if he were stopping himself from crying. He grabbed the trash, and ran out the front door.

"That was a mistake," Steve realized.

"I was curious how much time would elapse before you realized the flaw in your plan." Stephen glanced at his watch. "Four minutes and thirty-six seconds. Extremely far off on that one."

"Can't get your shirt back, huh? Wouldn't have done me much good, anyway." Stephanie pointed to her chest.

Stephen and Steve both cringed.

"This is why you'll always be the weaker sex," Stephanie snorted.

Steve started to tear through his drawer. "I have to have more than one blue shirt."

"Do you really think your dad's girlfriend would screw you over this badly?' Stephanie asked.

Steve scanned his room as he answered. "I have no idea what she'd do. She's kind of ruthless. Her last report was this exposé on a husband and wife research team at Tarp Scientific that lied about the results of an experiment. It was such a harsh takedown that the state took away their kids."

This made Stephanie do a double-take. "Wait. Really?"

"Yeah. She devastated their lives." Steve watched Stephanie

to make sure she understood how dire the situation was. "She's a hard core journalist... or wants to be, at least. She's always talking about finding that one piece that would transform her from regular Nicole Davies to 'Nicole!'"

Stephanie ran to the bedroom door and peeked out. Then she dashed back to Steve, her eyes frantic as she grabbed his arm. "Your Dad is dating Nicole Davies? *The* Nicole Davies?"

"Yeah..." Steve wanted to step away from Stephanie, but her grip was too strong.

"That's huge." Stephanie shook Steve hoping he would understand. "How are you so calm about this?"

"She's just some local reporter in New Jersey. Who cares?"

"Interesting. On my world Nicole Davies covers astrophysics on her web stream." Stephen nodded approvingly. "It is rather informative."

"On my world she has her own media empire. TV shows. Magazines. Books. A whole cable network." Letting go of Steve, Stephanie sat on the bed and took a cleansing breath. "Her books... they're the best. She understands people in a way... it's amazing. It's magical. She's an icon of female empowerment"

"This is definitely not the same Nicole. And we need to get you out to the garage."

Steve looked back at Stephanie on the bed. "Get up." Then he stripped off the sheets.

"Good. You're back. Breakfast is ready!" Nicole held out a platter loaded with things that looked like pancakes, eggs, and bacon. Nothing smelled like those objects.

Steve peered around the huge stack of sheets he was holding. "Cool. Let me throw these in the wash first." He moved to the next step, timing it to match Stephanie's exact movements. To make his pile of sheets big enough to hide Stephanie from view, Steve had included all of his pillows. One wrong step by Steve and Stephanie would be smothered under an avalanche of two hundred thread count cotton.

"Do it later." Dad ran over to the stairs. He stopped just shy of seeing Stephanie crouched behind the sheets. His father leaned even closer, smiled, and whispered, "Eat it while it's still hot. I'm not sure what it will turn into when it cools." Steve was only able to exhale when Dad jogged back to help Nicole set the table.

At the bottom of the stairs, Steve slowly placed his laundry basket on the floor. Stephanie followed it down, staying exactly behind the basket, until she lost her balance and landed face-first on the floor.

"Ow!" Stephanie yelped.

Steve turned the basket over, covering Stephanie with his sheets.

"What the—" she protested.

"Yum!" Steve said too loudly. "Breakfast!"

"What was that? It sounded like a dog." Dad looked at Steve. "Did you change your shirt again?"

"Yup." Steve sat down at the table and reached in front of Dad to spear a stack of pancakes. It took him two tries to penetrate the pancakes' thick hide. "So, tell me about your trip."

"Well, the drive up was nice," his father started. "There was this stretch of road that was covered by trees on both sides. Like a tree tunnel."

"Except for how strong the sun was through the leaves." Nicole rubbed her temples. "It was like a strobe effect. It started giving me a migraine."

"Oh." Even if he wanted to, Steve could not say another

word. His mouth was frozen shut in a gummy pancake mess.

"The hotel was on this beautiful lake," Dad explained. "It was on top of a mountain. So part of the trail around the lake was carved right into the side of the mountain. It looked amazing."

"But after that drive I needed a nap." Nicole was shaking her head in exasperation. "Like that could ever happen."

"Our room was next to the elevator." Dad looked to Nicole to make sure he was relaying the information correctly. "It wasn't the quietest room around."

"Grand Central would have been quieter. People were coming and going all the time. Not the best place to try and get rid of a headache."

Dad looked down and chewed his eggs.

"But that hike must have been worth it?" Steve asked between mouthfuls of food. The sooner that plate of paste-like breakfast was done, the sooner he could get Stephanie out to the garage.

"We left before we had a chance." His father forced a smile.

"I didn't get any sleep. I would have been miserable on that hike." Nicole kissed Dad on the cheek. "Thank you for understanding."

Nicole pushed her plate full of uneaten food over toward Steve. "You eat mine. I'm not hungry." Steve was too busy gasping for any moisture to wash down his current mouthful of food to respond. "I should head home," Nicole added.

"Already?" Dad wiped his mouth with a napkin. "I thought we'd have the weekend."

Steve was having a hard time judging how sincere his dad was being.

"I really need to get some sleep. Once bags form under your eyes, they never go away. That's not good for on-air talent." She kissed Dad on the forehead with as much passion as she had greeted Steve earlier.

"Well, let me walk you out at least." Dad grabbed her bags and walked her to the front door, past Steve's pile of sheets.

Steve's mouth was so dehydrated, he had to scoop his breakfast out with his fingers. When the door slammed shut, he leapt over to his clothes and freed Stephanie.

"Did she make you her tofu scrambled eggs?" Stephanie stared past Steve into the kitchen. "She cooked those for the president once."

"Did the Secret Service shoot her?" Steve pointed to the back door. "Dad's in the front yard. You have to go now."

Stephanie walked toward the back door, straining her neck to catch a glimpse of Nicole in the front window.

Steve bounded back up the stairs and dove into his bedroom.

"What are you doing?" Steve asked Stephen.

"Doing some cognitive warm-up exercises." His attention stayed locked on the book and notebook in front of him.

"You have to go. We don't have much time." Steve checked his watch. Only a few seconds had passed, but he had no idea how long his dad would take to say goodbye to Nicole. Steve went to shut the book Stephen had open, but stopped. "Are you doing my homework?"

"I find doing rote repetitive tasks lessens my levels of stress and allows me to focus on larger issues."

"That's AP Physics! It's going to take me all weekend if I'm lucky."

"I apologize." Stephen started to rip a page from the notebook.

Steve grabbed his hand. "Hold on. Wait." Flipping through the pages, he studied Stephen's handwriting. It was nearly identical to his own. "These are all correct."

"Of course they are." Steve turned more pages in the notebook. "You did next week's problem set, too."

"I'm concerned that in order to make any progress determining what opened the dimensional rift, I will need access to more advanced equipment. However, based on our interactions, I fear I may have been displaced into some kind of primitive feudal society with only basic scientific advancements."

They both froze when they heard feet stomping up the stairs. Steve didn't realize he had been holding his breath until he heard his dad walk into the hall bathroom and shut the door. When he heard the water for the shower come on, Steve opened his door and gestured for Stephen to walk out first.

They had just stepped into the hall when the handle to the bathroom door turned. There was only a second for Steve to react. Yanking his hat off, he slammed it on Stephen's head then he leapt back into his room. This left Stephen alone in the hallway as his dad walked out of the bathroom.

"Left my shampoo in my bag." Steve heard his dad say to Stephen. Steve could only hope that Dad remembered about the shampoo before he took off his clothes for the shower. "Why do you keep changing your shirt?"

"I do not understand the question." Steve cringed at the level of condescension Stephen had in his voice as he answered.

Daniel was quiet for a moment "Whatever. Listen, I was thinking. I may offer to take Nicole away again next weekend. Would you mind that?"

"If you wish." At least Stephen was starting to sound a little more civil.

"Great! I realized that maybe I wasn't being fair to Nicole. I was expecting her to be more like Mom."

"If I am not mistaken, Mother also enjoys the outdoors." From the floor on the other side of his bed, Steve's blood ran cold when he heard Stephen use the words *Mother* and *enjoys*. His mind raced as the silence stretched between Stephen's remark and his dad's response.

"Yeah, she did," Daniel agreed. "And if I'm being honest, all day yesterday I kept thinking how much your mom would have liked it there."

"It is unfair to expect Nicole to share Mother's interests."

Stop saying Mother! Steve smothered his face in his hands to keep from screaming.

"You're absolutely right." Dad said.

"Perhaps you should have her select the activity you engage in next weekend." Steve was now convinced that Stephen may be actually doing this just to mess with him.

"That's a brilliant idea." Steve heard Dad kiss the boy that he thought was his son. "Thank you. This may have been our first adult conversation. I like that a lot. I'm going to go call Nicole right now."

Dad's footsteps were moving away from the bathroom to his room when Stephen stopped him. "You left the shower running."

Laughing, Dad changed direction. "Now you're starting to sound like me."

As soon as Dad was in the bathroom, Steve sprinted into the hallway and dragged Stephen down the stairs.

When Josh was born, their mom had to sacrifice her home office for a nursery. Dad promised he'd build her a new one over the garage. Two kids in the house tested his ability to come through on that promise. But he finally finished it. Mom only got to enjoy it for a year before the accident.

After she was gone, Dad wouldn't go up there again. Being in her old office never upset Steve like he thought it would. With her journals still piled neatly on the desk, it felt like she had just run out to the store for a few minutes. Steve didn't live in denial that she was coming back someday. He knew that was impossible. What mattered was that he could still feel her presence somewhere in his life.

So he had adopted the room as his own and just moved in among her belongings. Maps of galactic empires mixed on the walls with in-progress equations scrawled on whiteboards. Long boxes full of comics sat next to file cabinets full of dissertation notes. And an Xbox and small TV sat next to her laptop. The only other furniture was an old fold-out couch and a coffee table. On the desk was Steve's inspiration. It was a candid picture of his mom in her Stepstone lab, leaning against a support pillar by a water fountain. She was reading through a stack of data. It was her favorite part of the lab.

The other Steves had made themselves at home in the room. Stephanie was laid out on the couch, watching Buck tear through a box of comics. Stephen had pulled a journal from the stack on the desk.

Before he could open it, Steve snatched it from his hand. "Please don't go through these. They were my mom's and... they're private."

"Melissa Buchmann is my mother as well," Stephen argued. "I have as much right to read what my mother wrote as you do."

"No. She wasn't your mom. I mean, she *was*. But not that one." Steve slammed his fist on the table. "Just... they aren't yours. I don't want anyone reading them."

"As you wish." Stephen nodded in agreement, but his eyes drifted back to the stack on the desk.

"These are amazing!" Buck declared. "On my world, Everlast and their government proxies stopped production of the Reflex comic years ago. So much has happened since." He held up a pile of comics for the others to see.

"Great. I'm happy for you." Stephanie hugged a pillow. "What about the rest of us? Are we just going to live here forever? Let's hear it, Stephen. Any ideas?"

"That's not a simple question to answer." An equation on the whiteboard seemed to puzzle Stephen. He erased one variable, stared for a moment, then wrote the exact same thing back in its place. "First, we must determine how we were brought here."

Steve stood up. "You said we need equipment. I think I can help with that."

Chapter 7

It was past nine when the Steves left the garage. Steve's dad always let him work out there until all hours of the night, knowing that he could trust his responsible son on his own. His dad was usually asleep when Steve came back into the house. Sneaking out would not be a problem. At least, that's what Steve assumed. He'd never done that before—never. There had been plenty of white-collar-level offenses against his dad, like talking back or downloading a movie he wasn't supposed to see, but outright lying was something he'd never do.

The walk to Dr. Hicks's normally took ten minutes, especially considering it was all downhill. Tonight it took much longer. Each Steve pointed out every tiny difference between their Longview and this one... *every* difference. Stephanie was feeling very nostalgic. She had moved away from this neighborhood years ago. Stephen was shocked by the antiquated look of the houses. None of his world's advancements had been incorporated into the buildings. He was baffled at how he didn't see one infraction generator on the whole block... whatever that was. The ability to move freely down the street without checkpoints was causing Buck to skip—literally.

The muffled alarm coming from Dr. Hicks's house should have worried Steve. The other Steves were very concerned about it, especially Buck. But Dr. Hicks's safety never crossed Steve's mind. As Hicks often pointed out, the alarms on his equipment were calibrated to factory preset levels and his experiments typically exceed OSHA norms. Basically, every time Dr. Hicks baked, he set off the smoke detector, but the cookies always tasted great.

Even though Dr. Hicks had long ago given him an open invitation to his house, Steve felt that may have been revoked considering their awkward interaction the day before. With the other Steves getting more and more worried about the alarm, Steve led them around back to the basement entrance, where he had them wait outside in the yard.

"Dr. Hicks!" Steve yelled as he opened the door and stepped inside the house. Here, the alarm was unbearable. Steve covered his ears as he descended the stairs to the basement.

What was normally an orderly laboratory was in chaos. Deep cracks peppered the walls. Papers were scattered everywhere. Burn marks ran up one side of the room. A cart of equipment was toppled over and bent in half. Glass shards crushed under Steve's feet as he walked further into the basement lab. Whatever happened here couldn't be good for Dr. Hicks's research... or his health.

The past few years had been hard on Dr. Hicks. Before the accident, he and Steve's mom had been the golden children at Stepstone Labs. Well, Mom had been the real star. She had developed the plans for the Wireless Energy Transmitter. It would be able to send electricity through the air to a receiver without any physical connections. It would change the world. Dr. Hicks had been with her from their first days at Stepstone and was just as devastated by her death as Dad, Steve, and Josh. When Stepstone's investigation into the accident firmly placed the blame on Mom, Dr. Hicks was appalled. Nothing was wrong with her theory. It should have worked. Gary Trouter, Stepstone's CEO, had himself approved her research. He knew her findings were solid. Dr. Hicks wasn't going to let Mom be the scapegoat just to appease Stepstone's investors.

Going to the newspapers was Dr. Hicks's first mistake. Doing a live interview on the six o'clock news was his second. Full of righteous anger, Dr. Hicks didn't sound like a champion for his disgraced colleague. He sounded like a raving lunatic. His animated explanation of the theory behind the WET became a meme. All five minutes of him frantically writing on the back of index cards had gotten ten million views on YouTube.

Trouter fired Dr. Hicks immediately. While the rest of the world moved on, Dr. Hicks vowed to exonerate Steve's mother and prove her theory worked. For the past five years, he had been doing that with his own money.

In the center of the room, two feet poked out from beneath an overturned, large metal box with a tuning fork on top. Cables and power cords spooled out from the side of the box, which appeared to have fallen off the cart next to it. The box must have been heavy enough to topple the owner of the feet, which were not moving. Panic coursed through Steve as he stood next to what were most likely the remains of Dr. Edward Hicks.

The flashing red light and alarm were ratcheting up the tension to absurd levels. Steve went to grab Dr. Hicks's feet, but hesitated, having never touched a dead body before. That was fortunate, since it was during those few seconds that Dr.

Hicks chose to lift up his knee. Steve jumped. Then the other knee moved. Dr. Hicks was not dead.

Scanning the walls, Steve found the alarm speaker. Beneath it was a red button. It was either a panic switch or a kill switch. Steve decided that pressing it could not possibly make things worse, so he ran over and hit it. The deafening alarm immediately turned into deafening silence. That, Dr. Hicks noticed. He dragged himself out from under the metal box. As he sat up, his back was to Steve. It wasn't until he stood and turned that he saw Steve standing next to the alarm shut-off. Jarred by Steve's sudden appearance, Dr. Hicks jump back in surprise.

"Sorry," Steve offered before Dr. Hicks could get upset.

"Steve! Why—Were, uh, we—" Dr. Hicks struggled to orientate himself as he stood. "Did we have plans today?"

"No..." Steve started.

"Whew. That's a relief. I don't have a concussion." Dr. Hicks rubbed his head. "Were the neighbors complaining about the alarm again? It's been going off all day and it just became background noise to me."

"No... I need your help," Steve tried to explain.

Closing his eyes, Dr. Hicks let out a deep sigh. It was one of sheer exhaustion. It was also the sigh of an annoyed parent having to deal with one too many requests. "This isn't the best time. Maybe next week."

"We can't wait that long."

"You'll have to!" Dr. Hicks snapped. "I'm not going to be much help to you right now. It turns out that I've wasted the last five years of my life." He emphasized his frustration by flinging his screwdriver. Steve watched the screwdriver land harmlessly on the other side of the lab.

Dr. Hicks came over to Steve. "Don't let this change your mind about your mother. The failure is not hers. It's mine. Her theory works. I know it."

With the arrival of his others, Steve had completely forgotten that Dr. Hicks had been close to testing his device. He looked at the blast pattern on the wall. "Is that what happened here? You tested it?"

"Unfortunately." Dr. Hicks hung his head.

"So, no transfer occurred?"

"For .006125 seconds there was a minimal energy transfer. Then the couplers must have overloaded. That's what I've been trying to determine."

That was almost no time at all. But for just a second, his mother's theory worked. It didn't prove the accident wasn't her fault. But at least it would discredit anyone calling her a fraud.

"I was being rude." Dr. Hicks walked away from the tuning fork device. "You said you needed my help. What can I do for you?"

"Yeah. Um... so... I was in the woods alone. All of a sudden I felt a rumbling, and then something rushed through my body..." Steve saw the growing look of confusion and discomfort on Dr. Hicks's face and realized how creepy he sounded. He quickly added, "A dimensional rift opened."

Any fatigue Dr. Hicks was feeling vanished. He leaned forward. "As in a tear in reality connecting two alternate dimensions?"

"Yes."

"What makes you think this is what occurred? Were you ingesting drugs?"

"No. He was entirely sober."

Dr. Hicks stumbled backwards as another Steve entered the lab. Then a second followed. When a girl, who looked like Steve's long-lost sister, walked in, Dr. Hicks lost the power of speech. This menagerie of Steves filtered through the lab, examining everything. Dr. Hicks watched as the first duplicate went straight to the device in the center of the room.

"Did... did... did they come from the dimensional rift?" Dr. Hicks asked Steve.

"Yeah. And we need your help to figure out how the rift opened," said Steve.

"That might not be necessary. I believe I can formulate a hypothesis right now." Stephen pointed to the tuning fork device. "Were you attempting to create a Wireless Energy Transmitter?"

"Yes..." Dr. Hicks was stunned. "How do you know that?"

"Every child knows what this is. You can't matriculate from the sixth grade without being able to construct one."

The expression on Dr. Hicks's face wavered between astonished and this-guy-is-messing-with-me—and back again.

"He comes from a super-smart planet," explained Buck.

"We are all from the same planet, just different dimensions," clarified Stephen. "These settings are all wrong."

"Excuse me?" said Dr. Hicks. Scientific wonder or not, this interdimensional traveler had just questioned his math.

"The frequency is far, far too low. And the energy output is much too high. No wonder your receiver overloaded."

Dr. Hicks positioned himself in front of the device so that Stephen could not adjust the settings. "How else could you get electricity to convert to vibrations?"

"Small, rapid pulses of high frequencies."

It left Dr. Hicks speechless. That hadn't occurred to him at all. The solution was simple and elegant. Dr. Hicks could only laugh.

Stephanie walked up to Dr. Hicks to get a closer look at him. "I thought your name sounded familiar. I know you... or at least you on my world."

Dr. Hicks froze, unable to look away from Stephanie. "You

are like Melissa reincarnated." Stephanie backed away from Dr. Hicks as the scientist got more excited. "You even move the same way she did."

Buck walked over to Stephen to study the device. "So how did this thing bring us here?"

"It's rather complicated to summarize into layman's terms." Stephen looked away from the group. "Suffice it to say these incorrect settings triggered a cataclysmic event, which opened the rift."

"If that brought us here, can it take us home?" Stephanie asked.

"Once it is repaired, all we must do is replicate these settings and another rift should open," Stephen declared.

"Well..." Dr. Hicks looked at Steve. "It's not that simple. Making this first device took me nearly five years. I could repair it, but..." He did some quick calculations in his head. ". . . best case, it would be at least a year before I had all the components."

"A year?" Buck was panicked. "I can't just stay here for a year. I have people depending on me."

Stephanie was also starting to panic. "There has to be something we can do to repair this more quickly. There are four of us to help."

"It would not require four people." Stephen was irritated. "A small child should be able to do this on his own."

"In your nerd universe maybe." Stephanie glared at Stephen.

None of the Steves spoke. A day ago, they had been going about their lives, and now they would be trapped in another dimension for a year, maybe longer. The only Steve not defeated was Steve himself.

"I know how to get you what you need." Steve jumped up. "The lab at school."

They all looked at him. "A high school lab?" asked Buck. "I don't think a bunch of Bunsen beakers will be much good."

"Bunsen burners," Stephen growled. "And of course they wouldn't help. They are for chemical reactions. But your point is valid. There is no way that any high school in this primitive dimension would have the necessary equipment."

"You don't understand—"

"What if we just stole it from that Stepstone place?" Buck said. "I could lead the raid. Security on this world is a joke." He studied the group, trying to decide who would join him on his mission.

"You don't have to do that," Steve tried again. "My school—"

"Now we're talking," Stephanie applauded Buck.

"We don't—"

"Steve's right!" Dr. Hicks clarified. "That Steve—the one I know—he's right. Sinatra Edison's lab is supplied by Stepstone. The equipment there is state-of-the-art. Every component we'd need would be there."

"Regardless, we'll still be stuck here for months. That's unacceptable." Panic was rising in Buck's voice again.

"Not necessarily." Dr. Hicks pointed toward Stephen. "Clearly, you know this technology. Would you be willing to assist me?"

"I could help assemble another WET device," Stephen agreed. "Any child on my world could."

"I want to help, too!" Steve blurted. His enthusiasm stunned the others. But he wasn't about to miss out on this physics lesson. "Three of us working on it will go that much faster, right?"

"That would not expedite anything." Stephen stood in front of the WET to illustrate his point. "In fact three people working on a device this size would interfere with each other more often than facilitate actual progress."

"That's true," agreed Dr. Hicks.

"Please. This was Mom's life work." Steve was pleading with Dr. Hicks. "I want to see it finished. Please. For her... let me help."

"Of course." Dr. Hicks nodded. "But don't you have to go to school?"

Looking around the room full of his doubles, Steve smiled. "Yeah. But I bet I could find someone to cover for me."

Chapter 8

Being trapped in a crowded, narrow entryway was hell for Buck. The massive crush of bodies trudging forward at a glacial pace drove him crazy. There was no way out except to follow the lemmings to their destination and hope that it wasn't a trap. Because if it was, the lemmings would panic and people would be hurt.

"Dude, breathe. It's fine." Noah patted Buck on the back, causing him to tense up even more.

"There's nothing *fine* about this situation." Buck scanned the people around him.

"That's true. We shouldn't have to go through a metal detector to get into school. But that's the messed-up world we live in."

A mass of high school students behind them stretched down the steps of Sinatra Edison back to the street. Ahead of them, just past the entrance to the school, was an airport-grade metal detector manned by two tired security guards. Each kid had to wait for a green light before they could move forward. Despite the potential for delays, the line moved quickly. Noah and Buck had only been waiting for ten minutes and were a handful of students from the front.

"That is all the more reason you should have let me prepare the way I wanted to." Buck gritted his teeth.

"Well, you definitely can't bring a machete to school. Sorry." Noah whispered *machete* as softly as he could, but the doughy Sci Sider in front of them still spun around when he heard the word. "Calm down. He's talking about an art project," Noah said, just before the Sci Sider stepped through the metal detector.

The tablet screen mounted on the side of the scanner caught Buck's attention. One guard, who couldn't have shown less interest if he were watching a PBS fund-raiser, pressed a button on the screen after each student passed through the gate, causing a digital *WHOOSH*. "What does that sound mean?" Buck asked Noah.

"Sounds like something was being emailed."

On the other side of the gate, a second guard waved Buck forward. Although "wave" would imply far more passion in the task than what was demonstrated.

Buck stood his ground. "What are you sending?" he demanded of the guard.

The guard tilted his head to the side. The look in his eyes said very clearly, *Are you kidding me right now?*

"I want to know what you're doing!" Buck directed this to the guard holding the tablet.

That guard answered by looking back at the line of irritated students spilling out of the door. Noah pushed Buck forward. "Just go! It's fine," he hissed.

Locking eyes with the gate guard, Buck stepped into the metal detector. He braced for a challenge from the guard, or maybe an assault from shock troopers hidden in one of the classrooms. Instead, the light turned green and the guard waved him forward, muttering "Smart-ass."

"This won't work at all if you get Steve thrown out of school," Noah said to Buck after he passed through the scanner.

"I *am* Steve," insisted Buck.

"That's the spirit." Noah patted him on the back.

Buck pointed to a security camera on the ceiling. "Who do you think is watching those videos? Where are they being sent? Are they going to the government? Your only protection is knowing what they already know about you."

"Fine. We'll look into that. But that's not why you're here today," Noah reminded him.

"Right..." Buck grumbled.

Before Stephen could start gathering components from the school, he needed to take inventory of Dr. Hicks's lab. Since Steve had insisted on helping, that only left Buck free. The idea of pretending to be Steve was bad enough to Buck, but he had also been given a task: sign Steve up to try out for the play. Buck had agreed to help mainly to avoid having to spend the day hiding in the garage with Stephanie. Also being able to use the bathroom whenever he wanted without having to sneak into the house was a plus.

"Your first class is down this hall." Noah pointed in the general direction of the hallway. "Second from the end on the left. So I'll meet—"

A pale Sci Sider with her face buried in her phone passed them. Noah abandoned his instructions. "Kayla! My inspiration!" he called to her.

There was a glimpse of recognition on her face as she looked back at Noah. It was quickly replaced with irritation and an eye roll. "What?!" Kayla sniped.

"My painting is turning out amazing, but it would be better if I didn't have to work from memory to get your beautiful hair color right." Noah impressed himself with how smooth he sounded.

Kayla was way less impressed. "That's so creepy." She returned to her phone, leaving Noah's pride in her wake.

"Nicely done. I'll pretend like that never happened," Buck promised.

"That'd be cool." Noah handed Buck a flyer. He pointed to a room number on it. "This is on the Art Side of the building. I'll meet you here after class to sign Steve up for tryouts. Have fun today!"

Most of the class were in their seats when Buck entered the room. Only two empty seats remained. Considering Steve's lack of self-esteem, Buck assumed the seat closer to the back was his regular spot. When no one around him reacted, he knew he had chosen correctly.

Just after Buck reached into his bag, a handful of lanky fingers zipped Buck's arm inside it. "Nice haircut. Did you do it yourself, dill weed?"

In fact, Buck had. Since Steve's father and now everyone at Sinatra Edison had seen Buck with a buzz cut, Buck had also given a similar haircut to Steve and Stephen. Their new looks didn't work quite as well on them as they did on Buck.

"Justin..." Buck ventured. When there was no correction, he continued, "Let go of my bag."

Justin smiled at the challenge. Then he zipped it tighter, pinching Buck's skin.

When Buck was ten, he was caught after curfew by three Everlast Youth Agents. They were like the Hitler Youth of his world. He was in another town at the time and didn't recognize any of the hulking teens who had surrounded him.

Under normal circumstances, Buck would have been given a demerit, which was a PC way of saying "beating."

That day, Buck experienced the benefit of anonymity. The Everlast Youth soon learned that the short kid they had stumbled on was a highly trained member of the Resistance. Buck took out all three without messing up his clothes. One hand would be more than enough to take out the skinny nerd in front of him.

Justin was startled by how quickly Buck grabbed him. Instead of wrestling Justin's arm away, he simply squeezed two pressure points on his wrist. The shot of pain did the trick. Justin snapped, "Jeez, you spaz. Calm down. I was just playing."

"Yeah." Buck let go of Justin's wrist. "Me too."

Justin rubbed his wrist, then snatched the flyer from Buck's desk. "*The Trial of Terrible Terry*? You trying out for the play so you can be with the other Art Sider animals? Makes sense. I never thought you belonged with the Sci Siders. I can't wait to see you dancing out your feelings on stage." Justin stood up and pranced in front of Buck's desk to illustrate his opinion of art.

For over an hour the night before, Steve had explained his relationship with Justin. At no point did Buck get a satisfactory answer as to why he didn't just beat the crap out of this kid. Seeing him in person now, Buck really didn't understand why.

Buck grabbed a fistful of Justin's shirt and pulled him in close. "Sit down and shut up!" he growled.

The burst of laughter from Justin stunned Buck. "Oh my God! You're like a caveman. Who let you into this school?"

When the rest of the room joined in laughing with Justin, Buck let him go. He looked around, recognizing how immediate the class's reaction was. They all had thought the same thing as Justin. Maybe Steve had sent the wrong version of himself for this assignment. Buck sat down before he could see that in the corner of the classroom, Madison hadn't joined in on the laughter.

Chapter 9

Kieron's chair squeaked as he rocked back and forth. "How did you keep it all together? Having long, drawn-out conversations with your mirror images... that's just too surreal to process."

"At first it was." Steve smiled to himself. "If Noah and Dr. Hicks hadn't also seen them, I would have started to wonder if I was going crazy. But the more I talked to them, the more I realized how different they were from me. Then it stopped feeling like I was talking to myself."

"Where do the repairs stand on the WET?"

"Stephen has the list of equipment he needs from school. It shouldn't be too hard for him to get. We can check out almost all of what we need from the lab."

"So Stephen will also be going to school in your place?"

"Easier that way. He knows exactly what he's looking for."

"So if this was just prep work, why did you have to send Buck to school in your place?"

"The WET was my mom's dream project. I didn't want to miss anything Stephen and Dr. Hicks were doing."

"They were basically just cleaning up. Doesn't sound that exciting to me. It's interesting that the day you send Buck just happened to be the

same day that you were going to sign up for the play tryouts."

Steve shrugged his shoulders. *"That's just the way it worked out."*

"Is it?" Kieron's chair groaned as he leaned forward across the desk toward Steve.

If this had been a real recording, Kieron would have cut out the twenty seconds of dead air as Steve debated his answer. *"It's this self-regulating silent agreement thing. No Sci Sider has tried out for the play in forever. Technically we're allowed to, but it would mean going against my side of the school. That's a lot to stand up to. Once Sci Siders found out—especially Justin—I don't know... they already hate me enough as it is."*

"I know it's silly." Steve shook his head. *"It would just be easier for someone like Buck. He can deal with that kind of pressure... I can't."*

When Steve came downstairs and went into the dining room, Josh paused his work in his sketchbook to stare at his brother. "You've been in and out of the bathroom for like an hour! What's wrong with you?"

"I really had to go." Steve hoped that his little brother would not have any follow-up questions. There was no toilet in the garage. Buck, Stephanie, and Stephen had to take turns sneaking into the house to use the bathroom. During the day when no one was home, it wasn't an issue. After Josh got home it became quite a challenge. Steve had been running traffic control, making sure Josh was distracted in the dining room while one of the others snuck back to the garage and the next person took their turn. This would be their last chance to go until everyone was in bed. Dad would be home from work in half an hour. It was only going to get more complicated then. None of the other Steves, except Buck, seemed to be cool with his suggestion of using a bucket in the garage room. And Stephanie absolutely forbade Buck from doing it.

If Steve couldn't let his dad know about the doppelgängers, he definitely couldn't let Josh find out. In his whole life Steve had never known Josh to keep a secret for more than three minutes. This he would blab about to Dad instantly. Then who knows what would happen. Dad may try to keep it from Nicole. That just didn't seem realistic to Steve. Daniel was always saying how honesty is the cornerstone of any good relationship. Even if he didn't tell her, she had so wormed her way into Dad's life that she would figure out something was going on sooner or later. Then there would be a story. Then they'd take Steve and Josh away from their dad, just like they did with those researchers' kids at Tarp Scientific.

Steve decided to ignore the comment from Josh, who appeared to have other things on his mind. Spread out across the dining room table was an array of 1970s Dungeons & Dragons manuals. The books were well-worn, with plenty of dog-eared pages. Josh was carefully studying the profile of a troll. He had copied the top half of the troll exactly in the sketchbook in front of him, but the bottom half seemed to be giving him some trouble.

Dad had been thrilled when Josh first discovered his D&D materials. Of course, he had left it on the bottom bookshelf in the living room, hoping that one of his sons would be interested in his favorite childhood game. While Steve had breezed right past them on his way to his dad's old comic book collection, Josh was a different matter. He had been drawn to the books from the beginning. Unfortunately for Daniel, Josh never wanted to actually play the game. He just loved the characters' origins and their worlds. It would later be his gateway to the ever expanding world of fantasy fiction.

Before Josh could ask any more questions, Steve looked over at the troll in the sketchbook. "That looks pretty good."

"No, it doesn't." Josh furiously attacked the legs of the troll with his erasure. "I'm trying to draw his legs to look like he's walking, but it just looks like his legs are weird and short." Josh flipped back a few pages in his sketchbook and showed Steve his previous aborted efforts.

"Maybe it has to do with the line weight?" Steve offered.

Josh looked over at his big brother. "What's that?"

"I don't know exactly. But Noah is always complaining about it when he looks at comic books." Pulling out a chair, Steve joined Josh. All day he and Stephen had been helping Dr. Hicks straighten up the lab. The three of them had been so absorbed, they didn't stop until Steve had to rush home to meet Josh after school.

Josh considered the suggestion for a minute then went back to drawing. "Hey, Steve, can I ask you something?"

"Go for it." Steve took one of Josh's pencils and a discarded sheet of paper and started his own crude version of a troll.

"Is Nicole going to dump Dad?"

"What?" Steve had been expecting Josh's normal Echelons of War-based questions.

"Aunt Leslie said that it was a bad sign that Dad and Nicole came back from their trip so early."

"I don't know." Steve focused on his drawing.

"I hope so," Josh announced. "I'm getting sick of her."

The quickest way to sow discord in the house was to get Josh riled up about something. Steve didn't want to stoke the fire of his dislike for Nicole. So he said nothing, which Josh immediately noticed.

"What? You *like* her?" Josh challenged Steve.

"I do..." Steve said, lying more to himself than to Josh.

"No, you don't. You leave the room whenever she comes over."

"Not all the time."

"Stop faking. You don't like her either." Josh pulled Steve's paper away to get his full attention. "You should say something to Dad."

"You say something, if you hate her so much." Steve grabbed back the sheet of paper.

"I tried. But Dad went into this whole thing about how he wasn't trying to replace Mom. And Mom would always be our mom. I know *that*. Half the kids in my class have divorced parents." Josh poked his finger at Steve. "He won't listen to me, but he'd listen to you."

Steve patted his brother on the head like a dog. "I have to do some stuff out in the garage."

"No. You have to say something," Josh whined.

Steve pulled over Josh's sketch pad and pointed to his latest pass at the troll legs. "Wow! That's getting better. It looks like he is really running."

Josh, completely falling for Steve's distraction, looked at the page. "Yeah! It does look better, doesn't it?"

"This is pointless!" Stephen pushed back in his chair.

"Stop being a limp and go!" Stephanie shoved the deck of cards back at Stephen.

"Hey, you found Candy Land." Steve laughed as he walked into the garage. "I loved playing that."

"Where's the strategy in this game? What could a child possibly learn here?" Stephen lifted a card with a yellow square on it. "Gooey Gumdrops! I have to remain here until I draw *another* yellow card. This is insanity."

"You're being a sore loser." Stephanie pulled a yellow card from the top of the deck. "Lollipop Woods, here I come." She held the card up to Stephen's face. "In case you were wondering, this is what yellow looks like."

"You're being an unappreciative winner," Stephen said

solemnly.

"It's better than being a loser." Stephanie made her piece prance to its spot.

"No surprise there," Stephen grumbled.

"So did I," Stephanie added. "But Science McComputer Nerd here had never heard of it."

Stephen flicked his game piece and walked back to the computer. "I am wasting time playing a child's game."

Stephanie leaned back. "At least you got to leave this room today."

"You used the facilities once this morning after the Buchmanns left the house. Then another time after I returned from Dr. Hicks's home." Stephen thought for a second, then added, "I would theorize that you also went into the house for lunch as well. Logic would say you used the facilities at that time as well."

"Thanks for the recap." Stephanie lifted her arm and directed her armpit at Steve. "Take a whiff."

Steve declined the offer. "I left you towels for the shower."

"Doesn't help when I have to put on the same clothes I've been wearing for three days." Stephanie sniffed her sleeve and reeled back from the smell. "You have extra clothes you loaned the guys. I didn't want to ask before because I thought it'd upset you, but did you keep any of your mom's old clothes?"

A memory of his dad cleaning out Mom's closet hit Steve. It had taken Dad more than a year after she died to do that. The finality of that task had devastated an eleven-year-old Steve. To alleviate Steve's pain, Daniel had agreed to store the boxes in the attic. Mom's stuff would be here, but out of sight. He said it would help them move on.

"We should have a few things.' Steve looked at Stephanie. "But it'll probably be too big, won't it?"

"I doubt it. My mom and I share clothes now all the time." Stephanie crinkled her face. "Unless your mom was crazy fat."

"No. She wasn't."

"Excellent. Now that we have settled that matter, let's discuss dinner." Stephen strode across the room. "Do you have an Iranian restaurant that delivers?"

"Wait." Stephanie held out her hand. "I also need underwear. That situation's getting real dire."

"There's probably some in my mom's stuff." Steve offered.

"Nope. Not wearing your dead mother's old underwear." Stephanie realized what she said. "Sorry. That was mean."

"Yeah, but you're right. That's weird." Steve wasn't sure how to ask the next part. "Uh... so... what?"

"I'll buy my own underwear." Stephanie shook her head. "Just give me some money, please."

"I want new undergarments as well," said Stephen.

"What's wrong with mine?" Steve was hurt. "They're clean."

"Did you use a thermal sterilizer?" Stephen asked.

Rapid, Stormtrooper-like clamoring up the stairs brought them all to their feet. The door burst open and Noah and Buck flew inside. Noah immediately headed to his normal spot on the couch.

"This you is exhausting." He said to Steve, nodding toward Buck. "Everything is a conspiracy and is out to get us."

"Spend five minutes on my world and you would under—"

"We're not on your world!" Noah buried his head in a pillow.

Steve's face dropped. "So it didn't go well today, huh?"

"No, it went fine." Buck tried to relax his stance, but got stuck when he wasn't sure what to do with his hands. "I did what you asked me to do. I signed up for auditions."

"No one gave you any trouble?"

"If by 'trouble' you mean detained against my will without a trial, beaten, and tortured for no reason... then, no. No one gave me any trouble."

Steve looked to Noah for a translation. "Dude got some pretty harsh looks from everyone when he walked in. I don't even think he noticed."

"That's great!" Steve smiled. "That must have made me look awesome!"

"Yeah. Except for how crazy he was." Noah tossed aside the pillow. "Mr. Tension here freaked when they asked him for your name and email address."

"Why do they need that information?" Buck asked. "Who are they compiling it for? Who else has access to it? That's their first step in taking over. These are important questions that you must ask—"

"It's just the drama club!" Noah looked up at Stephanie. "When do I get to take you around?"

"As soon as hell freezes over." Stephanie pushed the pillow back down onto Noah's face.

"You can never be too careful," Buck mumbled to himself. "Oh, here." He handed a stapled stack of papers to Steve. "Those are the lines you have to memorize for tryouts."

Steve studied the pages, then set them on the desk. Dealing with the possible fallout from signing up had been his main concern. He hadn't really given much thought to auditioning.

"Who are the Creationists?" Buck asked.

"The next evolution in rock 'n' roll." Noah shot his fist into the air, wiggling his index and pinky fingers.

"They're this Art Sider band at school," explained Steve.

"They're playing tonight at Read Aloud. I think that's what she said the name of the book store was." Buck tried to remember. "Some girl said I should go. Or maybe you should go. This has been a really confusing day."

"What girl?" All Steve cared about now was the answer to this question.

"Madelyn? No. Madison."

The ground fell away from Steve. His heart worked overtime as blood rushed to his head. "Really?" he asked.

Noah was on his feet. "Wait! When did this happen?"

"While you were convincing that girl to show you her toes. Madison saw me sign up and started saying how great it was I did that."

"Dude!" Noah turned to Steve. "Dude!"

"I know!"

"I have no comprehension of this situation," Stephen grunted. "And I am very content that way."

"Madison is *so* into you." Noah lifted Steve's arm to victory.

"You're reading way between the lines," laughed Stephanie.

"Never," Noah dismissed her, turning back to Steve. "We have to go tonight."

Now reality started to settle in. Steve could clearly see himself at the show, standing silently next to Madison. At no point in this scenario did he imagine them talking or dancing or him doing anything that would impress her.

Watching Steve's face drop, Noah grabbed him by the shoulders. "You got this. I'm going to be there with you the whole time."

Buck's laugh jarred everyone in the room. It was violent and intense. "If he's helping you with this girl, you have no chance."

"Hey!" Noah protested. "You don't know anything about me."

"In less than eight hours I watched six different girls reject you. It was humiliating." Buck shuddered.

"I'm not going to be able to do this." Steve sank to the

floor.

"You know what? Buck's right. I can't do anything for you tonight." Noah walked over to the couch. "What you need is someone to help break the ice with Madison, right? Who better to talk to a girl than another girl?" Noah put his hand on Stephanie's shoulder, who pushed him away.

Chapter 10

The heart of Longview was its main drag, called Side Street. It had everything a small town needed: a movie theater, a pizza place, and an ice cream shop. But the heart of Side Street was Read Aloud Book Store. It was opened in the early 2000s by David and Sebastian, a gay couple from Queens, New York. At first glance, Read Aloud was just an independent bookstore with a coffee bar. What made the store special was the small stage in the back. Every weekend, the store was packed with both Art Side and Sci Side Sinatra Edison students listening to one of the school's many upstart garage bands.

Steve had never been to Read Aloud for a show at night... or during the day. This whole experience was new for him. It was so new that his dad didn't know what to say at first when Steve asked to go to the mini-concert. He thought he would have to beg for permission. But Daniel actually seemed relieved that Steve wanted to go out at night. Maybe Steve was more of a nerd than he originally thought.

As soon as they walked into Read Aloud, Steve knew he was in trouble. Everything about the store that night was outside of Steve's comfort zone. The Art Sider band called the Creationists, whose very name was intended as a "screw you" to Sci Siders, was playing in the performance space. They were loud—too loud for Steve to have a casual conversation. All the tables had been moved away to make room for the crowds, so there was no place to sit.

Even worse, the room was divided as usual according to section. On one side of the room were the Art Siders, stoned and dancing to the music. On the other side were Sci Siders, tragically uncoordinated and swaying. The Art Siders had camped out at the front of the performance space, blocking easy access to the Sci Siders. Standing dead center among the Sci Siders was Madison—blocked off from every casual walk-by Steve could imagine.

Stephanie followed Steve to an empty corner in the back of the performance space. He leaned against the wall and watched Madison sway with the rest of the crowd. Stephanie studied the band, who were all rocking long hair and '90s plaid.

"I don't get what they're wearing," Stephanie said to Steve.

"Huh?" Steve pointed to his ear.

Stephanie leaned closer and yelled, "Why is the band dressed so stupidly?"

"They're being retro. Grunge." When Stephanie responded with a blank stare, Steve continued. "Did you have Nirvana on your world?"

"Wasn't that Courtney Love's husband's band?"

"I guess so."

"That crappy band was popular here?" Stephanie shook her head in disgust. "He was such a sponge. He got famous off of her success and then drove her so crazy that she killed herself. Such a loser. I can't believe these idiots idolize him."

"Yeah, it turned out a little differently here."

As the song died down, Steve focused back on Madison,

who was drifting away from the pack. Before she escaped, the lead singer mashed his guitar and launched into the next song. Madison leapt back next to her friends and continued to sway away.

"I don't get why I'm here." Stephanie pointed to Madison. "Noah said she likes you."

"No. His *hypothesis* is that she likes me. We have yet to run any tests to determine if that is scientifically accurate." Steve responded as quietly as he could over the roaring music. "If you get to know her, you can find out for sure."

"You can also find out by asking her out."

"But then she could say no."

Stephanie stared back at Steve, waiting for a better excuse.

"So... go make friends with her." Steve nodded in Madison's direction.

Folding her arms in front of her, Stephanie shook her head. "If I have to do this for you, what are you going to do for me?"

Steve's head whipped around. The band was about to finish their set. "I'm helping you get home."

"You were going to do that anyway. I don't really care if you get a girlfriend or not."

With a flourish, the Creationists finished their last song. Now was the time. "OK. Sure I'll do something for you. What do you want?"

"To meet Nicole."

"No!" Steve barked into the temporary silence of the room. Everyone turned around to find Steve staring back at them. When the house music started up a moment later, distracting the crowd, Steve pulled Stephanie closer.

"I can't do that."

"Why not?" she demanded.

"Because as soon as she finds out about you, she'll get a

camera to do a story. Then they'll take us all away. Even Josh."

"I can't imagine Nicole would do that."

"She has. And would again. Why do you want to talk to her so badly?"

"I want her advice."

"Whatever kind of guru she is on your world, she's definitely not that here. Believe me."

"Maybe. But I'm never going to have a better chance at meeting Nicole. Even if she's not exactly Nicole. I really want her advice."

"Advice?" Steve shook his head with determination. "Absolutely not."

"Fine." Stephanie turned and headed for the door.

The dance floor was clearing and there was now an opening to Madison. Steve reached for Stephanie's shoulder. "Maybe there's a compromise."

Stephanie stopped and looked back at Steve. "Such as?"

"It's too dangerous for you to talk to her directly. But what if I ask her your question for you?"

Time crawled forward as Stephanie considered his proposal. Behind him, the crowd was dispersing. Madison was leaving soon.

"I'm supposed to be your cousin, right?" Stephanie asked.

"Yeah. So you'll do it?" Steve's face lit up.

"Sure. Why not? What's my name? Our parents didn't name us Steve and Stephanie."

"Oh yeah..." Steve hadn't thought of this. He studied Stephanie's face, trying to decide the perfect name for her. His brainstorming was interrupted when she suddenly started rolling her eyes and twitching her head. Those gestures were so confusing that he almost missed being tapped on the shoulder.

He turned around to face Madison. A light shimmer of sweat was on her forehead from the heat of the crowd. She was still bopping from the music as she smiled at Steve.

"I can't believe it," Madison said, beaming.

Steve froze. He had run dozens of simulations of this moment. None of them started this way.

Madison leaned closer, as if trying to avoid being overheard. "You really signed up to audition? That's so cool!" She glanced behind her to make sure none of the Sci Siders heard her talking. "I could never do that."

"Um... yeah." Steve tried to reply.

"Why not?" asked Stephanie.

This was happening faster than Steve could handle. "My cousin," he offered.

"Hi, I'm Natalie." Stephanie shook Madison's hand.

"That's a good one." Steve realized what he said out loud, but no one else had noticed.

"Why couldn't you try out for the play?" Stephanie demanded.

Madison looked over her shoulder again. "Because it's an Art Side thing."

"I have no idea what that means." The minutiae of Steve's life was wearing thin with Stephanie.

"Sorry. She's not from around here," Steve informed Madison. Then he explained to Stephanie. "The play, drama club, choir, all those type of activities are just for Art Sider students."

"So it was against the rules for Buc—*you* to sign up?" Stephanie asked.

"Not really against the rules," Madison chimed in. "Just frowned upon. Like, no Sci Sider would want an Art Sider on the Mathletes squad. People are very territorial around here. But I love *Terrible Terry*! It would be so much fun to be in it. I was so jealous when I heard what you did."

Steve didn't even try to stop the smile that exploded on his face.

"If he can work up the courage, you definitely should be able to," said Stephanie, patting Steve on the back.

Madison smiled and shook her head. "No way. I could never do that."

"Don't be such a wimp." Stephanie pushed Madison. "Who exactly is stopping you?"

Steve's smile was obliterated. He was trapped in the passenger seat of a car plunging off the side of a bridge.

Madison's silence was so powerful it muted the noise of the crowd. Steve looked from Stephanie to Madison and back again. There had to be a way to fix this. Maybe if he started laughing and made Madison think Stephanie was joking.

Then Madison smiled. "You're right. That's crazy." She looked at Steve, whose jaw was now on the floor. "Do you think there's still time to sign up?"

"Maybe. I'm not sure," was all Steve could manage.

"You know what? It doesn't matter. I'm going to go there and audition anyway." Madison stood up taller.

"You can borrow his script," Stephanie offered.

"Yeah. I'll bring it in tomorrow." Steve had finally caught up.

"Awesome! Thanks." Madison looked back at her group. The band was gathering their instruments from the stage and her friends were putting on their coats. "We're going to get some pizza. You guys want to—"

"Yes!" One day Steve would learn subtlety.

Madison glanced at the overeager Steve, then grabbed Stephanie's hand. "Come on. I want you to talk to my friend Tina. She's scared to take her driver's license test because her dad says having a girl on his insurance will be too expensive."

Steve waited while Madison introduced Stephanie to her friends. He should have joined them for this part, since it was likely a lot of those girls didn't actually know his name. But Steve needed a moment to burn his conversation with Madison into his memory forever.

Chapter 11

Weekends were supposed to be relaxing. So far this Saturday had been the most stressful of Steve's life. It started with him sitting bolt upright in bed with the horrifying realization that today there was no work or school. After several days, he and the other Steves had found a good rhythm for their weekday morning routine. That basically involved them waiting until Daniel left for work and Josh left for school. Then Buck would quickly come in and get ready to take Steve's place at school. After that Steve and Stephen would get ready and go to Dr. Hicks's. That let Stephanie have the run of the house for a few hours. Steve had completely forgotten that, on the weekends, they were all home all day. That meant food and bathroom access for the other Steves had to be carefully thought out. Steve had not even come close to doing that.

In a panic, Steve had found his dad and convinced him that they needed to make an immediate run to the wholesale club to beat the weekend rush. Dad was confused, but agreed. Nicole had spent the night and seemed happy to join them. Steve suspected that the real reason she wanted to go was that she liked getting recognized by shoppers. Convincing Josh to delay his normal weekend binge-fest was harder, but he ultimately relented. Two hours later, they pulled back into their driveway with a car loaded down with massive boxes of snacks and various impulse buys.

Steve studied the garage, trying to catch any movement in the room. If the Steves were up there, he couldn't tell. But it had been two hours, they had to be out of the house by now. Steve suddenly had a clear premonition of Nicole walking into the house and seeing Stephanie, Buck, and Stephen together on the couch, watching TV.

"I'll take the meatballs in before they melt." Steve dashed to the back of the car, just as Dad was opening the trunk. He grabbed the box of frozen meatballs before his dad could register what Steve had said. Josh and Nicole, who were waiting on the other side of the car for Dad to distribute items for them to carry in, just watched as Steve ran with a single box into the house.

Steve rang the doorbell a dozen times as he unlocked the door. He stepped inside to silence, scanning the living room for any indication that could give away that other people had been there. Then, the door slammed shut behind him. Before he could turn around, the lock clicked and a hand covered his mouth.

"We're still here." Buck whispered as he muffled Steve's scream. When Steve's shrieking faded, Buck uncovered his mouth.

"Why?" Steve turned and saw Stephanie standing next to Buck.

She shook her head and pointed upstairs. "Stephen is in the shower."

There was banging at the front door, then Josh started yelling. "Open the door! Why'd you lock it?"

"Are you kidding me? You had hours." Steve started pushing Buck and Stephanie away from the front door toward the stairs.

Stephanie put her arm around Buck. "Princess here took forever in the shower."

"It's a luxury. Kill me." Buck shrugged off Stephanie as he turned to run up the stairs. Stephanie smiled as she followed him

"Open the door!" Josh banged harder this time.

"Sorry, the wind blew it shut." Steve shrugged as he opened the door.

"Move." Josh was balancing five boxes of varying sizes. None of which should have been stacked together. The pile wobbled to the left and right. Josh kept it from falling, defying all the laws of physics. He headed directly to the kitchen, followed by Nicole, who carried a pack of napkins, but was mostly spotting Josh in case his pile collapsed.

Dad entered next with all the remaining items in a perfectly arranged stack. The heavy case of water bottles was on the bottom. Two boxes of cereal, laid side by side, were next. Then a container of snack bars and a brick of toilet paper rounded it out. The whole thing was completely blocking his line of sight. Like with the luggage, he was only making one trip.

"Couch," Steve warned his father just before he plowed into the furniture.

Dad's rapid dodge of the couch caused his tower of goods to teeter. With some minor adjustments he kept it upright as he maneuvered into the kitchen. Steve heard a grunt, which must have been his dad setting down his burden. That was immediately followed by an angry growl. "What is this mess?"

"I didn't do it." Josh's quick denial sent a chill through Steve. He ran into the kitchen. Nicole and Josh were examining the counter, which was littered with crusted-over bowls. Two frying pans sat caked with what appeared to be an attempt at an omelet. That was at least what Steve had deduced based on the pile of cheese, peeled onion, and cut-up peppers next to the stove. Josh had been telling the truth. This wasn't him. This was the work of a Steve or even multiple Steves.

"Was this you?" Dad gingerly touched a bowl full of a filmy yellow liquid. "The kitchen was clean this morning."

"Um... I forgot. I wanted a snack. But then we were in a rush to leave." None of what Steve was saying made sense to him, so it certainly couldn't have made sense to his father.

"Clean. This. Up. Now!" Dad's face was getting red. It was the closest he got to exploding in anger.

The room went silent. An odd expression crossed Nicole's face, then she took a step out of the kitchen and into the living room, where she froze. "Is the shower running?"

"No." It was the dumbest thing he could say, but Steve's brain had melted. Stephen was still in the shower.

"I think it is." Nicole went to the stairs and looked up toward the second floor. "Yeah. It definitely is."

Dad eyed Steve as he went into the living room to confirm for himself. When he reached the stairs, he turned back to Josh and Steve. "Did one of you leave the shower on?"

"I took a bath Thursday. I'm good till Sunday," said Josh.

Nicole wrinkled her nose. "That's a little too long to go between baths."

Before Dad could say anything, Steve ran to the stairs. "Oh yeah. That was me." He tried to laugh it off. "I forgot. I started that water to warm it up when we got home."

"That's ridiculous.' Dad's anger was growing exponentially "You know how much water you're wasting?"

"The world is on the verge of a water crisis." Steve saw that Nicole was ramping up for a TED talk on the environment.

Before she could get out another factoid, he dashed up the stairs. "Sorry. I'll get in now."

Thankfully the bathroom door wasn't locked as Steve burst into the room. Keeping his eyes closed, Steve shut the door behind him. The water was still running and he heard humming. It was risky, but Steve opened one eye quickly to check that Stephen was still actually in the shower. Steve was relieved that he didn't get an eyeful of a naked Stephen. Although it was an irrational fear since it was truly nothing he hadn't seen before. But the idea of seeing himself naked from the outside was too much to fathom. Besides, that's not the way he wanted to discover if they did have any physical differences.

The humming continued. Stephen hadn't heard him come in. "Stephen." Steve realized he was being too quiet when Stephen didn't respond to his name. He tried again a little louder. Still, nothing happened. He debated pulling back the shower curtain, but that was an action that no doubt triggered terror no matter what dimension one was from. "Stephen." Steve was as loud as he could be without anyone outside the bathroom hearing him.

"Ahhh!" Stephen thrashed at the shower curtain until his head... and thankfully only his head poked out. "This is unfair. I am still allocated five more minutes. We agreed upon equal time." Stephen was shouting over the shower water that streamed down behind him.

"I know, but my dad, Josh, and Nicole are home." Steve lowered his voice, hoping that Stephen would take the hint.

He didn't. "That is of no concern to me. I will get an equal amount of time as Buck had, which will not include the time this exchange is taking." Stephen returned to his shower and pulled the curtain shut.

There was a knock at the door. Despite the steam filling the bathroom, Steve's blood turned to ice when he heard Nicole's voice. "Steve... is everything OK? I heard you yelling."

He couldn't speak.

"Steve?" She asked again.

His first attempt at "I'm fine" came out as a wispy wheeze. His second attempt was much too loud. "I'm fine! Just singing. I mean rapping. Sing-rapping."

"OK." That was followed by her footsteps leading away.

His head was pounding and he couldn't catch his breath. Steve didn't know how much longer he could keep up this arrangement. Three people couldn't live in the garage room forever. He wondered if they could start staying with Dr. Hicks. He had the room in his house. But it was risky. They would be too vulnerable to being exposed if they were separated like that. It would be too easy for one of them to walk out on the street at the same time Steve did.

Anticipating all the contingencies to keep the other Steves hidden was exhausting. It was one thing keeping ahead of his dad. At least he was predictable. The spontaneous irrational actions of his ten-year-old brother were much harder to plan for. But there was no avoiding it. Steve's family couldn't find out about the other Steves.

Josh would try to keep the secret. Even Dad might. But they wouldn't be able to hide that something was wrong from Nicole. Josh would flip out for days if he knew. He may not say anything, but he would be an insane spaz. Dad was just too honest. Mom always said that Dad couldn't lie, because he never had enough practice. Every Hanukkah, she could tell the moment Daniel had bought her big present. Mom said his whole demeanor changed. He became stiff and awkward, conscious of every word. Nicole was an investigative journalist. She would figure those two out instantly. It was a wonder she hadn't suspected something was going on with Steve. But then again, she didn't seem to understand anything about him. So that wasn't that surprising.

But Steve knew Nicole would eventually learn about the other Steves. She was an actual trained reporter. She was always saying how vigilance and observation were the key to uncovering the best stories. The most devastating secrets, she said, were not kept by shady, mysterious people, but by the guy next door. Soon enough she'd realize her boyfriend's son had the best secret of all. Steve needed to get them out of the house. There was no way Nicole, Josh, and Dad wouldn't eventually notice three extra people in the house.

After what was far more than five minutes, Stephen shut off the water. "Turn around." Steve did as Stephen instructed and faced the door.

It seemed like another five minutes passed before Stephen proclaimed himself ready. Steve went into the hall first. He heard his Dad and Nicole downstairs and the faint whispers of the TV. That meant Josh had begun his weekend binge in the back room den. Steve ushered Stephen into his room, where Stephanie and Buck were waiting.

Buck shut the door and looked at the others. "Steve, if you just keep your family from looking in the backyard we can climb out the window and get back to the garage."

"No, we can't." Stephanie crossed her arms and sat on the bed. "We'll just hang out here today."

"You can't. It's too risky that Josh will barge in here. He always does." Steve was relieved when he saw Buck nodding in agreement.

"How about you distract them and we can slip out the back door." Buck directed that offer more to Stephanie, for her approval, than Steve.

"Yes. That would be far more realistic." Stephen seemed relieved to be excused from physical activity as well.

With his orders in hand, Steve went downstairs. Dad and Nicole were in the living room. Daniel was flipping through the newspaper. He was maybe the last person in all of New Jersey to still get an actual newspaper. Nicole was on her phone. From the back room, Steve heard Josh cheering on someone in a battle he must have been watching. No one had noticed Steve on the steps and he took that time to examine the room for any inspiration. When he found nothing there, he went into the kitchen. Everything from their shopping trip had been put away. Although the breakfast mess was still strewn about. Steve would have to deal with that before it started to reek. Then it occurred to Steve what he needed to do.

"Where's the sliced turkey?" Steve tried to sound as panicked as possible as he ran into the living room.

"What sliced turkey?" Dad lowered his paper. He got very concerned when he saw how distraught Steve was. "We didn't get any."

"Yes we did! Five pounds!" If so much wasn't at stake, Steve would have been enjoying this improv exercise more.

"I don't remember that." Nicole didn't look up from the phone.

"I know we did. I picked it up myself. I remember. I couldn't decide between oven-roasted and maple-glazed. Then I remembered that the maple glazed gets kind of gummy after a few days. So, I went with the over-roasted." Coming up with those details excited Steve and reminded him why he wanted to be in the play in the first place.

"OK." Dad shrugged. "Go check in the car."

That wasn't what he wanted. As Steve walked through the living room to the front door, he tried to come up with a new emergency to get them out of the house. Then, he decided the easiest answer was to continue playing the role of "Distraught Teenager Looking For His Turkey." He went through the motions of going out to the car and looking in the trunk. Returning to his role, he slammed the trunk shut and ran back into the house.

"It's not in the car." Steve scared Nicole with his abrupt entrance. "Where is it?"

With a sigh, Dad sat forward. "Maybe someone dropped it when they were carrying it in."

"Then we *need* to find it." Frantically, Steve waved Dad and Nicole toward the door. "Please help. We have to check every step of the front walk. It'll go bad out there. That's a ton of meat. It'll attract bugs and... raccoons... maybe even a bear from the park. This is really dangerous. Come on! We all have to search for it."

Dad and Nicole shared a look. Steve realized that if he was trying to convince Nicole everything was normal, this was the absolute wrong way to do it. The alternative, however, was far worse. When they grudgingly stood up to help, Steve went to the hall leading to the back room.

"Josh, you have to help us look for the turkey we dropped."

"We didn't get any turkey." Josh yelled back.

"Fine! Whatever!" Steve was practically screaming to make sure Buck, Stephanie, and Stephen clearly heard the next part. "Stay in the back room, watching the TV with your back to the door. Who cares?!"

"You're *so* weird!" Josh laughed.

Steve ignored that and shouted up the stairs. "OK. I'll be outside with Dad and Nicole... who are already out there... not in the living room."

To their credit Dad and Nicole were taking the search seriously. Dad divided the path from the car to the house into imaginary sections that they methodically searched. Steve felt bad when he saw how intently Nicole examined every centimeter of her areas. At the same time he was proud of how convincing his performance was. The farce went on for five minutes, yielding only a lost battle axe from one of Josh's *Echelons of War* action figures. When Dad and Nicole had made their way to the car, Steve dashed to the corner of the house that gave him a partial view of the garage. In the second floor office window, he saw a hand waving. Steve took that to mean that his diversion had worked.

"You know what?" Steve chuckled, hoping this would soften the blow for Dad and Nicole. "I just remembered. I never did get the turkey."

"What?" Dad stood up, then ran his hand along his lower back. He must have been stiff from bending over that long.

"Yeah. I remember putting back the honey-glazed turkey because it would be gummy and was reaching for the oven-roasted one when Josh came over to tell me that he found those sour gummies we liked. I never did get the turkey. So funny."

Without a word, Nicole returned to the house. As Dad followed, he looked at Steve. "Are you getting enough sleep?"

He was not, but he wasn't going to let his dad know that. "Yeah. Sure. I'm sorry about that. I just really like that turkey."

"Apparently." Daniel ruffled Steve's head.

Feeling bolstered by a house free of extra Steves, Steve jogged inside and up the stairs to his room. He couldn't stop himself from letting out a quick shriek when he found Stephanie waiting on his bed.

"Didn't you see Buck's signal? I never got my turn to shower." Stephanie held up her dry towel.

"Are you OK?" Nicole called from downstairs.

"Uh..." Steve's mind was racing. "I stubbed my toe. I'm OK. I think."

Pushing the door shut, Steve tried to reason with

Stephanie. "I just pretended to take a super-long shower. I can't pretend I'm taking another one."

"Too bad. I didn't ask to be stuck in a disgusting garage for who knows how long. I want to at least feel like a normal human being."

"Just one more day. You can be the first one to shower tomorrow."

Stephanie didn't offer a counter proposal. "Open the door and check that no one's there."

"But—"

"Or, I just walk out there."

Steve didn't bother arguing. The hall was empty when he stepped into it. He waved Stephanie out. Before she shut the bathroom door, Steve yelled downstairs. "I forgot to wash my hair. I'm taking another shower right now. Here I go." At that Stephanie shut the door and turned on the water.

Since he couldn't be seen outside the bathroom for the next few minutes, Steve went back to his room and crawled under the bed to hide. As he settled into his quiet seclusion, listening to the shower water run, he began to process how many close calls he had just that morning with Nicole. At any moment today she could have discovered the others. What would happen if it took more than a month to get them home, and she moved in while they were still in the garage?

All Steve could think about were those kids and their parents at Tarp Scientific. That story Nicole had done on them had been in his mind all morning. Steve hadn't seen the report himself, but she talked about it enough that he might as well have seen it. Those scientists had been working on a synthetic second skin. It was supposed to help people working in extreme environments, protecting them from cold, rain, even fire. Except it didn't work. So they altered the results ... or something. Steve didn't know those details. It was what happened because of Nicole's report that he focused on. New Jersey Child Protective Services took the couple's children away. All because of questionable scientific practices. Steve was hiding interdimensional travelers. He had even participated in the research on the device that brought them to this world. If that became public knowledge, who knew what would happen to his family? All he could think of was Josh being taken away from Dad.

Nicole could not find out about the other Steves. Even if he had to lie to the most important people in his life. It was for their own good.

Steve was shaken out of his spiral when he heard the absurdly loud flush of the toilet in the upstairs bathroom. He realized the shower was off and it was time to retrieve Stephanie. Crawling out from under the bed, he snuck into the empty hall, then lightly knocked on the door. He whispered, "It's me," before turning the handle. Just in case she wasn't ready, he didn't push the door open immediately. When he heard no objections, he opened the door and waved Stephanie out.

"Is the bathroom free now?" Dad's voice was coming from halfway up the stairs.

Stephanie dashed into Steve's room, mere seconds before Steve's dad's head appeared.

"Yeah. It's all free." Steve forced a huge smile.

Dad studied Steve. "Is you *hair* clean now?"

"Uh-huh..." Steve had to fight the urge to run his hand through his very not wet hair. It was very short now. Maybe Dad wouldn't notice that it was dry.

That was another addition to what Steve assumed was his dad's expanding list of Steve's weird behavior. Steve didn't want to know what his dad thought was the reason Steve was taking back-to-back showers. It may well be worse than the truth.

Daniel hadn't taken a full step into the bathroom when he erupted again. "How many towels did you use?" He came back to the hallway carrying a mountain of wet towels for Steve to examine.

"I like to be really dry?" Steve couldn't stop himself from answering with a question. Even he was baffled by how three people could use that many towels.

Dad let them drop to the floor. "Wash these." He started back to the bathroom, then stopped. "And you still haven't cleaned the kitchen. I want that done by the time I get out."

"OK. I will." Steve felt the injustice of getting in trouble for something he didn't do. It was magnified when Dad slammed the bathroom door shut behind him.

Waiting until Dad started the shower, Steve led Stephanie to the stairs, praying that there was enough hot water left to keep Dad from completely losing his mind. Steve went down first, leaving Stephanie in the upstairs hall. He found Nicole on the couch with her laptop out. Josh was still huddled away in the back room. Steve stood in the living room for a minute without Nicole giving any sign that she noticed him. Her attention seemed entirely focused on her work. With Nicole's back to the stairs, it would be possible for Stephanie to get at least as far as the kitchen without Dad's girlfriend looking up. Daniel took fast showers. Stephanie couldn't stay up there much longer.

Steve leaned back toward the step and waved for Stephanie to come down. She was nearly silent as she stepped into the living room. When she saw Nicole, Stephanie froze. He eyes bulged out of her head and she covered her mouth. It was the only time Steve had ever seen Stephanie show even a hint of excitement. When she started to point at Nicole and mime begging, Steve had to pull her into the kitchen.

They were far too close to Nicole to risk speaking. But, at least now if she turned around, they were out of her line of sight. Now, Steve had to get Stephanie all the way out of the house. Before he could figure out the next step, Stephanie pulled him closer and whispered in his ear.

"You *have* to let me meet her. Please! You have no idea." Despite how quiet her voice was, Steve felt the intensity of her need to go back into the living room. She might as well have been screaming in his ear.

Shaking his head Steve stepped back into the living room. He needed Stephanie out of the house immediately and the fastest way to do that was to get rid of this distraction. "Hey, Nicole, Dad said he needs your help with something upstairs." Steve's brain was fried and he couldn't come up with any more details.

She continued typing for another few seconds, then shut her laptop and looked back at Steve. "Sure."

As Nicole got up, her eyes remained fixed on Steve. The longer her glare lingered, the more Steve was convinced she knew something was going on. Another few seconds and he would confess, just to end the awkwardness.

Nicole pursed her lips. "Are you OK?"

She knows! Steve mustered his resolve. He had to maintain his composure. "Yeah. Totally fine. Sorry. Dad said he needs—"

"You don't need to be sorry. You shouldn't be so hard on yourself. It weighs you down. I see how defeated you seem."

Steve ran his hand over his face, trying to feel what it was she was seeing. "I'm fine. You should really go see what—"

Nicole reached for his hand and pulled it from his face. "You were wrong about the turkey. It wasn't the end of the world. Forgive yourself for your mistakes. You..." She squeezed his hand for emphasis. "*You* are the only one who can." Then she clasped her other hand over his as if she had bestowed her blessings upon him. With a final closed-mouth smile, she went up the stairs.

Stephanie appeared instantly from the kitchen, her voice barely under control. "She is so smart. She wrote a whole book about that on my world. It was life-changing. I have to talk to her!"

Halfway through her gushing praise, Steve had started pulling her toward the door. When Steve heard soft, padded feet clomping from the back room, he wrenched the front door open and pushed Stephanie outside. Seconds later, Josh turned the corner into the living room.

"Who were you talking to?" Josh scanned the room that now only contained one Steve.

"Uh..." Steve looked at the front door he was standing next to. "I thought I saw the turkey."

"We didn't buy any!" Josh shook his head.

"Oh yeah!"

"You are the dumbest smart person I know."

This time when Steve laughed, it came easily. The absurdity of this morning had pushed him over the edge.

"I didn't ask you to send up Nicole." Dad said as he came down the stairs. "Why would you—" He stopped in front of the door to the kitchen. "You still didn't clean this up."

Before Steve could answer, Josh chimed in. "He was too busy looking for the turkey again."

"You were?" Dad came over to Steve then started sniffing. "How do you smell this bad after two showers?"

Chapter 12

There was too much laughing. That was the first thing Stephen noticed as he and Noah entered Sinatra Edison. If people were laughing, then they couldn't be taking their task seriously. School was a serious pursuit that offered a chance for advancement, but it also demanded all of one's attention. At least, that had been Stephen's experience.

Distractions were everywhere in this school. There were PA announcements, posters, petitions, bake sales, tickets to buy, tickets to sell—it was endless. This was a mall, not a place of learning. How much time did these morons waste in pursuit of other activities? It was no wonder that Steve was so pathetic. Hard work was second nature to Stephen. On his world, he spent every free second he had studying to keep up with his classes. Even then, it was never enough.

This was not what Stephen should have been doing. His time would be best served continuing repairs on the WET. Dr. Hicks's design had proven to be extremely haphazard. Not only was Hicks handicapped by this world's prehistoric scientific knowledge, but he didn't even have access to the best that their primitive technology offered. The WET was in some cases held together with gum and duct tape. To successfully reopen the rift, they would need proper materials. If Steve was to be believed, the laboratory facilities at this school would have everything they required.

Steve's class schedule was shocking to Stephen. Instead of devoting his entire day to the sciences and math, it was diluted with English, social studies, and health... whatever that was supposed to be. There was no time wasted on extraneous pursuits like liberal arts in Stephen's dimension. Those classes were reserved for the lost cause Dreg students— anyone on Stephen's world who wasn't a member of the esteemed Science Order. The calculus and physics classes Steve was just now taking were taught on Stephen's world in elementary school. By high school, students were expected to be running their own experiments and making discoveries. It was far more demanding... at least to Stephen.

Perhaps the biggest distraction was Noah. His overexplanation of mundane social interactions was excruciating. The hierarchy of the students was painfully obvious. Sci Siders were far more revered than the Art Side students, who were enjoying their last expressions of free will before beginning a lifetime among the Dregs. As Noah pointed out which hallway to walk down and when each class started, Stephen refrained from reminding Noah that a child could read a map and look at a schedule.

Every class that wasn't science- or math-based tested Stephen's resolve. There was a class simply called "history" that boiled down the whole of humanity's experience on Earth to a fifty-three-minute lecture. English class was just some form of book club that discussed works of *fiction*. On Stephen's world, English classes taught the most effective way to write scientific papers.

By the time he arrived at physics class, Stephen was livid. His patience for this adult kindergarten was at an end. He was ready to show off his vast scientific and mathematical skills.

A familiar lanky form lowered itself into the seat in front of Stephen. Justin spun around. "I believe you're in the wrong class. This is physics, Art Sider, not drawing."

At that moment Stephen found it hard to remember in which dimension he was currently residing. The Justin on his world had delighted in mocking Stephen for making fewer scientific discoveries than he had. Justin also enjoyed comparing Stephen's intellect to that of the size of boron, which is the smallest element of the periodic table with an atomic radius of ninety picometers. It was a devastating insult.

Here, however, the situation differed. "I am precisely where I need to be. You are the one who has to re-sync your Tellstar GeoCrystal." A GeoCrystal was a computer on Stephen's world that predated their current Quantum molecular computer drives by twenty years. Tellstar was a low-end brand of electronics. On Stephen's world, no one would have laughed at this joke either.

"Oh my God!" Justin flung his hands in the air. "You can't even get *Doctor Who* references right. I can't believe you signed up for that play. How clueless are you? Life is over for you on the Sci Side."

"That statement is greatly misinformed," Stephen blurted.

"Ooh!" Justin reared back in mock horror. "Are you going to try to hit me again, you Art Sider barbarian?"

"How dare you—" Stephen was cut off when Mr. White entered the room.

In one clean motion, Mr. White set down his briefcase and

removed a stack of papers. "You have fifteen minutes."

He walked up and down the aisles, setting down a single sheet of paper. At each desk he paused, seemingly to study the terror in each student's face. He didn't, however, do that for the girls. Instead, letting the paper flutter down, as if their efforts were beneath him. The room was immediately silent, except for the scratching of pencils on paper. Stephen read the first page, then looked back at the rest of the class furiously writing out equations.

"Is there a problem, Mr. Buchmann?" Mr. White called from behind his desk. "You do understand what a pop quiz is, don't you?"

"I do." Stephen had been prepared for this concurrence. Dr. Hicks and Steve had both mentioned Mr. White. Still, it was a shock to see the man, who was in his dimension, the CEO of Stepstone, a Fortune 500 company, reduced to teaching remedial science lessons. Removed from his tailored suits, this man inspired no awe, only pity.

"Good. Then get to work. You, especially, will need all fifteen—make that fourteen—minutes."

For Stephen, each problem on the quiz was simpler than the one before it. He could not understand why everyone required so much concentration. This was as simple as differential equations that he had learned in elementary school. Still, this was Steve's life, not his. He saw no harm in helping him for now.

"Another question?" Mr. White adjusted his glasses on his nose when he looked up to see Stephen standing over his desk.

"I have completed this examination." Stephen handed him the pack.

"Oh, you have?" Looking up at the clock on the wall, Mr. White scoffed. "In three minutes?"

Stephen shrugged. "I procrastinated for a minute because

initially I assumed this must be some form of farce."

"Is that so?" As Mr. White took out his red pen, the class looked up from their quizzes. No one had ever finished one of Mr. White's quizzes in the allotted time. This was going to be a bloodbath.

No effort was made by Mr. White to suppress his smile as he X-ed through answers on Stephen's quiz. At one point, he laughed so hard that he started tearing up. With a mixture of horror and delight, everyone in the room watched, no longer concerned about their own grades.

"I hope that was worth it," Mr. White remarked as he handed the decimated quiz back to Stephen. "Go sit down. I'm offended that you would waste my time with this idiocy."

When Stephen was ten, he once visited his mother at work, and got to meet Timothy White. It had been so awe-inspiring, Stephen had lost the power of speech. He had no such issues with this version of the man.

Stephen studied the quiz then placed it back in front of Mr. White. "You are in error. Each of these is correct. This is basic math. I can perform these calculations in my sleep."

"I guess you got up too early, because this is the work of an idiot." He handed it back to Stephen.

"I AM NOT AN IDIOT!" Stephen slammed the paper on the desk, knocking over a model of the solar system. His face was red. Everyone in the room gasped. Stephen pointed to the first question. "In this problem, 'Daredevil Johnny,' as you call the human subject, would have 206.439 kilograms worth of force exerted on his body at this point. Here it would be 179.64 kilograms and here 204.783 kilograms. How is that incorrect?"

Two dozen heads looked down to check their answers.

"You did not calculate the normal and friction forces affecting him." Mr. White tried to stand, but because Stephen was so close, he couldn't move his chair.

"That's irrelevant." Pointing to his equation, Stephen stepped through the problem. "Weight and centripetal force remain constant. All that is required is to calculate the change in direction."

"That's an oversimplification of the—" Mr. White stopped as he processed what Stephen had shown him. "I see what you did... that... that actually works." His pen hovered over the X for a moment before he scratched it out.

"Thank you." The red rage in Stephen's face dulled some. "Now, explain your thought process for problem number two."

Red ink splattered Mr. White's shirt when he snapped his pen in half.

Dr. Hicks pitched forward when Steve dropped his end of the board. Before the whole shelf toppled to the ground, Hicks was able to catch himself. He set his end on the ground and watched Steve revel in Stephen's recap of the day.

"You did what?" Steve shouted.

"I have procured the materials from your school that we shall require for the first phase of the repairs," Stephen explained. "When we enter Phase Two, I'll have to—"

"You told off Mr. White?" If Stephen had told Steve that he was giving him a space shuttle, he wouldn't have been happier. "In front of the whole class! And you were right. That's awesome!" Another thought occurred to Steve, and his joy disappeared. "He must have been pissed."

"Indeed. He was extremely upset." Stephen began laying out the diagnostic tools he had checked out of the school lab. "That man operates in opinions. Science is provable fact. Once

I demonstrated my equations for the other answers, he was forced to give me full credit."

"You made him go through the whole quiz?" It took a moment for Steve to process what Stephen had said. "What did you get?"

"A 120, which makes absolutely no sense. How can I get more than 100 percent of the questions correct? That is mathematically impossible."

"Bonus questions." Steve ran over and hugged Stephen, who froze in place. "A 120! That's the highest grade I've gotten all year. Hell, that's the highest anyone's gotten. How?"

"That is a child's class. How are you having difficulty with it?"

"That's the thing! I'm not having trouble. He just has it out for me. Any answer I give is the wrong one... according to him at least. I can't believe you called him out on it... and got away with it." Steve had to sit down. "He's going to hate me so much now."

"His feelings are irrelevant," Stephen declared.

"Doesn't matter." A smile crossed Steve's face. "If you did that for me on the midterm, I'd get an A in the class. It wouldn't matter how much he hates me. After this year I'd never have to deal with him again."

The vacant expression on Steve's face disturbed Stephen but didn't surprise him. He moved back to get some space. "Can we return to the matter at hand? If the internal circuitry is still functional, that will save us several weeks of work."

"Just calibrating the same settings as before should reopen the rift. And you all can return home." Dr. Hicks began pacing the floor. "This is bittersweet. I wish Melissa were here to see this. Her theory would have changed the world."

Laughing, Stephen went to the tool bench. "On this world, a design this simple qualifies as extraordinary? Then projects that I completed in third grade would make me a god here."

Chapter 13

"I'm done. May I be excused?" Steve started standing up without waiting for an answer.

"Hold on..." his dad said through a mouthful of food. "That's all you're going to eat?"

"Yeah, I'm full." Steve looked down at his plate. The pork chop was only missing a carefully cut-out corner. The roasted broccoli and mashed potatoes appeared to be untouched.

"OK." Dad shrugged and looked at Nicole, who was sitting next to him. Across the dining room table, Josh was devouring his second helping of everything. "Is there something wrong with the pork chops?"

"No. They are delicious." Nicole proved her point by cutting off another piece. "I love how much you do with such a... simple recipe."

"Yeah. They're fine, Dad." Steve turned to go into the kitchen.

"Don't worry. He'll eat later." Josh reached for more mashed potatoes, not noticing Steve freeze in his tracks at that comment.

"What do you mean?" Dad asked.

"When he does his homework out in the garage, he takes out tons of food." Josh had already finished his newest helping of potatoes.

"That's not true." Steve was being consumed by panic. He didn't think his little brother had noticed him taking dinner out to the other Steves in the garage. Steve had been very wrong. "It's just a snack, not that much."

"You already finished off that whole giant box of frozen pizza we got on Saturday." Josh mimed Steve eating all those pizzas.

"You're secretly eating alone?" Nicole turned to Dad. Her look was an unmistakable *This-Is-A-Serious-Concern* expression. "Do you feel judged when you eat in front of others?"

The plate in Steve's hand started to feel heavier. The others had been complaining about having pizza for dinner every night. He was going to let them have his food to help mix things up. "It's nothing. I just have been working late and get hungry."

"Yeah, but if you eat your dinner—" Before Dad could finish offering his obvious advice, Nicole reached over to touch his arm.

"We're not judging you, Steve." Nicole's voice was surprisingly warm. If she hadn't been so completely wrong about the situation, it would have been comforting. "We just want to help you."

"Help him do what?" Josh followed that up with a satisfying belch. "Excuse me."

"Hold on." Dad rested his hand on top of Nicole's hand. "Do you think Steve has an eating disorder?"

"No. Wait." Steve set down his plate on the table. This was getting worse by the second.

"I don't know. But I have reported on this issue enough to

notice some troubling warning signs." She studied Steve. "Do you see how tired he is? How tense he always seems?"

"I promise, it is just school." Of course Steve was exhausted. When he wasn't working on the WET with Dr. Hicks and Stephen, he was running around sneaking in supplies to the garage. That included digging through mom's old clothes in the attic for the ten minutes he had during the day before Josh and Dad got home. Then walking two miles with Stephanie to Lower Sable, the next town over, so she could buy everything she needed, which was much more than a package of underwear. Steve had zeroed out his allowance money on an assortment of shampoos, body washes, deodorants, and tampons. He had no idea being a girl was so expensive. The guys were no less demanding. Stephen insisted on having a completely unblemished apple every night. That was in addition to his hyperspecific instructions for what temperature he wanted his pizza served. Buck was devouring more food than Steve thought possible for one person. Buck could not get over the variety of snack foods on this world, and demanded that Steve bring him everything. It was more than the pizza that had been scarfed down. On his own, Buck had finished off a wholesale club-sized box of frosted cereal, a tub of licorice, and three bags of pretzels. Needless to say that meant even more times Steve had to sneak Buck into the house to use the bathroom.

"Is that why you've had to go to the bathroom so much?" Josh giggled at his question.

"You do seem to be in the bathroom a lot more often." A crease formed on Dad's face. Steve knew this meant he was starting to consider Nicole's theory.

"Stop talking about what I do in the bathroom." Steve couldn't look at anyone at the table. "It's not any of that stuff. I just don't like pork chops anymore. OK? I swear that's all it is. They taste gross." Steve walked into the kitchen and dumped his food into the trash. Now he would have to find another way to feed the Steves.

There was nothing quite as unnerving to Steve as being out in public with the other Steves. Granted, it was after midnight, and the streets of Longview were completely empty. That still didn't mean someone wouldn't see them.

But after the inquisition at dinner, Steve couldn't get food to them until well after Nicole had left and Dad and Josh were asleep. So they had gone to the hot dog place on the edge of town. It was the only restaurant open this late, plus no one Steve knew ever went there. He ordered a half dozen hot dogs, endured a withering look from the guy behind the counter, who must have assumed that they were all for Steve, then joined the others as they ate behind the restaurant, out of sight from passersby.

After they finished, the other Steves immediately ignored his request to head back home. They insisted on continuing this excursion. Steve sympathized. It had been almost two weeks, but being confined to the garage was getting to them. The room was nice and spacious when Steve was by himself, but when all four of them were there, it was claustrophobic.

They had no destination. That combined with yet again sneaking out of house had unnerved Steve. Within a few block he completely forgot about his worries. Steve had thought that sneaking over to see Dr. Hicks had been a thrilling experience. But aimlessly wandering at night turned out to be the most amazing feeling ever. All of a sudden, his boring town held a world of new possibilities. He could go anywhere and do anything. Was this what college was like?

That excitement was short-lived.

"I require a more expansive explanation than, 'Because,'" Stephen told Steve.

"They're private," Steve said.

"You are withholding scientific knowledge." Stephen went to run his hand through what used to be his bowl-cut hair. Instead, he found his new, unsatisfying buzz cut.

"I'm not. Trust me. It's just random thoughts." Steve sped up to walk next to Stephanie and Buck, leaving Stephen to trail behind.

All evening Stephen had been pressuring Steve to let him read Melissa's journals. Normally Steve left them in the garage office, but when Stephen first got up there, he immediately started reading through them. So Steve had taken them to the house and hid them in the attic with Mom's old clothes. Most of the entries were mundane records of her daily activities: going to work, picking up the boys from school, hiking in Mountainside. There was nothing scandalous or offensive. They were Steve's private connection to his mom, and he didn't want to share.

Stephen hustled to catch up to Steve on the street. "It could very well be that those random notes she wrote down contained the first inkling of a brilliant discovery. Who better than I to uncover them?"

"He said no," Buck barked. "Let it go."

Stephen curled back into himself.

"Your town is awesome." So much sarcasm was dripping off of Stephanie they could have sold it as a perfume. The group had reached the far end of Longview and were near the north entrance to Mountainside Park.

"Sorry," Steve shrugged. "There's not a lot we can do without being seen."

"We'll definitely be spotted if we stay out on the street."

Buck scanned the road.

"Hold on!" Stephanie pointed behind them. "I just saved the night."

They all turned to face what Stephanie was looking at—the Longview Jungle Golf Course and Arcade. It was a mecca for the town's under-twelve set and rested on the edge of the park. There were lines to get in during the summer, but once fall came and the leaves changed, it emptied out.

"Anyone not have mini golf on their world?" Stephanie was already crossing the deserted street. "I can explain the rules."

"I think it's closed for the season. There's no way we can get to the clubs," Steve pointed out to the others, who were already crossing the street.

"Yeah, that's real tight security they have there." Stephanie pointed to the mini golf course that was only protected from the outside world by a three-foot high wood rail fence. "I bet Mr. Resistance Fighter here could jimmy open the lock to the clubhouse." She patted Buck on the back.

"Any activities involving targeting are banned on my world." Buck was a kid on Christmas morning. "I haven't played Putt-Putt since I was five! Gimme a hairpin or something."

Between Josh and Steve, the two of them had been to Longview Jungle Golf several hundred, maybe several thousand, times. It had been the site of birthday parties, school trips, and boring Sunday afternoons. The waterfalls and animatronic lion obstacles had long ago lost their challenge for Steve. He could play the course blindfolded. Tonight, though, the thrill had returned.

It didn't take Buck more than a minute to pick the lock on

the clubhouse door. There had been enough moonlight for them to easily play most of the holes. But the fake palm trees and ornamental thatch huts had left a quarter of the holes in absolute darkness. Those became the best ones.

"Fascinating," Stephen commented.

"You mean how badly I'm kicking your ass," Buck called out as he swung his club. His ball barreled down the course until it was swallowed by the darkness of the cave at the end of the green.

"Hardly. Rather, I think it's fascinating that we have all putted from the right side of the tee." Stephen placed his ball on the green and stood on the right side to illustrate his point.

"Why's that weird?" Steve asked as he watched Buck blindly walk into the cave. "We're all the same person."

"No, we're not!" Stephanie laughed. "You're scared of everything. Buck and I aren't."

Steve ignored that all-too accurate fact. "But we all liked the same type of pizza."

"That's because you only had one kind at your house." Stephanie hit her ball just to the left of the cave. It rolled into a tiny hole, then reappeared in a second section of the course below them.

"So none of you like pepperoni and olives?" Steve asked.

"No!" Stephanie and Stephen said together.

"I do!" Buck echoed from inside the cave.

"It's not crazy for me to think that we'd like the same things, is it?" Steve wondered.

"Do you like graham crackers and ginger ale when you get your period?" Stephanie asked.

"STOP SAYING STUFF LIKE THAT!" Buck shouted.

Stephanie walked over to Buck. "You're never going to be as tough as you pretend to be if that kind of talk upsets you so much."

Stephen took his shot. His ball had been aimed at Stephanie's shortcut hole but instead bounced off the side of the cave.

"But we do have some stuff in common." Steve insisted. "Buck loves Reflex."

"Kind of." Buck leaned on his club. "I've been reading the newest ones in the garage. They're totally different from the ones I read as a kid. I mean, he's a clone now with a bunch of new powers. It's kind of not the same character. Which doesn't mean I'm not pissed that I won't be able to see the movie. That would be amazing."

"I just figured we'd have something in common." Steve followed the group to the next hole, forgetting to take his turn.

"What about our parents?" Buck jumped down to the next section.

"Even they're different." Steve pointed to Stephanie. "Your parents are divorced." He looked at Stephen. "Your parents only had one kid." Then he faced Buck. "And your mom is Sarah Connor."

"No. Her name is Melissa Buchmann, too," corrected Buck.

"It's from *Terminator*... a movie... forget it." Steve twirled his club as the others lined up for the next hole. "At least our moms are all physicists, right?"

"Naturally," Stephen noted. "She heads her own research division at the Stepstone on my world."

"Actually, my mother works at Tarp Scientific in North Ridge." Stephanie pointed to Buck. "And your mom's not even a scientist. She's the leader of the resistance or whatever."

"Well, now she is," Buck explained. "But she worked as a physicist until those Everlast Security jackasses shut down her lab."

"Maybe they share similar personalities?" Steve was

intrigued.

"My mom's strong, confident, and a natural leader," Buck started.

"So's mine." Stephanie's enthusiasm seemed to dim the more she talked about her mother.

"My mother is just as demanding." Stephen stood up straight as he began to list her traits. "She has the highest of standards and expects nothing less from me... no matter how hard I try."

Steve had stopped twirling his club. Stephanie put her arm on his shoulder. "Sorry. Was that hard for you to hear about our moms?"

"A little." Steve looked down. "I guess that's what my mom was like, too. Sort of. She was smart and tough. But that's not how I think of her. I remember how happy she was. How she always smiled when she saw me and Josh in the morning."

Stephanie hugged Steve. Stephen was quiet as they gave Steve a moment. The reflective silence was broken a few seconds later by a loud sniffle. Buck, who had his back to them, blew his nose, then turned to face the group. His eyes were watery.

"Come on! Are we playing or what?" Buck said, trying to hide the wavering in his voice.

"Sure." Steve smiled and picked up his ball. "My turn."

He placed the ball on the green. The first part of this hole dropped away immediately and appeared to empty into a stream. Steve knew this was an optical illusion, and if he hit the ball just right, it would bank around the stream to the hole. He pulled the putter back and gave it a tap—

"FREEZE!"

The searchlight cut across the course and passed over the Steves. Before the light could find its way back, Buck pulled all of them down. As they lay flat against the ground, they saw two patrol cars in the parking lot. An officer was in one, operating the searchlight. Two others got out of the second car.

"WE KNOW YOU'RE IN THERE. COME ON OUT!" a thin-framed silhouette yelled into the darkness. He and his beefy partner walked onto the course.

"We are so screwed," Steve whispered. "We have to get out of here. Who knows what they'll do when they see all of us together?"

"Don't panic. We can figure this out," Stephanie assured him.

The officer in the car swept his light across the trees behind the course. The beam barely penetrated the darkness of the park behind them. Steve estimated that he and the others were maybe twenty yards from the edge of the forest. There was no way they would make it if they tried to run for the woods. But if some of them distracted the cops on the course and another took out the searchlight, they would have a shot.

"I have an idea," Steve whispered. "We can lose them in the woods—"

"I would barely venture to call that a plan." Stephen cut him off. "I have formulated a better idea."

Steve wanted to object but doubted he could have a better idea than Stephen.

"The three of us..." Stephen quietly indicated Stephanie, Steve, and himself. ". . . will sprint toward the parking lot, leading the officers to believe we are fleeing toward a vehicle." He pointed to Buck. "You will remain behind, then proceed in a stealthy manner to disable that searchlight. Once that objective has been completed, the rest of us will reverse direction and proceed into the park."

Steve started to point out that this was his plan but realized that he had not actually told them his plan.

"Are you sure they'll follow us?" Stephanie whispered.

Buck grunted. "They'll always take the bait."

"But both of them?" Stephanie was doubting the plan.

"That's a good point," Buck started. "We should split up. Steve, head to the arcade. Stephanie and Stephen, head to the parking lot. But we have to wait until they find us first. Otherwise, they may not see you running."

"The major concern will be how long do we remain concealed in the reservation." Stephen studied the dark forest behind them.

"I've spent plenty of time in this park," Steve offered. "We can just keep going through the woods."

"And then we will become disoriented and die of exposure." Stephen rolled his eyes.

"I know the way. Mom and I hiked these woods all the time." Stephanie pointed to a ridge of raised trees. "Once we're inside, everyone head toward those trees. You should able to see them easily."

"Get ready." Buck had been watching the cops. They were getting closer. "Go, now!"

Buck kicked over a ceramic giraffe. As soon as it hit the ground, the spotlight zeroed in on their hiding place. Steve popped up, followed by Stephanie and Stephen. Shielding their faces from the searchlight, each pair ran in their separate directions. The heavier cop and his thin-framed partner each took off in separate directions, hot on the tail of their night's biggest catch.

After patiently counting to ten, Buck sprinted toward the police cruisers. The officer operating the searchlight was busy bouncing the beam between the two groups. He didn't notice Buck sneak between his car and the other patrol car. Reaching into the window of the empty car, Buck found the handle of the search light. He aimed it at the other car, flipped it on, then hit the horn. The officer operating the search light turned to face the cacophony and light coming from the his right. He was instantly blinded by the other car's search light. Buck dashed behind the cars, then doubled back toward the woods. On the golf course, the heavy cop and his thin-framed partner stopped their respective chases and turned back to the parking lot to see what was happening. While they had their backs turned, the others sprinted toward the woods. It was too late when the officers noticed where the Steves were headed.

"GET BACK HERE, NOW!" the beefy one yelled into the woods.

When his partner joined him, they stared into the eternal darkness of the park. "We're going in there after them, right?" the thin officer asked his partner.

"Hell no, Nichols!" He shook his head and turned back to the squad car. "So far as I'm concerned, it was just a bunch of raccoons."

"If you say so, Johnson."

"I do. Let's go eat." Officer Johnson yelled to the third officer, still recovering his eye sight. "Hey, Bobby, you want to get some hot dogs?"

Finding the trees Stephanie had selected turned out to be harder than she imagined. There were several terrifying moments when both groups thought they would be left for dead in the woods. Once the patrol cars pulled out of the parking lot, Steve turned on his cell phone flashlight. Buck saw it immediately and found his way to him. Stephanie and Stephen took longer. Stephen had insisted on calculating their location based on the position of the stars. After Stephen's third start-over of his calculations, Stephanie saw Steve's light and dragged Stephen along.

Stephanie took the lead as they hiked along the edge of the park. Steve had started to recognize landmarks as soon as they began their trek. Even so, he still doubted his own sense of direction and was glad to have someone else taking responsibility. He was less worried about them dying in the woods than he was about being humiliated if he sent them down the wrong path.

They only walked through the woods for twenty minutes. Buck figured that, by that time, the cops had definitely given up their search. The group exited the woods near Dr. Hicks's house. Compared to the trees, it almost seemed like daylight as they walked past the streetlights. The group felt every minute of it being three A.M. as they trudged up Steve's street to his house. Tonight, no one would complain about where they slept as long as they got to sleep.

As they made their way up the block, Steve looked at the darkened world around them. While all of these people had been asleep, he had played two rounds of golf, tangled with the police, and ran through the pitch-black woods. He was exhausted and had never felt so alive. Having these Steves around was changing everything.

Chapter 14

Standing on the railing of the back deck, Buck reached up to the windowsill above him. It was just out of his grasp. He'd have to jump for it. That would be risky, but the situation was dire. Taking a deep breath, Buck visualized his goal and leapt for the ledge. It was large enough for him to get a good grip when he grabbed it. Then, it was a matter of one simple pull-up. He was able to get his elbows on the sill, and brace his feet against the side of the house. He couldn't hold this long. Looking in the window, he saw his chance, and knocked.

Inside the room Steve yelped and dropped some papers on the floor. It took him far too long to come over to the window. Buck was losing his grip. He knocked again. That seemed to spur Steve into action.

"What are you doing?" Steve whispered as he opened the window, letting in the early morning sun.

Buck jabbed his hand into the room, readjusting his grip on the inside of the window. When he had both hands inside, he pushed himself up the wall with his legs until he could get a knee on the sill. His heart was pounding more than he imagined. He would never admit it out loud, but that had been insanely risky. When his breathing slowed, he swung his legs into the safety of Steve's room.

"I need to use the bathroom." Buck kept his voice low, despite the urgency.

"Why didn't you wait? We're all leaving in fifteen minutes." Steve kept an eye on the door.

"That would have been too late." Buck looked away from Steve. "I may have had too many of those hot dogs last night."

Steve smiled. "You put a ton of onions on yours."

"Don't remind me." Buck snuck to the door of Steve's bedroom. "Can you check if the coast is clear?"

Buck was sweating now. Steve must have noticed the color rushing from Buck's face. He set down the papers he was holding and opened his door a crack. After a moment, Steve began waving his arm around frantically. Buck was afraid to move too quickly. Then Steve said very loudly and very awkwardly into the hall, "Hi, Dad!"

Buck rolled under the bed and came face-to-face with a very old pair of socks. He watched as Steve's feet came back into the room, followed by his father's. Being silent and stealthy had never been a problem for Buck. His stomach was another issue. The bed above him was not going to muffle these rumblings.

"Steve, I was thinking a lot about dinner last night." Steve was still standing by the door, blocking his dad from coming into the room. "I didn't mean to put you on the spot. I just want you to know that if you have any problems—"

"Dad, I don't have an eating disorder. I swear." Buck didn't know what Steve was talking about, but he needed to wrap this up very soon.

"I know. I just want you to remember that if you have a problem... any problem, no matter how big, you can talk to me... or Nicole."

"OK. I will." Steve moved forward but his dad's feet remained still.

"Nicole may have been overreacting a bit, but, well, she really cares about people and truly wants to help." Steve's dad paused. "That may be what I love most about her. She is always trying to help. That's why she did that story on Tarp."

"Right. The researchers and their kids." Buck could her the bile in Steve's tone.

"Exactly. I think I'm really lucky that I found someone like her, who is so smart and compassionate. It's very rare. Don't take it for granted when you find it."

"I won't, Dad. I have to finish getting ready."

"Yeah. Of course. Me too." Before Steve's dad's feet turned away, they took a step forward and Buck heard a kiss. "I love you, boychick."

Buck stopped paying attention. He was overcome with envy. Steve sounded irritated by his father. Buck would do anything for another moment of sappiness with his own dad.

The sheets on the side of the bed were lifted up. Steve's head appeared. "Dad went back to his room. Go."

Buck wasted no time as he sprinted out of the room into the bathroom. If he had waited a moment longer, it would have been a very messy disaster. It wasn't until Buck flushed that he remembered how loud that toilet was. The noise triggered yelling from downstairs. He inched into the hallway, careful to make sure no one was up there.

From the kitchen he heard Steve's dad yelling. "If you want a ride, we're going in two minutes."

"Yeah. I don't want to be late." Josh echoed his father from downstairs.

"OK!" Steve yelled back from his room.

Buck stepped into the room. "You weren't waiting for me,

were you?"

"No." Steve was frantically flipping through the stapled stack of papers he had been holding before. "I'm just not sure about this anymore."

When Buck got closer, he recognized the script for the play. "The audition. What? Are you nervous?"

"Kind of. There's been a lot going on and I'm not sure I'm ready." Steve flung the pages onto the bed. "This was a stupid idea."

Picking up the pages, Buck laughed. "Nah. There's nothing to worry about. It's easy. You're just trying out for the assistant." Buck straightened up. "*Here's the file. I've highlighted the relevant information.* It's like two lines. No big deal."

The frantic look in Steve's eyes was replaced with awe. "You just did that on the spot?"

"No. I've been stuck in that room for days. I must have read this script a dozen times."

"You are really good."

Buck didn't argue the point. "Whatever."

Now Steve was smiling. "You should audition for me."

"No." Buck forgot that they were supposed to be whispering. "You wanted to be in the play. You do it."

"I do." Steve lowered his voice more, as if to compensate for Buck's outburst. "But, I didn't have time to get ready. You already know this."

"Forget it!" Buck was back to whispering as he pushed the script into Steve's hands. "I'm not here to live some fantasy life. This is what *you* wanted."

"Steve!" His dad called from downstairs. "We're going."

"Yeah!" Josh bellowed.

"Please." Steve offered the script back to Buck. "I don't want to screw this up because I didn't have time to prepare. All you need to do is say two lines. You'll be great. If you get the part then I'll start rehearing and be ready."

"No. It's wrong. And weird to keep pretending to be you."

"You are me. But, I get it." Steve looked around his room. His actions were jerky and desperate. Then his gaze settled on a stack of comic books on his desk. "How about this? You do this and I'll let you take my Reflex comics back with you when you go home."

Buck had seen this before. It was stress. Steve was overloaded. Hiding the three of them from his family must have been harder than he was telling them. It was like being a double-agent. That was high pressure.

"Steve!" His father's voice was getting grave.

"Please." Steve said.

Buck was quiet for a moment. "Just the old Reflex comics. I don't want the new ones."

When Buck walked into the auditorium, something surprised him. He was actually excited to audition. Before that week he had never heard of *The Trial of Terrible Terry*, but after all his repeated readings in the garage, he loved it. *Terrible Terry* was a courtroom comedy about a small town recluse who hires a recent law school grad to stop the big-city rich guy from tearing down his house and putting up a mini mall. It was the funniest thing he'd read in years. (It was also the only funny thing he'd read in years.)

Steve wanted Buck to read for the part of the assistant to the town millionaire, Mr. Farnsworth. Most of the assistant's scenes were with Mr. Farnsworth. The only way this part could become great is if it were played by Jon Blaze (a really famous pre-Everlast comedian on Buck's world).

Yellow Post-it notes marked the pages where the assistant

actually had lines. Buck had memorized them long ago. In fact, he had learned most of the other parts as well. There was not a lot to do in the garage.

"I think this is a trap."

Buck clenched the back of the seat in front of him. His heart raced as he scanned the auditorium for possible exits. When he whipped around, he was met with a sweet face smiling back at him.

"I never feel safe in a room with this many Art Siders." The girl laughed.

Adrenaline drained from Buck's body and his heart slowed down. One of the first things he learned in the Resistance was to maintain a good poker face at all times. Nothing was more important to remaining undercover than being in control of one's emotions. Buck nodded and smiled back at the girl, hoping she would continue talking so he could figure out who she was.

"I love this play. I've watched the movie version a million times. I'm so glad your cousin talked me into trying out."

Right! This was Steve's crush, Madelyn... or was it Marilyn? No, her name was Madison. Buck had met her briefly while signing up for the auditions. She was cute in a mousy way, but not Buck's type. His one girlfriend so far had been bulletproof-tough. Crystal didn't back down from anything. In fact, it was her obstinate nature that led her to tell off that Everlast agent. Granted, that forced her to go into hiding, quickly ending their two-week romance.

"Did you decide what you're trying out for?" Buck asked. Whether or not she was Buck's type, he owed it to Steve to do as much flirting as possible. Based on his limited time with Steve, he was certain that flirting was not a strength Steve had.

"Sabrina. Might as well go for broke, right?" Madison held up her left hand and crossed her fingers for luck.

Sabrina was the female lead of the show. She was the daughter of Terrible Terry, the recluse. One of Buck's favorite scenes was Sabrina begging Mr. Farnsworth to let her father stay in his house. When that fails, Sabrina awkwardly tries to seduce Farnsworth, who as it turns out is gay.

"That's a great role. I bet you'd be awesome in it."

"I don't know. Maybe." Madison smiled and looked away as her cheeks blushed slightly.

Yeah, she was definitely not for Buck. Crystal thought modesty was more pathetic than actual self-doubt.

"All right, people, listen up!" Mr. Salinger, the sponsor of the drama club and resident director, made his way up the stairs to the stage. When he got to the last step, he made a dramatic leap onto the stage. His jiggling paunch undermined the effort.

"We're going to run these auditions in groups. The first will be for Terrible Terry, Rick Cherry, and John Highland."

Buck was surprised at how excited he was to see these parts performed in person. This was a great scene. John Highland was Farnsworth's ruthless, big-city attorney. His career was made on the backs of widows swindled out of inheritances and injured workers denied insurance payouts. He had never lost a case or showed an ounce of warmth. Rick Cherry was the naive, bright-eyed recent law school grad hired by Terrible Terry.

"Anyone up for those parts will be reading the courtroom showdown scene. It's on..." Mr. Salinger held out his hand, which lingered untouched. Mr. Salinger looked off-stage. "CRYSTAL!"

A very awed and overwhelmed girl came running up with a script. Her heavy cat-eye glasses slipped down her nose as she flipped through the book, then placed it in Mr. Salinger's hand. Buck's heart stopped. If he hadn't heard her name, he would never have recognized her. The Crystal he had known was a fierce warrior. Watching this girl on stage made him question what he'd ever seen in his Crystal.

". . . page eighty-one of your scripts," Salinger finished.

He held the script out to Crystal. She was still recovering from getting him the script the first time, and jumped when it suddenly appeared in front of her again. Salinger's arm remained still while Crystal remembered her job and swapped the script for a clipboard. Without making any eye contact with Crystal, Mr. Salinger pulled the clipboard back from her.

"Bill Amarone, Darren Abrams, and Christopher Walls, you're up first." After reading the names off of the clipboard he flung it back to Crystal, who stepped out of Mr. Salinger's way as he made his way down from the stage to his perch in the auditorium. He was not to be bothered with such mundane tasks as carrying things.

Buck leaned forward as the first group started their scene. Darren Abrams, who was reading Terrible Terry, played him drunk... very drunk. Bill and Christopher may have read their parts well, but Darren's performance was like a black hole, drawing everything around it into this dismal abyss.

Mr. Salinger waited a full second after they spoke their last line before grabbing back the clipboard and reading off the next group of names. "John Graziano, Phillip Blade, and Kristian Thomas. Next!"

Two guys stood up from the audience and ran onto stage. One was tall and slim. The other was a ball of focused concentration. The tall one stared out into the darkness of the theater, waiting for his next direction. The ball of concentration bounced on his feet to keep his energy going. Buck laughed when he recognized the ball of concentration as Kristian Thomas. On his world Kristian had become a legend in their school. During a routine Everlast security sweep of the school, they had found contraband in his locker. Kristian was so scared when the agent asked him about it, he pissed himself. From then on, everyone called him "Flood."

Tension built on stage while they waited for the third to appear.

"Who are we missing?" Mr. Salinger barked.

Crystal bobbled the clipboard, recovered, and pointed to a name.

"Why is John Graziano wasting my time?" No one on stage had an answer for Mr. Salinger. "Then he has lost his opportunity. I need someone to read the role of Highland for these two very patient gentlemen."

Mr. Salinger turned to the rear of the auditorium, looking for volunteers. He was met with dozens of faces intensely preparing for their roles, none of which were for Highland.

"I don't have time for this!" Mr. Salinger had a very packed schedule of being busy. "You."

Buck flinched when he saw Salinger's finger aimed at him. He looked behind him to find only Madison.

"Today, please!"

Madison mouthed "Good luck" as Buck jumped up and jogged to the stage. He spent enough time around military personnel to know what "today" meant. With one smooth motion, he vaulted onto the stage.

Phillip, the tall kid, watched Buck as he settled into position next to him. "Aren't you a Sci Sider?" he asked.

The ball of concentration, also known as Kristian, stopped bouncing. "He totally is! What's going on?"

"What's the holdup now?" Mr. Salinger hollered from his pool of shadows.

"This kid is a Sci Sider," Kristian whined. "They can't audition."

The auditorium full of Art Siders bristled at this. Buck

stared down at Kristian. He was pretty certain that he could scare Kristian badly enough right now to get him to wet himself on stage.

"Actually, I can." Buck locked eyes with Kristian. "That a problem?"

"You think you can act?" Phillip asked. "I'd like to see that." He began a series of stilted mechanical movements and a robot voice. "Emotion does not compute! Error! Error!"

Every Art Sider in the auditorium burst out laughing.

"Quiet!" Mr. Salinger cried. The roar of laughter died down to an acceptable chuckle. "I'm afraid Mr...." He looked at Crystal, who shook her head. "Who exactly are you?"

"Steve Buchmann."

"I'm afraid this Sci Sider is right. He can try out. What role are you auditioning for?"

"The assistant."

"That's harmless enough. So let's just get his humiliation over with." He leaned back into his pool of shadows. "Begin when you're ready."

Kristian eyed Buck like he was trying to steal his phone.

"*Your honor, I'll be calling Mr. Winecart to the stand,*" Phillip said, assuming the role of Rick Cherry, Terry's attorney.

Kristian took his time sitting down on a metal folding chair on the stage. He was playing Terry as a paranoid homeless man.

"Wait! Stop!" Salinger snapped. "Sci Sider, where is your script?"

"I have it memorized," Buck said.

Phillip and Kristian looked at the scripts in their hands. "That's bull!" Kristian exclaimed. "No, you don't."

Direct challenges like this always helped Buck focus. It got him out of many unpleasant situations on his world. He nodded to Kristian. "Let's find out."

"Get on with it!" Mr. Salinger screamed.

When Buck first read *The Trial of Terrible Terry*, he recognized who John Highland was immediately. Well, who he reminded him of at least. He was Lieutenant Aaron Johnson, the overweight head Everlast officer in his version of Longview. This man was intense and unyielding. He brought the toughest operatives to tears. The most unnerving part was that he always did it with a smile.

A tiny smile crept across Buck's face. *"Mr. Winecart. Can you tell me when you first saw your house?"*

"Hold on... give me some time. I needs to do some math-a-matical computations." He wrote a series of figures in the air. The audience chuckled. *"That would be nineteen hundred and sixty-two."*

Kristian mimed taking out a handkerchief and aggressively blowing his nose. This got a few more laughs from the audience.

"And is that the year before your wife passed away?" Buck relished being on the other side of an interrogation, even if it was just pretend.

"Oh, my poor Delores!" Before Kristian could mime taking out his handkerchief again, Buck pulled an imaginary one from his pocket and handed it to him. The gesture caught Kristian off guard, but he played along by miming taking it and blowing his nose. This got a huge laugh.

"Let's discuss something more pleasant—your loving daughter, Sabrina." Buck found Madison in the audience and winked at her. Steve owed him big time. *"What year did she graduate from high school?"*

"I'll never forget. That was 1963."

Buck nodded. The thing about Johnson, the Everlast officer who was inspiring Buck's performance, was that the closer he got to breaking someone, the nicer he got. Buck chuckled warmly, as if he were remembering his childhood in that house. "*So just tell me one more thing... When did you actually buy the house?*"

"*Like I said, 1962.*"

"*That is when you moved into the house. When did you buy the house?*"

Kristian stared off, looking for a voice to give his character an answer. He jumped when Buck got in his face. His voice was hard stone granite now. "*You never bought that house, did you?*"

The audience gasped at the turn in Buck's tone. They had been lulled by his charms as well.

Kristian was so intimidated by Buck's full wrath that he lost his character for a moment. "I... I... I... have an—"

He had another line, but Buck cut him off. "*Let the record show that Mr. Winecart failed to answer the question. Your witness, Mr. Cherry!*"

The silence in the auditorium was only broken when Phillip began clapping. The other Art Siders soon followed. Kristian stared bullets at Phillip, who was now giving a standing ovation.

"What role were you auditioning for, Mr. Buchmann?" Mr. Salinger asked as he approached the stage.

"The assistant."

"Not anymore... Mr. Highland."

Chapter 15

"You've had an eventful couple of weeks." Kieron Gill lifted himself up and adjusted his pants.

"Where I'm at now is exponentially past 'eventful.' We're making great progress on the repairs to the WET. The housing is fixed. Now we just have to repair the circuits. I can't believe that every day I get to work on an actual Wireless Energy Transmitter. My mom's life goal and I'm going to be able to see it functioning. Then I will be able to see it do something even more amazing."

"Open a dimensional rift?"

"I can't imagine how cool that will be. The others don't really remember much about going through the rift. They fell in when it opened. But I may be able to actually study it!"

Kieron chuckled. "Speaking of studying, I have to ask... You haven't been to school since the other Steves showed up."

"Yeah. We've set up this system. Stephen goes in for my physics class, then Buck covers for me the rest of the day. When Stephen gets back, he fills me in on what Mr. White is covering in physics."

"That has to be an experience, being tutored by a version of yourself from a scientifically advanced dimension."

"Kind of. He doesn't have a lot of patience for it. The other day I was asking him about Bell's theorem and its connection to quantum physics. But everything he said I already knew. It was like he was just reading the textbook back. I kept trying to get him to actually have a conversation about it and he flipped out. He said he didn't have time to hold my hand. It was... embarrassing."

"He sounds temperamental."

"Does platinum melt at 1,768 degrees Celsius?"

Kieron and Steve laughed.

With a final chuckle, Kieron got the interview back on track. "But sending the others to school in your place is not just about the WET, is it?"

Steve looked into the mic. "Not entirely. I'm certainly not going to miss seeing what Dr. Hicks and Stephen are doing. That's scientific history. I can't learn that in school. No one in this dimension knows about that stuff."

"But..." Kieron leaned forward, urging Steve to confess.

"Well, it was amazing when Stephen was able to fight back against Mr. White. I just couldn't ever do that. From now on I know Mr. White will rip apart anything I turn in. I'll have to defend myself as well or better than Stephen did. But I'm not nearly as smart as he is. If I'm wrong once, Mr. White will destroy me. At least this way I can have a bunch of A's in place to give me some wiggle room when I do go back."

"Makes sense." This was Kieron's move—concede a small point before really trapping a guest. "Then why did you have Buck audition for you?"

"You should have heard Buck practicing. He was so good. And I just hadn't had any time to get ready. It made more—" Steve sighed. "That's not true. I had been practicing. But I was really nervous and as soon as I heard Buck, I knew he'd get the part with no trouble. I mean, I know I'll be able to do the part. But if I messed up during the audition, I'd never have that chance. I didn't want to risk being embarrassed."

"Clearly, if you were willing to give up your comic collection."

"Yeah..."
"What did it cost you to get Stephen to go to physics for you?"

It was *his* fantasy interview. If Steve didn't want to have an imaginary conversation about letting Stephen read his mom's journals, he didn't have to. He flung open the door to Read Aloud and headed to the sci-fi section.

"Hey, Natalie, was that your cousin talking to himself?" Madison pointed to Steve across the street as he walked into Read Aloud.

"Probably." Stephanie shrugged.

"Steve was amazing at the auditions! It was crazy." Madison turned right and led Stephanie, who she knew as Natalie, into the pizza place. Madison, as always, was followed by her friends Sherri and Tina. "I'm so glad you talked me into trying out, Nat."

Stephanie winced at her nickname. "That was all you. You stood up for yourself, you got the part."

"She didn't get just any part. She beat out all those Art Siders for the female lead." Sherri wrapped her arms around Madison.

Tina latched onto their walking hug. "She was so awesome they made her Sabrina over *all* the Art Siders. They are so mad about it."

"You've pissed off so many Art Siders," Sherri echoed Tina.

It was taking Stephanie a lot of effort to keep smiling around Sherri. She knew, logically, that this Sherri wasn't the same Sherri who had tormented her in middle school, but the similarities in the mannerisms were uncanny. Just like the

Sherri she had loathed, this one was a sycophant, latching onto the alpha girl in the pack and willing to do anything to please her, even if she destroyed another person in the process.

Madison blushed. "I don't know what got into me. I think Steve's audition just inspired me. I was so determined to get the part."

Sherri looked at Stephanie. "It's all because of you." In the same breath, she shifted topics. "I love this shirt. So vintage." Sherri ran her hand down Stephanie's arm. Stephanie did her best not to pull her arm away. Her deal with Steve was still in effect, so she had to continue pretending to be friends with these girls.

"Thanks." Stephanie forced a smile. "It was my mom's." In a sense, it was. Steve had dug out a few boxes of Melissa's old clothes, which fit Stephanie pretty well. They were five to ten years old, but apparently vintage was a good look for her.

Each girl ordered a plain slice at the counter. Over the past week Stephanie had eaten her fill of pizza, but thought it was best to go along with what the others were doing. Madison then led them to a table by the front window that overlooked Main Street. Sherri and Tina rushed to grab spots on either side of Madison. Before Stephanie had to decide whether she would sit next to Tina or Sherri, Madison nudged Tina and patted the chair next to her. Both Tina and Sherri settled into chairs across the table.

Where she sat didn't matter to Stephanie. She was still preoccupied by their conversation from a few minutes earlier. "So he really doesn't call on any of the girls in class?"

"Nope," Tina answered. "Never."

"But why?"

"Mr. White just hates girls, I guess," Sherri offered.

This was not sitting well with Stephanie.

"He doesn't hate girls. He just doesn't think we're any good at science." Madison folded her pizza slice in half and took a bite.

"And you just accept this?" Stephanie could not understand why these intelligent women were acting like pathetic men.

"There's nothing we can do." Sherri shrugged and folded her pizza as well.

"Especially after what happened to Becky." Tina tried to mimic the fold, but as the cheese slid around, she gave up. The mention of Becky got Stephanie's attention. Like with Sherri, Stephanie knew a Becky back on her world.

Sherri bumped Tina, who almost dropped her pizza. "What was that for?" Tina whined. Sherri arched her eyebrows in Stephanie's direction. "Oh... right." Tina shrank back behind her pizza.

The secrets... they were Sherri's lifeblood. Well, definitely for the Sherri from Stephanie's world, and most likely they were for this Sherri as well. On her world she had been a victim of Sherri and her secrets. They had cost her all of her friends. If Stephanie had been home, she wouldn't have taken the obvious bait. Instead, she found new strength by visualizing getting personalized advice from *the* Nicole Davies.

"What?" Stephanie asked with as much interest as she could fake.

Tina and Sherri looked to Madison for permission to tell the story. Madison's eyes danced between the two, gathering consensus.

"It's something about your cousin..." Madison began.

"It's not necessarily a bad thing," Tina offered.

"It was kind of sweet, actually." Sherri smiled, trying to make it better. To Stephanie, Sherri's smile was like a shark rolling back its eyes before it attacked.

Every instinct Stephanie had told her to go. This felt like a typical Sherri trap— offering up what seemed like helpful information, but was really intended to drive Stephanie away from someone. That was what had happened with her friend Becky in middle school. Sherri said Becky's dad forced Becky to be friends with Stephanie so he could get close to her mom. Becky's dad was a chemist, who wanted to work at Tarp Scientific, where Stephanie's mom was CEO. Becky's dad had no such aspirations, but at the time Stephanie believed Sherri, and dramatically told off Becky. Not even two days later, Sherri said she didn't want to be friends with Stephanie because she had been so mean to Becky.

"There's this girl in our class... Becky Anderson." When Madison said the name, Stephanie's heart skipped a beat. Had Madison heard her thoughts? It took Stephanie a moment to focus back on what Madison was actually saying. "So smart and so nice. But she's... on the heavier side."

"Justin and all the idiot Sci Siders guys call her Big Beck. It's really mean," Tina added before bursting out laughing. Sherri only lasted a second before losing it herself.

Stephanie took a cleansing breath. Her Sherri's actions had ruined middle school for Stephanie. Her mom had been the one who helped her heal by the time she started high school. She told Stephanie that friends were a weakness and a liability. Their dramas were a distraction. Stephanie's mother hadn't become a CEO by wasting time worrying about her friends. She remained focused and worked hard. As soon as Stephanie adopted that philosophy, her life got better. No one could hurt her if she didn't open herself up to the abuse.

Madison composed herself first. "Mr. White was doing the same thing. No matter how many girls raised their hands to answer a question, he never called on any of us. It was like we weren't there. After a while we gave up."

"Except for Big Beck." Tina was a little too excited to be able to freely throw around the nickname.

Sherri shook her head. "We have to stop calling her that. I know I laughed, too, but I've been thinking a lot about it. Justin came up with the name to cut her down. We have enough trouble with men taking away our power. We can't help them. OK?"

Tina and Madison nodded. Stephanie was shocked. There was no irony in the statement. By this point in her life her instincts were on full alert for insincere Sherri traps. This didn't feel like one of them.

Tina continued, now more careful in her choice of worlds. "No one else knew the answer, except her. So, she raised her hand and just kept it up."

Madison took over the story, "It was crazy. He wouldn't look at her, but Becky wouldn't put her hand down. It felt like that went on forever. Then Steve raised his hand."

"And he *never* raises his hand in class," Tina added for color.

"Well, he *used to* never," Sherri corrected. "But this was a few weeks ago, before he became Mr. Know-It-All."

Stephanie shrugged her shoulders to preemptively pretend that she had no idea why her cousin was magically transformed into a physics genius. It certainly wasn't because he had been replaced by his double from another dimension.

"It was the perfect controlled experiment." Madison bit her lower lip in frustration. "It one hundred percent proved our theory. Becky was the *only* person who had her hand up and he totally waited for a guy before he called on anyone."

Sherri was shaking with excitement. "But this is the best part. Mr. White calls on Steve and asks for the answer. And Steve says 'I don't know, but Becky does. She's had her hand up forever.'"

"Mr. White was so mad that he broke a pencil in his hand. I swear." Madison's nodding head verified Sherri's claim.

"And then Mr. White railed on Steve for the rest of class. Becky was humiliated. It was brutal." Sherri seemed to Stephanie to genuinely be disturbed by how her friend had been treated. Maybe Stephanie had been wrong about this Sherri. She was even more surprised to hear that Steve had once had a backbone.

Any joy in telling that story had faded for Madison and Tina as well. Their faces dropped. This only enraged Stephanie, who stood up. "You have to do something about him!"

"We tried." Madison shrugged. "My mom called the principal, but he just said we were overreacting. That Mr. White is a highly respected physicist. And the school is lucky to have a teacher, who worked at Stepstone."

Stephanie looked at each of the girls. "So that's it? Are you just giving up? That ignorant man is robbing you of an education."

A look of true confusion crossed Tina's face. "Weren't you paying attention? He'll flip out if we do anything."

"I can't afford to fail another quiz." Sherri looked to the other girls for support. "My GPA has already dropped to 3.923."

"Natalie, what are we supposed to do?" Madison stood up to calm down Stephanie. "Mr. White thinks science is a man's world. He's said it dozens of times. We can't change that."

Stephanie put Madison's hands in her own. "Yes, you can. Like Nicole always says, 'You have all the power in the world.'"

"Who's Nicole?" Madison asked.

"A very smart woman," said Stephanie. Then she got back on track. "What would the guys in your class do if he stopped calling on them?"

"Nothing," Madison said. "They'd just sit there and take it like sheep."

"Exactly! That's why men are the weaker sex."

Sherri and Tina clapped at this.

Madison wasn't convinced yet. "OK. What would you do if you were in our class?"

Chapter 16

Before Mr. White finished writing the problem on the board, Stephen knew the answer. He had learned about the light invariance principle in fourth grade. It had taken him a few weeks longer to learn it than the rest of the class, but he eventually got it. That had been his parents' first warning sign. But it didn't matter on this world. Here, he was light-years ahead of everyone.

Usually.

Today, every female member of the class was raising her hand to answer, no matter what the question was. It struck him as odd that they would all know the answers to every question—especially considering that up until this point, only eight percent of the girls would raise their hands on any given day. This indicated to Stephen that there was some ulterior motive at work.

While their end goal was not clear, it was evident that their efforts had no effect on Mr. White. As usual, he continued only calling on the male class members. Stephen thought this was shortsighted on Mr. White's part. However, it offered

Stephen a break from his task.

His campaign had been extremely successful. There had been four quizzes since Stephen had assumed Steve's place in class. On the first two, Mr. White had initially graded them 68 and 59 percent respectively. He had taken issue with Stephen's choice of formula. As Mr. White had phrased it, they were "sloppy shortcuts."

As per his agreement with Steve, Stephen argued each point with Mr. White. Stephen did not understand the theories enough to use a shortcut, so he was forced to "show his work." This allowed Stephen to easily walk Mr. White through his thought process. Each paper was subsequently given a score of 100 percent. The other two quizzes were graded far more liberally.

Keeping up his grades in school on his own world was far more difficult. Academic success dictated every aspect of life there. It was not a question of Stephen being unwilling to work hard. His every waking hour had been dedicated to study. Yet his grades had continued to fall. With each decline, his parents' patience grew thinner. There had been talk of a remedial school. His family would have been devastated. But with a 2.9 GPA, he would never be hired in any lab. At least with a remedial degree he could get work as a lawyer or an architect. His parents were convinced that was the best future for him.

Stephen had been past desperate. The research he had found in his mother's tablet was in a file of other discarded ideas. There would be no method for anyone at school to discover his indiscretion.

That was before he arrived on this primitive world where the mundane thrived. Just a few hours of research had shown Stephen that most of this world's leaders had no advanced degrees. Research corporations were headed by glorified accountants. Competitive positions on his world that would only be open to the most elite of candidates were available to people based solely on social relationships. It was astounding.

"So if h remains constant that means the velocity would be what?" Mr. White turned away from his equation on the board. He was met with a sea of hands that only belonged to the girls.

When no boys in the class attempted to answer, he continued, "Since this example takes place in the vacuum of space, friction will not affect the outcome."

Stephen had known the answer to every question posed in class so far. But, acquiescing to Steve's request, he refrained from "overdoing it." So he had sat out several questions today. This would be the fourth time. That screamed of failure to Stephen.

As soon as his hand was up, Mr. White pointed at him. "Mr. Buchmann."

"The velocity would be 16.823 kilometers per second."

"Exactly. Do you all see what Mr. Buchmann did—"

Without a word, every girl in the class stood up and walked out. There were no drawers slammed shut or other dramatic gestures. They just left. The murmurs of the boys in class were louder than their exit.

"Excuse me. Where do you ladies think you're going?" Mr. White asked as the last of them headed out the door.

From his desk Stephen could still see Madison standing in the hallway outside of the classroom. She had linked hands with a girl to her left and Becky to her right. Becky was glaring back into the room at Mr. White with a look that chilled Stephen.

"All year, you have refused to call on any of the girls in your class," Madison announced. "If you don't think we are a part of this class, then we're leaving. When you have apologized for marginalizing us and promise to change, we'll return."

They didn't wait for a response. Madison led them away. Everyone except for Becky, who lingered outside the door long enough to flip the bird back at Stephen.

The anger of the large girl confused him, but he was not as confused as Mr. White was. "What just happened here?" White bellowed.

The roomful of boys all shrugged their shoulders.

"That's a massive overreaction! I don't think they fully understand the repercussions of their..." Mr. White trailed off. The heat of his red face faded, quickly being replaced by a pale white that matched the board behind him.

He studied the classroom in its new state. More than half of the chairs were now empty. In the hall, several other teachers had gathered to watch the girls' parade.

"I should go talk to the principal." Mr. White was speaking just above a whisper as he headed toward the classroom door. "Start on the problem set on page 164."

"How old?" Dr. Hicks nearly dropped the welder in his hands.

Stephen grabbed the loose panel before it fell again. In the midst of Dr. Hicks's shock, Stephen had almost lost a finger. His face burned red. "Pay attention!" Stephen threw the panel at Dr. Hicks's feet.

"So sorry." Turning down the flame, Dr. Hicks set the welder on the bench to his left and lifted up his welding mask. "It's just astonishing how early you learn calculus on your world."

"Dangerously so." Stephen seethed as he took off his protective gloves and rubbed his hand. Since Stephen had come there straight after school, they had been working without a break for over three hours. The entire time Dr.

Hicks had been quizzing Stephen on the minutiae of life on his world. This was their standard topic of conversation, and he was beginning to tire of it. They were coming very close to finishing the repairs to the WET. Stephen estimated that they were 75 percent complete. It was only a matter of days now.

"Here they used to wait until college to teach calculus," said Dr. Hicks, oblivious to Stephen's sudden mood change.

Without Dr. Hicks reacting to him, Stephen's anger fizzled... some. "No wonder scientific advances are so infrequent on this backwoods world. By the time one finishes their course work, one would be twenty-two or twenty-three years old."

"Actually, with grad school and post doc, you're talking closer to thirty or thirty-five years old."

"That is a colossal waste of time. Is there any interest in science or math on this world?"

"Oh yes! Absolutely!" Dr. Hicks gazed off, trying to think of a good proof of his statement. When none came to him, he decided that Stephen may be right. "Well, now that I think about it, that's probably why funding for this initial WET device was a nightmare. Trouter recognized that your mom—well, uh, Steve's mother... and your mother, too—regardless, he approved the proposal immediately. The shareholders, however, needed more convincing. Trouter was a coward. He would have given up. But Melissa... she never backed down. She had the brilliant idea to create a scale model first."

Stephen looked away. For every excruciating minute Dr. Hicks spent asking about life on Stephen's world, he spent twice as much time talking about Melissa Buchmann. Dr. Hicks would be disappointed to learn how little she had thought about him. Stephen assumed that was the case based on how infrequently she mentioned him in her journals. Perhaps her lengthiest mention of Dr. Hicks was his recommendation for recreational activities at the Jersey Shore.

The journals had proven to be entirely worthless to Stephen, which was all the more frustrating considering how much effort it had been to get them. When Steve had begged Stephen to assume his place in Mr. White's class, the only price Stephen demanded was access to the journals. Even in the face of such a clear, beneficial arrangement, Steve had anguished over the decision for hours. Stephen had hoped they would provide a detailed explanation of how Melissa had developed her theory for the WET. On his world those journals certainly would have. Instead, she had filled each one with ramblings about her family life. One mundane memory followed another.

Dr. Hicks was still drifting through nostalgia. "The first model was barely strong enough to power a tiny flashlight. The board went nuts. Once they could visualize it they approved the WET project right away. Your—Melissa and I got to work the next day. But as you know, scaling up is rather complicated. As the level of energy increases, the vibration wave inverses."

And that was where he lost Stephen. Nodding his head, Stephen listened to the list of theories and principles that allowed Wireless Energy Transmission to exist. He understood none of it. In school, Stephen had learned how to make the WET and dozens of other mainstays of his world through simple rote. He knew the components. Why they worked was another matter. Like a child with a baking soda and vinegar volcano, he could make it go boom, but never understood why it went boom.

Up until middle school, that hadn't mattered. Then it suddenly mattered a lot. Classes became about theory and expanding on preexisting formulas. Stephen couldn't keep up. The only child of Daniel and Melissa Buchmann, their contribution to the advancement of society, was a failure.

When he tried to rectify the situation, he became a pariah.

"So after the accident, the board backed away." Dr. Hicks had traveled through his pleasant memories of toiling in the lab and was now in the depressing present. "It's funny. After they saw the first model, some accountant on the board had valued the WET at eight billion dollars. Can you imagine?"

The number struck Stephen. For him, that was like trying to put a cash value on the introduction of the first solar cell. These simpletons had no idea how the WET would transform their world. His mind raced through a series of childhood projects and toys.

The Buchmanns' refrigerator had reeked of rotting food when he first opened it. The stasis field generator he had made in summer camp when he was ten would keep produce fresh forever. A simple multiphasic scanner, like the one he made for Science Scouts in fifth grade, would revolutionize medical treatment. The quantum storage unit he played with in his room would make those asinine mobile devices obsolete. Every one of those things Stephen could make in his sleep. He was suddenly starting to see some positive aspects to remaining on this world.

Chapter 17

"*Do you really think you can take me? We both know you'll lose.*"

Steve pounded his fist on the table. "*I have never lost. Never!*"

There was silence. Then cheers.

Stephanie and Buck stood up from the couch and applauded. Stephen remained on the couch in the back room of the Buchmann house, laboring over a laptop hooked up to a mobile phone. If he was impressed by Steve's performance... well, he wasn't.

The Steves were enjoying a rare afternoon in the house. Over the past couple of weeks that they had been on this world their time in the main house had been limited to sneaking in to use the bathroom. Today, Dad had taken Josh for a long-overdue haircut, leaving the house empty for at least an hour. For the first time since getting there they were all in the house together. They were enjoying the spacious luxury of the Buchmanns' back room den. It was an enclosed porch in the rear of the house with a sectional couch and a large TV. Steve had spent many hours there watching cartoons. Its relative seclusion made it his favorite room in the house. This afternoon it was his performance space.

Buck nodded. "Remember, there's more room on the stage when you cross in front of Phillip."

"He's the tall one playing Rick Cherry?" Steve asked.

Buck lost his enthusiasm for Steve's performance. "You need to start going to rehearsals."

"Soon." Steve looked away from Buck. Rehearsals had started immediately after the cast had been announced. With the WET nearly completed, Steve had asked Buck to fill in for him, so he could help finish the device. In their spare time Buck taught Steve the blocking. All of that had cost Steve something more than just his prized comic collection.

"Highland is a lot bigger part than the assistant. You're already a week behind," Buck continued.

"I know." Steve looked at his watch and found a way to change the subject. "We should start getting ready."

"That can wait," Buck declared. "Me telling you what we did in rehearsals can't replace actual firsthand experience."

Steve sighed. "You promised you'd go to rehearsal for me and I'm letting you take my place at the *Reflex* screening."

"That's not the point. Proper preparation is essential for any mission. I can't tell you how many times training has saved—"

"Do you know what Madison did today?" Noah announced as he stormed into the back room.

"Yes! We know!" Steve was irritated with Noah's entrance, but happy for the distraction. He closed his script and left the back room, heading to the living room.

"I already told them." Buck had more to cover from rehearsal, but he followed Steve, Noah, and Stephanie. Stephen paid no attention to everyone leaving him behind.

"She led all the girls in a walkout," Noah continued, as the Steve parade wound through the living room and up the stairs.

"Everybody at school was talking about it."

"We know." Steve bounded into his room and flung open his closet.

"The question is, will it make a difference?" Stephanie stood by Steve, looking into his closet, surveying his clothes. After a moment, she pulled two polo shirts, one black and one navy

"Madison thinks it will," said Buck as he entered the room and walked to the window. "That's all she could talk about at rehearsal today. Speaking of which, I need to show you the deposition blocking."

"I know," Steve muttered. "We'll do it this weekend. Let's just get through tonight first."

"What's going on tonight?" Noah wedged himself between Stephanie and Steve and peered into the closet.

"Madison invited us to a party." Buck was looking out the window, scanning the yard.

"You're kidding." Noah's eyes shot open. "You're going to a drama club party with Madison?"

"Not me." Steve pointed to Buck and Stephanie. "They are. I have to go to dinner with Dad and Nicole."

"You don't *have* to," Buck noted.

"I promised Stephanie." Steve watched her examining the shirts. "It may be the last chance I get to ask Nicole her question before the WET is ready."

"I'm so, so confused." Noah plopped down on the bed, his shoes landing next to Steve's pillow. "Why can't Smarty Pants go do that for you?"

"My name is Stephen, and I'm doing more than enough as is," Stephen snapped as he walked into the bedroom, the laptop still in his arms. "Your world's internet speeds are maddingly slow."

"That's a good point." Stephanie held up a black polo and a

navy polo, studying them in the light of the room. "This isn't the best use of resources. Wasn't the whole reason for this charade to get you and Madison together? You should go."

"I agree with her." Noah smiled at Stephanie. "You need to go."

"I can't. Stephen won't do it, and Buck has barely said three words to Nicole," Steve explained. "Besides, Buck has a rapport with Madison. I thought it would be better if he went."

"This is a needlessly complicated plan." Stephanie tossed the navy polo to Buck. "Not to mention criminally manipulative."

"We're the same person. It's OK," Steve pointed out.

"No, you're not!" Stephanie yelled.

"It's not like he's going to start making out with her and then pass her off to me," Steve argued. "All Buck has to do is ask her out and leave."

"You're hopeless," Stephanie declared.

"I think it's pointless, too. She likes you." Buck looked at the navy shirt. "Why don't I just wear the black one?"

"A little color is better." Stephanie handed him some jeans.

"No one will be able to tell the difference in the dark," Buck muttered.

"Is this girl so vapid that you believe she wouldn't be able to detect any difference between the person who schedules a date with her and the person who actually accompanies her on said activity?" Stephen picked up the discarded black polo from the bed.

"She's not vapid." Stephanie pulled the shirt out of his hand. "She's very smart."

"In that case, it would follow that she would be more attracted to someone with a great intellect." Stephen crossed his arms, proud of his logic. "So maybe I should attempt to woo this young lady."

"That's dumber than Steve's plan," Noah snorted as the others started laughing.

No one noticed Stephen stepping toward Noah with his fist clenched.

Stephanie crossed in front of him as she pulled Steve out of the room. "We need to discuss what you're going to ask Nicole."

When Buck started to change his clothes, Noah followed Stephanie and Steve down the stairs. Stephen dropped the black polo back onto the bed as he left the room.

Chapter 18

Stephanie knew that if one more person bumped into Buck, there was going to be bloodshed. The small house party Madison had invited them to really did mean *small* house. Every square inch of the place was packed with Sinatra Edison Art Siders. As per the school's custom an Art Sider party meant no Sci Siders allowed. An exemption had been granted to Madison and Buck, who they knew as Steve, because they were in the play. Moving from the front door into the living room had taken ten minutes. The house was filled with yelling, smoke, and pounding bass. It was a nightmare with pizza.

Stephanie watched girls flitter from one group to another, all of them seeming to talk at the same time. "What can they possibly have left to say to each other? They spend all day together talking."

"I know! It's awesome, right?" Noah bopped through the crowd. The legs of his far-too-long-for-him dress pants kept getting trapped under the heels of his vintage Vans. He straightened his powder-blue tuxedo jacket and moved to a group of sophomore Art Siders who had no idea who he was.

"This is pointless," Stephanie shouted. "We won't be able to find Madison in this nonsense."

"We'll never find Madison like this!" Buck barked as a backwards-hat-wearing senior shoved past him. Buck clenched his fist so hard his knuckles turned white.

"That's what I just said," Stephanie replied.

"What?" Buck yelled.

"We can't leave yet." The noise of the room covered the panic in Noah's voice.

"You're here!" Stephanie heard a voice project over the noise of the room. Then a pair of arms wrapped around Buck from behind. "I'm so glad you're here," the voice repeated.

Watching Buck tense up after being grabbed from behind, Stephanie was quick to defuse the situation. "Hi, Madison!"

Madison stepped in front of Buck, who appeared to relax once he saw his assailant. Before either could say anything else, they were both enveloped in a giant hug. This time it was Noah, emerging from the crowd. "There she is! We were looking for you."

Madison looked at Buck. "You were?"

"Yes," Buck answered with the same warmth as if he were being interrogated.

"Good thing you found me." If she heard Buck's tone, she certainly didn't notice it.

Noah released Madison and Buck. "I have only one question. Where's the keg?"

"In the kitchen." Madison leapt from Buck's side and grabbed Stephanie's hands in hers. "Natalie, you have to hurry and catch up."

"Catch up to what?"

Madison had turned her attention back to Buck and missed Stephanie's reply.

"That's a great idea, Natalie." Noah stepped aside to clear a path for Stephanie.

"I don't understand what she's talking about." Stephanie ignored Noah's urgings.

"Drunk. It's time to get drunk!" Noah pulled her with him toward the kitchen.

The whole time Buck had been in the house, he'd seen nothing but throngs of kids. Within a dozen steps, Madison had led him to a couch in a den that only had a few other people in it. They were all Art Siders from the play. Some worked backstage. The rest were cast. Sitting in an armchair, clutching a plastic cup overflowing with beer, was Kristian. On his lap was a giggling freshman Art Sider wearing a low-cut shirt and a very hard-working Wonderbra.

This kind of party was completely foreign to Buck. What drinking he had done was with his resistance troop after a mission. And that was purely to commiserate. The most any one at those gatherings was after was to lessen the pain of their lives. Everyone here was happy. It was unnerving, but he liked it.

Christopher, a pudgy Art Sider sitting on the crowded couch, leaned forward. "Big Steve! There he is! Dude, do your Salinger impression."

"Yeah!" Madison pushed him into the center of the room. "Go."

Buck nodded, then closed his eyes to find his character.

"All right, people, listen up!" Buck stormed across the room then back again. "We're going to run through this whole play in ten minutes, whether you know your lines or not! CRYSTAL!"

The laughter drowned out the noise of the party. Madison

smiled and squeezed Buck's arm. A clearing opened on the love seat and she guided him to it. If there was any residual anger toward these Sci Siders in the midst of the Art Siders, a few play rehearsals and a lot of alcohol had dissipated it. As Madison and Buck sat, she rested her hand on his knee. For someone new to an Art Sider party. Madison seemed very at ease. Buck assumed that Madison had started drinking early and quickly that night. In his experience that meant she had not done it much in the past.

"What is the deal with his blocking in the opening scene?" Christopher asked. He was the understudy for all the male roles in the play and as such made some connection with almost everyone there.

"Tell me about it," Phillip complained from his spot on the floor in front of Kristian. "We're all crowded on one side of the stage. I feel like if I take a step in the wrong direction I'll smash someone's foot."

"Yeah, that's my foot you keep stepping on," Madison said.

"Sorry about that," Phillip continued. "But that's my point. I'm, like, three feet taller than you and I'm standing in front of you. That's crazy."

"It's a huge waste of space," Buck agreed.

"Really!" Kristian slurred from his chair. "I bet you have some Sci Sider formula for the most efficient distribution of bodies per square meter. Would you pretty, pretty please enlighten us Neanderthal Art Siders with your fancy book learning?"

Kristian's bloodshot eyes locked on Buck. The resentment dripped from his face and silenced the room. Buck sat up ready to square off with Kristian. After the Kristian on Buck's world had his accident in front of Everlast, he had become the punchline of every joke at school. That had made him an outsider, which also made him a danger. Buck learned that

Kristian had gotten his revenge on his classmates by pointing the finger at any student who had said anything negative about Everlast. None of them actually had. Everlast didn't care and quickly detained each student Kristian had singled out.

"It's a really simple formula." Madison smiled, putting her hand on Buck's shoulder. "It's 'beer times big mouth over the square root of embarrassing jackass.'"

Even the tight-shirted freshman on Kristian's lap laughed at that one.

Listening to Tina and Sherri talk was like listening to an echo. One spoke and the other repeated the exact same information. Once Stephanie noticed this, she found it impossible to follow the conversation. As soon as the two of them had seen Stephanie enter the kitchen, they had swarmed her. In a series of double statements, they told her about walking out of Mr. White's class.

"Mr. Terlington told us—" Sherri said.

"Mr. Terlington is our principal," Tina explained.

"He told us the walk-out totally got his attention and that he would form a committee to listen to our complaints about Mr. White," Sherri finished.

"He is totally setting up a committee to deal with Mr. White," Tina echoed.

"But that doesn't mean we're getting off the hook for cutting class," Sherri continued.

"We are kind of in trouble for leaving class," Tina elaborated.

Despite their annoying speaking pattern, Stephanie was surprised to find herself enjoying listening to Sherri and Tina. They had been so excited to see Stephanie, which was a new experience for her.

"Sorry that took so long." Noah slid in between Stephanie and Tina. "There are a lot of people here tonight looking to get drunk. So what are we talking about?" He handed one of the beers to Stephanie, who froze when she took hold of it. Being at a party was new enough for her. Drinking was completely foreign. Stephanie's mother had drilled into her that nothing good could come of drinking. She said that alcohol led to a loss of self-control. If she wanted to succeed, she could not afford one slipup.

"Everyone is talking about their walkout." Noah looked at Stephanie. "And it was all your idea, huh?"

"It was totally her idea," Sherri exclaimed.

"She's full of great ideas!" Tina gushed.

"She said we should—" Sherri started.

"He knows the story," Stephanie said, stopping another Sherri/Tina run. She hadn't intended to be so abrupt and the result was an awkward silence. With each passing second, Stephanie regretted her bluntness.

After what felt like a year to Stephanie, Tina smiled knowingly. Her gaze shifted from Stephanie to Noah, who Stephanie just noticed was staring at her. "OK. I gotcha. We understand, don't we, Sherri?" Tina's smile grew.

Sherri followed Tina's gaze to Noah. "No. I wanted to—"

Tina pulled Sherri away. "We'll see you in a little while." Then Tina turned and mouthed to Stephanie, *He's cute*, with fourteen silent *U*'s. That was completely lost on Stephanie.

"Wow! That was the least subtle blow-off I've ever seen." Noah raised his glass to toast her.

"Sorry. I just didn't want to hear that story again. Did you?"

"Not really."

"OK then." More silence followed. Out of need to do

something, Stephanie took a sip of her drink, forgetting it was beer. She did not try to hide her reaction. "Ugh. This is awful."

"Yeah, but I've heard it gets better the more you drink." When Noah looked down at the cup in his hand, Stephanie noticed that it was untouched.

"Great... so why am I here again? Madison could care less."

A crowd of guys carrying a freshman, painted green, on their shoulders pushed their way past Noah and Stephanie.

"It's a party. Who doesn't want to go to a party?" Noah shouted.

"Me." Stephanie took another tentative sip. This time she only winced a little. Without saying anything to Noah, she walked away, knowing that he would follow.

"So you never go to parties on your world?" Noah asked as he trailed behind her.

"How often do *you* go to parties?" Stephanie took a third sip.

"That's irrelevant. I always *want* to go. When else can you hang out with all of your friends completely free of parents and teachers?"

Stephanie pointed to his cup. "For someone so excited to party, why haven't you had any yet?"

Noah looked at his beer. For a moment he dropped his bravado as he hesitated to take a drink. It was the first time that night that Stephanie felt like she wasn't the only party newbie there. When Noah finally took his first sip, his whole body shuddered. Stephanie laughed at him.

"It is really bad." Then Noah took another sip.

Even though the party was getting louder, Stephanie no longer had any trouble hearing Noah. Maybe the beer was helping with that. She had also found the rhythm of the room and was able to move about without wanting to punch anyone. In the corner of the living room, just next to an upright piano, she found a space free of people and sat on the floor. Noah looked around for free wall space. Finding none, he sat in front of Stephanie.

"Why are you helping us?" she asked. Her voice was soft. The corner provided protection from the noise of the party and made it easier for Noah to hear her.

"Steve's my best friend." Then Noah realized something else. "Which I think means all of you are my best friend, too. Maybe... I'm not sure how that part works."

"So you get dragged into this ridiculousness just because you're friends with Steve? That doesn't seem right."

"But that's the point of friends. They make life more interesting."

"Or do you mean complicated." Stephanie downed the rest of her beer.

Noah looked back at the party. The music pounded. "I feel like you haven't learned the true meaning of Christmas yet," he said to Stephanie.

"What?"

He reached down and took her hand in his. "Get up. We're going to dance."

"I'm not dancing with you," Stephanie said. But she didn't pull her hand away.

"Come on, please. It's an amazing experience." Noah helped her to her feet. "Who knows the next time I'll get invited to a party. I want to do it all."

While Noah was leading her to the dance floor and his back was safely turned away, Stephanie let herself smile.

All that the watered-down beer did to Buck was make him have to pee. Alcohol was tightly regulated on his world. Only

NSA-approved people were allowed to purchase it. Forget getting an older brother to buy beer—forty-year-olds had trouble getting alcohol. All Buck drank was a 100-proof homemade concoction brewed in the hidden depths of the Park. It supercharged his tolerance.

Then the room tilted to the left.

OK, maybe he was the tiniest bit drunk.

Madison giggled and fell into him. That made her laugh harder. Tara had just finished her rendition of "American Pie" as sung by a longshoreman. Half of the circle of cards they were sitting around had been picked away. The cup in the center was brimming with a mixture of beer, schnapps, and wine. Whoever drew the fourth king and had to drink it would never forget why this game was called Circle of Death.

Christopher studied the cards before him. Closing his eyes, he waved his hand over them, using his fingers like a divining rod. He slowed over the cards to his left, honing in on one tilted slightly away from the others. He let out a cleansing breath and turned over the card—a three.

"Crap!" he yelled. "I thought this would be a jack. I could feel it."

"You were so close, baby." Susanna, an adoring sophomore hugged him.

"I was debating between two cards," Christopher explained. He pointed to another card without turning it over. "I'm going on record as saying that this is a jack."

"Just drink!" snapped Kristian, sucking the fun out of the moment.

Christopher downed his beer as ordered. To avoid further inflaming Kristian's wrath, Susanna quickly snatched the next card. It was a six. All the girls in the circle laughed and picked up their cups. Tara and Madison bumped their hands together when they both reached for the same cup. The two girls burst out laughing. When they tried for the cup a second time, they bumped hands again. The explosion of laughter that time infected everyone else in the room.

Except one person. Kristian barked, "Hey! It's a six. Girls drink!"

"We're trying," Tara said through laughter-induced tears. She and Madison then reenacted their fist-bumping, to the delight of the room.

"Here!" Kristian grabbed two cups and handed them to the girls. "You're holding up the game! I thought Sci Siders were more efficient than that."

Madison mumbled, "Sorry," as she took her cup. They both downed their beers. Tara placed her cup upside down in the middle of the circle and blew a raspberry at Kristian. As Madison set her cup down, she swayed backwards. Buck leaned over to steady her.

"You OK?" he asked.

"Yeah..." he took a deep breath.

"Finally!" Kristian grabbed a card and showed it to Christopher. It was a jack. "I believe this is the one you were looking for!"

"Oh, man!" Christopher laughed.

"I get to make a rule." Kristian studied the circle. His gaze settled on Madison and Buck. "Here's one. If you're not an Art Sider... drink!"

Kristian cracked open another beer and reached for Madison's cup. At the sight of more beer, her skin tone turned green. It took all of her willpower to take the cup from Kristian. As she put it to her lips, Buck grabbed the cup out of her hands.

"You've had too much," he said to Madison. It took a little longer than normal for the shock of this action to register in her beer-soaked brain. When it did, she smiled at him.

"What are you doing?" Kristian stood up. "I pulled a jack. I get to make a rule. You have to follow the rules."

Kristian reached for the cup in Buck's hand. He easily dodged Kristian's reach. Kristian made two more failed attempts for the cup before stopping. Even through his drunken haze, Kristian recognized how much faster Buck was than him.

"She's not drinking anymore." There was no debate in Buck's voice. "It's just a game."

"Is that what you think? That all the Art Siders do is play games?" Kristian kicked at the circle of cards, resulting in a chorus of "Hey"s and "Watch it"s from the group.

Kristian made his way through the circle of cards toward Buck and Madison, who were still sitting on the floor. As he crossed the middle of the room, Buck jumped to his feet. He had been in plenty of situations like this. When resistance fighters drank homemade moonshine in the woods, things could get ugly. And when they went bad, they went bad fast. Taking a step forward, Buck put himself between Madison and Kristian.

"Sit down, dude," Tara barked to Kristian. "You're being an ass."

"No one asked you, back-stager!" He spun around to Buck and Madison. "You two don't belong here. Time to go!"

"Hey!" Phillip snapped. "That's not cool. You need to take a—"

As he struggled to stand up, Kristian pushed Phillip back to the floor.

Then he reached down for Madison. Just as he was about to make contact, he stopped.

Buck had locked his hand around Kristian's wrist. In another fluid motion, he hit Kristian in the center of his chest with his open palm. The high school star was airborne for a second, then landed flat on his back. Beer spilled everywhere.

The rest of the Art Siders in the room just watched Kristian on the floor, trying to catch his breath. He was more stunned than actually hurt. Still, no one rushed to his side.

There wasn't a sound in the room

Then Christopher screamed, "Yeah! That was awesome!"

"Sorry about that," Phillip said to Buck. "He gets that way sometimes."

"He's been having that coming for a long time now," Tara agreed.

"That was the coolest thing ever!" Christopher gushed. "Have you taken stage combat classes?"

Kristian managed to sit himself up. He was taking short breaths and didn't bother to try to talk. There was no tension in the room now. His threat had been neutralized. Still, they all watched Kristian's moves carefully. As he got to his knees, Phillip's face dropped.

"I guess I should make sure he gets home," Phillip pouted as he helped Kristian stand. "I'm his ride."

There were no "I'll get you for this" speeches from Kristian as Phillip walked him out of the room. He had been stunned into sobriety. The others tried to reconstruct the remnants of their game. Through all of this, Madison could only do one thing: watch Buck.

"You want to keep playing?" Christopher offered to Buck. "You guys don't have to drink if you don't want to."

Buck looked back at the group as he helped Madison onto the couch. When she sat down, she patted the spot next to her. Her glassy eyes were locked on to him.

"I have to pee," blurted Buck as he ran out of the room.

At first, Stephanie had been acutely aware of the music they were dancing to. She listened to the lyrics of songs, some of which she knew and others that didn't exist on her world. As one song faded into another, she got lost in the movement of the crowd. Noah twisted her around and hopped up and down the same way no matter what the music was like. She would have assumed that was the way people danced on this world, if there hadn't been a room full of other people there dancing normally.

All the living room furniture had been pushed against the walls and the throw rug was rolled up in a corner. Someone had left a few small lamps scattered on tables around the room. It made it easy for Stephanie to forget where she was. When they started dancing, Noah paid too much attention to what she was doing. It made her self-conscious. But then Tina and Sherri pushed their way through the crowd to join them. Under other circumstances, their joyful squeals would have put Stephanie on guard. Here, they were infectious. The girls held hands and spun around in circles, completely unconcerned with who was near them.

In her conversion to a dancing machine, Stephanie had lost track of Noah, who had been pushed away by Tina and Sherri. But he had never been one to take a hint. Noah danced just outside their group, and when Stephanie saw him, she smiled and waved him inside their circle. Her inhibitions were gone now. She shimmied, shook, and grinded herself against Tina, Sherri, and Noah. There were no words, just movement. Stephanie was connected to a larger group for the first time in her life.

"I need another beer," Tina yelled over the music.

"What?" Sherri screamed.

"Beer! More beer!" Tina yelled again.

"I need to pee, too," Sherri answered.

"Just come on!" Tina pulled Sherri off through the crowd.

Stephanie tried to continue dancing, but hearing human voices for the first time in thirty minutes had taken her out of her zone. Her bouncing and gyrating slowed. Noah stopped when he saw Stephanie losing her enthusiasm.

He leaned into her ear. "That's a good idea."

"Going to the bathroom?" she screamed back, causing everyone around them to look over.

"No. Taking a break. I need to get something to drink. You want anything?"

The crowd around them continued dancing, but Stephanie felt her connection slipping away. If she left, that feeling would be gone. But just standing here, she was only hanging on to a memory.

"Sure." She walked off ahead of Noah, who followed her.

Earlier in the night, the kitchen had been mobbed with people waiting in line for the keg. Now that it was empty, the harsh fluorescent light had chased everyone to darker regions of the house. All that remained were knocked-over stacks of Solo cups and puddles of beer. Noah found two clean-ish cups in the middle of an intact stack and filled them with tap water. Stephanie didn't realize how thirsty she was until she downed the first cup in one gulp. An open window brought in a breeze that chilled her sweaty skin.

When Stephanie shivered, Noah took off his jacket and handed it to her. "Here."

"I'm OK," she said.

"Take it. I'm too warm right now."

A door behind them opened from the backyard, bringing two seniors and more cold air with them. They bounded through the kitchen into the house as the door slammed shut. Stephanie sighed and took Noah's jacket. "Thanks."

"No problem."

Stephanie slipped her arms into the tacky tuxedo jacket and they disappeared. Her whole body was swallowed up by its bulk, making her look even smaller than she was. This was the first time she had ever worn a boy's jacket. She immediately succumbed to its warmth, comfort, and the faint trace of cologne.

"You have some moves," Noah said.

"You don't."

"I am very passionate. That counts for a lot."

"Whoever told you that was lying."

"Jeez! You don't pull punches. Are you ever happy? Or are you always mean to people?"

"Shut up! You're an asshole." Stephanie's smile vanished as she turned away from Noah. She looked down at the blue jacket. One of her fingers wormed its way out and stroked the material.

"Sorry," Noah said, but she didn't turn back around. "Are you seriously mad?"

Noah waited for a response. When he didn't get one, he walked around to face her. Tears were running down her cheeks. She pulled away from him, hiding her face.

"I was just kidding around. I didn't mean anything," Noah tried again.

"I know," she said, wiping her eyes with the sleeve. "Sorry."

"You're not mean," Noah said. "You're actually nice."

"I'm not." Stephanie's voice was tired. "That's why I don't have this."

"Have what?"

"Friends."

"Of course you have friends. You're a great person."

"No girl I know has ever done that before. Just danced with me. Or wanted to just hang out with me. Those girls did.

They would have talked my ear off all night. And even after I pushed them away, they still wanted to dance with me. I don't understand."

"They like you."

"Why? I'm a bitch." Stephanie was pleading with Noah for honesty.

"Yeah. You are." Noah quickly followed up, not wanting to set her off again. "But not in a bad way. You're strong. You're funny. You're passionate. Madison doesn't have to like anyone she doesn't want to like. But she thinks the world of you. So do Tina and Sherri. You took the time to help them solve their problem. That's what friends do."

"I didn't do anything."

"You listened and cared. That's all anyone can really do."

"That's it? That's all I have to do to have friends?"

"Well, it's not that simple. You have to make plans and spend time together."

Stephanie considered this newfound knowledge. "Thank you."

"For what?"

"For not taking a hint and letting me push you away."

"My pleasure!" Noah smiled proudly.

Another set of feet trampled by them through the kitchen. The back door flew open and the group disappeared into the darkness of the yard. In their wake was another breeze. Stephanie pulled the jacket in tighter around her.

"Here." Noah lined up the sides of the jacket and buttoned it up for her. She watched his eyes trace up her body to her face. When he finished with the last button, she took hold of his hands, pulling him in closer. His lips lingered in front of hers for a brief second before she kissed him. Noah was so surprised he had almost forgotten to enjoy the moment.

As quickly as it started, the kiss ended. Stephanie pushed

him back. "What am I doing?"

Noah could only watch as Stephanie ran off into the night with his jacket.

Stephanie made her way up the walk past a junior boy who was standing on top of a central air unit next to the house, trying to reach the gutter above him. Two of his friends raced over to him with a bed sheet tied to a trophy. They began taking turns trying to throw the jerry-rigged grapple hook onto the roof.

Stephanie was trying to avoid the swinging trophy when she ran into a familiar polo shirt.

"Did you do it?" Stephanie rubbed her tear-soaked eyes. "Can we go?"

"Um... actually, I'm not Buck."

Stephanie realized the shirt was black. "Steve, what are you doing here?"

"We finished dinner early and—"

"Did you ask her?" Stephanie instantly forgot the trauma of her kiss. "What did she say?"

"Can I tell you later? I—"

Buck appeared and caught the trophy grapple hook as it fell in front of him. He tossed it into the yard and the juniors chased after it.

"What are you doing here?" Buck checked over his shoulder to make sure no one saw them together.

"We finished dinner early and I... well... I... I just... You didn't ask out Madison already, did you?"

"No." Buck looked at his feet. "It got a little intense. She was drunk and was looking at me... a lot. I'm not you. It didn't feel right."

"You got her drunk?" Stephanie pushed Buck.

"No! She got herself drunk." Buck looked at her jacket. "Is that Noah's?"

Stephanie ignored Buck. "So if you're here, does that mean you're going to do what you should have been doing in the first place?"

"Yeah. Where's Madison now?"

"In the back room."

The Circle of Death game had never resumed. It had done its job. Everyone was drunk and doing half-remembered monologues for the group. Christopher was using a toy light saber as a cane as he performed lines from *A Midsummer Night's Dream*.

"Have you conspired, have you with these contrived to bait me with this foul derision?" Christopher drove the light saber into the carpet to emphasis the word *derision*.

"Hold on!" Tara screamed way too loudly. "That's a girl's part!"

Madison rolled into Tara's side laughing hysterically. "Girl's part!"

"No it's not!" Christopher said as he tried to remember why he thought that. "It's just not."

"Yeah. It is," Madison said between laughing fits. "It's Helena's girl part!"

Tara snorted, setting off another laughing fit.

"Steve!" Madison yelled as she struggled to lift herself off the plush couch.

"Is that what you call your girl part?" Tara asked the empty spot where Madison had been sitting.

As Steve entered the room, Madison steadied herself as much as possible and ran over to him. "Tell Christopher that he's a lady in *Midsummer Night's*."

"You are a lady in *A Midsummer Night's Dream*," he said to Christopher.

"See!" Madison bowed and pointed to her source material. Then she wobbled a little. He reached out and grabbed her before she toppled over. "You saved me! Twice!"

"Did I? That's very nice of me."

"It was. I'm glad you're back. I missed you."

"I bet you have." He stepped closer to her. "I've been meaning to ask you something."

Madison smiled. "What?"

"Will you go out with me next weekend?"

"Yeah. I'd love to."

"Sensational. I have another query for you. Has anyone informed you how resplendent you look tonight?"

Madison blushed. "Do I?"

"Indubitably." Then Stephen kissed her.

Chapter 19

"OK. I admit it. I chickened out." Steve threw his hands up in mock surrender. "I didn't have to go to that dinner. I could have asked Nicole Stephanie's question anytime. It's just that I'm terrible at parties."

"Have you been to many parties?" Kieron stared Steve down.

"None, actually. But I know me. I would have been all self-conscious. Buck's fearless. If you calculate all the variables, Buck has an 83.7 percent higher chance of successfully asking out Madison than I would."

"That makes sense. But asking out Madison is not what I was talking about."

Steve rocked back and forth in his chair. "Play practice?"

"Yup. First, you just wanted him to brave the Sci Siders and the Art Siders to sign up. Then, you worried you would blow the audition. But now you've got the part. What's the problem?"

Steve went quiet. Kieron waited patiently. "It was more than I wanted. I was just hoping to be up on stage. Apparently Buck was so good that they gave him a lead role."

"You don't think you can handle that?"

"I can handle it!" Steve declared. Then his determination waned. "I just need to work up to it. They're expecting me to be as good as Buck *was. What would have happened if I'd gone to the first rehearsal and sucked it up? They would have kicked me out. I need to get as good as Buck. Then I'll go to rehearsals."*

"Alright. There is a logic to that," Kieron conceded. "Did you hear her?"

"Huh?"

"Steve! Don't be rude. Nicole was asking you a question." Dad ruffled Steve's hair. "That's not as satisfying with your new haircut."

Out of habit Steve went to fix his shaggy bed-head hair and felt his new buzz cut. Then he turned to Nicole. "Sorry. What were you saying?"

"I was just asking if you boys liked tofu." Nicole was standing next to the car, waiting for Dad to find the right button on the fob.

"I don't think so." Josh looked to Steve. "We don't like tofu, right?"

"You've never had it." Dad found the button and unlocked the car.

"Shotgun!" Josh yelled.

"Not today," his dad ruled. "Nicole sits up front."

Nicole gave a flat, closed-mouth smile as she opened the passenger door. "Sorry. I get car sick in the back."

Josh flung his head toward Steve, looking for support. In the Buchmann house, the rules of shotgun were sacrosanct. This was mainly because Daniel let his sons shift the manual transmission into neutral at stop lights in a feeble attempt to get anyone else in the family, besides him, to fall in love with driving stick shift. Steve just shrugged and got in the back.

"I think you'll love this restaurant." Nicole buckled her seat belt and checked her makeup in the visor mirror. "Everything is vegan."

The restaurant was crowded and a line had formed outside. Fortunately, Daniel had made reservations guaranteeing a quieter table in the back. Nicole was concerned she would be hounded by locals recognizing her from the news. It was never actually an issue.

Dinner dragged on for over two hours. Not only was the service slow, but Nicole sent her dish back twice because of cauliflower that she suspected was really broccoli gone bad. It was only when dessert was served that things picked up. That was mostly because the vegan chocolate mousse Josh ordered was loaded with sugar.

"It's so awesome!" Josh accidentally launched a gob of mousse from his spoon in his excitement.

"Josh!" Steve warned as he wiped a mound of mousse off of his face... which he immediately tasted. It was a crime to call it chocolate, but it was much better than his eggless carrot cake. Steve had been trying to figure out how to ask Stephanie's question without his dad and Josh grilling him about who this mysterious new friend was. He had tuned out their conversation and was now having trouble following what Josh was talking about.

"The Echelon prince has lost the Crystal of Repetition. But it turns out the Celestines have it in the mines.'" Josh jumped out of his seat to act out the scene, using his dad as a stand-in for the evil Celestines.

"Josh, sit down," Dad said.

Josh sat down, continuing his story, unfazed. "They're using it to make millions of clone warriors. The final battle is going to be epic. I gotta pee."

Josh was up again and heading for the bathroom.

"I have to use the restroom, too." Dad stood and leaned over to Nicole. "You'll be OK?" he whispered.

She nodded and gave Steve another flat closed-mouth smile as Dad followed Josh to the bathroom.

"Have you ever read any of those 'Ekelone' books?" Nicole managed to mangle the title of the book despite how often Josh mentioned it.

"No..." Steve checked behind him to make sure his dad and Josh were out of earshot. "Um, Nicole, can I ask you something?"

"I'm usually the one asking questions." She laughed at her joke. "But sure. Fire away."

There were a lot of details Steve was going to have to change in Stephanie's question. If Steve thought Nicole paid enough attention to his life to be suspicious about this mysterious new girl, he would have pretended it was a guy friend. Regardless, he wanted to get this over with before his family returned.

"So I have this friend at school whose mom wants her to go to boarding school." Really it was an elite all-girls academy on Stephanie's world that was a fast-track program for future business leaders. From the way she described it, the school sounded like a cross between bar exam prep and indentured servitude.

"And your friend doesn't want to go?" Nicole prompted Steve.

"Not really."

Nicole steepled her fingers as she considered this information. "In my experience boarding schools lead to amazing opportunities later in life. I wish I had the chance to go to one myself. Your friend is lucky."

"So you think she should go?"

"Does she have a reason she doesn't want to go?"

"No..." Maybe Steve had left out too many details. When Stephanie explained the situation to him, it sounded clear that she shouldn't go. "It just seems like a change she doesn't really want. Like it's being forced on her."

The closed smile returned to Nicole's face. "I see. This is about something that's happening to your 'friend' that feels out of 'her' control." The quotes around *friend* and *her* were so obvious that Steve almost left the table.

"I think you should tell your 'friend'..." Steve winced when Nicole rested her hand on his. "...that change is a wonderful part of life. And that no one gets anywhere if they're afraid to take a chance."

Nicole took a drink of water, as if that was all there was to say on the subject. When she set the glass back down on the table, Steve noticed something different in Nicole's demeanor. She softened. Her voice became warmer. Yet, she commanded authority and confidence. "But, change is complicated. It's rarely something you seek out. And when it comes, it's hard to recognize it as anything good."

Nicole paused and looked past Steve toward the bathrooms. She lowered her voice. "I'm going to be very honest with you right now. I never imagined this would be my life, going out to dinner with you, your father, and your brother..." What she was saying should have infuriated Steve, but the way she said it was weirdly comforting to him. It was as if they were the only two people in the restaurant, and she was talking to her oldest friend in the world. "I was dating another man before your father. This was about four years ago. I loved him very much and I thought we were going to spend our whole lives together. Then he cheated on me. It almost destroyed me. Everything I had dreamed of was gone. But I wasn't going to let his weakness make me weak." Steve didn't hear any sadness in her voice. It sounded more like pride to him.

"I threw myself into my work. I was promoted to on-air talent. Then I got a job at your father's station. I was impressed with him right away. We became closer." She paused and smiled. "Your dad is very special person. He is strong, dedicated, and honest. More than that, he's resilient. When he lost your mother, he had every right to shut down and never open his heart again. But he did. And I was the person he chose to welcome into his life."

Nicole hesitated. To Steve she seemed scared to continue. When she did, she had regained her confidence.

"This is the brutally honest part. I never wanted to have kids. The man I was with before your father... he and I had always been in agreement about that. But your father already had a family. That was the change that I had a hard time recognizing as good— at first." She squeezed Steve's arm again. The smile that followed was real. It was the most natural smile Steve had ever seen from her. "I know this hasn't been easy. I'm trying. I really am. You and Josh are so wonderful. You are part of what makes your dad such an amazing man. More than anything, I want to be a part of that. And I hope your 'friend' learns to love the change in 'her' life like I did."

"Yeah..." Then Steve shoveled some flavorless carrot cake into his mouth, more confused than ever.

"You're not going to stay out here all night again, are you?" Dad hit the close button on the garage door opener. Josh had already bolted into the house to use his sugar rush to finish reading his Echelons book.

"No..." Steve had hoped that the others would be back from the party and he could find out what Madison had said.

That would have to wait until morning. "I'll come in with you."

"Good." He put his arm around his son's shoulder. "I really enjoyed tonight. I hope you did, too."

"I did." Steve avoided looking directly at his father, afraid that he would instantly see Steve was lying.

Dad got quiet while he figured out how to deal with the next topic. "So... Nicole told me about your... question tonight."

"Oh..." Steve's mind raced to come up with a new fake friend to explain his question.

"I want you to know that no one could ever replace your mom," Dad explained.

"I know. That's not what—"

"I'm not sure that you do. You've had to go through so much the past few years. It meant that you had to grow up a little too quickly. But there are still some things that you're too young to understand." Dad motioned to the bench on the porch and they both sat down. "I loved your mom so much... she was my everything. We created an amazing life together. We started a family."

A wind chime that Steve's mom had made, which was hanging from the porch, seemed to distract Daniel for a moment. "I never want to replace Mom. I don't want to even try. Because of that I didn't think I would ever find anyone special again. But, then I met Nicole. She's smart and driven, but more importantly she cares about people. She'll do anything to help anyone. You see it in every story she does."

Steve thought the kids of the Tarp Scientists taken away from their home might feel differently about Nicole's reporting. Then he felt guilty for thinking that after his dad had been so open with him.

"I'm very lucky that someone as amazing as Nicole feels

the same way about me as I do about her." Dad smiled, then he sighed and looked at Steve. "But I'm worried about you. I don't want you to feel like you have to leave because Nicole is moving in. Do you really want to go to boarding school?"

"Oh God, no!" Steve rubbed his temples. "I think she really, really misunderstood me."

Dad chuckled. "That didn't sound like something you'd want to do. It's just that you've been so stressed lately. And I know you've been having some trouble at school. I thought maybe you were looking for a new solution."

"Actually, things at school are going pretty good now."

"Yeah?"

"I brought my grade up in physics by nearly twenty points. And I think the play is going to turn out really great."

"That's wonderful." His father pulled him in for a hug. "I feel like we should be having this talk over a beer."

Steve stood up. "I'll go get us some."

Dad wrestled a laughing Steve back down to the bench. "Get back here. Maybe when you're sixteen."

Taking a moment to let them both settle, Dad patted Steve's shoulder. "You've been in such a funk the last few months. It's good to see you laughing again, boychick. That makes me really happy."

"Good." Steve looked down and smiled.

"You know what? Screw it. Fifteen is close enough. I'll let you have a few sips of my beer. Just don't get drunk. You don't want to be hungover for *Reflex* tomorrow."

The back door flew open and shut as Dad went to the kitchen. Steve sank into the chair and thought about the movie that he would not be seeing tomorrow. In the corner of the yard, a buzz-cut head appeared. Buck sprinted across the lawn like he was avoiding a spotlight on a watchtower. Once he'd vaulted up the stairs of the garage, he looked back, pointed at

Steve, and gave a thumbs-up.

Missing the sneak preview of *Reflex* was suddenly all worth it. Buck had asked out Madison and she had said yes. When Buck was safely inside the garage room, Steve jumped up and did a little dance.

He stopped his celebration when a thought crossed his mind. It looked like Buck was wearing the black polo. Maybe he had been right. In the dark, no one could tell the difference between that and the navy one.

Chapter 20

"Politicians are why we're late!" Daniel proclaimed as he, Josh, and Buck emerged from the depths of Penn Station and into the heart of New York City. "They scream about how bad taxes are. Then they act like heroes when they get rid of them. Then surprise, surprise! There's no money to fix a stupid stoplight!"

For the last fifteen minutes, the Buchmanns had been stuck on a New Jersey Transit train as it waited for a signal delay on the Jersey side of the tunnel to be fixed. The second the train stopped, Daniel launched into a tirade about the poor state of the country's infrastructure.

Buck was still in shock that they were able to just get on the train in Longview and go to New York. No security clearances were needed. None of them had to show IDs. The conductor just notched their paper tickets and kept moving.

On his world, travel into New York City was strictly regulated. Everlast considered the city a high-value target and went to extreme measures to protect it. Buck had been to Manhattan twice that he could remember. Once when he was six, before Everlast Security took over, when he went to see the Rockefeller Center Christmas tree with his family. The second time was on a class trip when he was twelve to see a government sanctioned exhibit at the Metropolitan Museum of Art. Each kid in the class went through a full pat down before they got on the train. There was a second search of the students before the train entered the city. Once they got to Penn Station, they were ushered into an armored transport that left through the basement. The whole trip into the city, including one hour at the museum, took six hours.

Actually walking the streets of Manhattan was almost too much for Buck. People were everywhere, rushing down the sidewalk, talking, buying lunch, eating lunch, selling lunch, kissing, screaming, laughing, crying—it was absolute chaos. It was freedom and it was beautiful.

"Come on, we'll take the F." Daniel led them across the street toward a subway entrance. "Maybe we'll be lucky and the trains will actually be running."

In the middle of the street, Buck had an unobstructed view of Times Square. The lights hypnotized him. There was no propaganda or the oppressive dark colors of the Everlast logo. In front of his eyes was the end result of what his family and the resistance on his world were fighting to achieve.

"Are you crying?" Josh tugged Buck onto the sidewalk. "You have been so weird lately."

Buck smiled down at Josh, then pushed past him. "Come on, hurry up!"

Tonight was Buck's reward for everything he had been doing for Steve: trying out for the play, going to rehearsal, and flirting with Madison. The truth was, as much as he protested, he was enjoying it. For so long, all he had known was a life of conflict. He had never dreamed about doing a bunch of silly activities like acting. But it had come to him surprisingly easily.

He found himself walking through scenes in his head. Part of Buck hoped they would be stuck on this world long enough that he would actually get to perform in Steve's place.

Once the Buchmanns were within sight of the theater, Daniel allowed himself to smile. "Boys, I may be more excited about this than you are."

"No way!" Josh bellowed. "You never even read the comic!"

"So? This movie is supposed to be amazing," Daniel explained. "I can be excited to see a movie with my boys."

"Fine. But we're not going to explain any of the post-credit stuff." Josh looked up at his brother. "Right, Steve?"

"Promise." Buck nodded.

"Is that so?" Daniel picked Josh up and swung him around. "You better tell me everything or you'll be too dizzy to watch the movie."

Josh squealed and Buck laughed. His dad used to do the same thing to his Josh. In the past six months he had come to doubt if he'd ever see that again. Without thinking, Buck raced over, caught Josh's feet and hoisted them up onto his shoulders. They were now in position to march Josh to the imaginary roasting pit. That was Buck's part in the game they were playing. At least, it was on his world.

"Steve, what are you doing?" Daniel asked the teenager he believed to be his son.

Buck's face went blank. He had gotten caught up in the moment. Settling on a reasonable excuse, he prepared to explain himself.

"We have to clean him first before we can cook him." Daniel started swinging his half of Josh back and forth. As the adrenaline faded, Buck joined Daniel.

By the time they found their seats in the theater, Josh's cheeks were red from laughing so much. Daniel handed a box of licorice to each of the boys. Buck couldn't stop smiling. Normally he would have been worried that such an overt display of emotion would blow his cover. But he figured Steve would have been that overjoyed to be here as well.

The theater was packed. Some people were actual members of the press, attending the advanced screening so that they could write reviews of *Reflex*. The majority was composed of people like Daniel, who pulled strings to bring their family or friends to see the hottest movie of the year.

The last time Buck had been to the movies, he was eleven. Watching any movie at this point would have blown him away. When the first shot appeared on screen of Reflex in costume, he starting bouncing in his seat. The movie was loosely based on the "Turned Tables" storyline from the comic. A lot had been changed, but the major plot points were still there. That included one of the most famous sequences from the story: when the elite ninja assassin squad invaded the home of Jake Reynolds, aka Reflex. Every fan in the theater knew what was coming as soon as they saw the recreation of the iconic shot of ninja hanging upside down over the sleeping hero.

The ninja invasion began with all the windows in the house shattering. A roar of approval erupted in the theater. This was what they had been waiting to see.

Buck broke out in a cold sweat. His fingers dug under the armrest. It felt like he was plummeting down an elevator shaft. The screen went fuzzy and Buck's breathing became rapid.

He turned to Josh and Daniel. They were enthralled with what they were watching. No one else around him seemed to be reacting like this. Buck looked back at the screen and immediately felt nauseous. He dropped his head in his hands, trying to escape the sensory overload he was experiencing.

As soon as he closed his eyes, he saw a clear vision of his bedroom on his world. It was six months ago. There was a pounding at their front door. Boots trampled up the stairs. His dad was yelling. There was a crack. Then his mom screamed. Then Josh was crying. Guns were in Buck's face. He was on his knees in the living room.

They dragged his unconscious father out the front door. There was a gash over his right eye, dripping blood. A second trooper carried Josh over his shoulder like a sack of laundry. Another trooper threw a packet of papers on the floor in front of his mother. It was a list of rules his dad had violated by launching an investigation into Everlast's connection to the massive terrorist attack that paved the way for their rise to power. Josh was taken as collateral against further retaliation.

The battle in Reflex's house continued to rage on screen. Every punch and broken piece of furniture made Buck wince. He took a deep breath and focused on the back of the seat in front of him. As he felt his heart beat returning to normal, Buck looked again at Daniel and Josh. Both cheered the fight in front of them. For the first time, Buck understood how far away from home he really was.

Chapter 21

All the indicators on the front of the WET were green. It emanated a low hum, barely audible a few feet away. Dust underneath the device was pushed away from it in waves by the supersonic vibrations of the tuning fork on top. When the receiver across the room lit up and the fan attached to it activated, Dr. Hicks squealed. Then he started dancing in a circle. Stephen cringed when Dr. Hicks hugged him.

"It works!" Dr. Hicks panted. "She was right! Look at that. It's beautiful."

He ran across the room and examined the readings on the receiver. His eyes were wide. "One hundred percent? There is no signal loss. None!"

"As I had explained to you." Stephen studied the control panel on his phone. He had found a discarded, outdated mobile device in Dr. Hicks's lab. With a simple grade school mnemonic, he had updated the operating system to handle his computing needs.

For weeks he had maintained how simplistic reconstructing the WET was for him. And it was. But the admiration with which Dr. Hicks looked at him was addictive. Stephen had managed to impress a leading scientific mind on this world.

"It's so quiet," marveled Dr. Hicks. The first time Stephen had been assigned to assemble a WET, he had to use everyday household items. (Household items were far more impressive on his world.) It had taken him a week longer than his classmates, even though it was supposed to be just an overnight assignment. When he turned in his attempt, the teacher threw it out. It had sounded like an unbalanced washing machine. Stephen worked for two more weeks to correct the problem.

"Steve will be blown away. You can all go home." Dr. Hicks came back to examine the WET.

"Yes. We will now be able to return to our home dimensions." Stephen stepped away from the WET to get some space from Dr. Hicks.

The actual purpose of repairing the WET had slipped Stephen's mind ever since he had kissed Madison. He was not enamored with her in any sense. The act of osculation had been pleasant enough, but Madison was not appealing to him. What he did enjoy was knowing how easily he could achieve a desired goal on this world. The others thought he was incapable of romance. They had found the idea preposterous—just as it was on his own world. They laughed at him. Here, on this world, he was their superior, and they mocked him. Stephen had proven how mistaken they were.

Dr. Hicks powered down the WET. "I thought we'd have a little more time. I still have so many questions about your dimension and what you have discovered."

Stephen was hesitant. "I'm not sure it is wise to discuss that."

"I understand your concern. But this isn't a violation of any temporal situation. We are from parallel worlds. Nothing you tell me would affect the timeline on this world."

"True..."

"Do you use hydrogen-based engines for space flight?"

Stephen nodded very slightly, hoping to discourage any more conversation.

"How did they deal with the thrust of the engines not being able to overcome drag from the magnetic funnel?" The excitement in Dr. Hicks' eyes was childlike.

"Can we try to remain focused on the task at hand?" Stephen reprimanded Dr. Hicks.

"Of course. The WET." Dr. Hicks inhaled deeply to maintain his cool. "When the Wireless Energy Transmitter is implemented on a wider scale, how do you compensate for power fluctuations?"

"I don't believe I understand your question." Stephen turned away from Dr. Hicks.

"One of the uses Melissa and I envisioned for the WET here would be as a way to power electric cars on the road. Like a cell phone network with WETs all over the country. Someone would subscribe to a provider and have access to wireless energy wherever they went. But when you're talking about cars, their power needs can vary dramatically. Not to mention they are traveling at high speeds. The sudden shifts would lead to overloads all the time. How do you avoid the network shutting down?"

"That is a complicated topic." Stephen began typing on his phone. "We should recalibrate the WET to the incorrect settings you initially were utilizing."

"But this could save years of trial and error. Not to mention save lives," Dr. Hicks pushed. "I always argued that it would be best to minimize the units of energy sent out. Make that uniform, then vehicles absorb only what they require. Melissa, on the other hand, said that the transmitter should be designed to modulate. What's the best way?"

"Was your transmission rate 64.97?" Stephen was determined to avoid this conversation.

"Is the transmitter even capable of being modulated, or would that limit the amount of raw power it can handle in the first place?"

"That's irrelevant." A drop of sweat rolled down Stephen's face.

"What's irrelevant? The power source?" Dr. Hicks examined the battery casing on the WET. "If the power source is too weak, all you'd be doing is lighting up small devices. The WET is ubiquitous on your world, right?"

"Naturally."

"How does it handle large power surges?"

Stephen's breathing became more rapid. "This has no effect on our task," he snapped.

"Actually, it does. Reopening the rift long enough for all of you to enter could require more energy than when you arrived. I'm concerned if this device can handle it."

"It can!" Stephen thrust the phone controller toward Dr. Hicks, poking him in the chest. "This will work!"

"I was very nearly killed the first time I tried this. Please tell me. How do you know it won't overload again?" Dr. Hick rubbed his chest, noticing just how hard Stephen had poked him.

"I just know!" Stephen barked.

"We have some time. I want to understand—"

"No!" Stephen screamed.

Dr. Hicks stepped back. Stephen saw some form of realization cross Dr. Hicks's face, who seemed almost frightened when he spoke again. "You don't really know how the WET works, do you?"

Stephen's reaction was far from subtle. He grabbed Dr.

Hicks by his shirt. "I know more than you do!"

Dr. Hicks pushed Stephen away. "We're dealing with technologies that can transcend dimensions. Anything less than a complete mastery of the sciences involved would be reckless and just plain stupid. You're a fraud!"

All Stephen saw was red. This technological kindergartener was calling him a cheater and a liar. Those words stabbed at Stephen. They had followed him across dimensions. They echoed in his head. Once again they rendered him powerless. The terror of their implication shattered his very being. They took away everything. Who was this man... this ignoramus... to cast about such insults? The people of this dimension were lucky to have enough scientific knowledge to make fire. They were too stupid to even know what those labels could truly do to him.

"I made this work!" Stephen advanced on Dr. Hicks. "Not you! I did what you couldn't. I know how to do things you've never even dreamed about. Everyone on this world should be awed by my presence. I am the greatest scientific mind you will ever meet. The gifts I could bestow... your sad world would talk about my work for a thousand years."

Dr. Hicks tried to back away but bumped into a cabinet. "You can't stay here."

"Why not?" A wrench on the floor caught Stephen's eye. "It is a much better alternative."

Stephen picked up the wrench. Dr. Hicks realized his intended target a second too late. The wrench flew straight toward the WET, striking it directly in the control panel. Dr. Hicks ran over to the device. The control panel was devastated.

"The regulator!" Dr. Hicks tried to remove the panel but a spark arced out, forcing him to take a step back.

When Stephen saw the receiver glowing brightly, he

immediately regretted his outburst. "Get away from there," he called to Dr. Hicks.

Before Dr. Hicks could process what Stephen had said, the WET surged. A pulse of energy blasted out of it, knocking Hicks back across the room. His head smashed onto the floor. A desk next to it shot back toward Stephen, pinning him to the back wall.

He remained there, motionless, waiting for another reaction. For ten minutes, he watched as the WET spun down to an inert husk. The room was silent. The machine had shorted out the power, including the alarms. When he was certain there would be no aftershock, Stephen pushed himself free of the desk. He surveyed the lab. It was once again in ruins.

In the corner, the closet door remained intact. They had stored most of the unused components borrowed from Steve's school there. Stephen quickly surveyed what was inside of it. Steve would be joining them soon. Stephen didn't have long to gather what he would need to start his new life.

Chapter 22

In the corner of the hospital waiting room was a tiny table surrounded by tiny chairs. A random assortment of toys was scattered on top of it. The toys had no age consistency. An infant's pop-up toy was next to a one-legged Ninja Turtle, which was lying on top of a baby doll. Steve could not understand how those uninspired selections would comfort any kid stuck here.

A man and woman were the only other people in the waiting room with Steve. He avoided making eye contact with them for the first hour that he was there in case they started crying. All they ended up doing was staring down at their phones, showing no emotion—happy or sad. This was Steve's first time in a hospital waiting room and he was certain that all anyone did in one was cry. Although he wasn't crying, so that disproved that theory.

Steve was still trying to process what had happened. Dr. Hicks's lab was destroyed again, and Steve had found him unconscious in the corner. Stephen was nowhere to be found. The WET was in ruins. Once Steve had called 911, things moved quickly. The ambulance arrived. Paramedics took Dr. Hicks away. It wasn't until Steve arrived at the hospital that he had time to think.

Nothing made sense. The last time Steve had been in the lab, the WET repairs had been nearly completed. They were supposed to test it that afternoon. If something was wrong, Stephen would have noticed. And where was Stephen? Steve had searched the house while he waited for the ambulance. It was possible that they had opened the rift and he had returned home. If so, why wouldn't he get the others first?

Across the hall from the waiting room was a vending machine with snacks. Steve fished in his pockets for cash. All he had left were two singles. It had been weeks since he had last collected his allowance. (So which Steve was getting all of his money?) Cheez-Its would be his dinner tonight.

"I love these." Steve gave a start when Stephanie reached from behind him to snatch a handful of Cheez-Its from the bag as soon as he opened it. "Any news?"

"Nope." He stuffed a handful of crackers in his mouth. "He's still in a coma. They think he may be like that for a while. That's all I know."

"Sorry." Stephanie paused a respectful moment before crunching her next Cheez-It. "I know this isn't the best time, but..."

"Nicole said you had no good reason not to go to that school." Steve pulled the Cheez-It bag away from her. "Then she said some stuff about not avoiding change."

Stephanie leaned back in her chair, contemplating Nicole's advice. "Are you sure you explained the whole situation to her?"

"I told you she wouldn't be any help."

The couple sitting on the couch just to their left looked up from their phones at the same time. Making no effort to be subtle, the man pointed at Stephanie and Steve, then whispered to the woman. She nodded in agreement.

"Are you twins?" the woman blurted.

Steve froze, forgetting his cover story.

"We're cousins," Stephanie explained, saving him from his own panic.

"You look exactly alike." The man laughed. "So weird."

"You are," Stephanie replied through a mouthful of Cheez-Its.

The man's smile turned into a frown as he registered what Stephanie had said. She didn't wait for him to respond.

"You need to come back to the garage." Stephanie reached for more crackers. "Buck is being really weird about being around your dad and Josh. He won't go in the house. Your dad doesn't know you're not home. He almost came up to the garage room looking for you. Your family hasn't seen you all night. At least Buck pretended to be you long enough to convince him everything was OK. Also, we're hungry."

"I know. I know." Steve pulled at his buzz-cut hair, grasping for the frilly comfort that seemed like it had been gone for months. There were too many things to keep track of. "I can't leave until Dr. Hicks wakes up." Steve turned away from Stephanie. But the only other way to face was toward the now-angry couple.

"You should be careful with him. He's a loon," said Stephanie.

"No, he's not," Steve whispered sternly, trying not to raise his voice.

"Yeah, he is. At least the one I know is. He's crazy obsessive. You should see him around my mom. It's sick. You said it yourself, he's careless. He probably couldn't wait and tested it before it was ready."

"He wouldn't do that." Steve almost launched into a tirade

but stopped. The damage to the WET was different from the first time. It looked like it had been smashed from the outside. "I think. I don't know. It's possible."

"We need to find out what happened to Stephen. And we need to figure out our next step. Are we trapped here? Mind your own business!"

The couple's heads snapped down to look at their phones. It was a poor attempt to cover that they were listening to the very loud Stephanie. Steve jumped up and pulled her out into the hall, spilling the Cheez-Its as they left the waiting room.

"Can you not let the whole world know what's going on?" Steve whispered.

"Stop hiding." She was making no effort to speak any more quietly. "We have some decisions to make."

Steve checked the doors leading to the rest of the hospital. Stephanie rested her hand on his shoulder. "They'll call you when he wakes up."

Steve nodded. Back in the waiting room, the couple had been intently studying Stephanie and Steve. As she turned, Stephanie caught sight of the couple. She leapt back toward the door and flipped them the bird. They both dropped their phones.

"Stephen abandoned us!" Buck slammed his fists on the table. Everything in the garage room jumped.

"I don't think he did," Steve said calmly. "I don't. He wouldn't. He's... us. We wouldn't do that to ourselves." Steve nodded confidently. "I'm positive."

"Then where is he?" Buck stalked across the room.

"Stop pacing. You're making me nervous." Stephanie was sitting on the couch with her arms crossed.

"Where else does he have to go?" Buck demanded. "He doesn't know anyone else on this world. It's only logical that he went into the rift."

"The WET didn't open a rift." Steve stood to face Buck.

"How do you know that?" Buck moved Steve to the side to continue his laps of the room.

"The evidence doesn't support that hypothesis," Steve explained. "The receiver was intact. The accident that brought you here overloaded the receiver."

"Stephen fixed that, right?" Stephanie looked up from the couch.

"True." Steve turned to her. "However, to open the rift we need to replicate those conditions. That didn't happen."

Buck stepped in front of Steve. "That makes sense."

Steve smiled.

"So now we need to find Stephen so he can fix the WET again."

"How long will that take?" Stephanie grabbed Buck's arm to stop his pacing. "Who knows where he went or why? Something happened and he ran."

"Or was captured," Buck suggested.

"By who?" Stephanie demanded.

"I don't know." Buck sighed. "That's what makes them so dangerous."

Stephanie chuckled. "You're losing it. Look, there is an easier answer, Steve."

"Huh?" Steve was still basking in his previous victory.

"You've been working with Stephen and Dr. Hicks," Stephanie said. "Can't you fix it on your own?"

The room was quiet as Steve registered the request. In the time he had worked with Dr. Hicks, he had seen the designs enough to understand the basics. Over the past couple of weeks, Stephen had fleshed out the details of how the WET should operate. But none of that could replace actual knowledge and experience. Assembling it wrong could do even more damage than the past two times.

The longer Steve stood there, the tighter Buck clenched his fists. "That's what I thought. I'm going to go search for Stephen. I don't know about you but I want to actually go home."

Before Buck could reach for the door, Steve blurted, "Wait! I can do it."

"I'd have more faith if it hadn't taken you twenty minutes to say it." Buck turned the doorknob.

"No! I can do it... I think. But I need your help. It'll take me some time. I need you to cover for me—"

"No!" Steve and Stephanie both leapt in reaction to Buck. "I'm done. I'm not playing pretend anymore. This is your life. Not mine. You want to be in the play, you be in the play. I'm going to figure out how to get us home."

The door slammed as Buck stormed down the stairs. Stephanie looked at Steve. A look of horror crossed his face. "Oh, man... I have to go back to school tomorrow."

Chapter 23

Passwords were pointless. At least they were to Stephen. The right algorithm could crack any password in seconds. On his world, biometric scanners were the only acceptable form of security. It was no surprise to Stephen that computer systems on this world were constantly being hacked.

Even an advanced tech lab such as Stepstone hadn't left behind the relic of the password. This was fortunate for Stephen. It meant he had no trouble breaking into their high-security research facility. He had installed on his phone a simple code cracking program. It was actually a game he remembered from his preschool programming class. In fact Stephen had managed to get in so fast that it actually looked like he worked there.

When Stephen first fled Dr. Hicks's house after the explosion, he didn't have a destination. This was not his world. He knew no one. And yet he did know a version of Longview. Out of habit, he found himself walking a familiar route—to Stepstone. On his world, his mother was a vice president at the research company. Stephen knew the facility well.

No matter which world they were on, scientists had a common trait: when they were working, they could process no other stimuli. Once Stephen was deep inside the facility, no one noticed the fifteen-year-old redhead in their midst, even if he was wearing jeans and carrying a grocery bag. He moved confidently through the building, which was laid out exactly like the version on his world.

On either side of the long hallway were large glass windows overlooking a production line. This was where Stepstone created their signature batteries. People clad in white isolation suits carefully assembled various components. Stephen shook his head in despair. That was one of the possible fates that awaited him if he had returned to his world—a technician toiling for the benefit of the upper class.

A heavy sound-proof door blocked his progress. Beyond it were the real labs, where the bleeding edge technology (for this world at least) was being developed. The equipment he needed was there.

"I forgot my badge," Stephen told the guard, who controlled passage through the door.

The guard studied Stephen. "You an intern?" he asked.

"Yes. I started yesterday and left my ID at home. I am very sorry, but my supervisor said I need to give this to someone in the administration office." He presented his grocery bag. "I don't want to screw this up already."

The guard sighed, shook his head and pressed the buzzer, unlocking the door. "Don't forget it again."

The silence on the other side of the door surprised him. If he closed his eyes, it would be like being in a sensory deprivation chamber. Plush carpet lined the floors and acoustic tiles ran along the walls and ceiling, muffling his every step. Industrial-strength air filters removed any odors from the area.

It took another five minutes for Stephen to work his way to

the administration offices. Since the corridors were almost identical to the ones back on his world, he started to fear he might run into his mother at every corner. Part of him wished he would see her once he completed his mission.

Walking through the door to the administration offices was like exiting an air lock. The sterility of the hallway was replaced with a warm, inviting waiting room. Plush leather couches lined two walls. Lite FM music wafted from hidden speakers in the walls. Half a dozen plants around the room were being nourished by warm incandescent lights. A mahogany desk was the only thing preventing access to the offices beyond the waiting room.

"Hi," Stephen announced to the assistant manning the desk. "I'm here to see Gary Trouter."

A young woman looked up from her computer and studied Stephen's face. She may have been only two years out of college, but the severity of her expression made her look twenty years older.

"Is that right?" she told Stephen more than asked him. "Do you have an appointment that I was not aware of?"

"No. But he will want to see me."

She laughed and reached for an intercom button on her phone. Stephen lightly touched her hand, stopping it in its path.

"Please tell Mr. Trouter that Melissa Buchmann's son is here to see him. And that I know how to repair his Wireless Energy Transmitter."

Gary Trouter was an imposing man in person. It was not just his size. He was over six and a half feet tall and built like an NFL quarterback. It was how he held himself. That was something he got from growing up on the streets of Newark, New Jersey. He always looked like he was ready to fight—even in board meetings. This made negotiations with him very difficult. He liked to get right up in his opponent's face. Without fail, they all backed down.

What none of his opponents had known was that he had not thrown a punch in twenty-five years. Yes, he had been in plenty of fights growing up in Newark, but he hadn't won any of them. It wasn't until he went to MIT that he discovered that being a large black man, who stood like a thug, scared people. There was no need for actual violence if he projected the aura of violence.

The version of Gary Trouter that Stephen knew wasn't a CEO. He was just his mother's coworker. He could be intimidating, but Stephen had only ever known him to be a dedicated scientist. That gave Stephen some confidence, and he needed all of it that he could get. Trouter's bravado may have been an act, but it was very, very, very convincing.

"I'm sorry," Trouter bellowed. "You want me to give you access to my most advanced lab... completely unsupervised?"

Stephen nodded.

"And you'll give me a working version of the Wireless Energy Transmitter?"

Stephen nodded again. This time he smiled to show his confidence.

"Stop smiling!" Trouter barked. "Did Hicks put you up to this? Just tell me now and I won't call the cops."

"No." Stephen dropped his smile. "He has nothing to do with this."

Trouter's nostrils flared as he stared at Stephen. "Steve, I know how important that project was to your mother. And how hard it must have been to lose her like that. But understand, that technology was a dead end."

"You're wrong." Stephen stared back at him. "I found my mother's notes. You were right. There was a flaw with her theory. But, I have determined what it was and I have corrected it."

"I'm being gentle with you." Trouter rose and looked down at the seated Stephen. His voice got more intense with each word. "But I will not have a fifteen-year-old boy come into my office and tell me what to do. You can either leave on your own or I will have security—"

Stephen reached into the grocery bag at his feet and pulled out the model version of the WET he had taken from Dr. Hicks's closet. He placed the mini receiver on Trouter's desk, then activated the portable WET. It gave its small hum and the LED on the receiver turned green.

"I've seen this before." Trouter put his huge hand over the WET receiver and switched it off.

"No, you haven't." Stephen pressed another button on the WET control panel. The deactivated receiver in Trouter's had come back to life. Then the lamp on his desk turned on—as well as his laptop, ceiling fan, printer, and cell phone.

The receiver dropped onto the desk as Trouter backed up to the wall. "How are you doing this?"

"I told you. I have corrected her calculations." Stephen smiled. "And if this has impressed you, I have additional ideas that I am certain will intrigue you."

For two hours, Trouter grilled Stephen about the plans for the WET. Stephen played coy on the details, pretending he did not want to show his hand until their deal was finalized. It was a convenient way for Stephen to cover his inability to answer Trouter's more complex questions.

By the time Stephen left the office, he had secured his future. He would develop a working prototype of the WET and give the designs to Trouter. In return, Stephen would get a percentage of the profits and continued access to the facilities. When he turned sixteen, he would be a millionaire many times over. Every few years after that, Stephen planned to introduce another invention from his world. He would become *the* scientific mind on this world. If he was to be branded a cheat, he may as well profit from it.

Unfortunately, he was not the only Stephen Buchmann on this world. Sharing this improved life with Steve would not be possible. Once Stephen constructed a new WET, he would remedy that issue.

Chapter 24

Walking the halls of Sinatra Edison again was very surreal for Steve. He had been out for the past several weeks, but to everyone else, he hadn't missed one single day. It was like walking into the middle of a conversation and no one explaining what they were talking about. Stephen and Buck had changed a lot of Steve's relationships with people. Some he was aware of, but most were surprises. An Art Sider had run up to him laughing about "lady parts." His history teacher seemed very concerned that he had some kind of concussion. Maybe the most unnerving thing was Justin.

"Hey, man," Justin greeted Steve as he walked into physics. "You see the new Spitzer telescope images NASA posted this morning?" This didn't sound like a jackass Justin trap question. It was legit, or at least it sounded that way. Steve mumbled a no just in case.

"I'll send you the link after class. It's awesome," Justin said.

A faint whiff of strawberry-scented perfume sauntered its way toward Steve. Excitement coursed through his body, followed by a wave of fear. This was his typical reaction to

Madison walking into class. While keeping his head down, Steve peeked up to get a glimpse of her fresh, morning beauty. His jaw dropped when she waved—at him—while smiling!

What was this new world?

"Let's pick up where we left off Friday," Mr. White began before the door had even shut. "As Mr. Buchmann so astutely pointed out, calculating the time it would take to travel from Earth to the Alpha Centauri system would in fact be altered by the presence of a theoretical exoplanet outside that system. How would we reconfigure the formula to determine that time?"

Dozens of hands went up. Steve's remained down. He had an idea about the answer, but he wasn't 100 percent certain. There was no need to ruin it with a guess.

"OK, Ms. Anderson, what would you do?" Mr. White asked.

Throwing all subtlety out of the window, Steve turned his whole body around to look at Becky. His mouth hung open as he watched her answer Mr. White's question. Mr. White had actually called on a girl. When she finished giving the correct response, Steve faced the front of the room. His mouth remained open.

"I assume, Mr. Buchmann, that based on your expression you disagree?" Mr. White stopped his glasses from sliding further down his face and pushed them back into place. "I really don't feel like arguing today. Just tell us what you think the right answer is."

"Um..." Steve had to forget about the new dynamic in class and do some actual physics in his head. Becky had included the same variables in her equation that he had initially thought to try. That made him feel a little more confident, but that could just mean they were both wrong. In that case, he could make things worse for Becky once again. He took a chance. "No. I agree with Becky."

Mr. White took off his glasses and rubbed his temples. It was his classic frustrated-beyond-belief move. Well, this new world order was fun while it lasted.

"I can't seem to win," Mr. White declared. "There goes my lesson plan. I'd set aside twenty minutes today to debate this with you. Yes. She's right."

Steve exhaled, realizing that he hadn't taken a breath the whole time. Mr. White didn't launch into a tirade directed at him. That was an improvement. But he apparently expected mega-debates every time Steve raised his hand. That could be a problem.

For the first time all year, Steve hadn't been counting down the seconds until the end of class, so he was surprised when the bell rang. As he gathered his books, he was grabbed in a bear hug from behind. Everything in his hands dropped to the floor.

"You are very cute for someone so clumsy." That was Madison's voice. Steve's head exploded. "Would you run lines with me at lunch today?"

"Um..." Steve squirmed to the left and the right, trying to figure out how to turn around and face Madison.

"If you have something else to do, that's fine." Madison let go of him.

Free of her grasp, Steve started to breathe again. At this rate, he was going to asphyxiate himself by third period. "Lines. Yes. We can run lines."

"Awesome!" Madison did a little hop of excitement. "I'm still having trouble with the scene we're running today. I'm not sure if Sabrina is supposed to be happy or sad. It looks like her dad is about to lose his house, but she's falling in love with Rick Cherry. It's—"

"Whatever." Justin stepped in front of Madison. His tall

frame cast a flagpole-like shadow on her face. "I don't get this Art Sider crap. And we have some unfinished business."

Neither Stephen nor Buck had mentioned anything about Justin since the first day they had started filling in for Steve. This had to be about Steve being in the play. Justin wasn't going to let that rest.

"There is the small matter of the Maze Campaign." Justin held up a tablet with a detailed map of a maze on the screen. Dragons and trolls lined various halls of the maze. "You promised that we would finish it this week."

"Oh, right..." What the hell had Stephen done? Was he friends with Justin now? That would make Steve's life easier. But at what cost? "Sorry. I need to work with Madison. How about tomorrow?"

Justin became a puppy dog, happy to get the tiniest bit of affection from his owner. "Yeah, that'd be awesome."

As Justin scampered off to his next class, Madison smiled at Steve. "See you at lunch."

"Totally."

It hadn't occurred to Steve at all that asking out Madison might have additional perks, such as being able to have lunch with her. This was turning out to be an amazing day. Not even the bleak look on Noah's face could dampen Steve's mood. Noah was looking at the tiled floor, shutting out the chaos of the school around him. Steve sprinted to catch up with him.

"Wait up!" Steve called.

Noah glanced over his shoulder long enough to register that it was Steve, and then he continued. "I told you. The cameras aren't tracking us."

"What?! What are you talking about?" Steve asked.

"Wait. Which one are you?" Noah studied Steve's face.

"It's me!" Steve spread his arms as if he'd finished a huge musical number.

"Oh!" Noah brightened for a second. Then his smile faded. "Oh... I didn't know you were coming back."

"Neither did I. A lot of crazy stuff happened yesterday." Steve followed as Noah plowed through the hallway.

"Are they still here?" Noah looked worried.

"Yeah. We had a setback."

"So they'll be here a little longer?"

"Yup."

Noah considered this. "Did any of them say anything about the party?"

"Like what?"

"I don't know. Maybe Stephanie heard something interesting from Madison." Noah was being oddly vague.

"Even better. She wants to go out!" Steve waited for Noah to match his excitement.

"Stephanie does?"

"What? No. Why are you asking about Stephanie?"

Noah stopped walking. "I'm not. You are."

"I'm talking about Madison. Why are you... Do you have a thing for Stephanie?" That was enough to wipe away Steve's smile.

In a desperate attempt to avoid eye contact, Noah pulled out his cell phone. "That's crazy."

Steve leaned closer to Noah. "You can't have a thing for her. She's me."

"I know!" Noah's anger shocked Steve. "I don't. OK? I don't."

Their conversation was interrupted by the bell, followed by a rush of students going to their classes. When the hallway cleared, Steve was left by himself. Since they were twelve,

Noah had shared every detail of every crush he'd ever had with Steve. No matter how badly Noah was shot down, he remained positive and immediately proceeded to his next object of desire. In all those conversations, Steve had never heard as much passion in Noah's voice as he just did.

Standing behind the curtain, Steve could see the whole stage, which was lit by a solitary work light. The rest of the auditorium was dark. One folding table at stage right stood in for an office desk. At the back of the stage, a crew member was painting the office backdrop. Kristian, Phillip, and Madison were standing around the desk flipping through their scripts. Steve had not stepped out on stage yet.

Buck had carefully shown Steve all of the play's blocking so far. And Steve had been a good student, memorizing lines along with Buck and studying the layout of each scene. In theory, he could replace him at any time. In reality, he had still never said one single line in front of anyone except the Steves. This rehearsal would be the very first time he'd ever stepped on stage.

That may have been a mistake.

"People!" Mr. Salinger proclaimed. "Let's have quiet."

Since no one on stage had actually been talking, they shrugged and set down their scripts.

"Crystal! What are we doing today?" Mr. Salinger barked.

His poor student assistant jumped, but she managed to keep her script open to the right page. "The negotiation scene."

"The ne-go-ti-a-ti-on scene!" he repeated, breaking the word into syllables. "Let's see some magic people!"

Mr. Salinger flopped into a seat, propped his feet up on the chair in front of him, and tented his fingers to study the scene. The set crew continued their quiet painting, as Kristian, Phillip, and Madison took their positions at the desk. Steve tensed up and listened for his cue line: *"May I continue?"*

"So this here's the trial? Don't look nothing like it does on Perry Mason," Kristian started. He had assumed the hunched-over stance of his character, Terrible Terry, the recluse.

"No, Daddy." Madison held Kristian's hand. The gesture conveyed the warmth her character, Sabrina, felt for her father. *"This is the deposition."*

In all of his "rehearsals" with Buck, they had never actually practiced the scenes with other people reading lines. One question was running through Steve's head: Did he enter *after* Phillip said the line, *when* Phillip said the line, or *just before* Phillip said the line? These were small differences, but considering how far Steve had to go to cross the stage, a few words could make or break a scene. If he entered too early, the audience would see him and it would ruin the surprise reveal. If he came in too late, the audience would think there was some kind of screwup.

Phillip, who played lawyer Rick Cherry, dug through a stack of papers until he found a folder underneath and opened it. *"May I continue?"*

Steve hesitated for a second, then launched forward. He had been concentrating so hard on when the line was said, he never made a decision on when to enter the scene. Now it was way too late. He moved quickly to make up time while trying to look like he was walking casually.

"STOP!" Mr. Salinger yelled.

Steve froze mid-step. The scene was ruined because of him. That would be the end of his big debut in the play. Forget another date with Madison. She may not even want the first one after today. Maybe he could talk Buck into fixing things tomorrow.

"Phillip, you're killing me." Mr. Salinger as he walked up onto stage, Crystal trailing behind. "You take that long digging for a prop and you'll lose the audience."

That answered Steve's question: start moving before his cue. He allowed himself to breathe. After today, Steve would be able to pass one of those Navy SEAL diving tests.

"From the top," Mr. Salinger turned around and saw Steve standing in the middle of the stage. "My apologies, Mr. Buchmann."

Steve headed to his mark, backstage. He now had a lot more questions for Buck. This was harder than he thought. Missing all those rehearsals was definitely a terrible idea. He had a lot of work to do.

"You got a big ol' do-over, didn't you?" Kieron turned his head away from the mic to finish chewing his sandwich.

"Yeah. Kind of." Steve tried not to look directly at Kieron's mouth.

"That's great. But what my listeners really want to hear about is your work on the Wireless Energy Transmitter. It was a groundbreaking piece of technology for this world. And now you have to put it back together by yourself."

"Yeah. It's going to be a challenge, but I can do it." Steve pumped his fist in the air.

"Talk me through this. Dr. Hicks is still in a coma. But you have access to his plans?"

"I found them in the lab. There were in bad shape from the explosion. But I can make out a lot of it. Plus, I helped with the reconstruction of the last one."

"What about the components?"

"Well, the WET Dr. Hicks and Stephen were working on has parts

that can be salvaged. I can still find anything else I need in the school lab."

"How long do you expect this to take?"

"Buck and Stephanie have been here nearly three weeks. I'm going to work as fast as I can."

Kieron lowered his head and glared at Steve. "Really?"

Steve sighed. "It took Dr. Hicks five years to do this. And he invented the stupid thing! I just can't take that long. That's not fair to the others. I can't imagine if I were trapped on another dimension away from my family. That'd be awful."

"What about Stephen? If Buck finds him, do you think he'd help?"

"I don't know. I kind of doubt it. He has nowhere else to go on this world. There's a reason, whatever it may be, that he hasn't come back."

"So, if they are ever going home, it's all up to you."

A cold wave washed over Steve.

Chapter 25

"What should I do with my hands?" There was a look of panic in Steve's eyes.

"Don't let go is what you should do!" Buck grunted as he hoisted the destroyed WET off the ground.

On the other side of the device, Steve was struggling to unfasten a latch. Buck's face was turning red. Steve didn't have much time left.

"No. I mean, in the play. What do I do with my hands?" The panel on Steve's side popped open and he nodded to Buck, who got to set the device back down. He stepped back, rubbing his arms.

"When I'm standing on stage I feel very conscious of my hands. Should I be holding something all the time? Should I put them in my pockets?" Steve put one hand in his pocket and held a screwdriver in the other to test out the pose.

"I don't know. Just do what people do regularly." Buck walked away from Steve. He had been staking out Dr. Hicks's house, hoping to find Stephen. Except for Steve's garage, Stephen should have no other place to go. Instead, Buck saw

Steve, through a window, struggling in the lab and decided to help. Now he was regretting that.

"That's what I can't figure out." Steve counted off on his fingers. "I've done a number of informal studies. First, I analyzed what people did in the show. Seventy-two percent are always holding a prop. Thirteen percent keep their hands in their pockets or folded in front of them. The remaining 15 percent do a combination of all these actions. In the general public, the numbers are drastically different. Eighty-four percent just let their hands hang free. Twelve percent have their hands in their pockets. The remaining 4 percent use some kind of crutch object... a phone, a pencil, food..."

Buck glared at Steve. "Do whatever you think your character would do."

"That's what I'm trying to figure out. What would he do?"

"You get to decide that. It's what an actor does." Buck examined the box of components Steve had taken from the school lab.

"Just tell me what you did and I'll do that." Steve thought his argument was clear-cut.

"No!" Buck barked. Steve flinched. "You wanted to be in a play. Be in the play."

Steve snapped. "I'm trying. Not only do I have to catch up in school, I have to fix the WET and take care of you and Stephanie. I get up at five every day to do laundry so Dad doesn't notice the extra clothes and towels we're using. It's just all so much. Figuring out what I need to do in the play is hard. But you were there during all of the blocking. I don't want to screw up all of that."

"So what?" Buck threw his arms in the air. "What's the worst that will happen if you suck? If you forget every line in the play! Nothing!" Buck answered his own question. "Nothing happens. No one dies if you screw up. It's a stupid play. It's make-believe!"

His anger highlighted lines and creases that Steve had never seen in his own identical face. They were hard and sad. It was the first time Steve had seen this side of Buck and it brought him out of his self-pity. Buck was always intense, but it had been controlled. Maybe this was the kind of fury he needed to survive on a world where he couldn't trust anyone.

"I'm sorry," Steve offered.

Buck took a step back. "No. I'm sorry. It's not your fault you live on this cushy world."

"I forget about what it's like for you back home," Steve admitted. "But I swear I'll get you back there soon." Steve smiled, trying to reassure Buck.

"How?" Buck swept his arms around the devastated lab, ending at the untouched box of components. "This will take you years. Stephen is the only one who can do this. We have to figure out where he is."

Steve's face dropped. More to himself than Buck he declared, "I can do this. I can. I will get you home so you can help your family."

"Right." The face that turned back around this time was very familiar to Steve. It was the same confused fifteen-year-old who was struggling with the world around him. "Like I know how to do that either. I'm just kidding myself that I can help Dad and Josh at all."

"If your mom is anything like my mom was, she'll figure out something." Steve put a hand on Buck's shoulder. "I know she will."

"It's funny," Buck said. "On this world, the building they're being held in is abandoned. I could just walk in and get them. On my world it's a fortress."

"You're in the way."

Stephanie towered above Noah as he sat at the top of the stairs leading up to the garage room. He got to his feet and hopped up onto the landing.

"Are you alone?" Noah asked.

"Why?" Stephanie took another step back. "What are you going to do?"

"Nothing!" Noah had rehearsed a much smoother opening line for this conversation. "I just wanted to talk to you alone for a few minutes. Is that OK?"

Stephanie groaned. "You're the clingy type, aren't you? It was one kiss. Get over it."

"It was more than just a kiss and you know it."

"It was just a kiss." Stephanie stepped around Noah and into the room.

Noah followed her inside. She was waiting on the couch. "You have a serious problem with hints, don't you?" she said.

"We had a moment. I saw it in your eyes," Noah argued.

"It wasn't even that good of a kiss. Come on."

"Not the kiss. I'm talking about right before it." Noah motioned to his eyes. "We connected."

"So what if we did?"

"Why did you run away afterwards?"

Standing up, Stephanie motioned to the garage room around them. "Look where we are! I'm from another dimension, living in the home of my male version—your *best* friend by the way. How screwed up is that? Do you think we can just start dating?"

"Dating?" Noah smiled.

"You know what I mean." Stephanie turned red. "Hooking up. Hanging out. Going steady. Whatever you want to call it... we can't do it."

Noah's smile faded. "Why is your first instinct to push people away?"

"This isn't a normal situation. It doesn't count."

"Everything counts. What's the matter with following your feelings? Taking a chance?"

"It's not that simple," Stephanie protested.

"Of course it is. Just do it. Sometimes you get hurt... a lot of times you will. But sometimes it'll work out. You'll never know until you try."

Stephanie's finger jabbed Noah in his chest as she emphasized every word. "My. Life. Is. Just. Fine. Stay. Out. Of. It."

Noah rubbed his chest where a welt was already forming.

"You're alone. Let someone—anyone, it doesn't have to be me—let them in. Life's so much better that way."

"Who the hell do you think you are, telling me how to live my life?" Stephanie's words were harsher than her tone. "Just go."

"Hey, Noah! What's up?" Noah turned and came face-to-face with Steve.

Steve patted him on the shoulder as he entered the room. His face was sweaty from the walk back from Dr. Hicks's. Buck followed and only nodded in his direction.

Steve flopped on the couch and started fanning himself with a stray comic book. "What are you guys talking about?"

The silent, blank expression on Stephanie's face scared Steve, who sat back up. "Did something happen?"

"No," Stephanie said in a whisper.

"What happened?" Steve was really alarmed now. Buck keyed into the discomfort of the exchange and ran to a window to check the perimeter.

"Nothing," Noah offered. "Everything's fine."

"No, it's not!" Steve blurted. "Look at her."

"It's nothing. I promise. She's fine." Noah smiled, trying to force the rest of the room to smile with him.

"Tell me what happened!" Steve demanded. "She looks like she's going to cry."

This woke Stephanie up. "You want to know?"

"You don't really need to—" Noah tried to stop her.

"You're the one who's all about the joys of 'letting people in.' Let's share with your best friend." Stephanie faced Steve. "We kissed. Noah and I made out at the party the other day."

"You what?" Steve's eyes locked on Noah.

Buck burst out laughing.

"It wasn't like that," Noah said, trying to calm Steve down.

"I asked you not to hit on her!" Steve was furious. "You promised me that you wouldn't. What's wrong with you?"

"Calm down." Stephanie stepped in front of an approaching Steve. "I'm the one who kissed him first."

"*You* kissed *HIM*?" Buck asked through tears of laughter.

This revelation didn't change the situation for Steve. "How screwed up are you? This is worse than if I had a sister and you hooked up with her. She's me! You made out with me!"

"It's totally different," Noah tried to explain.

"Just get out of here!" Steve yelled.

"I—"

"Go!"

Noah looked to Stephanie, who shrugged her shoulders. "Aren't friends great?" she asked.

Chapter 26

Steve hovered behind Nicole as she sprinkled some kind of herb onto a very thin pancake. It smelled awful and was taking forever. Steve tapped his foot to speed her up. As it was he would barely have time to eat breakfast, let alone stop at Dr. Hicks's lab on the way to school. After Noah's bombshell Steve had been too wound up to go to sleep. Plus he needed space, so he went back to work on the WET. That had gone well... really well... much faster than he imagined it would. Between Dr. Hicks's plans and the salvaged parts Steve had finished reassembling the device last night. That had made him forget Noah's betrayal, even though he had stayed up until after midnight to do it. He still needed to test it and had planned to do that this morning before school.

That euphoria faded when he got back home last night. Dad and Nicole were still up, watching some movie in the living room. There was too much of a chance they would catch him sneaking back in, especially considering that he had made such a big deal about pretending to go to sleep before he snuck out. He wasn't ready to face Stephanie either. So he sat in the cold on the lawn for an hour before they finally went to bed. Now he was waiting for the world's slowest cook to finish making a breakfast that he would hate. And based on the small portions she had made for Josh and Dad, there wouldn't be any leftovers for Stephanie and Buck. Steve would have to split his food again, but he had to eat enough not to make Nicole think he wasn't anorexic or something. Steve's head started to spin trying to keep it all straight. His fists slammed on the table, causing all the silverware to jump.

"What the hell was that?" Dad glared at Steve, who just now realized he had lost his cool.

"You are being a spaz." Josh eyed Steve. "You've been a spaz all week. You get all jumpy when I walk into the room."

Those must have been times when Buck was in the house. Steve lately could only remember being exhausted any time he had a quiet moment at home. It hadn't occurred to Steve that he would have to explain to his family why he was being crazy when it wasn't even him.

"Boychick, are you OK?" Dad ruffled Steve's hair. "Are you sure you're not taking on too much. School. The play. That's a lot."

Steve ground his teeth and nodded. He did not need to be reminded.

Nicole stopped her slow work on his breakfast. "What you need to do is prioritize you." Then she returned to her cooking.

"Uh-huh." All Steve was doing was prioritizing versions of himself. The last thing he needed was Nicole getting suspicious. "You're right. I'll do that right now. I'm going to take a walk before school. You can just wrap up my crepe. I'll eat it later."

Steve left the table before anyone could ask any questions. At least Stephanie and Buck would have leftovers in the fridge to eat this morning.

"C-minus?"

Even though it had long since dried, the red ink seemed to still be bleeding through the paper. It just lay there at the top of Steve's quiz, begging for a bandage to cover it up. Dozens of other wounds littered the page. X's and question marks were everywhere. A war had been fought and Steve had lost—badly.

Mr. White handed out the last of the graded quizzes to the class. Every smile and fist pump made his C-minus seem that much more pathetic. Steve's grade wasn't a complete surprise. When he first started taking the quiz, all Steve could think about was Noah and Stephanie. How could Noah do that to him? There was also the play weighing on his mind and the new problem with the WET. Of course Nicole popped into his head. Getting past those distractions was hard enough. Then there was the quiz itself.

He had been baffled by the first problem, even though he understood the general concepts. He just hadn't learned the formulas or how they were applied. Maybe missing three weeks of school had been a bad idea. Stephen's tutoring sessions had been suspiciously lacking.

This quiz had covered some complex mathematical concepts. It would take Steve a lot of time to catch up to this level. Still, he hadn't been entirely wrong. On the last problem he had used the wrong formula, but it was basically the same idea. His answer was off by .00004. That wouldn't fly at NASA, but should have earned him full credit in high school.

For some reason, the room was suddenly quiet. Steve looked up from his quiz to find Mr. White hovering over him.

"Go ahead. Let's hear it." Mr. White gestured to Steve. "What did I do wrong? How did I incorrectly force you to use an inferior method to solve those equations?"

Steve could feel the eyes of the entire class on him. Arguing for that last problem would mean the difference between a C and a B. His GPA in this class needed all the help it could get. Stephen would have argued his way up to an A. But Steve wasn't from a world of scientific geniuses.

"No... you were right," Steve muttered.

"I know," Mr. White declared as he returned to the front of the room. "So that's basic wave function. It's fine if you're dealing with theory in a lab. Now we need to factor in time and the realities of the universe."

Ice shot through Steve's veins. That was just "basic" wave function? They were already moving on to the complex stuff. Steve considered running from the classroom. But that would involve going past Madison's desk. There was no need to wreck another part of his newly fixed life.

Flipping through his notebook, he found an empty page and began copying the new equations from the board. This may be over his head now, but if Steve worked hard he would be able to catch up and understand it. Unfortunately, the amount of information that Mr. White presented to the class that day was astounding. Steve had filled twenty pages of his notebook with equations, sample problems, and solutions. Each page was more alien than the one before it. He didn't even feel any relief when the bell sounded. All it meant was that he could tally up exactly how screwed he was.

"That was awesome!" Justin spun around to face Steve. "I had never thought about the connection between Heisenberg's theory and gravity before. Insane stuff."

"Definitely," was all Steve could offer. Sometime over the past few weeks Justin, the bane of his existence, had become his best friend. Actually, he had become Stephen's best friend... well, more like lackey. It was unnerving.

"I want to take a stab at some of these homework equations. Do you think we could work on them together at lunch?" The look on Justin's face was just shy of a lovestruck teenager asking out a girl.

"Maybe?" Steve considered the possibility that he could use Justin to help him catch up in class. That would mean spending more time with Justin. Steve wasn't sure it was worth it.

"Cool." Justin tried some elaborate finger-snapping maneuver that should have ended with pointing his fingers at Steve like guns. Instead, he just bashed his knuckles together and winced in pain as he headed out of class.

"I was waiting for him to leave," Madison whispered from behind Steve.

He caught a whiff of her perfume as he turned around to face her. Every concern he had about class was gone in an instant. She had her hair back in a ponytail and Steve became hypnotized by the unobstructed view of the soft skin of her neck.

"I have an idea," she continued. "I know we talked about seeing a movie on Friday. But I was wondering if you would mind going to an art show instead."

"Um..." Steve tried to process all the new information he was getting. To the best of his knowledge, there hadn't been any discussion about what he and Madison were doing on their date.

"I know there's the whole Art Side/Sci Side thing," she explained. "But I think we're past that, right? And there's this guy who does paintings using equations. He substitutes colors for variables and solves them. I saw it online. I can send you a link. It looks awesome and I think you'd like it."

"Yes!" She was thinking about what Steve would want to do. Whatever those paintings looked like, Steve decided that he would love them. "That sounds great."

"Oh, good." Madison gave a little hop of joy. "See you at rehearsal."

As Madison weaved her way out of the class, Steve found a new burst of energy. Physics was not going to get the best of him. There was nothing on that quiz or in class today that he couldn't learn. He was going to get an A on the midterm. Better yet, he was going to nail every problem and then destroy the bonus question. Who needed sleep this week? It was decided.

"I knew you couldn't keep it up," Mr. White announced from behind his desk. The class had emptied, leaving just Steve behind. "You could only lawyer me on these quizzes for so long."

Mr. White got up from his desk and walked over to Steve. "Consider this fair warning. There will be no wiggle room on the midterm. None of your alt-physics will help you. This will be the single most difficult test you will ever take. Ever!"

A huge smile crossed Mr. White's face. He patted Steve on the back, which seemed like a genuinely warm gesture. The smile was the most evil thing Steve had ever seen.

Walking felt strange. The sudden emotional shifts of the past hour left Steve with wobbly legs. By the time he made it into the hallway, most everyone was in their next class. He didn't have long before the late bell sounded, but running was not an option right now, so he would just have to be late. This physics midterm was going to be impossible. Even if he dedicated every spare second of the next week to studying, he would be lucky to get a B. There was no way he would be ready.

Not that he had any spare seconds for anything. When he went to test the WET this morning before school, reality came crashing down around him. Nothing worked. Steve was certain the conversion circuits were set up according to the plans. There was just no reaction happening. He was at a loss on how to fix it. It should have been working.

When Steve got to the stairs, he froze. Noah was at the top, staring back down at him. Their face-off ended a few seconds later when Steve charged up the stairs, his head down, avoiding any eye contact with his friend. He only made it halfway up the stairs before Noah stepped in front of him.

"Get out of my way," Steve ordered.

"No. I need to talk to you for a second." Noah wouldn't move.

"I don't want to talk to you." Steve stepped to the left to get around Noah, but he shifted to block Steve.

"Please. You don't understand."

"I think I do. You have no respect for me as a friend. Pretty straightforward." Steve turned around and headed down the stairs. He would find another way to class.

Noah followed. "I'm sorry. I really am. If it makes you feel any better, she shot me down."

"Good!" Steve headed down the hall to use the stairs on the other side of the building. "You deserve it."

"I deserve it?" Noah slowed down. "Why do I deserve to have my heart broken?"

"Because you betrayed your friend!" Steve's voice echoed through the empty hall.

Noah raced to catch up with Steve. "For your information, I like Stephanie. I really *like* her, like her."

"You like every girl you meet. Then you do something stupid and she never wants to see you again. This is already a screwed-up enough situation. I didn't need you complicating things."

"I wasn't trying to complicate anything." Noah realized something. "And why are you the only one who gets to do something crazy to be happy? Why are you so special?"

"Obviously I'm not!" Steve got to the other stairs and sprinted up them.

"Who are you and what have you done with the real Steve Buchmann?"

Mr. Salinger was waving his script around while poor Crystal scrambled to gather up loose pages. All Steve could do was stand on the stage in front of the entire company and take the abuse. At this point, it was just the cherry on top of a very, very bad day. Justin had been entirely useless as a study buddy. While doing the problem set, he talked nonstop about the role-playing game Dungeon Caravan—his mouth full of food the whole time. Not one word was said about the actual problems.

In social studies he got an F on a paper that he didn't know he had written. Apparently whichever Steve had been in school for that assignment was from a world where the civil rights movement had never happened. On that world, there was no such thing as racism. Steve's teacher, who was African American, didn't think that was funny.

Then rehearsal started. From the first scene, Steve was having trouble. He was so focused on the blocking that he couldn't concentrate on his lines. Most of what he said sounded like a tired robot. The one time he actually was able to emote with any conviction, he stepped on Kristian's toe. On the bright side, Kristian's overreacting to his injury was the most solid performance of the afternoon.

As the rehearsal went on, the actors started to become distracted by Mr. Salinger's irritated complaining from deep in the theater. After Steve missed a cue all together, Mr. Salinger threw something so hard that glass broke. From then on, rehearsal only got worse. Steve was completely conscious of his every movement and every word that left his mouth. It was painful for everyone involved.

Now Mr. Salinger was raging at him. "We open next weekend! Next weekend! I'm looking at day-one-level rehearsal performances. Steve, if you don't want to be in this play, tell me now so I can get a replacement."

"No, I want to be in the play," Steve said to the floor.

"What?" Mr. Salinger hollered.

"I want to be in the play," Steve repeated with slightly more enthusiasm.

Mr. Salinger jumped up on stage and stood right in front of him. "What was that? I didn't hear that."

Out of the corner of his eye, Steve saw Madison. He couldn't make out her exact expression. But he was certain it was whatever someone's face looks like when they decide they no longer like a person.

"I WANT TO BE IN THE PLAY!" Steve screamed in Mr. Salinger's face. He wasn't sure what the play's director wanted him to do, but it felt great to let a little of the pressure go.

Mr. Salinger nodded and stepped away from Steve. "That's more like it." He then moved to the center of the stage. "Let's call it a day. We're not going to get anything more done today. But tomorrow! Tomorrow! The sun better shine like it has never shone before. Tomorrow!"

The cast fled the stage before Mr. Salinger could break into song. Steve looked to where Madison had been standing. She was dashing backstage—avoiding all eye contact with Steve. Instead of looking into the eyes of his crush, he got a face full of Mr. Salinger.

"Steve, I need a moment with you." He ushered Steve down the stairs and up the main aisle. "This is your first play, right?"

"Yeah."

A soft chuckle emerged from Mr. Salinger. "It happens every year. Some phenom appears from the depths of the school to wow us at auditions. Blows us away at every rehearsal. Then about this time, just before opening night... total meltdown."

"I wouldn't call it—"

"Total. Melt. Down." He spun Steve back toward the theater's seats. "In a few days, this auditorium will be packed with everyone you've ever met in your life. All of them waiting for you to wow them."

For the first time, Steve realized just how large his school's auditorium was.

"This can go one of two ways, Steve. You brush off tonight, come in tomorrow and continue on your path to magnificence. Or, you complete your... Total. Melt. Down. What's it going to be?"

"I want to—"

"No!" Mr. Salinger spun Steve back toward him. "Don't tell me. *Show me*. Come in tomorrow and show me what I can expect on opening night. OK?"

"Yeah. Thank you, Mr.—"

"Because if you don't wow me tomorrow, you're out and Christopher takes your place."

Chapter 27

Watching this rehearsal was the most enjoyable event Stephen had witnessed since he arrived on this world. The director's passion for perfection was diametrically opposed to the absolute pointlessness of this endeavor. That made his dissatisfaction with Steve even more hilarious. Several times, Stephen found himself physically covering his mouth to stifle a laugh. Hiding in the shadows, all the way in the back of the auditorium, Stephen could not hear every insult the director leveled at Steve, but the expression on his face filled in any gaps.

Stephen had assumed this rehearsal would not go well for Steve, given how his day had been going. With work on his WET nearly complete, Stephen had decided to check on this world's version of him. After all, he planned to assume his place here soon and wanted to be kept abreast of his status. He had overheard a bit of the altercation in the hall between Steve and Noah. While maintaining a friendship with Noah was of little consequence to Stephen, it served to add to Steve's deteriorating mental state.

During rehearsal, Stephen searched through Steve's locker and saw his latest academic achievements. It stung Stephen that the history paper he had expertly written received an F. The physics quiz, however, was embarrassing considering how easy the subject was. Although Steve's solution for the last problem was impressive given that he clearly had no understanding of the subject matter. Stephen would have enjoyed arguing with that simpleton Mr. White over that one. Not that Stephen had any interest in continuing the farce of his education after he sold the WET to Stepstone.

Over the past several days, Stephen had been getting a preview of the perks of his new life. By hacking the primitive security of the website of a nearby hotel, he had been able to secure a comfortable place to stay. It wasn't up to his world's standards of comfort, but it was far superior to the garage room. Granted Stephen had no income yet, however he had made the reservation using a false identity and the disinterested twenty-something working the front desk never asked Stephen for any identification. In that seclusion Stephen had mapped out the details of assuming Steve's place in this world. Obviously, there couldn't be multiple versions of himself in this dimension. Buck and Stephanie would be happy to return to their worlds. Steve, however, would require more convincing to get him to vacate this life. Without much effort on Stephen's part, Steve was already destroying his scholastic career. His time in this theatrical production was clearly limited. Stephen imagined that offering Steve a chance to leave those failings behind would be enticing. But, alone, that was not enough.

The inability to reactivate the WET would be a key component in this scheme. Stephen had visited Dr. Hicks's laboratory last night after Steve went home. Dr. Hicks had given both him and Steve a spare key to the house. Steve had made impressive progress on the WET. In fact, Steve's version was complete. That was why Stephen had rewired the circuit boards. It was a small modification, but one that would take Steve several days to discover.

With the only working WET, Stephen would have leverage over the others. To return home, they would happily coerce Steve to acquiesce to Stephen's demands. One final motivation needed to be introduced.

Stephen unlocked his modified phone and began typing out his message.

Chapter 28

The text simply read, "Have to cancel our date." Steve studied the message for any hint of why Madison had canceled. Maybe there was an extra number of spaces that served as a secret code to Steve, pleading to find her because she had been kidnapped. Sadly, the spacing was absolutely consistent. There was no frowny face or TTYL. This was bad.

His finger hovered over the reply button. Should he ask her why? Should he ask to reschedule? Would that look desperate? Would that make it worse? Noah's advice would be perfect now, if Steve had any interest in talking to him.

He swiped down to refresh the page. Maybe she had sent a follow-up. Nope. Nothing.

"Could you please put your phone down?" His father gestured with his fork.

"Yeah. And then eat this!" Josh pushed a bowl that had a single string bean in it over to him.

Steve picked up the dish and slammed it in the center of the table. His dad and Josh burst out laughing and Nicole gave her flat, cold, lifeless smile.

All of dinner had been like this—an annoying array of unfunny inside jokes. For the past ten minutes, Dad and Josh had been making each other crack up over that uneaten string bean. He had been in a bad enough mood from school and rehearsal. The text from Madison had been the final straw.

"Oh! I keep forgetting," Nicole blurted. "I found the perfect desk for the back room."

"That's great!" Dad said. "Where?"

"Why are you putting a desk in the back room?" Steve asked.

"For Nicole's office," Dad explained.

"What office?" Steve looked around the table for an explanation.

"We talked about this already. Remember? You said you liked the idea," Dad reminded his son.

"To get rid of the back room? No, I didn't!" As soon as Steve said the words, he realized that his father must have had that conversation with Buck or maybe even Stephen.

"Uh-oh! Now look who's the last string bean," Nicole stated stiffly. Dad and Josh burst out laughing.

Steve didn't.

"That's *our* room..." Steve mumbled.

Dad watched as Steve repeatedly scooped up a pile of mashed potatoes with his spoon, then dropped them back down on his plate. "Maybe we'll all go look at the desk and see what we think," he offered.

"I call dibs on any secret compartments!" Josh proclaimed.

"The desk is going to be for grown-up work." Nicole returned her attention to her plate.

"I'm ready for dessert," Dad declared. "Who wants to put the last string bean out of its misery?"

Josh, Nicole, and Dad laughed as if it were the first time that joke had been made that night.

Without saying a word, Steve jumped up and grabbed the dish with the sole-surviving string bean. He pounded it against the side of the trash can to make sure it was finally out of their lives. Tossing the dish on the counter, he began clearing everyone's plates. His display killed any joy in the room. Josh pushed back from his seat to make room for the sullen Steve tornado. Dad eyed Steve as he grabbed his plate then moved on to clear Nicole's.

"Actually, I'm still working on it," she informed him.

Steve let the plate drop back to the table and stormed over to the sink. The clanging and echoing of plates against the stainless steel made any conversation in the kitchen impossible. Dad and Nicole exchanged a look.

"I think it's time to start homework," Dad said to Josh.

"Sure," Josh agreed. Normally, he would protest starting his homework, but being caught between his dad and Steve at times like this never ended well for him.

"Can we have a few minutes?" Daniel whispered to Nicole, who quietly got up from the table.

"What are you doing?" He reached over Steve's shoulder and turned off the water.

"The dishes." Steve turned the faucet back on.

"What's gotten into you?" his dad barked.

"Nothing's wrong. Everything is fine," Steve said to the sink.

"Are we back to this again? Would you just say what you're thinking? Is it the back room? We don't have to put a desk there if it's that big a deal."

"I don't care about the desk." He drowned a sponge in dish soap, then let the water from the tap run over it, making a mountain of bubbles.

Dad turned off the faucet again. This time he kept his hand there to keep it off. "Stop. You're doing it again. You're not talking to anyone. You're bottling something up again. And then letting it erupt in these pity-party tantrums that ruin the whole night."

The soapy sponge sprayed blue gel when Steve threw it at the sink. Before Dad had time to react, Steve was up the stairs and had slammed his door. In the dark isolation of his room, the anger seeped away. For the first time all day, he felt like he could breathe. There were stacks of notes to read through, problem sets to solve, lines to memorize, and advanced energy transference contraptions to repair. All of that would have to wait while Steve enjoyed his pity party.

Chapter 29

In the middle of the morning on a weekday, Willie's Waffles in Lower Sable was busier than Steve expected. Lower Sable was the town next to Longview. Each town in the area had their own version of the definitive New Jersey diner. Residents of the towns were fiercely loyal to theirs. Urban myths sprang up in each town about the other town's diner: rats in the kitchen, hair in the food, the cook is a serial killer. None of the stories were true, but they guaranteed that people from one town never ate in the other town's diner. That meant that Steve and Stephanie could safely eat at Willie's Waffles without running into anyone they knew.

For all the differences between the various Steves, the one constant seemed to be appetite. Stephanie had ordered the "Long Haul Special," a meal designed to keep truckers satisfied. It consisted of an omelet, hash browns, sausages, and a stack of pancakes. Steve kept pace with the "Hibernation Sandwich"—two omelets and bacon sandwiched between two pieces of French toast and served with a side of hash browns.

"That would be a terrible idea," Stephanie said between

bites.

"I would just ask Madison why she broke the date," Steve insisted. "Not beg her to go out."

"Still going to seem desperate. The last thing you want is to appear desperate."

He considered this as he finished off his breakfast sandwich monstrosity. The last few bites had been extremely difficult to keep together since the grease from the omelets and bacon made everything slide. Left with a handful of breakfast food, Steve just tossed all of the remnants into his mouth.

"Hut awout uhn uhh-muhl," he struggled to say through a mouthful of food.

"Send her an email?" Stephanie asked.

Steve nodded.

"Then you get to wait for her response and obsess. Did she get the email? If she got the email, did she read it? If she read it, did she write back? If she wrote back, did it get lost in cyberspace? Do emails actually get lost in cyberspace, or is that just something we tell ourselves so we don't feel like a loser?"

"So there's nothing I can do..." With great effort Steve swallowed. "But there is something *you* can do."

"No!" she blurted, spitting a mouthful of food at Steve.

"Please talk to Madison for me?" Steve asked, his eyes a heartbreaking reflection of her most pathetic moments. "I'll ask Nicole another question for you."

"What's the point? She's definitely not like *my* Nicole." She shoveled in the last bite of her food.

"I'll do anything."

"No!"

"Why not?"

"It's none of my business."

"Of course it is. She's your friend and I'm... you."

"What difference does it make if we are friends? Her love

life is her own business."

"When you date someone, you date everyone in their life. You're doubly involved."

"You and Madison never went on one single date." Stephanie speared a stray strip of bacon on Steve's plate.

"That's a technicality. The point is, friends talk about their lives. Who they like. Who likes them. Everything. So you should go talk to Madison for me."

Stephanie's ravenous chewing of the last bacon strip slowed down as she listened to Steve. "I don't think I can."

"Sure you can. Girls talk about that kind of stuff all the time."

"That's the thing." Stephanie found a straw wrapper and started twirling it into a tiny ball. "I don't really know how to do that. I'm not used to this 'friends' thing."

"Really?" Steve said louder than he intended.

Stephanie flicked the tiny straw wrapper ball at Steve's face. "I'm not contagious or something. Calm down."

"Sorry," he said as he pulled the wrapper ball from his mouth.

"I have had friends before, but we just never stay that close."

"But you're really..." Steve paused, searching for the most accurate way to describe Stephanie that was also positive. The word search was very noticeable.

"Nice?" Stephanie suggested.

"Yeah!"

"No, I'm not." She swirled her straw in her water glass. "It's the way I've always been. Mom drilled into me how strong and focused I needed to be to make it in the world. And to avoid distractions, like friends."

"That's crazy," Steve insisted.

"Are you sure your friends have never created any kind of

drama that caused distractions in your life?"

Steve didn't respond.

"I'm talking about Noah," Stephanie told him.

"Yeah. I know." She had a good point. "But to be fair you did kiss him first." Another thought occurred to Steve. "Yeah. Why did you kiss him first?"

Stephanie pushed her glass away and slumped in her seat. "I don't know. He was being nice. I was having fun."

"Do you *like* him?" Steve was having trouble with this thought and what the implications were if this version of himself liked his best friend. Would that mean he should have feelings for Noah?

"No." She sat forward. "No. Absolutely not. It was just a thing that happened in the moment. I don't think he understands that?"

"Yeah." Steve felt relieved. "Noah can get kind of carried away and do really dumb things like... you know... Look I didn't say friendships aren't complicated."

"If they're complicated distractions, then what's the point?"

Her logical argument was confusing Steve. It took him awhile to remember his point. "To have someone to talk to. That's the reason. Someone who will care. I mean, if I were still talking to Noah, I would have called him right away when Madison texted. None of you cared that Madison dumped me. He would have."

"Would he actually have had any helpful advice?"

"No. Probably not. But he would have listened. Maybe made some jokes. I don't know. But it would have made me feel better."

As they stared at their empty plates, the waitress placed the check in the center of the table. Steve stood up to take out his wallet and walk to the register. He turned back to see that Stephanie hadn't moved.

"Do you really think Madison considers me a friend?" she asked.

"I think so, yeah."

She stood and followed Steve to the cash register. "What time does rehearsal end tonight?"

Maybe it was the blinding late afternoon sun blaring through Read Aloud's front windows, but Stephanie was having a hard time recognizing any of the titles on the shelves. The din of the Creationists had distracted Stephanie the first time she was in the store, and she hadn't noticed the books. Now, as she followed Madison, Tina, and Sherri up and down the aisles, the strange titles were giving her a headache.

Not all of them were strange. Stephanie recognized plenty of books in the classic literature section. It was modern fiction that started to get hazy. As best as she could tell from studying the publication dates, somewhere around the 1970s was when all the unfamiliar books started appearing. Past that time, they all seemed like they were written by obscure male authors— Tom Clancy, Stephen King, Dan Brown, John Grisham. On her world, they were the kind of writers whose books were only found in indie stores in Manhattan.

"What about this?" Madison held up a book. On the cover was a pair of shoes hanging from the branch of a tree next to the title *Endings*.

Tina frowned. "Eh. A little derivative. I liked the premise and the characters. But I thought it was going to be more 'Ralph' and it turned out to be 'Susie.'"

"No, thank you!" Madison quickly put the book back on the shelf then dusted off her hands. All three of them burst out laughing. Stephanie just watched.

This had been going on all afternoon. The three of them seemed to have their own language. Everything reminded them of something else. All of those events had been boiled down to a single code word, such as "Ralph" or "Susie." It was impenetrable to an outsider. Being that outsider was what Stephanie had wanted to avoid. If they were her friends, like Steve claimed, they would actually try to have a conversation with her.

"I can't find anything," Madison sighed.

"I know what you mean," Sherri agreed. "Nothing is speaking to me."

"Yeah, everything is so..." Tina slumped her shoulders forward and crossed her eyes.

"Exactly," Madison squealed.

At this point, Stephanie was too irritated to even roll her eyes again. Maybe that was her problem. Stephanie could see herself doing it. Before any new experience, she had already made up her mind about it. That was exactly what her mom did.

"You should reread something." Stephanie's lips cracked a little when she opened her mouth. It had been almost a half hour since she had last spoken.

"Yeah?" Madison considered.

"You said you were in the mood for something that was like that 'Eagles' book. Why not read that again?"

Sherri crumpled over laughing. This set off Madison and Tina. Stephanie was chilled watching Sherri. It immediately brought her back to her world. That Sherri had tormented her and turned all her friends against her. Stephanie turned away. It served her right for ignoring her instincts.

"Wait!" Sherri reached for Stephanie's shoulder. "I'm sorry. We weren't laughing at you."

Stephanie stopped but didn't turn around. This was a

typical Sherri trap. She had fallen victim to it before.

"Eagles isn't the name of the book," Madison explained. "It's a stupid joke thing."

"When Madison first started reading that book, she talked about it all the time," Sherri continued.

"Finally, I asked her what the name of the book was," Tina added.

"And she totally blanked," Sherri tagged back in.

Stephanie took a chance and turned around. Madison hung her head in shame. "I was reading it on my tablet. I hadn't looked at the cover in forever."

"She rattled off all of these names," Tina said. "She couldn't remember what the title was, but she insisted *Eagle* was part of it.

"Then I opened it," Madison confessed. "The title was *Soaring Hearts.*"

The three of them were crying with laughter now. This time, Stephanie didn't wince at their reaction. Before Stephanie could think about it, she was smiling. Maybe it wasn't the funniest story—well, it was kind of funny—but she stopped before she laughed out loud. That was another trap she'd fallen for. It happened all too often in middle school—laughing along with a joke Sherri made, only to be called out for not actually getting what was funny.

As the girls recovered and moved down the aisle, they revealed a shelf of books that froze Stephanie in her tracks: *Text Friends, The Summer of Me, Down the Hall.* Teen Romances! It was half a step above porn on her world. Her mom called books like these "mind garbage" and said Stephanie would be better off staring at the wall than reading them. Stephanie loved these books.

In a frantic burst, she pulled every title that seemed even remotely interesting. Her arms were overflowing by the second shelf. The selection was mind-blowing. Vampire love stories. Dystopian love stories. College love stories. College break-ups. Vampire break-ups. When she couldn't hold her books anymore, Stephanie sat on the floor. She opened the book closest to her and started reading.

"What are you doing?" Tina asked.

Reality splashed its cold water in her face. For a brief second, she had thought on this world that these books weren't verboten. But Tina's tone was so full of scorn. It was seventh grade all over again.

"They... fell." Stephanie searched for a better explanation.

"Oh, there you are." Sherri stood over Stephanie.

It was fun while it lasted. Stephanie began placing books back on the shelves. Maybe she could come back later and buy a couple of books before she returned to her world.

"Are you crazy?" Madison balked. "You can't put that one back. It's the best in the series."

Madison grabbed a copy of *Glances at Dawn*. A pale boy wearing a worn leather jacket lay across the cover. His passionate eyes stared deeply into the soul of a virtuous-but-tough teenage girl. Gravestones littered the background.

"Or did you read this one already?" Madison handed the book to Stephanie. The tone in her voice was genuine.

"No. I haven't read any of them," Stephanie admitted.

"You haven't? You have to read it! It's so amazing!" The passionate actress in Madison took over. "It's this super-realistic take on vampires. Very scientifically accurate."

"Yeah! They're all terminally ill," Tina jumped in. "Just on the verge of death. They are infected with this neuro-virus that never lets them fully die."

Madison interrupted, "The virus is fascinating and pretty accurate. Basically, it has a symbiotic relationship with the human body. The virus attacks the host cells, almost like a cancer. But instead of killing his host, the virus starts taking over the functions of the dead cells. The author got her PhD in oncological medicine."

Stephanie was starting to understand why Steve was so into Madison. She was this unique balance of a free-spirited artist tempered by an organized, inquisitive scientist.

"Uh-huh—so this girl, Tulip, falls in love with this guy, Dean." Tina was getting breathless. "He's had the disease for decades."

"It's all about how their love overcomes all obstacles," Sherri added.

"My mom would kill me if she ever caught me with this book," Stephanie admitted.

"Really?" Sherri blurted.

"She thinks books like these kill brain cells," Stephanie explained.

"Oh my God!" Sherri hugged Stephanie. "My mom's the same way. She says I'm wasting my 'gift.'"

"That's awful!" Stephanie caught herself, not meaning to insult Sherri's mother. "Your mom's not awful. Just—"

"It's OK." Sherri smiled. "It's true. Like, I can't be into two different things?"

At that moment, Stephanie's disinterested facade crumbled. The floodgates were open. "I tried telling my mom that once. She said I must not be very serious about my future." This was the first time Stephanie had said that out loud. It was invigorating. "What does she know about my future? Who is she to tell me what I should be doing?"

"Totally. I've done more in high school than she did getting her master's!" Sherri declared.

Tina watched patiently. When there was a slight pause in the conversation, she jumped. "The science stuff is all great, but the best parts are all in book two. Because her best guy friend gets the disease. And she gets all worried about him."

"Don't tell her what happens!" Sherri blurted.

"I'm not going to spoil anything," Tina promised.

Then Tina spoiled everything. Stephanie didn't mind at all. She loved hearing every detail. "She's at this party with them. And Dean is all 'I'm too old for a high school party.' And he leaves and Robert's there. That's her boy BFF. And they totally make out. But she freaks and runs off."

"Just like you did to Noah!" Tina didn't realize what she said until Sherri elbowed her. "Whoops."

"Sorry," Sherri explained. "We promised each other we wouldn't talk about that unless you brought it up first."

"Really?" Stephanie was impressed by their restraint. Fortunately for Sherri and Tina, who were doing their best to not force the issue, she was still riding high from opening up about her mother. "I'm glad you did. It's been so weird."

Tina and Sherri were bouncing, waiting for the gossip.

"How?"

"Is he a good kisser?"

"Did you break his heart?"

"Is he stalking you?"

"Did you make him cry?"

"Were you super-drunk?"

"He's kinda cute."

"Was it a pity kiss?"

"I like his eyes."

"You were doing him a favor."

"I'm obsessed with his hair."

"He won't do better than you."

"I'd make out with him."

"I bet he dies a virgin."

It was an avalanche of questions and statements. For the first time in her life, Stephanie wasn't worried about carefully wording her answer so that she didn't trigger some catty response.

"Noah came over the other day to talk to me—" Stephanie started.

"Oh Em Gee!" said Tina.

"I didn't know what to tell him. I didn't want to hurt his feelings, but I'm just not into him. I think he got the message. And he even seemed OK with it. What got weird was with Steve—" Stephanie stopped when she saw Madison's face change. Curiosity turned to intense concern. Stephanie said nothing and just watched Madison waiting for her next words. With one small slip, she'd ruined all of her progress. The silence just lingered. Sherri and Tina waited for Stephanie to continue. Madison's face was growing stranger. Was she getting angry now? Stephanie had nothing to lose. "I'm sorry. You probably don't want to talk about my cousin. I wasn't thinking."

Now Madison looked confused. "Why not?"

"Because you canceled your date with him. It's none of my business and I wasn't trying to force you to talk about it."

"Canceled our date? Did he say we're not going out next weekend?"

"No. I meant yesterday."

"What are you talking about? We had a great time. That's why he asked me out again."

Chapter 30

"Now which one of us is the genius?"

Steve stepped aside with a flourish to unveil the grand structure behind him. It was the same structure that Buck had been scrutinizing since they had started to make their way through the cracked, busted up parking lot leading to it. A faded sign hung over the main entrance reading "Longview YMCA." Ivy draped the walls that weren't already drenched in graffiti. Any opening had been sealed with moss-covered boards.

"How is this supposed to help?" Buck made a half-hearted effort to pull off one of the boards covering the main doors.

Built on the edge of Mountainside Park, the building housed Longview's YMCA until the 1980s, when a new modern facility opened closer to downtown. It had remained vacant since then. Now it was mainly a target for urban explorers, vandals and teenagers on a dare.

"You said that on your world this is where your brother and your dad are being held. But on this world, it's an abandoned building. We can study it and find ways to sneak people out. Perfect, right?" Steve emphasized his point with another flourish toward the building.

"Did you think this never occurred to me?" Buck's rage flared up much more easily these days. Instead of being intimidated by it, Steve was just getting tired of it. "What does it matter what it looks like inside? I know what it looks like on my world. There are guard towers there. There. There. There. And there! Not to mention a ten-foot-high barbed-wire fence!"

Imagining those obstacles in front of the former YMCA added a nice healthy dose of futility to Steve's plan. "OK, but we still haven't been inside. Who knows what we'll find there?"

Steve marched to the door and tugged on a board. It moved so little he may have actually made it tighter. He tried another board. All he got for his trouble was a splinter. Only after Steve hopped around shaking his hand for five minutes did Buck relent. Without saying anything, he pointed to a tree several yards away. His finger traced up it to a line of branches, which were brushing up against an open second-floor window.

"Come on, genius." Buck leapt up to grab the lowest hanging branch.

Despite the appearance of the outside of the building, the floor on the second story was surprisingly solid feeling. It was the mossy, damp smell that reminded Steve that this was not a safe place to be and to watch his every step. He followed Buck down the hall towards the stairs. They passed a half dozen empty rooms. Without any furniture, Steve could only guess at their purpose.

When they got down to the first floor and were standing in the lobby of the main entrance, it occurred to Steve what he was doing. For decades in Longview the ultimate dare had been to sneak into the abandoned Y. Steve had never had any interest in even considering attempting that. Yet here he was.

Even though Steve knew better, he couldn't help be a little

scared that he would see *her*. The rumor that made the dare so exciting was that the Y was haunted by the ghost of a little girl who drowned in the pool. Unfortunately for the kids looking for a good scare, the old Y never had a pool. That was why Steve froze when they went through the double doors on the other side of the lobby. As they entered the cavernous room, they almost stepped into what at first appeared to be a pool. Only when Steve looked around the walls of the room did he see the basketball hoops. Beneath his feet the floor still had the remnants of the painted boundaries of the court— at least the part that hadn't been flooded and turned into a disgusting pond. Even with a crisp fall breeze, the air in the gym was dripping with humidity. An entirely separate ecosystem had evolved inside the building, and the gymnasium was the epicenter. Steve wondered how much water had to have leaked in over the years to maintain this nightmare pond and where it came from. This body of water looked like a permanent feature, not the result of a recent rain storm.

Buck stood on the edge of the court, surveying the room. Boarded-up windows lined the tops of the wall a good twenty feet above the ground. Only one crack let any light into the gym. It was a perfect holding pen.

"So what do you suggest?" Buck asked Steve. "I stop up the toilets and wait thirty years for the place to flood?"

"When you put it like that, it sounds hopeless." Steve picked up a basketball left by the bleachers. His fingers poked through the deteriorated rawhide, releasing a river of filthy water. Steve would never get that hand clean again.

"Assuming I could get past the guards undetected, it's over once I get in here." Buck waved his arm around the dead-end room. "I appreciate what you're trying to do. But there's nothing here that can help. On my world, this building is not a crumbling wreck."

"Maybe there is something here that would be helpful." Steve was grasping for anything at this point. He still couldn't get the WET to work, and returning to his old life had been a disaster. Things with Josh, Dad, and Nicole were tense and awkward. He desperately needed to do something right. "Maybe studying how the building fell apart would show you structural weaknesses. I mean something went wrong to cause this much water to flood in."

Buck considered this as he walked around the court. "That's an interesting idea. We could force a pipe to burst." He pointed to the indoor pond. "It would be a good distraction. I bet a small charge could rupture it."

"Yeah! Yeah! Easily!" Steve ran over to Buck's side. Then he stopped cold. "Wait. No. That's not a burst pipe."

"The roof's intact," Buck pointed out. "Where else would the water come from?"

Steve watched the surface of the pond. It appeared stagnant. A layer of algae covered the surface. Getting on his knees, Steve shined his flashlight across the surface of the water. In the corner of the room, just to the left of one of the basketball hoops, the algae was cleared away and Steve saw a ripple. It was a very tiny one, but it was there. Without thinking, Steve waded into the black lagoon.

"I wouldn't go in that water." Buck stood on the edge, careful to keep his shoes dry.

"I want to see something."

"It's a busted water pipe. I know I'm not the science guy in the group, but it's pretty obvious. Expansion and contraction of water trapped in these pipes over all these winters caused it to burst."

Steve peered around the basket. "That's not right. When they closed up this building, they would have turned off the water and drained the pipes. This water didn't come from the town's water system."

A splintered, water-logged door lay beyond the pond. The handle had long ago crumbled away. Steve put his fingers in the hole where the handle used to be and pulled. The swollen door didn't budge. Making sure Buck didn't see that, he tried again, this time bracing himself for a strong tug. The entire doorframe disintegrated, sending Steve tumbling backwards. His arms pinwheeled, grabbing for anything to save him from being completely submerged in the diseased swamp beneath him. Buck's strong arm snagged his shirt with mere inches to spare.

"Thanks," Steve said.

When Steve was steady, Buck let go and they peered into what once had been a closet. Now it was a high-end hotel for mold. At the bottom of the closet was a bubbling fountain of water. It wasn't a massive centerpiece type of fountain found on a front lawn. This was just a tiny trickle feeding a constant stream of water into the larger pond in the gym.

"See! A burst pipe," Buck proclaimed.

"Yeah!" Steve agreed. "But it shouldn't be."

"So they messed up and didn't shut off the water."

"Exactly! Look!" Steve pointed across the gym to a door under the bleachers. "The lockers are over there. And so are the bathrooms."

"OK." Buck had given up on following this chain of thought.

"They're all downhill and on the same side of the building. The water for this building is pumped uphill from the town reservoir."

"Sure," Buck agreed.

"See those pipes sticking out of the wall?" Buck looked on the opposite wall and saw a spot where some fixture had been ripped away, exposing two pipes. "That's as far as the pipes go."

Steve pointed back to the fountain in the closet. "This is something else. Come on." Turning back, Steve raced through the pond and out of the gym.

For the first time since meeting him, Buck was having a hard time keeping up with Steve as they dashed up the mountain. Buck was actually pushing himself. It would have been a good workout if he weren't so confused about their destination. Steve hadn't explained himself as they dashed back up to the second floor of the Y, then climbed out the window. Buck was surprised at how quickly Steve made his way down the tree, considering how hard it had been for him to get inside in the first place. Whatever his theory was, he was excited about it.

Steve was several paces ahead of Buck when he found what he was looking for. They had only gone about three hundred yards up hill. Steve's breathing was so labored, he couldn't speak and only pointed to the three-foot-tall concrete bunker. As soon as Buck got close enough to it to see he understood. The structure was sticking out of the ground in the middle of the woods. On top of it was a manhole cover that Buck assumed was designed to give maintenance workers access to what was buried underground.

"The aqueduct," Steve attempted to say with his limited air supply. "Pipe."

"This is part of the supply line to town?" Buck asked.

Steve nodded. "Exactly." His breathing was coming easier now. "They never used the aqueduct, but they set up the supply runs to town. Over the years, rainwater has entered the system. That's what made the aqueduct pipe under the building burst."

"But we don't know for sure." Buck crouched down and started to lift the manhole cover. Steve tried to help, but Buck waved him off. Planting his feet, Buck pulled the lid straight up. Beneath him was a ladder leading down into darkness. Buck's heart started racing. He had been in enough tight cramped spaces during missions to know how much he hated them. The crippling grip of claustrophobia was wrapping itself around his chest. But Buck had to push past it. He certainly couldn't let Steve know how scared he was to go down there. Setting the manhole cover to the side, Buck took the flashlight from Steve's hand and started climbing down the ladder.

"Where are you going?" Steve peered down past Buck into the unknown. All of Steve's enthusiasm from the sprint uphill dropped away.

"To see where this goes. You coming?"

"That's OK." Steve took at a step back.

"You wanted to help me, right?" Buck continued his descent without waiting for Steve to respond, mostly because if he heard one good reason that this was a bad idea, he would stop.

When Buck's feet reached the final rung of the ladder, he heard a splash that echoed all around him. Turning on the flashlight was no help. The area at the bottom of the ladder was barely wide enough for one person. Buck was basically standing in an upright coffin. That did nothing to alleviate his rising panic.

Above him, Buck heard clanging as feet made their way down the ladder. Steve's breathing was getting more rapid. Buck knew this was not exhaustion, but fear. He squashed against the wall to make room for Steve.

"Are you scared of the dark?" Buck was not trying to humiliate Steve, but he also didn't need them both freaking out right now.

"Uh... no?" Steve asked in response.

Buck angled the flashlight toward their feet and scanned the bottom of their micro-cell. On either side of them were pipes leading away. He bounced the flashlight between the two tunnels. They were roughly the same size, coming up to their knees and about three feet wide— even smaller than the space they were in now.

"Which one is downhill?" Steve asked.

Buck's eyes jumped from one tunnel to the next. "I don't know." The space inside the concrete box suddenly felt even tighter. He became aware of the overwhelming smell of death and rot around them. "I don't know," he repeated.

He needed to investigate these pipes to know for sure if they led to the abandoned Y. The thought of crawling through one of them in the wrong direction was terrifying.

"It's OK. This is easy to figure out." The calmness in Steve's voice surprised Buck. "Water flows downhill. Point the light at the water."

Buck obeyed as if Steve were his commanding officer. Steve took a piece of paper out of his pocket, balled it up and let it drop. When it hit the stream at the bottom of the concrete box, it was washed away to the right. Solving that helped Buck orientate himself, and calm him down.

That only lasted until he realized the next step. He turned back to Steve. "Can you climb up? I need some room."

Steve stepped onto the ladder and went up a few rungs, leaving enough space for Buck to get down on all fours. The water was cold and the bottom of the pipe was covered in a think sludge. It wouldn't make his journey any easier.

"I'll follow behind you." If Steve was nervous, Buck thought he was doing a good job of hiding it.

"No. Go back to the Y. Wait by that pipe. Start tapping on it. If I can get near it, I'll tap back." That was a good plan, but the truth was Buck also didn't want someone behind him in the tunnel, blocking his way out.

"Just yell, I guess, if you need anything," said Steve.

As Steve climbed up the ladder, Buck stared down the pipe. He turned on the flashlight. The darkness swallowed up the light, illuminating only two or three feet in front of him. What he saw did not inspire him to go forward. The inside of the pipe was coated with a black gunk. The stream of water rolled over what Buck hoped was a twig, but was most likely an animal skeleton. He had to crawl through three hundred yards of this tube. The pipe seemed to get smaller by the second. His head was pounding. His breathing was shallow. This was worse than in the movie theater.

Then Buck thought of his dad, unconscious, being carried out of his house. He thought of Josh, crying out for mom, as he was grabbed by the Everlast officer. They were on the other side of a pipe just like this one. His fears didn't matter.

Even on his hands and knees, Buck was too tall for the tunnel. Flattening himself out in the murky water, he army crawled forward. Keeping the flashlight in his mouth provided a little protection from the unknown. His progress was faster than he imagined. There were no obstacles. And once he got used to the water, it didn't bother him too much. Of course he'd need a six hour shower to rinse it off. Keeping his dad and Josh in his mind drove him forward. At first it was a desperate desire to free them. But, then random memories started popping in his head. Most were surprisingly happy ones. There was last Christmas when they woke up to fresh omelets that Dad had made using black market eggs from Canada. His favorite was of him and Josh pouring over the copy of Reflex they had hidden away in the attic. Josh liked to pretend Buck was Reflex and he was Reflex's newest sidekick.

Before Buck knew it, he heard a metal tapping. A few yards

later he entered another intersection where he could stand up. Above him the pipe ran right to where the tapping was. When Buck tapped back, he heard Steve yelp, then scream "We did it!" That declaration had been severely muffled by the thick wall. It took a few attempts before Steve understood him when Buck yelled for him to meet back at the manhole cover.

Buck couldn't stop smiling on the return journey through the pipe. This time the claustrophobia never came close to slowing him down. Everlast might know about this pipe. On his world it may be in worse condition. But it didn't matter. Buck had a chance. That was all he needed. When he emerged from the manhole cover, he grabbed Steve and hugged him.

"Thank you." Buck covered Steve in the grime and filth from the tunnel. Steve didn't seem to care.

"It's the least I could do." Then Steve heard a muffled sob. "Um... are you crying?"

"No." Buck whimpered.

Stephanie held the note up to show Steve and Buck as they entered the garage room.

"Was he here?" Buck grabbed the piece of paper from Stephanie.

"I didn't see him. It was on the couch when I walked in."

"Why does he want us to go to the aqueduct?" Buck let the note drop to the floor.

"The rift." Steve sat at the desk. "He must have a way to reopen it."

"Great." Buck smiled. "Perfect timing."

"Not really." Stephanie turned to Steve. "I talked to Madison. She never canceled your date. In fact, you two apparently had such a good time that you're going out again this weekend."

The chair clattered to the floor as Steve jumped up.

"I guess we know what Stephen's been doing," Buck noted.

"What do we do?" Stephanie looked from Buck to Steve. "Something isn't right."

"We find out." Steve walked to the door.

Chapter 31

When Steve saw Stephen standing in front of the aqueduct, he had a moment of déjà vu. There was a picture his dad took of him once in the same exact pose— one leg crossed in front of the other, arms behind his back, leaning against the aqueduct. The difference was that, in that picture, Steve was smiling. At that moment in the valley, Stephen was not.

"Thank you for coming so quickly," Stephen proclaimed as Steve, Stephanie, and Buck entered the clearing. The sun was well on its way down, and there were maybe twenty minutes of light left. His head titled to the side quizzically. "What happened to you two?"

"Don't worry about it." In their rush out of the garage, Steve had forgotten that he and Buck were still covered in muddy grime from exploring the pipes.

Stephen continued. "I imagine you all have some questions regarding my whereabouts for the past week."

"With Madison. We know," Stephanie snapped.

"You discovered that more quickly than I estimated you would." Stephen nodded his head toward her to acknowledge her minor victory. His hands remained behind his back. "That is of little matter. My main activities have been working to secure your return to your home dimensions."

Stephen then revealed what he had hidden behind his back: a phone.

"Are you going to call a cab to get us home?" Stephanie asked.

"No." Stephen completely missed her joke. "This has been programed to operate my WET."

"You built another WET?" Steve stepped closer, looking at the mobile device.

"It is completed and functional."

"Where is it?" Buck circled around to the right with his back to the aqueduct support and Steve and Stephanie to his left. Stephen was completely surrounded by all of the Steves.

"At Stepstone. I reached an arrangement with them. In return they provided me with components and facilities more suitable than Dr. Hicks's medieval basement." Stephen swiveled to keep track of the Steves.

"So why didn't you bring it?" Stephanie glared at him.

"The aqueduct is well within the range of my WET. A dimensional rift will still open."

"Hold on!" Steve held out his hands. "Everyone stop for a second. Why did you destroy the WET we were making with Dr. Hicks? I know you did something to it."

Stephen looked up at the tree line. "That was not my doing. Dr. Hicks insisted on replicating the faulty design he had used initially. I argued that he was risking the pro—"

"He's lying," Buck snapped. "Look at his eyes."

Stephen nodded toward Buck. "It is indeed difficult to fool oneself."

"What did you do? You almost killed Dr. Hicks!" Steve's face grew red.

That outburst caused Stephen to take a step back. His heels hit a rock and his arms flew out as a balance check. His right hand had a tenuous grip on the phone. Buck seized the opportunity and launched himself at Stephen, knocking him to the ground. The phone rolled out of Stephen's hand, away from both of them. It landed only a few feet from Steve, who dove onto the device. He was relieved when he checked the modified phone and saw the fall hadn't damaged it.

"Get off of me, you filthy dolt!" Stephen growled, his voice muffled by a face full of earth.

"Stop!" Stephanie rested her hand on Buck's shoulder. "Let him up."

"Thank you." Stephen spat out dirt as Buck released his grip. He got to his feet and looked down at his clothes that were now covered in the same grime that Buck had been caked in.

Steve pressed the home button on the phone. A control panel filled the screen, followed by a prompt for a password.

"It remotely activates the WET." Stephen reached out for the phone. Buck swatted his hand back.

Steve showed the others the screen. "It's password-protected."

"Yes." For the first time since they met him, Stephen was not slouching. "I installed additional security features to prevent you from operating the WET."

"Me?"

"Precisely you. I want to ensure that only I can open the rift." Stephen smiled as he glanced at the confused looks on Steve's, Buck's, and Stephanie's faces. "I apologize. You are missing an integral piece of information. I will be remaining in this dimension as the sole Stephen Buchmann. You three are leaving."

Steve felt something go cold inside of him. There had been

things he thought Stephen may have been planning. He might have been scheming to pull an inter-dimensional bank robbery. Or he might have tried to find a world with space travel. Or maybe he wanted to collect the best basketball players from each world and create the ultimate Dream Team. But this was not anything Steve had considered—to be exiled from everything he knows, spending his life on another world, knowing that an imposter was in his home with his dad and brother. That idea of complete isolation in the multiverse terrified him. It also made him really mad.

"The hell you are!" Steve growled.

Stephen smiled. "I think I am."

"You can't just take over my life?"

Stephen stepped forward and stood face to face with Steve. "I am quite certain I can."

"You're out of your—"

With no warning, Stephen slammed his forehead into Steve's head. The pain was blinding. Steve reached up instinctively with his free hand and covered the point on impact on his forehead. That left his other hand holding the phone relatively unprotected. Stephen took advantage of that and snatched the phone from Steve's hand. Buck charged at him, but Stephen was far enough away to have time to scramble up an embankment away from all three of them.

"No closer!" He held the phone in the air. "This is your only way home. I've equipped the WET with a fail-safe. With the press of a button, I can disable it permanently, trapping all of you here."

"Stephen, this is ridiculous. Steve's not going anywhere," Stephanie declared. "If we can go home, let's just all go back to where we belong. Don't you want to go back to your family?"

"No. This is not complicated." Stephen waved his arms around the valley. "I wish to stay here. In this dimension."

"I'm not going!" Steve declared. "You can't have my life!"

"Why not?" There was genuine curiosity in Stephen's voice. "You didn't want it. You forced it on us the very first chance you had. When you got it back, you made a mess of it. Everything you wanted, you have ruined. By the end of this term, your grade in physics will be so poor it will exclude you from any form of higher education. You are a failure at even that asinine theatrical performance in which you insist on participating. How embarrassing for you to be expelled from a child's make-believe game."

Steve took a breath, ready to refute the claims. Instead, he remained quiet. As much as it hurt to hear, this was all true.

"Shall we discuss your personal life? Is that how you wished it to be? Your father has replaced your brilliant mother with a woman who, under the best of circumstances in the universe, becomes a talk show host."

Stephanie looked at the others and shrugged.

"Let us not forget Madison, the object of your affections. A meek child, you were so terrified to ask her on a romantic excursion that all of us were required to assist you."

If the hate Steve felt for Stephen at that moment had powered lasers in his eyes, he would have burned a hole through his doppelgänger.

"You shouldn't be that upset," said Stephen. "You wanted to make your life the best it could be. Well, I am the very best your life can be."

"There is no way I am letting you stay." Steve was too mad to come up with a reasonable argument.

"I didn't imagine this would happen easily." Stephen looked at Buck and Stephanie to make sure they weren't trying anything. Then he focused back on Steve. "I will make this simple for you. If you do not leave when I open the rift, I will destroy your life. Everything that has ever mattered will be taken from you. I have an email prepared to be sent to several federal agencies detailing every action of the last several weeks. All of us will be rounded up to spend our lives as guinea pigs. Additionally, I have prepared a similar missive for your father and brother. It will explain in clear and concise terms how you deceived them and violated their trust."

Steve bristled at that. "That's not what I did—"

"It is *exactly* what you have been doing! Your scheme in school is a clear violation of the honor code. You had another person taking examinations in your place. That is grounds for instant expulsion. You are concerned that your family will feel betrayed—imagine how violated your beloved Madison will feel. After all, she thought it was you she was kissing... on multiple occasions!"

Steve surged forward. Stephen held the phone in front of himself as a shield, stopping Steve in his tracks.

"Asshole!" Stephanie threw a small rock, hitting Stephen in the chest. It wasn't enough to disable him, but it seemed to hurt him. "We're not going to let you do that to Steve!"

Rubbing his chest, Stephen glared at Stephanie. "Allow me to clarify. If Steve stays here, you all stay here. No one except myself has the code to activate the WET. The only circumstance in which I open the portal is when you all are standing under the aqueduct. Otherwise, you will join in Steve's misery."

Buck roared and managed to take only one step forward before Stephen taunted him with the phone. "Please show the others how much of an imbecile you are. Assault me with all your furious anger. It will do nothing to bring you any closer to opening the portal."

This deflated Buck and the others. There was nothing left to argue. Steve looked at Buck and Stephanie. It was clear what was on their minds: home. He had never intended to take their lives away just so he could be happier.

"This silent protest is a pointless exercise," Stephen proclaimed. "I have no qualms..."

Steve didn't hear the rest of Stephen's rant. One of the few remaining beams of sunlight in the sky reflected off a tiny speck on the aqueduct. It was a single drop of water that fell from the massive structure. A split millisecond later, Steve thought of the picture of his mother that sat on his desk. In that moment, he made a connection that had eluded him and Dr. Hicks for years.

"It won't work!" Steve blurted. "The WET won't work."

"Preposterous!" Stephen chuckled. "Of course it will."

"No. You're wrong. All you're going to end up doing is destroying the WET again."

"You have no idea of which you speak." Stephen looked to the others. "Ignore him. Get under the aqueduct! Or you will never go ho—"

"You can stand wherever you want. It's not going to work." Steve smiled. "If he activates the device, he'll destroy it, and most of Stepstone."

"This is a pathetic game. The WET works!" Stephen waved the phone in the air to prove his point.

"Maybe. But it won't open the portal. You haven't accounted for something."

"And what would that be?"

Laughing as hard as Steve was felt great. "I'm not telling you that."

"Enough of this."

Steve stepped under the aqueduct. "Go ahead. I'll be fine. Try it. See what happens. It won't take you more than a few weeks to make another one. Although, this time, you won't have any lab to use."

Stephen's fingers flew over the phone's controls. Buck

rushed up the embankment, covering the distance between him and Stephen in three strides. He wrenched the phone out of Stephen's hand.

Stephanie looked to Steve. "Are you serious? It won't work?"

"One hundred percent positive!"

"You have to tell him what's wrong with the WET." There was panic in Buck's voice.

"No." Steve crossed his arms. "I won't let him steal my life."

"What about our lives?" Stephanie pleaded with Steve. "We have the right to go home."

"You are all panicking for no reason," Stephen explained. His eyes shifted downhill toward the Stepstone Labs. "There is nothing he has figured out that I cannot decipher. I will run a full diagnostic. If I made an error, I will determine it. It will only take twenty-four hours."

"Great." Steve walked past Buck and Stephanie as he headed out of the valley.

"Nothing has changed," Stephen growled to Steve as he passed him. "Be back here tomorrow night. My terms have not been altered."

"Fine. See you tomorrow." Steve patted Stephen on the shoulder. "You won't figure it out."

Chapter 32

The walls of the back room den were wood paneled and the ceiling was painted forest green. In the dark it looked like the deep woods. Steve always found it calming to sit in there with the lights off at night, even though it also looked like a room in a horror movie. It had been two hours since the confrontation with Stephen by the aqueduct, and the magnitude of what Steve faced was finally hitting him. When he first got home, he was in a daze. Nicole told Daniel that it was how all performers were before opening night and reassured him that Steve was fine. It was the first time Steve had appreciated her advice. And under other circumstances, she may have actually been right.

Steve could have lost it all. He still could lose it all. As far as he could tell there were only two likely outcomes. First, Stephen could figure out what was wrong with the WET setup. He was incredibly smart, and now he knew specifically what to focus on. There was a chance he could solve this by tomorrow. If that happened, Steve, Buck and Stephanie all get sent away. Or, Stephen doesn't figure it out and ruins Steve's life with some tell-all email. What had Steve been thinking? All he did was postpone a world-shattering earthquake by a tiny bit.

"Dad said to leave you alone." Josh flicked on the lights in the back room and jumped onto the couch. "Nicole said you're meditating or something because you think you're going to suck tomorrow."

"She didn't say that... did she?" Steve squinted as his eyes adjusted to the sudden change in the room.

"Who knows what she's talking about. But the play's not until tomorrow, right? Why would you be worried now?"

Josh had a good point. In his obsessing over tomorrow night, Steve hadn't done the simple math. The twenty-four-hour deadline would fall after the play ended. No matter what, he would have to perform. Steve sat up. He would still have to prepare for the play. Now he was nervous.

The physics test!

Steve's blood ran cold. He most definitely had to take that tomorrow. There was no way he would be ready for it. Steve stood up and started pacing.

"You're really nervous?" Josh looked truly stumped.

"Yes. There's a lot of stuff happening tomorrow. A lot!" Steve could feel his heart starting to race. "I'm not sure it's going to work out."

"Of course it will."

"I don't think so. And it's going to be bad when I screw up."

"You won't screw up." Josh looked at his big brother. "You're awesome."

"Uh-huh." Steve had no patience to humor a ten-year-old and his simple logic.

"No, really." Josh jumped off the couch, unable to contain his growing enthusiasm. "You can do anything. You got into that stupid nerd school all by yourself."

"That's different." Steve slowed his pacing as he remembered the weeks leading up to the entrance exam. Getting into Sinatra Edison had been his dream since his mother had first told him about it as a kid. He had always imagined that when he was old enough to apply, Mom would help him study for the entrance exam. But she died years before that time came. So as the exam date approached, he started to question if he should bother at all. If he applied and didn't get in, it would be humiliating. He was the son of a ground-breaking physicist. How could he face anyone, including Dad, if he failed at this? But that wasn't what Mom had taught him about science. Every experiment ran the risk of failure. No one could make any scientific advances if they didn't face that risk. So for weeks Steve focused on nothing but passing that exam, taking practice test after practice test. On the day of the entrance exam, he had no doubts. He passed with no trouble.

"Do you know your lines?" Josh asked.

"Yes." Steve said.

"So, what's the problem?" Josh got distracted by a comic book lying on the coffee table.

Steve had not been concerned about memorizing his part. That had been easy. The blocking was what worried him. Although, he did have numerous notes in his script and he had been to a decent number of rehearsals at this point. If he went through the script again tonight, he would be ready.

That left the physics exam. Five minutes ago, it had seemed overwhelming. As Steve thought more about preparing for the Sinatra Edison entrance exam, he got inspired. When he let go of doubt, he had achieved what had seemed impossible. Now Steve *wanted* to take the physics exam. He wanted Mr. White to throw his hardest material at him.

"I think they should have had Crater in the Reflex movie."

Josh held up the comic and flashed the page with the character called Crater on it. "He's the best villain. Even though I liked the fight scene with Glider. But, Reflex could always beat Glider so easily. He could never stop Crater. Don't you think?"

"Yeah. Probably." Steve hadn't seen the movie. It was all because he had been so afraid of taking chances that he had the others living his life for him. At the aqueduct that night, for the first time in a long time, Steve had made a risky choice without hesitating. It could backfire on him. But Steve didn't think it would. In fact, he knew he was right about the WET.

Steve went over to Josh. "No. I definitely know he could."

As Steve turned to leave the back room, Josh stared at him. "Where are you going?"

Steve felt a burst of energy. He had a massive amount of work to do that night. But he was done being scared of failure. "I'm going to kick Glider's ass."

Nothing was going to stop him.

Chapter 33

"Crap..." Steve muttered to himself as he approached the school. The early morning sun had been shining right in his eyes the whole way from home. It was a hard way to start the day. It had also prevented him from seeing Noah on the sidewalk until he almost walked into him.

Standing on the sidewalk, directly in front of him, was Noah.

"'Crap'?" Noah asked. "That's what you think when you see me now?"

"No!" Steve struggled to shift gears in his head. "That's not what I meant. I was just thinking about physics. I wasn't ready for you yet."

"Whatever." Noah headed toward the school.

"Wait!" This conversation was on Steve's agenda but not until after he was done with physics. His impassioned plea for forgiveness was a pile of note cards scattered on the floor of his brain. "It's different than you think. There's this whole thing with Stephen and the others. And I really need your help. And I'm sorry."

Noah's backpack slipped down his arm as he spun around to face Steve. "So you're apologizing only because you need my help?"

"That's not it. I really am sorry."

"I don't think you are."

"Look, mistakes were made."

"There it is. You still don't think you did anything wrong."

Another apology got stuck in Steve's throat. The new awareness he had achieved after last night vanished. "I didn't!" Steve snapped. "You promised me—"

"I know! You said that a thousand times! Can you get past yourself for a minute? Everything that's happened in the past few weeks has been for your benefit. You never thought about what it did to anyone else."

"Stop turning this—"

"I'm not done yet!" Noah adjusted his bag. "I know how screwed up the thing with Stephanie was. But do you honestly think I would hurt my best friend for a random crush? I really, really liked her. And she stomped all over me. She didn't do it because she's you or whatever. She did it because she didn't like me. That hurt so bad. I would expect my best friend to understand that. I would expect him to try to make me feel better, not worse."

A crowd of students brushed by Noah and Steve, racing to get in the door before the first bell. Noah checked the time on his phone and followed the crowd toward the building. Steve watched Noah bound up the stairs, not sure he recognized his friend anymore.

Steve had been staring at the blue lines on his loose-leaf paper for so long that he could count the tiny red treads sprinkled throughout them. Five minutes had already gone by. Only forty-five minutes were left in class. Even Mr. White's opening threat of doom and gloom had not registered with Steve.

That was not how it was supposed to go with Noah. Guys didn't have emotional blowout fights. They got mad, then yelled and shoved each other. Then it was over. Originally, Steve had planned to finish the exam, then find Noah and apologize. Noah would have forgiven him. Then together they would have stopped Stephen and returned the other Steves to their worlds. Having the very core of their friendship ripped apart was not the plan.

Forty-four minutes left.

Well, one phrase from Mr. White did cut through the Noah clutter: "You'll need every second of this period to complete this exam."

Noah was crazy. That was it. He knew he was wrong and just wanted to turn it around on Steve. Right? That must be it.

Forty-three minutes left.

Being sleep-deprived was not helping matters. Steve had spent all night cramming. Then he ran lines until the sun came up. The blank pages in front of him just reminded him of what a waste all that studying was. He had been kidding himself that he could do this. Pretty soon he would completely fail this midterm, all because of Noah.

Forty-two minutes left.

Stop! he screamed in his head.

Steve slammed his fist down on his desk. Everyone in the room turned to look at him, including Madison. A little smile lit across her face that said, *It's OK, you're going to do fine.* Great! That was more guilt for Steve. Madison didn't know that she was smiling at the wrong guy.

A hand slipped into the aisle out of Mr. White's view. It belonged to Justin and it was making a thumbs-up sign. Was that for Steve? Were they that close now that Justin would risk Mr. White thinking he was signing answers during a test? Noah wanted nothing to do with him, but Justin would toy with suspension for him.

Forty-one minutes left.

He would deal with that later. He would worry about Madison later. This was not Noah's fault either. It was his own fault. And just like with the Sinatra Edison entrance exam, Steve could fix all of this. More importantly, nothing had even happened yet to be anyone's fault. There was still plenty of time to take this exam. Steve was more than prepared for it. In fact, he knew which formula to use for problem one just based on the first line.

Thirty-nine minutes later, Steve set his exam down on Mr. White's desk. And then he didn't move. Mr. White took a perverse pleasure in grading tests and quizzes in front of students. Watching them crumble before his eyes as their grade steadily declined was one of the few perks of his job. He was not actually allowed to force students to endure this torture. However, every now and then, there was someone masochistic enough to weather the humiliation. Today, it was Steve.

"Seventy-four," Mr. White smiled as he put down his pen. A lot of the exam was correct. Where it was wrong, however, it was a blood bath.

Steve's eyes raced up and down the exam. He couldn't walk out of there with a C. The bell sounded and a flurry of students passed him to turn in their papers. Madison gave his shoulder a supportive squeeze as she left the room.

"Mr. Buchmann, please leave." Mr. White waved toward the door. "I don't want to see you cry today."

Nothing could affect Steve's concentration as he analyzed the exam. On number three, he had lost a few points for skipping a step. Problem six, he had used the wrong formula. Numbers nine and ten were connected. That was where he had lost the most points. He reread his solution. The X next to it didn't make sense to him.

"It's Friday," Mr. White said. "That means I don't have to look at you for another two days. Get out."

Steve studied the problem. He had seen his errors in the other questions, but he couldn't figure out what he had done wrong there. His math was correct. Mr. White had made a mistake.

"If you don't leave now, your C is going to become a D."

This had been the situation all semester. Steve had never challenged Mr. White on any of his mistakes. Stephen had, and it had turned his GPA around. The side effect was that Mr. White was out for blood with Steve. Challenging him now could be devastating.

"You look like you want to say something," Mr. White said. "Or did you have a stroke? It's hard to tell with that blank expression."

Steve placed his exam in front of Mr. White and rested his finger on number nine. "This is wrong."

"I know. That's what the big, red X means." Mr. White chuckled.

"No. Your solution is wrong. That should be solved calculating gravitational potential energy."

"I wrote the problem. I know the correct answer."

"Plenty of physicists have discovered problems. Not all of them knew how to solve them at the time." Steve felt light-headed. It was amazing, standing up to Mr. White. Steve flipped his exam over and wrote out a formula. "I assume this is what you wanted us to use. The problem is, the bowling ball in your example is being swung in a circle." He jotted down some figures. "If you carry your logic through—"

Mr. White grabbed the pencil from Steve and snapped it in two. "I have put up with this long enough. You were wrong. Get out and get over it."

Fire burned in Steve's eyes. He took out another pencil and continued to scribble on the paper. "The energy would actually be less than if it were still. That makes no sense."

Mr. White snatched the paper away from Steve. His breathing was deep and fast. Either he was going to pass out or burst into flames. Steve remained at the edge of Mr. White's desk. Their eyes stayed locked on each other until curiosity got the better of Mr. White. He looked down at Steve's notes, then back to Steve, then to Steve's exam. The chair creaked as Mr. White leaned back and looked more closely at Steve's work. The second bell rang. Neither of them moved.

"Damn it..." Mr. White let Steve's paper drop to the desk. "Damn it!"

It took all of Steve's self-control not to jump up and down as Mr. White scratched out the X. Steve stood perfectly still. When he had the exam back in his hands, Steve maintained eye contact with Mr. White.

"Thank you." Steve turned and walked out of the room. It was only when he was in the hall that he looked to see that he now had an eighty-six—a *B*.

Of all the changes that had been made in Steve's life, the lunchroom was the most jarring. The Art Side/Sci Side divide was as strong as ever. Except, now, Steve didn't have to sit in the neutral zone. As soon as he walked in, Madison waved him toward where she was sitting with Tina, Sherri, and Becky. At a table behind her, Justin was trying to get Steve to join him. Somehow Justin was deluded enough to think that he was more enticing than a living, breathing girl.

"I can't believe you wanted to enter the Labyrinth," Madison said as Steve stood next to her.

"That's my worst nightmare." Tina shuddered at the thought.

"You have balls, Buchmann," Becky proclaimed. "I'll give you that."

"I just couldn't wait all weekend to find out my grade," Steve explained.

Madison pulled a chair out for him. "I'm more than happy to wait. When he sees what I put down for that bonus, he's going to dock me points."

Steve looked back into the cafeteria. The Art Side/Sci Side neutral zone was not completely empty. "I kind of have to take care of something. You mind if I skip lunch today?"

"Oh..." Madison looked up at him. "I was hoping we could run lines for tonight."

"I'd really like that. Can we do that after school?"

"Sure." She saw the weight in his eyes. "Is everything OK?"

"Not really." Steve turned to head towards the Art Side/Sci Side divide.

Noah had a large art pad, a few pencils and a sharpener spread out before him. As Steve watched his friend pick up a pencil to sharpen it, he wondered why he had never bothered to sit at the same table as Noah. No one from either the Art Side or the Sci Side used to want to sit with them. Yet they still followed the unwritten rule keeping the sides separated.

The sound of the chair being dragged across the floor quieted the whole cafeteria. Steve had not actually meant to draw attention this way. The chair was just too heavy for him to lift. Now all eyes were on Steve as he pushed the chair next to Noah's. All eyes, that is, except for Noah's. He was flipping through pages in his sketch pad.

"I had no idea..." Steve began. With the cafeteria so quiet it had come out much louder than he had intended.

Noah continued to turn pages until he found a fresh one. That was all Steve had really thought of to say. He was hoping Noah would fill in the rest like he always had. That only made the silence in the room more obvious. Steve leaned closer, keeping his voice low, so he wouldn't attract any more attention than he already had. "Noah, please talk to me."

Noah moved his pad away from Steve. This time Steve was slightly louder, still hoping that the rest of the cafeteria wasn't listening in. "Come on. I'm trying to explain."

The only response was Noah tearing out a page from his sketchbook, crumbling it up and throwing it in Steve's face. That elicited an "Ooh!" from the observers.

Steve looked out at everyone. He had lived for so long in constant fear of doing anything that would upset people. Why? Noah didn't worry about what people thought. Maybe to get Noah to listen to him, he needed to be more like Noah.

Steve stepped up onto his chair. "Thank you! Thank you!" There was now even more silence in the room. "Tonight, everything changes! Our two worlds, so long divided, will merge. Tonight, this sterile, cold Sci Sider will perform in the opening night of an Art Sider play." Steve mimed his head exploding. "Will I make a fool of myself?"

"Yes!" an Art Sider screamed out.

"Or will I change your entire world perception?"

"Traitor!" This time it was a Sci Sider.

"Will painters learn to love calculus? Will chemists become sculptors?"

The calls of "Shut up" and "Sit down" exploded

immediately from both sides of the cafeteria. Before they could grow violent, Noah reached up and grabbed Steve's arm.

"OK. Stop. You win. I'll talk to you." Noah glared at Steve, who jumped down from the chair. "What are you trying to prove?"

"That you were right. Sometimes it's worth it to take a risk."

"And sometimes it screws up everything." Noah closed his sketch pad.

Steve slammed his hand down on it. "Yeah, but it shouldn't have. That was all on me. Not you."

Noah nodded in agreement.

"I'm sorry. I was being a terrible friend. I dragged you into the weirdest thing that's ever happened to anyone ever, and you never hesitated for a second to help me. You had every right to walk away. Even after I blew up at you, you didn't turn us in."

"Man, you know I wouldn't do that."

"I know. And that's what makes what I did so much worse. I'm sorry. And the next time a girl me shows up, I'll support whatever you want to do."

"Really?"

"Absolutely. But if I find out I have a sister in another dimension—hands off!"

"Fair enough."

"So will you forgive me?"

"Yes..." Noah became even more serious. "Only if you can get me into the after-party for the play. Those drama parties are dirty and I want in."

"Deal."

Neither of them were about to hug each other, especially not in public. A gentlemanly fist bump marked the end of their argument.

"The only catch," Steve continued, "is I may not be here then."

"Where are you going?"

Every person taking a seat in the auditorium destroyed a tiny bit of Steve's confidence. Standing backstage and peeking through the curtains, so no one could see him in his John Highland, business suit costume. Steve watched as the audience piled in. He couldn't look away. The more people arrived, the less he wanted to go on stage. He checked the time. It was still possible to find Buck and have him take his place. Steve was certain he would ruin everything.

"There are *so* many people out there." Madison's head appeared next to his, watching the audience through the miniscule break in the curtain. "I didn't think about this part."

"I just thought it would be people we knew. I don't recognize anyone out there." Steve tried to sound like he wasn't scared out of his mind, but his voice kept cracking.

Madison put her arm on Steve's shoulder and pointed out to the crowd, keeping her finger close to Steve's face. "I see my mom. I hope she likes the show. She was so worried that I was spreading myself too thin."

"Yeah. Tell me about it." As the crowd found their seats, it became easier to see people. Steve spotted Josh, sitting next to Dad and Nicole. In that second his nervousness disappeared. The smile on Josh's face was pure pride. He was there to see his big brother. Steve knew that no matter what kind of performance he gave, Josh would still be smiling just as big at the end of the show. Now it didn't matter if there were five million strangers watching Steve, as long as his brother was there.

"Come on." Steve let the curtain shut. "We have a show to do. And we're going to be amazing."

Madison's confidence dipped. "You really think so?"

"Yes." That afternoon, he and Madison had run their lines. Each one sparkled with energy. They were ready. "And I know that audience will love you."

Her face lit up. "Thank you." Without warning, she leaned forward and kissed Steve.

It was his first kiss, and it was no quick peck. Her lips lingered on his. Her tongue touched his. Her body was pressed against his.

"Break a leg." With a hop of excitement, Madison spirited away toward the dressing rooms. Steve was left in a daze.

He remained in that state as the play started. His euphoria was only heightened by the audience. They laughed. The audience was laughing at Steve. And it was exactly when he had wanted them to. Well, it was *almost* exactly when he had wanted. He had dragged out his lingering stare a little too long. They saw where he was headed and started laughing before he could say the actual funny part. It was opening night; nothing could be perfect. All that mattered was that they were supposed to laugh at this part and they had.

"*Is that really how you want to start your testimony, Miss Winecart,*" Steve—no, his character, John Highland—asked Madison's character.

Madison huffed in response and folded her arms. It was perfect. It was adorable. Steve was happily lost in the scene. He gently asked John Highland's questions, nodding along to her answers. His interactions with the other characters had gone well—not great, sometimes a little rough. If he had rehearsed those scenes more often, they may have reached a new level. Steve understood this and the audience could tell. But this was a very forgiving crowd.

"*I would like to enter into evidence Exhibit A.*" Steve handed a sheet of paper to Madison. "*Do you recognize this, Miss Winecart?*"

Madison studied the paper. "*This is the letter from the city ordering my daddy to leave his house.*"

She stretched her arm out to hand it back to Steve. Just before he could grab it, she let go, and the paper fluttered to the ground. Madison stared bullets at Steve, although he knew that anger was directed at his character and not at him. As Steve bent down to pick up the paper, the audience roared with approval. Buck never mentioned that she did that. It must have been something she just came up with.

Standing up, Steve placed the paper on the judge's bench, then dusted his suit off. As he spun around, he saw a glimmer in Madison's eye. Her moment of improv had paid off and she was loving it. Looking at Madison, there was only one thing in Steve's mind: their kiss.

Unfortunately, that was all that was in his mind. "*Don't you mean...*"

And then silence. The next line had left his head. His eyes darted around the set as if the words he was supposed to speak were written on a wall. The excitement he'd seen in Madison's eyes was now concern, bordering on mild panic.

"*Don't you mean...*" he tried again hoping to jump-start his brain.

Nothing.

Out of the corner of his eye, he saw something large being waved around off stage. Steve turned his head enough to see Mr. Salinger waving his script binder. He had opened it to the current page in the script and was pointing to the line Steve was supposed to say. Even if Steve could have read twelve-point font from that far away, Mr. Salinger's frantic motions would have made it impossible. When Mr. Salinger's attempt to save Steve failed, he threw his binder in the air. Crystal, standing as always next to Mr. Salinger, watched the heavy script flip through the air. It arced down toward some metal folding chairs. She dived to the ground, catching it just before it could bounce and become a clanging nightmare.

Watching Crystal's death-defying catch was enough to snap Steve out of his loop. *"Don't you mean Mr. Farnsworth's house?"* With renewed confidence, he spun back to face Madison. *"Because that's certainly what the city calls it. Isn't that what it says, Miss Winecart?"* He pointed to the sheet of paper resting on the edge of the judge's bench. Madison was forced to stand and retrieve it herself. The audience loved this.

Either five seconds had passed during Steve's memory lapse, or it had been two hours. Steve never wanted to know how long. He had recovered and the play had continued. He had faced massive humiliation and survived. He had more than survived. His performance had been pretty good. The whole cast had been good. By the time they reached the curtain call, they were all feeling a surge of excitement.

In the darkness after the last scene, the cast lined up on stage for their final bow. Steve remembered his fear of the crowd from barely two hours ago. Now, he couldn't wait to look out into the audience, confident in his performance. As the curtain pulled aside, the cast was greeted with a theater full of people, applauding. It was more intense than Steve had ever dreamed it would be.

One lone figure leapt to his feet. In the glare of the lights, it took Steve a moment to recognize that the leader of the standing ovation was Josh. Their dad and Nicole joined him. The rest of the theater soon followed as the curtain closed again, obscuring Josh from view.

All the euphoria of the show drained from Steve. The reality of the next few hours hit him. When he saw his dad and Josh after the show, he would be saying goodbye to them…

possibly forever. All day, he had been ignoring the reality of his situation. Whether or not Stephen figured out what he did wrong, he could still destroy Steve's life. And it wouldn't just be Steve's life that was hurt. Dad and Josh would be left to deal with the aftermath. It would be just like with his mom all over again... maybe even worse.

The house lights came on and the cast went wild. Steve backed away from them. While the rest of the cast celebrated backstage, Steve slipped into the dressing room and changed. He wanted to have enough time with his dad and Josh before he had to go back to the aqueduct.

Steve grabbed his bag and jogged past the audience members filing out of the theater. Before he got to the back of the auditorium, he could hear the din in the lobby. It was packed. Steve weaved in and out of people, dodging proud parents taking pictures of their kids in full costume.

As he passed Phillip, Steve patted him on the back. "Great job tonight!"

Phillip tilted his head and squinted at Steve. "Yeah..."

Steve hovered in front of Phillip, waiting for a reciprocal, "You were great, too." Instead he got a continued stare.

"OK... see you later then." Steve backed away. Maybe it hadn't been that good of a show. Or had he been that bad that his castmates couldn't even pretend to compliment him?

Steve moved to the outer edge of the room, hoping for a better view to find his dad and Josh. On the back wall, he ran into Kristian, who still had on his Terrible Terry beard.

"Good show," Steve said to Kristian.

"Yeah, I saw you pulling this stunt with Phillip just now," Kristian snapped.

"I... what?"

"Listen up, here's some advice. Stop fishing for compliments. I already told you that you did good tonight, Sci

Sider. Get over it."

Ice ran down Steve's spine. He hadn't considered this possibility.

"You're back!" Madison smiled.

Steve spun around to face Madison. "I never left. I've been—"

"I saw you get in the car with your dad and brother like a minute ago." Madison looked at him. "Why did you change your clothes again?"

Chapter 34

"You were so awesome!" Josh was bouncing in his seat. "You were really acting! On stage! In front of people! It was so cool!"

Daniel looked back at his sons in the rearview mirror. "Steve, you really were fantastic. I've never seen that side of you before. I am so proud of you."

"Thank you," Stephen said as he looked out the window, smiling. All he had ever wanted was his parents' praise. It felt good, even if it was technically for Steve, not for Stephen. Leaning back, watching the porch lights blur together as the Buchmanns' car raced up the mountain toward home, Stephen knew he had made the right decision about tonight.

He had spent all day at the Stepstone lab studying the circuit boards of the WET. Everything was working properly. Steve was obviously bluffing. There was nothing wrong with the WET. Still, he doubted himself. There was no way Steve would have come up with a feint that quickly. He clearly believed he had discovered a fatal flaw in Stephen's work. That was not a chance Stephen had been willing to take. Gary

Trouter was expecting a working WET device on Monday. If something went wrong and it was destroyed, that would ruin Stephen's plans for his perfect life.

What the *hell* did Steve know?

It took all of Stephen's self-control not to melt down into a sniveling, crying child. Steve was not smarter than him. That was impossible. He was not going to let that ungrateful simpleton steal this life away from him. He and Steve were at a stalemate. His previous plan of action had to be abandoned. His new one was much simpler. If he couldn't threaten Steve to abandon his life, Stephen would simply take it from him.

His new plan started before the play had ended. First, there was a quick visit to the dressing room while the entire company was on stage for the courtroom scene. Before the final curtain call, he returned to the lobby. While the applause died down, he hid in the restroom. After a few minutes, he came out and found Daniel, Josh, and Nicole.

"You were fantastic!" Daniel exclaimed.

"So cool!" Josh exclaimed.

Nicole continued, "I have to admit I was impress—"

"Yes. Thank you." Stephen cut her off. Their praise was delicious. However, there was little time to bask in the glory. He needed to remove the Buchmanns from the lobby before Steve and the rest of the cast entered. "Can we go home now?"

"What's wrong?" Daniel asked, feeling his forehead.

"My health is not the issue. There is something very important that I wish to discuss with you."

"What is it?" Daniel whispered as he leaned in closer to Stephen.

"I do not wish to have this conversation here. We will talk at home." Stephen didn't wait for agreement and led Josh, Daniel, and Nicole to the exit. They had nearly reached their goal when the auditorium doors burst open and the exuberant cast made their triumphant entrance. There was more applause. The new commotion would provide Stephen with a renewed distraction to cover his exit.

"Hey!" A hand grabbed Stephen, but he did not slow down.

"Good show!" the voice continued. Stephen glanced back and saw the tall one named Phillip, who was smiling at Stephen as if they had cured cancer.

"Yes. And good job to you as well." Stephen pushed past him, running directly into Kristian. His build was similar enough to Steve's to give Stephen a start.

Kristian clasped Stephen by his shoulders. "I had my doubts about a Sci Sider in the play. Frankly, I still do. But tonight, I was proven wrong."

This was not going to be a short speech. "Thank you. You were sensational as well. Inspiring." Stephen put his hands on Kristian's arms and guided him to the side.

From that point the crowd in the lobby had thinned out. Stephen pushed Josh in front of him to keep the group moving. Just before they passed the last cluster of people, Stephen saw Noah. It would be impossible to convince him that he was this world's Steve. Stephen turned the group around and headed for the other exit.

"Where are you going?"

Stephen was seized from behind. He quickly registered that his assailant was too short and had arms that were too thin to belong to Steve.

"That was... SO. MUCH. FUN!" Madison squealed.

"Indubitably," Stephen agreed. "And you were excellent, Madison." He turned to Daniel. "Would you pull up the car? I'll be out in a minute."

"And who is this young lady?" Daniel asked.

"Please, just get the car."

Daniel eyed Stephen, clearly stung by how easily he was dismissed. Without saying anything else, he led Josh and Nicole outside.

"Are you leaving?" Madison asked as Stephen continued to edge toward the door.

"Yes."

"But you can't. Not yet," Madison pleaded.

Stephen looked around the room, trying to spot the familiar red buzz cut.

"Everyone is talking about going to the diner. You have to come!"

"I would very much like to. However, Josh is not feeling well. We need to get him home." Stephen was at the door now.

Madison was not giving up her pursuit. "You can stay. I'm sure Kristian will give you a ride home after. I really want to celebrate with you tonight."

Over her shoulder, Stephen saw Noah making his way through the crowd. Wherever that one was, Steve would not be far behind. Stephen pulled Madison through the doors in one smooth motion. Once safely outside, he wrapped his arms around her.

Brushing her hair aside, he whispered in her ear. "All I can think about is you. Nothing would give me more joy than spending the evening with you."

Stephen heard her gasp and he smiled. Manipulating Madison was so simple for him. As she stared up at him, he kissed her. It was the best performance of any Steve that night. Out of the corner of his eye, he saw the Buchmann family car approaching. "Tomorrow night," he said, "I will be all yours. I promise."

Madison watched as Stephen walked to the street, arriving

just as the car came to a stop. She waved. He only nodded in response. The car was several blocks away before she went back into the lobby.

Every bump in the road knocked Steve into either Noah or Madison. The back seat of Kristian's fifteen-year-old, two-door sedan car was barely big enough for one adult, certainly not for three. If this car had shocks, they were too weak for even this tiny rattlebox. The majority of Kristian's focus while driving was on finding the right song on his phone. In the front seat, Phillip called out any life-threatening objects in their way. Each last second swerve only delayed them and irritated Steve more. Stephen was alone with his family, doing who knows what.

"Why can't we just go to the diner?" Kristian asked as he flicked through a list of albums on his phone.

"Cause Steve needs a ride home," Phillip explained.

"Why's that my problem?" Kristian settled on a song, looked back at the road long enough to dodge around a stray trash can, then changed songs again.

"You're castmates!" Noah explained. "There's a bond."

"What are you talking about?" Kristian looked back at Noah. Phillip gripped the dashboard as the car barely missed a curb. "You weren't even in the play."

"But I could still feel the love, man."

"Someone better be saving us the prime booth." Kristian's patience for this errand seemed to have expired.

As they turned a corner and headed up the mountain, Steve, who hadn't been able to find his seat belt, was tossed over on top of Madison. She hadn't said anything to Steve since they left the school. Once Steve realized that Stephen was with his family, he became desperate to get home. All he was concerned with was finding someone with a car. Madison was eager to help, but Steve's explanation of why he wasn't with his dad was clumsy at best. He muttered something about a forgotten bag, traffic, and a cat. His entire existence was on the line, coming up with yet another lie was not on his list of priorities.

The first person Madison went to for a car was Kristian. He also happened to be the only classmate she knew who owned a car. Kristian's post-performance euphoria was just powerful enough to make him forget his dislike of Steve.

While Madison was getting transportation, Noah came over. Earlier he had seen who he thought was Steve turn away from him in the lobby. Steve realized how frantic he was being because Noah asked no questions, but was immediately ready to help. If nothing else, Steve had his best friend back.

"I'm still confused." Madison scooted free of Steve. "You got out of your dad's car because you forgot your bag. But you left without getting it."

"It's really complicated," Steve ventured.

"If you don't want to tell me... that's fine..." Madison completely turned away from Steve.

"I promise I'll explain. I just can't—"

The car made a sudden left turn, sending Steve flying into Noah. They were now speeding toward his house. Getting home had been Steve's main priority. He hadn't thought about what would happen when they arrived at his house and came face-to-face with Stephen.

Steve turned to Noah, who he was smashed into the tiny back seat next to him. This was a bad place to subtly ask for help distracting Madison. "Will you... um..."

"Get out? Yes!" Kristian blurted.

The car caught a little bit of air as they entered the Buchmanns' driveway. Kristian tapped Phillip on the shoulder and pointed to his door. Since the car was a two-door the only way out was through the front seat. Kristian wasn't getting up for anyone. Phillip opened the door and wrestled the seat latch until it came halfway forward.

Madison grabbed the back of Steve's shirt before he could follow Noah out of the car. "Wait! Will you please tell me what's going on?"

"Not here!" Kristian pointed to the door once again. "I. Am. Hungry!"

There was no dignified way for them to get out of the car. Steve snagged his foot on the doorframe and barely caught himself before face-planting on the driveway. Madison scooted across the back seat, then deftly stepped over Steve.

"You're kind of freaking me out." Madison reached down to grab Steve's hands and help him up.

"I'm kind of freaking myself out. Literally." He smiled at his joke. Madison didn't. "I just can't explain right now. I promise I will."

"In or out?" barked Kristian.

"You should go with them." Steve glanced over at Noah, looking for backup.

"Yeah. Let's go to the diner. Steve will catch up with us."

"Nope! Drama club only! Phillip, sit! We're leaving in five seconds." Kristian revved the engine to prove his point.

Phillip pulled back the seat gallantly to make room for Madison. "After you, Madame."

"Phillip, you're a straight up weirdo-creep," Kristian said as he revved the engine again.

"I don't want to leave you. I'll just wait and go with you." Madison stepped away from the car.

"You heard the lady. Phill-UP, we're Phill-OUT!" The car lurched a bit as Kristian put it in reverse. The motion threw Phillip off balance. He managed to catch himself just as the car started rolling backwards.

Steve needed Madison to be somewhere else. There was no way Steve was going to try to explain to Madison what was happening in a rushed fifteen seconds. Stephen's words to him at the aqueduct were clear in his head. He wanted to apologize to her and tell her the truth. This was just not the time. First he had to stop Stephen. He made one last attempt. "Madison, it's probably better if you go with them."

"Great idea!" Noah jumped back toward the car to make sure Phillip didn't slide the seat back yet. "Go with Kristian and celebrate his moment of glory." Noah couldn't help himself and rolled his eyes during that last part.

"Excuse me!" Jamming it into park, Kristian opened the driver side door and sprang out of the car. "What did you just say?"

"Nothing." Noah's face was panicked. "I didn't say anything."

Kristian, leaving the car running, walked toward Noah as if he were in the climactic scene of a family drama. "I heard what you said—"

"The Crystal of Repetition!"

It was Josh. It was a scream of pure excitement that sent a chill through Steve. The Crystal of Repetition was a magic stone from Echelons of War. It let the user make multiple copies of himself.

This couldn't be good.

"I'll be back in a minute. I would like to change my clothes," Stephen shouted down the stairs.

When he entered Steve's room, Stephen could sense something was wrong. He had not assumed that the other

Steves would wait around while their fates hung in the balance. As soon as he stepped completely into the room, a hand covered his mouth.

"Shh," Buck whispered.

Stephanie emerged from the dark corner behind the desk and quickly shut the door. Buck walked Stephen into the room and sat him in the chair. "Where is everyone else?" Buck asked in a hushed voice.

Following his lead on volume, Stephen whispered back, "Downstairs."

This relaxed Stephanie, but only made Buck edgier. "Is there really something wrong with the WET?" he asked through gritted teeth.

That changed the balance. They thought they were talking to Steve. So Stephen would give them Steve. "What are you doing here?"

"Quiet," Buck snapped. "We're asking the questions. Where have you been?"

"The play was tonight," Stephen explained.

"Oh yeah!" Buck's voice got five octaves higher with excitement. "How'd it go?"

"Can you stay focused for a second?" Stephanie said.

This was going to be enjoyable. Stephen let a smile slip out. "It was awesome!" That sounded like an overly simplistic enough review, worthy of Steve's pedestrian descriptive abilities.

"What about the dinner scene? Did the tray-passing bit work?" Buck was now completely focused on the play.

"Flawlessly!" Stephen hadn't seen any of Steve's performance.

"Are you kidding me?" Stephanie shook her head in disgust with how quickly Buck had veered off topic. Boys had shorter attention spans than puppies. "If you don't tell him what's wrong, we'll be stuck here!"

Letting out a heavy sigh, Stephen looked down. This was mainly a move to buy time until the urge to laugh passed. His orchestration tonight had been primarily focused on dealing with Steve. The others thinking he was Steve added a delightful level of obfuscation to the night. He relished what he was about to say.

"I know we were trying to deal with this ourselves." Stephen paused to really nail the pathetic whimper of Steve's voice. "But I didn't know what else to do."

Watching their eyes as they each jumped to different conclusions was pure ecstasy. The tension was too much. Stephen was definitely going to laugh if one of them didn't speak soon.

"What did you do?" Buck growled.

"I couldn't lose my family," Stephen pleaded. He was really feeling his character now. "I'm sorry."

Stephen turned his head to the door. "Dad!" he yelled. "They're up here!" This was the perfect cap to the conversation Stephen had just been having with Daniel, Nicole and Josh. They were having difficulty believing his claims of interdimensional travelers. This would remedy that.

"Are you crazy?" Stephanie blurted.

When Buck heard the footsteps racing up the stairs, he started scanning the room for a weapon. The lights flipped on as soon as Daniel burst into the room. His eyes danced from one Steve to the other. No matter what dimension they were from, each Steve recognized the look on Daniel's face. This was primal, don't-mess-with-my-family dad rage.

"What the hell is this?" Daniel pushed Buck to the side and grabbed Stephen, who he had spent the past hour with. "Get away from my family."

With the boy he thought was his son behind him, Daniel

looked at Buck and Stephanie. His head swiveled around the room, looking for some sign of a deception. Repeatedly, he tried to speak and no words came out. Nicole and Josh had followed him into the room. Nicole was on the verge of hyperventilating. Josh didn't have that problem at all. He was very familiar with this situation.

"So cool," Josh muttered before shouting, "It's the Crystal of Repetition!"

"Get him out of here," Daniel instructed Nicole. When she didn't move, he snapped again, "Nicole! Now!"

That woke her up. She grabbed Josh by the shoulders and tried to turn him around.

"No way. I'm staying," he protested.

"Josh, go!" Daniel had never used any tone like that with his youngest. Josh backed away. Nicole took his hand and turned toward the hallway. Her scream shocked everyone in the room. Blocking her way was yet another Steve.

Chapter 35

Over the past several weeks, Steve had envisioned this very nightmare scene. His dad would discover the Steves together. All hell would break loose. Being the smart kid that he was, Steve had practiced what he would say and how he would calm down his dad. In none of those situations did he imagine he would be the one barging in on the other Steves with his dad. It had thrown him off completely. Nicole's piercing screaming wasn't helping.

As Nicole backed away from the door, Steve stepped inside and surveyed the room. Everyone was glaring at him. The only person not frozen in place was Stephen. While everyone was looking in Steve's direction, he saw a smile creep across Stephen's face.

"Dad!" Stephen was getting back into character. "That's him. That's the one."

Before Steve had time to register what Stephen could mean by that, his father was charging toward him. Daniel grabbed Steve by the shirt and pushed him against the wall. Nothing could have prepared Steve for that. His father, his protector, was attacking him.

"I don't know what's going on here," Dad barked at Steve. "But no one threatens my son!"

It was the most hateful, soul-crushing thing Steve had ever heard in his life.

"Dad, it's me!" Steve struggled to say, fighting his first instinct to start crying. "It's Steve."

"No, Dad!" Stephen jumped to his feet. "Don't listen to him. He's been doing this for weeks, pretending to be me."

"No!" Steve tried to explain. "He's the one who's trying to steal my life!"

Stephanie and Buck traded looks. For as much time as they had spent with both Stephen and Steve, they were stumped now. Nicole pulled Josh closer to her, more to shield herself than to protect him. Josh's enthusiasm for the situation seemed to have evaporated as soon as his dad had attacked someone who looked exactly like his brother. Whatever was going on was very real and very dangerous.

"Ask them." Steve pointed to the other Steves. "They know I'm the real Steve."

"Excuse me?!" Stephanie snapped.

"What makes you the 'real' Steve?" Buck asked. "I'm just as much Steve as you are."

"That's not—"

Stephanie crossed her arms. "You're all fakes as far as I'm concerned."

"No, I mean tell Dad I'm his son," Steve pleaded as he pointed to Stephen. "And that he's the imposter."

"Stop it!" Dad let go of Steve and looked around the room. Everywhere he turned was a carbon copy of his son. "How is this possible? You're absolutely identical."

Then Dad's gaze rested on Stephanie. His eyes softened. Something in his throat caught when he spoke. "That's...

amazing. You look just like—"

"Steve with boobs!" Josh could barely breathe, he was laughing so hard. Tears were streaming down his face as he crumbled to the floor.

Josh's outburst failed to distract Dad. He just stared at Stephanie. "You look just like your mother—his mother—whatever. You're a mirror image of..." For only a second, tears welled in Daniel's eyes. That was just long enough for Nicole to notice. But another look around the room refocused Dad on Stephen and Steve. "All right. Which one of you is my son?"

"I am!" Stephen and Steve both shouted.

"Dad, this is what I tried to tell you downstairs." Unconcerned about spooking this man who looked like his father, Stephen approached him. "These... dopple-bambers appeared—"

Steve did a double-take when he realized that the key to Stephen's impression of him was to play dumb. "Doppelgängers! You know I know that word... dickhead!"

"It's like I was telling you downstairs, Dad. They appeared out of nowhere," Stephen continued, pointing at Steve. "And that one decided he wanted to send me to another dimension and take over my life. He forced the others to help him, too. He said he'd trap them here if they didn't. And he told me he'd destroy my life if I said anything."

"No! *You* said that!" Steve pleaded to the others. "You were there. You heard him!"

"We heard *one* of you say that." Buck looked from Steve back to Stephen, studying them for some tell.

"It was only when he tried to send *me* back to *his* world that I knew I had to do something." Reaching up to put his hand on Daniel's shoulder, Stephen took his performance to the next level. He forced out a single tear. "I lost Mom. I couldn't lose you, too."

Steve threw his hands in the air. "Oh, come on!"

"There's a simple solution," Stephanie said, pulling Stephen away from Daniel. "Stephen had a remote control for the WET device. Whichever one of these two has it now is him."

Before anyone could concur, Buck grabbed Stephen and pulled him to the other side of the room. The Secret Service didn't give pat downs as thorough as Buck's. When he had checked every inch of Stephen's body, he repeated his search. He still found nothing.

"Come on." Buck gestured to Steve, who willingly raised his arms. He ran his hands up and down Steve's legs and arms, checking pockets and inside his shirt and socks. When he plunged his hands into Steve's right jacket pocket, his face dropped. First he pulled out a Stepstone ID. Then he lifted out the phone slowly so he wouldn't set it off. He backed away from Steve.

"That's not mine," Steve pleaded. "I don't know how—"

Grabbing him with even more force than before, Dad dragged Steve into the hall. "No one threatens my son!"

"I AM YOUR SON!" Steve's world was chaos. All he had left was his desperate plea. "Dad, I'm your Steve! Not him!"

"Nicole, call the police," Dad ordered.

"No!" Stephen ran into the hall. "You can't."

"He's right." Stephanie rested her hand on Nicole's phone. "That will make this a thousand times more complicated." Then Stephanie realized who she was standing in front of, and completely forgot what else was happening. "I am so excited to meet you. I can't believe I'm touching your phone."

Lowering her phone, Nicole gave the most genuine smile Steve had ever seen from her. "Thank you. It's very nice to meet you, too."

"One of these two knows how to open the dimensional

rift. And one knows how to make sure it actually works." Buck glared at Steve and Stephen. "Although he may have been lying, too."

"I wasn't," Stephen blurted out before Steve could.

"Stop doing that," yelled Steve. "I'm the one who knows what's wrong."

"OK. If that's true, then tell us why it won't work." Stephen crossed his arms challenging Steve.

"No!" grumbled Steve. "Why don't *you* tell us?" It was a fourth grade move, but worth a shot.

"I asked you first."

"Yeah," Buck demanded of Steve. "Tell us."

"I can't." Steve could see himself being cornered and couldn't do anything to stop it. "Then *he'll* know."

Stephen nodded to Steve and mouthed, "Checkmate."

All of the Steves recognized Dad's massive sigh. It meant he was done discussing the situation. He was going to rule. His finger jammed into Steve's chest. "You were the one with this controller. Give me one good reason why I shouldn't think you're the cause of all this."

It hit Steve like a flash. It was so obvious. "Because my jacket was backstage during the play. He could have slipped it in then. Reasonable doubt, Dad. You can't convict on that."

Everyone turned when they heard the thud. Buck had punched a perfect fist-shaped hole in the wall. "He's right," he muttered. "No one was in the dressing room that whole second act. He could have slipped the controller in his jacket then."

When his dad let go of his shirt, Steve took a deep breath. It was the first time in what seemed like an hour that he felt any hope. The inkling of a plan was forming. He may actually get through this.

"I have an idea," he offered. "There are details of my life

that no one else could know except for you and Josh. Ask us questions you know only I'd know."

"I like this Steve's idea," Josh declared from the back of the room. Without waiting to see if anyone would follow, Josh raced into the hall and down the stairs. The tense standoff became a confused bunch of shrugs until Stephen followed Josh's lead. In the living room, two photo albums were strewn on the floor. Josh was frantically flipping through the pages. When it didn't have what he wanted, he tossed it aside.

"Be careful with those," Dad scolded.

"Here!" Josh presented a page to Stephen and Steve. On it were pictures of Aunt Leslie with Daniel, Melissa, Steve, and Josh. "Here's your first question. Is Aunt Leslie Mom or Dad's sister?"

"Neither," Stephen said quickly. "We just call her that. She's a neighbor Mom met when I was a baby."

"One point for this Steve!" Josh declared.

"That doesn't really prove anything," said Stephanie. "There's an Aunt Leslie on my world, too."

Clenching his fist Buck added, "Same here. But ours sold out my dad to Everlast."

From the pile of photo albums on the floor, Dad was drawn to one open page. On it was an eight-year-old Steve sitting on the steps of a colonial building. Heat waves could be seen pulsing in the background. Steve's face was red and his shirt was covered in sweat. The scowl on his face directly contrasted with the beaming smile on the face of three-year-old Josh, sitting next to him. Dad presented the picture to Steve and Stephen.

"Where was this taken?" he asked.

"Richmond!" Steve said confidently.

"Sorry." Stephen tapped the picture. "That's the capitol building in Colonial Williamsburg, right... Dad?"

"Yes." Daniel nodded.

"What? We've never gone there." Steve snatched the picture. His heart sank. Yes, they had been there. How could he forget that trip? He had been miserable the whole time. It was in the dead middle of summer in Virginia. When the picture was taken, Steve may have had a mild case of heatstroke. All he wanted to do the whole time was go back to the hotel, but his father insisted that they see all the sites. He had even tried to win Steve over with some ghost stories he knew about the older homes. Nothing had worked. The next two days had just been a series of screaming matches between him and Dad, broken up by swimming in the pool with his mom. Now that nightmare trip was going to screw him over again.

"Come on!" Steve pleaded. "Look how young I was. How could I remember anything about that sucky trip? Ask us something else."

"I don't know," Josh said, considering. "This Steve has two points now."

"Best of five. Please."

The others had taken their eyes off of Stephen and were focusing on Steve. They had already made up their minds.

"Fine," agreed Dad. "I'm not in any rush to pick the wrong Steve." He paced around the room, looking for anything to spark his next question. "OK," he said, looking at the phone. "Last year on Labor Day weekend, we were going to barbecue burgers, but you didn't want to wait for the grill to heat up. Instead we ordered takeout... from where?"

"Labor Day last year?" Steve asked. He could barely remember what they had for dinner yesterday. In his head he ran through all the places they usually ordered from. He decided to go with the family favorite. "I'm not sure. Chinese?"

That was a simple misstep that Stephen turned to his advantage. "Was it pizza? How do you expect us to remember that?"

"How could you forget about that?" Dad shook his head. "We ordered Indian and we all got sick!"

"It wasn't Indian, Dad." Josh took the menu from him. "It was the Mexican place. Remember the brown guacamole?"

Daniel's eyes were cold. He was beginning to feel the weight of this decision. "What was the first movie I took you to?"

It happened quickly and was only there for a brief moment, but pure terror crossed Steve's face. He had no idea what the answer was. The experience of seeing the movie was something that he would never forget. His dad had bought him candy and a soda. His mom had said no soda, but his dad said it was OK as long as she never found out. Steve remembered how big the cola looked in the armrest. At some point the movie got scary, and Steve buried his head in his dad's arm. When the scary part was over, Dad gave him the all-clear. None of that he would ever forget. The movie itself was lost to the fog of time.

"Well?" Dad asked. "Someone has to answer."

"I'm just waiting to see what he makes up," said Stephen.

"I don't remember." It was a whisper but everyone heard it clearly.

"*Rabbit Race.*" Stephen smiled. "There was the part with the tunnel and I got scared and buried my face in your arm." If Stephen had a microphone, he would have dropped it in front of Steve.

"How do you know that? You can't possibly know that! I didn't even know that."

"How could I forget? That was one of Mom's favorite stories."

"Her journals! You read that in Mom's journals!" Stephen had access to Melissa's old journals for weeks. It was all there for him to absorb.

"Or maybe I was actually there and remember it," Stephen pointed out.

"They both have a good point." The confidence Buck had in who was who was fading.

"I got one," Josh offered. "What's Dad's email password?"

"T1m3$t@MP," both Steve and Stephen blurted.

That was the last straw for Steve. Stephen had bled into every part of his life. He lunged toward Stephen but was stopped by Daniel. Just his presence between them chilled Steve and Stephen. For too long, Dad was silent. His eyes weren't focused on the boys but on Nicole.

"I'm sorry," Dad whispered to her. Then he took a deep breath and plowed ahead. "What do you think of Nicole?" He pointed to Stephen. "You first."

"Well, she'll never be Mom..." he started. It took all of Nicole's professional on-air experience to not react. "No one could be. But Nicole is really great. She's perfect for you. She's smart and funny. And I've never seen you happier. I'd love it if you guys got married."

Nicole stood her ground but whispered a "thank you." The joy she was feeling was wiped away when she looked at Daniel. His face was stone and he wouldn't make eye contact with her.

"Your turn," he muttered to Steve.

Since the first time Dad had introduced Nicole to Steve, he had asked this question. Every time, Steve had given an answer like Stephen's. It was a lie to keep peace in the house. It was a lie to keep Nicole happy. It was a lie to keep his dad happy. It was a lie he had been keeping for too long.

"I don't like her." Steve's voice shook. He was damning himself. "She's not right for you. Letting her move in is a huge mistake."

When Nicole gasped, Steve turned to her. "I'm sorry. I don't want to be mean. I know you're not trying to replace Mom or anything. But you know I'm right."

At this point, Steve had nothing to lose. He pleaded with his dad. "You aren't happy. Not really. You used to do fun stuff. We haven't played Pancake Poker since you started dating her. You loved Pancake Poker! I want to play that again. You said one of the things you loved about Mom was that she let you be yourself. Nicole doesn't do that. She's so wrong for you."

"That's enough!" Dad snapped. The other Steves were stunned. Confusion washed over Josh. Nicole was horrified. And Stephen couldn't help but smile.

"I guess it's pretty clear now," muttered Nicole.

"It is." Dad shook his head. "I can't believe I didn't recognize my own son."

He grabbed Steve by the shoulders and pulled him close. Steve braced for some assault. Instead he got a hug, a deep father-son hug. As shocked as Steve was, Stephen was even more so.

"What are you doing, Dad?" Stephen screamed.

"Don't call me that." Daniel kept Steve close. "You're not my son."

"Yes, I—"

"Stop it. Only my real son would know about Pancake Poker."

"Are you sure?" Buck asked.

"One hundred percent." Dad kissed Steve's forehead.

"It's awesome. I forgot about that," Josh said before remembering that Nicole was standing behind him.

"Do you really feel that way?" In a room full of inter-dimensional travelers, all focus had shifted to Nicole. "I'm that awful?"

"Honey. No." Dad reached for her arm, but she brushed him away. There was nothing else to be said. She headed straight for the door.

"Dad, I didn't mean—" Steve started to say.

"I know." Dad patted Steve on the shoulder.

"Where is he?" Stephanie barked. The group turned to see that they were missing one Steve. The answer came in the form of an engine starting. Buck was the first out of the door. Dad's car sped down the driveway, swerving around a confused Phillip and Kristian standing in the driveway.

"Where does he think he's going?" asked Stephanie. "We still have the remote."

"Exactly." Steve looked at the Stepstone ID and the remote in his hand. "Now he has to activate it manually."

Chapter 36

"It doesn't matter. Just go!"

Noah could hear the voices in the house behind him getting louder. Standing in front of him in the driveway, Kristian was puffing out his chest, literally and figuratively. If Kristian didn't still have his stage makeup on, it may have been a little intimidating.

"You said 'moment of glory' very ironically." Kristian was trying to channel Pesci from *Goodfellas*. The vibe he was really giving off was a desperate reality star just kicked out of the house. "Like that would be my only moment of glory ever."

That was exactly how Noah had meant it. "It wasn't ironic. You're hearing things. Go to the diner." Whatever was going on in the house was getting more and more heated. Noah had never heard Mr. Buchmann yell. He had been close to it many times, but the glare and low growl was his go-to angry mode. Today it was all coming out. At some point Kristian would peek outside his self-important bubble to notice the commotion.

Madison had noticed right away. "That sounds bad. Maybe

we should check on Steve."

"No!" Noah yelled. "We should stay out here, and you guys should go."

"I will," said Kristian. "But first I want you to promise me that you'll remember this moment when I'm on the cover of *Time*. Remember how you thought I'd peaked in high school."

"I promise you I'll never forget this moment."

"That sounds ironic, too."

Fumbling with the keys in his hands, Steve burst out of the front door. He only vaguely seemed to recognize there were other people in front of him. Heading straight for Steve's dad's car, he hit the unlock button on the fob and jumped in.

"So *now* he's going to the diner?" Kristian asked.

"Steve," Madison called as she walked toward the car.

Noah realized immediately that wasn't Steve. "Hold on for a second." Noah reached for Madison's shoulder to hold her back. Before he could say anything, Mr. Buchmann's car was in motion.

Not bothering with reverse, whichever Steve was at the wheel turned the car around on the grass and was going forty by the time he was back on the driveway. Phillip froze as the car raced toward him, then shakily swerved around him before making it to the street.

A stunned Madison looked back at Noah. "What was that abo—"

Noah watched Madison's face go blank when she saw another Steve race out of the house. He was followed by another Steve, and Stephanie, who she knew as Natalie. Her eyes danced back and forth. Noah remembered how vertigo-inducing it was when he first saw all of Steve's doppelgängers together.

A Steve approached Kristian very quickly. Kristian had lost the ability to form sentences. In addition to the absurdity of the situation, this Steve looked angry and very aggressive. "We need your car," he barked.

With his brain unable to process what was happening, Kristian just blinked.

"Your keys!" Noah knew this could only be Buck.

That forcefulness from Buck seeped through Kristian's brain just enough to trigger action. "They're still in the car," Kristian muttered.

"What the hell is going on?" Madison blocked Buck's path. "Steve... who... why..."

Gently tapping Madison on the shoulder, Steve said, "Actually, I'm the one you probably want to talk to." Noah knew this wouldn't go well when she backed away from Steve. "I can explain. But it's complicated. I promise I'll tell you everything after."

"After what?" she asked. "Who are they? Where did they come from?"

"A dimensional rift."

"A *what*? How long have they been here?"

"Long enough that you've met them all."

"All? Oh God..."

Even from where he was, Noah could see each second of the past few weeks run through Madison's head. Every laugh, every conversation, every kiss was instantly clear. It had all been a lie.

"I know it's confusing at first, but it gets easier telling them apart." Noah interrupted their moment. He was the only person there who had already experienced anything close to what she was going through.

Madison spun to face Noah. Anger was in her eyes. "You knew, too?" Then Madison's glare shifted over Noah's shoulder. He looked to his left to find Stephanie standing there. "Natalie did you know—" Madison's expression reached a new level of horror. "You're not his cousin, are you?"

"No. I'm one of his doppelgängers." Stephanie's face dropped. "I'm really sorry I lied to you. I know how awful that is. Especially when you were so nice to me."

Madison began looking between Noah and Stephanie. She shook her head. "You two made out! That's so weird." The enormity of the situation was crashing down on her.

At first Noah felt the pain of Stephanie's rejection again. But seeing how Steve's manipulation had hurt Madison so much, Noah realized something. He faced Stephanie. "I wasn't fair to you, was I?"

Stephanie was quiet.

"I guess we were both drunk." Noah was processing this new understanding as he spoke. "Not that it matters. I got the signals wrong. I do that a lot. I'm sorry."

"Well. I did kiss you first. That confused things. But I think I was pretty clear how I felt after that." Stephanie smiled. "Look, Noah, you're an OK guy. You just need to start *actually* listening to girls. Then you'll become a truly nice guy. Got it?"

Noah nodded, still wrapping his head around this new way of thinking.

"We need to go!" Buck barked from the car.

"Nobody is going anywhere." Mr. Buchmann came out of the house, followed by Josh and Nicole. "This whole situation is out of control. I'm not going to let you go off by yourself."

"I'm not by myself, Dad." Pointing to the others, Steve smiled. "We're in this together. And I know how to deal with it."

Before Steve could move to the car, his dad stopped him. "I know you can. I'm still going to help you. I almost sent you to God-knows-where. How did I not recognize my own son?"

Stephanie stood next to Steve's dad. "It's OK. He fooled all of us."

"I'm helping you. No arguments." Normally, an edict like this from Mr. Buchmann was non-negotiable.

Steve just pointed to Josh. "You have to watch him. Who knows what Stephen has planned?" Before his dad could make another demand, Steve continued, "I promise I'll be back." He hugged his dad.

"Let's go!" Buck got in the car and sounded the horn.

"Hey! Wait!" The car horn had snapped Kristian out of his haze. "No one drives my car but me."

"Then you're taking us to Stepstone." Steve led Kristian back to his car. Phillip stepped aside to let all of the Steves pile in.

Noah ran over. "I'm coming, too."

"There's no room," Steve said. "I know you want to help, but please let us handle this."

"If you need any backup..." Noah held up his phone.

"I know. Thank you."

The other Steves groaned when Steve pushed back the passenger seat and shut the door. Inspired by the excitement, Kristian threw the car in reverse and flew backwards. They were down the driveway and speeding through the street before Phillip realized he'd been left behind. Noah surveyed everyone there—Mr. Buchmann, Josh, Nicole, Phillip, and Madison. Each of them was looking to Noah to explain the most unexplainable thing he had ever experienced.

Chapter 37

In theory, the operation of a manual transmission vehicle was simple. In practice, it was far more complicated, especially if the operator was from a world with self-driving cars. Stephen learned this lesson after repeatedly stalling Daniel's car on the steep streets of Longview. To avoid this, he had driven closer to downtown Longview, hoping to find an easy straightaway. The winding roads of the old town offered no such magical passage. That devoured his head start, especially when he had to back track up the mountain to find the right route, stalling out the whole way.

When the car cut out on the final drive up to Stepstone, Stephen just left it on the side of the road. At this hour, the facility was mostly empty. He no longer had his ID, which he had left in the jacket Steve was wearing. But he had been assigned a passcode to access his lab. After a few failed attempts to remember that code, he was able to get inside. As he entered the lab, Stephen turned on the lights and headed straight for the WET—

CRACK.

Stephen fell on his butt and slid backwards on the freshly-waxed floor. It wasn't until his cheek started throbbing that he realized he had been punched... and hard. Standing over him was Buck, who grabbed him by his jacket and lifted him into the air.

"Password!" he barked.

From behind Buck, Steve stepped forward. He studied Stephen, then motioned for Buck to set him down. Steve had hoped to catch Stephen before he got to Stepstone, but unbeknownst to him, Stephen had gone on a useless detour. When they got to the virtually empty lab, they were able to walk right in with Stephen's ID. Steve's voice was measured and controlled when he spoke. "It's time for you to unlock the WET and for all of you to go home."

Buck raised his fist and Stephen slinked down to the floor. "Now," Buck growled.

Steve pulled Buck back. "Stop. This way won't work."

"It's the only way that will work at this point." Stephanie said when they all looked at her. "What? It's true. He's crazy and he's screwed us over. He deserves this."

"Maybe." The thought had been bothering Steve all day. "But he's us."

"He's an evil us," Buck snapped.

"None of us are evil." Steve argued. "I want to hear his side. Why he did it? Maybe we'd have done the same thing in his shoes."

From the floor, Stephen muttered, "You wouldn't be capable of doing this."

"That's not helping," Stephanie said.

"You have no choice." Stephen's mouth was already tender, making every word excruciating. "The only option left for you is to switch places with me. You won't be able to function in this shambles of a life you have now. I, on the other hand, could thrive."

"If you can, I can." Steve reached out and gave Stephen a hand, pulling him to his feet. "Why do you even want my life in the first place? You hate it here. You have this amazing tech wonderland to go back to." Once he was on his feet, Stephen pushed away from Steve.

"Yeah," said Stephanie. "You said this world is a backwater swamp."

"Hey!" Steve swept his arms around the state-of-the-art lab.

"His words." Stephanie pointed to Stephen. "Not mine."

"That doesn't matter." Stephen worked his way free of the group to an open space in the lab. "Because of your stubbornness, all of you will remain stranded on this world."

"Not going to happen." Buck advanced on Stephen, but Steve stepped in his way once more.

"Everyone just stop." Steve sighed and said to Stephen, "I don't belong on your world. You don't belong on this one."

Looking at the WET device, Stephen chuckled. "I will be very happy here, thank you."

"But you'll never really belong here," Steve argued.

"More than I belong there," huffed Stephen. "It's amazing none of you made the connection. Clearly, nurture wins over nature." On the floor was a flat panel that he picked up. "This is a battery. It powers the WET because your electrical grid is too weak. This battery will last decades and contains no harmful chemicals. I learned how to make it in kindergarten. I know of dozens of grade school projects such as this that will revolutionize your world. I will become the most celebrated scientist in history. Nothing else matters."

There was no lightning bolt moment for Steve. Everything just shifted and became clear. For weeks, Steve had only focused on the differences between himself and his doppelgängers. The differences were so glaring. It was fascinating, exciting, and frightening. One small twist in history and he could have been Buck or Stephen. One tiny click in his DNA and he'd have been Stephanie. What he ignored were their similarities. They seemed trivial. They all looked the same. What more was there to think about?

There was plenty. Here were four people from completely different worlds. Their families were different. Their societies were different. Yet, nature overcame nurture. Strip away the brash, the arrogant, and the domineering personalities, and what was left was exactly the same. In each of them was intelligence, concern, and ambition. All of it was wrapped up nicely and hidden behind a common fear.

Steve stared at Stephen. "You're afraid to fail."

The words cut through Stephen. "I'm sorry," he said, recovering. "Fail? I think I just described a very successful life. That you can't recognize that speaks volumes—"

"Not here. On your home world. That's why you won't go back."

"Ridiculous—"

"We all have the same problem." Steve looked to the others. "We won't try because we're afraid to fail."

"Why are you attacking us?" Stephanie glared at Steve.

"I'm not. My point is, we don't have to be afraid." He turned to Stephanie. "You push everyone away because some of your friends were awful to you in middle school. You're afraid that if you open yourself up again it will keep happening. But it didn't with Madison, Sherri, or Tina. They really liked you."

Steve faced Buck. "Same with you."

"That's not my problem," said Buck, ignoring Stephen. He turned toward Steve. "I'm not scared to be in a play or talk to a girl. The dangers I face on my world don't compare—"

"Kinda do." Steve was as shocked as everyone else that he

was saying this to Buck. "All you talk about is how if you screw up, you'll get your family killed. You are scared of failing. You should be. That's a huge risk. But no matter what, you are scared. And it keeps you from doing anything."

Stephen flinched when Steve turned toward him. "That's why you don't want to go back. You're afraid that you're not good enough. Like you said, science rules everything on your world. But the truth is, you aren't any good at it."

"That's preposterous." Stephen laughed. "Your understanding of science is medieval compared to mine."

"Not really." Steve began pacing the room, channeling a John Highland closing argument. "Otherwise, you would have figured out what's wrong with the WET."

"There is nothing wrong with—"

"There is. And that's how I know you're afraid to go home. You would have figured it out by now. You know about a lot of advanced technology, but you don't understand why they work or the theories behind them."

"How dare you?" Stephen marched toward Steve, but Buck grabbed him by the shoulders, stopping his advance.

"I should have noticed it when you tried to tutor me in physics. The reason you got so upset when I wanted you to explain a concept was because you didn't understand it."

"That was like trying to teach a baboon to read!" Stephen screamed. "With no effort, I was able to dominate your trifling class."

"You said it yourself. To you, that class was simple elementary school stuff. You know formulas and facts, but nothing else. You want us all to think you're a genius. And, here, you might be. But not on your world."

Stephen's face boiled red.

Steve kept pressing. "On your world, I bet they think you're kind of dumb."

SMACK.

Stephen's fist smashed into Buck's face. Buck was shocked at how much force Stephen put into his uppercut. It didn't hurt him, but it distracted him enough that he let go of Stephen. Steve backed away as Stephen charged toward him.

"I'm right, aren't I?" Steve smiled at his victory. "You're afraid people will find out how bad you are at science if you try."

Veins bulged in Stephen's neck as he screamed. "THEY ALREADY KNOW!" Stephen snagged Steve's shirt and pulled him to the ground. He smashed Steve's head on the floor and screamed in his face. "They know I'm a liar! They know I stole! Everybody knows! My life there is gone. I will never be able to get it back. That's why I want your life here!"

Buck lifted Stephen up in a bear hug. The back of Steve's head throbbed. Stephanie helped him to his feet.

"You don't deserve your life," Stephen whispered as Buck tightened his grip. "Everything is simple here. You could have anything you wanted, yet you struggled with it. That's pathetic!"

"That doesn't mean you can steal his life." Once Steve was steady, Stephanie walked to Stephen. "This isn't right. Let's just go home."

"The only acceptable life for me as far as my parents are concerned is in the Science Order. My mother had to use all of her influence just so I would be accepted into the Academy. But, I could not keep up. The program was beyond my capabilities. My performance was so poor I was nearing expulsion. Our mid-semester research project was my final opportunity. I was desperate. I found some discontinued research in my mother's files. It was brilliant. However, there must not have been any profitable application for it. She had abandoned it. The data had never been made public. Research fraud is an unforgivable sin on my world and still I turned in my mother's work as my own.

The Professorial Review Council informed me that my report had triggered a top-secret fraud notification. My parents were summoned and my mother recognized her work instantly. She was humiliated. I was expelled and banned forever from the Science Order. My parents were considering sending me to a Reform Institution when I fell into the rift. I am an outcast. There is NOTHING for me to return to."

While they watched Stephen try to regain his composure, the Steves imagined themselves in his position. It wasn't hard. They all had been hampered by goals that seemed unattainable. It was a simple jump in logic to understand how crippling it would be to live in a world where they would be ostracized for their failures.

"You really are an idiot." Steve laughed. That jolted the others out of their commiseration. Stephen remained still, drained from his outburst.

"Show a little compassion for your enemy," Buck added.

"Yeah, what happened to 'He's us'?" Stephanie said.

"He's totally us." For the first time that night, Steve saw a way out. He couldn't stop smiling. "It's the simplest solution in the world, and he can't see it."

In response Stephen grumbled, "Yes. The dimensional rift. That thought occurred to me almost immediately upon arriving on this world. However, as you so emphatically illuminated, my comprehension of it is sorely lacking."

"Then how about this?" Steve walked over to the WET. "You unlock it and I'll explain everything."

"Wait!" Stephanie stormed over to Steve. "Now you're going to help him?"

Buck pushed the now-docile Stephen to the side. "We went through all of this for nothing?"

"No. If Stephen agrees, you can all go home," Steve explained.

In the corner of the lab, Stephen stood quietly. His eyes were locked on the WET. The others waited as he considered the offer. After what felt like an hour, Stephen finally spoke. His voice was humbled. "That would be acceptable."

He walked to the WET, then knelt down to type in a code.

"If I were actually willing to return to my world." Stephen pressed a control key and the WET spun to life.

"What are you doing?" Steve ran over to the WET. The energy readings were increasing exponentially.

"Did I not make myself abundantly clear? No discovery I make—nothing I do—can remedy my situation. I would rather stay here and die." Stephen pulled a chair up next to the WET and sat down

Steve's eyes darted across the readout, then examined the battery attached to it. "He's set a timer."

"To do what?" Buck stood behind Steve, ready to punch something.

"It's going to begin transmitting." His voice was panicked. "Then it will overload and explode."

"You weren't bluffing, were you?" Buck asked Steve.

"No."

"Then let's get the hell out of here." Stephanie pulled Steve's arm.

"I would suggest haste." Stephen pointed to a clock on the wall. "You have only one hundred and twenty seconds."

Buck looked to the exit. "That's not enough time to clear the blast zone. Can you shut it down?"

"No." Steve's voice could barely be heard above the hum of the WET. Then he stood. "But I think I can save us."

Stephen's head snapped to the side to watch Steve. "Impossible."

Sprinting to the entry of the lab, Steve began examining the wall.

"What are you looking for?" Stephanie rushed to Steve's side.

"Some way to get to the pipes in the wall."

"Are you going to try to flood it so it shorts out?" Buck pulled a shelf away from the wall.

"No. It's what I realized at the aqueduct." Steve spoke quickly, but now the panic in his voice was gone. "Both times the WET had broadcast, it discharged massive amounts of energy that were intercepted by resonation that redirected the signal back to the transmitter, creating a sympathetic resonance. That resulted in a cataclysmic overload."

Stephen leaned back in his seat. His eyes were wide with terror.

Both Buck and Stephanie stopped their frantic search and looked at Steve. "That doesn't help us," Stephanie snapped.

"Right." Steve rubbed his head. "The WET sends out its signal through the tuning fork on top of it. That signal is supposed to go to the receiver. But in both cases, the levels were too powerful and the signal went too far. When Dr. Hicks tested his signal, it was caught by the aqueduct, which is basically one giant hollow tuning fork. The signal got locked in a feedback loop like when you put a mic in front of a speaker. Only with this, it built and built until it exploded."

"When my mom and Dr. Hicks tested their WET, the signal was intercepted by the pipes in the walls." Steve gestured to the archway above him. "Which were shaped like a giant tuning fork."

"So how is it going to help if we get to the pipes?" Buck was frantic now.

"We can dampen the vibrations. That's what I realized at the aqueduct. After Dr. Hicks activated his WET, I fell against the support leg. My mass making contact with the structure changed the frequency of the vibrations and opened the rift. It should do it again this time. As long as we do it before the WET reaches critical mass, nothing will go boom."

"Will that help?" Stephanie pointed to the wall. Steve smiled as he looked at the sprinkler nozzle in the upper corner of the ten-foot-tall arch.

There was a crash as Buck cleared everything off of a desk and started dragging it under the arch. Steve was turning to help him when a computer monitor hit him in the chest. Stephen pounced on top of him as he landed on the floor.

"Just let this go!" Stephen cried.

It took a moment for Buck to register what had happened. He let the desk drop and he turned to help Steve. Before he could get there, Stephanie waved him off.

"Keep moving the desk."

Buck hesitated before he realized nothing mattered if none of them could reach the sprinkler. Two scars were dug into the floor as he wrestled the desk across the room.

With his hands locked on Stephen's arms, Steve tried to push his double off of him. He had never been very athletic and doing a push-up with himself under these circumstances was proving impossible. He tried to lift up one knee to flip over, but Stephen had both of his legs pinned.

"Let him go." Stephanie grabbed Stephen from behind, wrapping her arms around his chest. "You're going to get us all killed."

"That doesn't matter." Stephen bent his head down toward his chest. Stephanie's arm was right in front of his mouth. He bit down. She screeched as she released him.

"You know what I know now," Steve began. "You can take that to your world. Let me open the rift."

"They will never believe anything I ever say again. I am a

pariah. I—OWWW!"

Stephanie dug her fingers up into Stephen's nostrils and pulled his head back. It distracted him enough for Steve to roll all of them to the side. When they landed on the floor, Stephen launched his head backward, hitting Stephanie in the face. She lost her grip on him.

Steve was on his knees when Stephen jumped back on top of him, trying to stop him from getting to the sprinkler. He drove his elbows into Steve's back, forcing him to smash his chest into the floor. As Stephen raised his arms up to pound Steve another time, Buck flew into him.

The two of them rolled away from Steve. Buck yelled over at him. "Go!"

The desk was resting just under the sprinkler. On the control panel of the WET, the timer had reached thirty seconds. Despite his aching body, Steve bounded onto the desk. He had to stretch on his tiptoes to reach the sprinkler, but was able to wrap his fingers around it.

THOOOM!

Just like before, Steve felt connected to the entire structure.

THOOOM!

Everything went black. In the center of the arch, a tiny pinprick of light appeared.

THOOOM!

The air around the lab shifted. Light returned, and the area under the arch appeared as two overlapping transparencies. The room was still.

Buck and Stephanie stared into the anomaly. On the floor, Stephen began scooting backwards into the lab. With one hand, Buck grabbed Stephen by the neck.

"I don't know how long this will stay open," Steve informed them.

Stephanie looked at Buck, then up at Steve. "I guess this is goodbye!"

"Yeah." Buck took a breath. "I don't really know what to say."

"Me either." Stretched out holding onto the sprinkler was not how Steve wanted to say his goodbyes. Under the best of circumstances, he didn't like the finality of those words. He had too much loss already in his life.

"Delightful." Stephen squirmed under Buck's grip. "That will save me from having to listen to your trifling emotional—"

Buck pushed Stephen forward. He tumbled into the distortion. The room vibrated as he disappeared into the rift.

"Was that necessary?" Stephanie asked.

"Did you want to deal with him anymore?"

Stephanie shook her head. "If I learned one thing from all this, it's that I'm glad that I'm not a guy." She hugged Buck and blew a kiss up to Steve. "I'm going to miss both of you."

"Me too." Buck tightened his hug. "This has been..." His throat caught and he stopped. When he looked up at Steve, he saluted him. "You renewed my faith in myself today. Thank you."

"I can't ever thank you for what you did for me." Ice ran through Steve's veins as his grip started to slip. He managed to hold on to the sprinkler with one hand. "You better go now."

Buck and Stephanie stepped forward into the distortion. Both of them started to wave to Steve but crossed the event horizon before they completed the gesture. A double vibration hit the room and jarred Steve loose from the sprinkler.

His feet landed on the top of the desk, but he struggled to find his balance, barely keeping from falling backwards onto the floor. When he was steady, he looked around. The lab was still and empty.

Chapter 38

"Just like that, they were gone." Kieron spread his arms apart like he'd just made a bird disappear.

"Just like that." Steve looked at the back of his hand, silent as he thought about his others. "It's funny. When they first got here, it was like living this surreal nightmare. After a couple of days, I actually got used to them being here. Now all of a sudden, it's just me by myself. I feel... alone. Like I lost a twin. Really a triplet. And an evil quadruplet."

"That may be the case, but you have your life back."

"Don't get me wrong. I'm happy for that. I'm just nervous. My backup is gone. Whatever happens now is all me."

"Talk me through the rest of that night."

"As soon as they were gone, I ran out of Stepstone. Dad was waiting when I got home. We talked a little. He had a lot of questions. I spent all day Saturday catching him up on the last few weeks."

"Was he upset?"

"Definitely. But he was more disappointed than upset. I had lied to him and hidden something huge about my life. He said I had been unbelievably irresponsible. The more we talked, the more I understood what he was worried about. They could have all been like Stephen. And they were living fifty feet from where Josh was. Who knows what could have happened?" Steve rested his head in his hands. "I can't... that would have been awful. I felt terrible after that."

"Speaking of Josh. How is he with all this?"

"Pissed." Steve smiled. "That was as close as he would get to the Crystal of Repetition, or whatever, and he missed his chance. I think I'm going to be paying for that for a while."

"You did a good job keeping this a secret until the end. But a lot of people know now."

"Well, Noah and I are good. He won't say anything. Before this weekend, I could have trusted Madison. Now, I don't know. Kristian and Phillip are complete question marks. That could get bad. Then again, they can say whatever they want. Stephen, Buck, and Stephanie are gone. There's no proof anymore."

"Except for the reporter who witnessed everything."

"Nicole. Right. Dad spent most of Sunday with her. When he got back, he wasn't in the mood to talk. I'm guessing it didn't go well. I feel really bad about that."

"This is it, then. You ready?"

"Yes. Absolutely."

A chorus of "Good job"s and "You were awesome"s greeted Steve as he entered physics. Justin stuck his thin, weaselly face right in front of Steve's. "Until Friday, I never understood the purpose of this school's art program. I still don't. But your performance was outstanding."

Some Sci Siders had gone to the play. That was a first. But Steve's joy was short-lived.

From the time he walked into physics, Madison wouldn't look at him. Steve had less-than-zero experience dating in the first place, let alone dealing with a breakup. Although technically, he had never dated her. That would probably not be worth mentioning.

He wasn't sure if he should try to talk to her, wait for her to talk to him, or ignore the whole thing. It only added to the confusion that Tina and Sherri seemed to be just as bewildered by Madison as he was. They cheerily waved to Steve when he walked into class. That stopped the second they saw Madison giving him the cold shoulder.

For as badly as that went, the rest of class was back to normal. Mr. White was on a tear after the exam. Steve was bombarded with questions all through class, but he was able to handle it. He had stood up to Mr. White and survived. Also, Steve had solved a mystery about inter-dimensional travel that had eluded some of the brightest minds in several dimensions. His confidence in his physics knowledge was pretty high.

Lunch provided the biggest surprise of all. As Steve and Noah took their new seats at the same table on the Art Side/Sci Side divide, Phillip joined them. This was their first guest all year.

"So. What happened?" Phillip took out a container of salad with a strong garlicky/fishy smell.

"Yeah. I've been waiting all weekend," Noah added between bites of a very dry hamburger. "Are they gone?"

Steve nodded. It was unnerving to have someone joining him and Noah at their isolated table.

Phillip noticed Steve's look. "Sorry. I can go if you guys want privacy."

"No, man. Stay, Phillip," Noah insisted. "It's cool."

"Yeah," Steve assured him, trying to ignore how much that salad made him want to send Phillip away. "But I need to know first, have you guys said anything to anyone about what happened?"

"Dude!" was all Noah needed to say.

"I swear!" Phillip crossed his heart. "I haven't said a thing. And neither has Kristian. Madison made us promise to keep this secret."

"Really?" That was not what Steve had expected to hear about Madison. "And Kristian was cool with that?"

"Not really..." Phillip played with his salad. "But he agreed on one condition. That Madison talk through all of her emotions with him. He thinks he can draw from it for future roles."

Burger flew everywhere when Noah started laughing. "No wonder Sci Siders hate us!"

In a blur, Madison walked past their table. Nothing else registered for Steve after that. He watched her sit down with Tina and Sherri. They immediately leaned in and fired a million questions at her. Every few moments, one of them nodded their head in his direction. It felt like the entire world was talking about him. Not once did Madison stop eating her food or look back at Steve's table.

"That's ice-cold," Noah said, noticing. "She's mad, huh?"

"I guess so," Steve replied.

"You haven't talked to her yet?" Phillip's mouth dropped open, revealing unchewed lettuce and tomato.

"No." Steve shrugged.

"You have to talk to her now." Noah scolded Steve, pointing at him with a french fry.

A month ago, that declaration would have been followed by a half hour of debate and strategizing on how to approach Madison. Instead, Steve stood and walked directly to her table. "Can I talk to Madison alone for a few minutes?" Steve asked Tina and Sherri.

"What did you do?" Tina asked Steve.

"Yeah," Sherri piled on. "You did something bad."

"It's OK," Madison whispered. "I'll talk to you two later."

"We'll be right there." Tina pointed to a nearby table.

"Actually, we may just wait with those guys." Sherri led

Tina to Noah's table.

A riot could have broken out behind Steve and Madison and neither of them would have heard it. Her silence dominated everything in the room. It was sapping any momentum Steve had.

"I'm sorry," he offered before he could lose his nerve.

Madison pushed her plate away and stared back at him. Her expression was the most frightening thing Steve had ever seen.

Steve started to explain. "I never meant—"

"To hurt me?" Madison snapped. "To lie to me? To play with my mind? To humiliate me? What exactly did you not mean to do? Who exactly am I even talking to?"

"I'm the Steve from this world. I swear."

"That doesn't mean anything to me. Have I ever spent any time with you at all?"

The pause while Steve tried to figure out that answer was the worst possible move Steve could make. All the anger Madison felt was replaced with horror.

"What were you thinking?" Her voice was just a whisper.

"I'm so sorry."

"I can't even complain about this to my best friends! They wouldn't believe me. The only person I've been able to talk to is that idiot Kristian. He's awful and I trust him more than you. Who were those people? Where did they come from?"

"They were versions of me from other dimensions. There was an accident that created a dimensional rift. It brought them to this world."

"And you thought you'd use them to play with my mind?"

"No. That wasn't the plan."

"There was a plan?"

"Sort of... They were going to help me do the things that I didn't think I could do. It just got out of hand. It hurt everybody in my life. I never thought—The only reason I let any of them near you was that I was too scared to talk to you. You're smart, talented, funny, and beautiful. I never imagined you could possibly like me."

"I did. Or one of you at least." For the first time since he sat down, Madison looked at him with something less than outright contempt. "Who was the one on stage Friday?"

"That was actually me."

"You did a good job."

"And you were amazing."

"Thanks."

Silence fell over the table again. Steve knew there was no way that Madison would ever forgive him. And he knew he didn't deserve it. Of all his deceptions those past few weeks, this one was the worst. She had thought she was giving him her trust and affection, and he had taken complete advantage of it. He had also robbed himself of a chance to actually get to know her. The end result of all of this was he still only knew her as a crush. Buck, Stephen, and Stephanie were the ones who actually got to spend time with her. Without another word, Madison stood up and left Steve sitting alone.

The dining room table was covered with books when Steve got home. Josh was going through every role-playing manual, fantasy world encyclopedia, and elfin dictionary in the house. A notebook filled with pages of research was open next to him. He barely registered Steve's presence in the room.

"What's all this?" Steve asked.

"None of your business." Josh closed the notebook and eyed Steve.

"Come on. Tell me." Picking up two books, Steve studied the covers. "This is a history of the countries in Echelon, and this is about spell casting in Narnia. Are you creating some cross-world fan fiction?"

Josh's ten-year-old hands whipped forward and grabbed the items away from Steve. "Leave that stuff alone." Flipping through the books, Josh found the page he'd been on and set them back down on the table.

"Jeez. Sorry. I didn't know it was some top-secret thing."

With more fury than he should have been able to muster, Josh flung his notebook onto the table. "You're not the only one allowed to have secrets!"

Steve took a step back. He had seen Josh angry before, but it had always been some form of unfocused tantrum. This was different. "You're right."

"It sucks, doesn't it?" Josh continued. "When someone hides things from you."

They had had various versions of this conversation over the past two days. None of them had been fights. Josh just wanted to know why Steve had hidden the others from him. Steve didn't know where this new anger was coming from.

"I told you," Steve explained. "I thought it was safer if you and Dad didn't know."

"That's stupid."

Little brothers are great at a lot of things. Cutting to the heart of the matter may be at the top of the list. "I was scared that if you knew, Nicole would find out. Then she would do a story on them... and us."

"You didn't trust me." These were the words of a boy trying to connect with his big brother. "'Cause I wouldn't have told."

"I know. I was being stupid. Next time my doppelgängers from another dimension come to town, I'll make sure you're the first to know."

"That's not funny!" Josh blurted.

Steve had wildly underestimated the course of the conversation. "Josh, what's going on?"

"If they come back again, we may not be able to figure out which one is the real you. Have you thought about that? We barely figured it out this time. What if you hadn't said anything about Pancake Poker? Then you'd be gone... just like Mom."

"No!" Steve pulled Josh into a hug. "I was never going to let anyone send me away from you. I promise I won't ever let that happen. I love you."

Josh relaxed into the hug. It was the longest embrace the two boys had shared. It lasted twenty seconds. "OK. You can stop crying now," Josh said.

"I wasn't the one crying." Steve laughed.

"Whatever."

"So what are you doing?"

"Coming up with a plan. If those double-gangers show up again—"

"Doppelgängers," Steve corrected.

"No. Double-gangers. Not doppel. That doesn't make any sense."

"Fine." Steve relented. "What is this?"

"This is called 'being realistic.' If they show up again, I'm going to find a spell that will let us figure out who the real you is."

"Yeah?"

In a split second, Josh had gone from angry to enthusiastic fanboy. Steve couldn't have been happier to see this side of his brother again. "It could work. See, all the magical devices in Narnia are real objects. Like a wardrobe. If I place an infusion spell from Echelon on one of those objects, I can make one of those mystical objects magical. Then it's just a matter of finding your charm from *Water Lords* and there it is—a Steve detector."

"Is there a spell that will clean up that table quicker?" Dad asked as he came into the dining room from the kitchen. He was wearing the only apron in the house. It was a print of Monet's *Water Lilies* and he had gotten it for Melissa for their first Hanukkah together.

"This is important research," Josh protested.

"I'm sure the world will survive if you have to wait to find the Infinity Gem until after dinner." Dad pointed to the books and then to the shelf in the living room.

"It's the Infinite Cloak!" Josh threw his arms in the air in despair.

"Clear the table." As Dad turned, he saw Steve. "Hi."

It was the kind of "hi" a casual acquaintance would give on the street. Dad never just said "hi" to his kids. He would launch into whatever it was he wanted to say. Maybe Steve had also gone too far with his dad.

"You want me to set the table?"

"If you want." Dad walked back into the kitchen.

Steve followed him. The plates were just to the left of the stove, forcing him to squeeze past his dad. By this point, Dad should have asked him a thousand questions about his day. So far, he hadn't even looked at his son.

Steve pulled four plates down from the shelf, stopped, then put one back.

Dad was taking a tray of potatoes out of the oven as Steve carried the plates to the dining room. Josh had cleared the table, but now all the books were stacked in the corner of the room. When Steve returned to the kitchen, Dad was standing in front of the oven, staring at the tray of potatoes as their sizzling slowed down.

"I heard what you were saying to Josh before." Dad turned and removed his oven mitts. "You need to know that you can trust me with anything. And that I will do everything in my power to protect you and Josh. I would never let anyone hurt you. Do you understand that?"

"I do, Dad. I'm sorry I didn't tell you. I really am."

Dad's eyes were cast down to the floor. He seemed to be gathering his thoughts before continuing. "You were wrong about Nicole. She would never do anything to hurt us." Dad looked up to find Steve's eyes. "If you had told her about the others, she would never have betrayed your trust. But more than that, she would never do any story that would hurt anyone. That's not who she is."

"Tell that to those kids." A month ago, Steve would have said that under his breath after Dad had left the room, and then flinched if he thought anyone heard. Now, he stood there, face-to-face with his father.

"What kids?"

"The kids of those Tarp researchers... the ones who falsified their research. Nicole did that expose on them and they took away their kids. How was *that* helping them? Imagine what would happen if she reported on us. They'd take me and Josh away from you. There's nothing you could do to stop that."

When Dad started laughing, Steve didn't know how to react. "Boychick, those scientist were experimenting on their kids. They had created a second skin application. The FDA rejected their research proposal, so they were testing it *on their kids*. The stupid thing asphyxiated them, sent them to the hospital. The state took away their kids because there were terrible parents. Nicole saved them. That's all she ever wanted to do."

The pain in his father's eyes shook Steve. Had he been too honest? "Dad, I—"

"No. Don't. You may have been wrong about her, but you weren't wrong about me and her. We weren't happy together.

We liked each other. But, that isn't enough. I knew something was missing. I wasn't being honest with myself. I had true happiness before... with your mother. With Nicole I had confused being with someone as wonderful as her with *actually* wanting to be with her." Dad paused. "I'm not going to expect you to understand that now. I'm a lot older than you and I'm still figuring out relationships."

"Dad." Steve hesitated. "Did you and Nicole break up?"

There was a sigh and Dad's shoulders slumped. "Pretty much. We're taking some time apart to figure things out."

"What did she say about Friday?"

"Tons. That was a lot for all of us to process. She did say she would keep all of this secret." Dad's hands reached around and untied the apron. Draping it on the counter, he turned back to Steve.

"That's not how I wanted to tell you about what I thought of you and Nicole."

"I wouldn't imagine it was. But I'm glad you did."

"So, you're not mad at me?"

"No!" It was clear and honest. "Well, yes. But not for what you said. I've wanted you to tell me your honest feelings about her for months now. I thought I'd given you plenty of chances to do that."

"You did."

"Then why did you hold that in for so long?"

"I was afraid." Steve looked at his feet.

"Of what? That I'd get mad at you?"

"No. That you'd be lonely again. You were so happy dating someone. I didn't want to take that away from you."

"Even if you thought she was the wrong person?"

"Yeah."

"Come here." Steve looked up to see his dad with outstretched arms. Without hesitating, he walked into the hug.

It had been so long since Steve had felt this protected. He wrapped his arms around his dad. The smell of Dad's old-man deodorant melted away the memories of the past few weeks.

"You worry too much." Dad roughed up Steve's hair as he released him from the hug.

"I know."

"Then stop. It's holding you back."

"I'm trying."

"Where's dinner?" Josh asked as he entered the kitchen. When he saw his dad and brother smiling at each other, he pushed past them to the stove. "That's not fair that you made me rush and clean off the table if you guys were going to waste an hour talking."

Taking out a spoon, Josh dumped the potatoes into a bowl. As he handed it to Steve, he picked up plate of string beans. "Have you told him what his punishment is yet?" Josh asked Dad.

"My punishment?" Steve was shocked.

"Don't worry about his punishment," Dad told Josh.

"Am I getting punished?" Steve asked.

"No. You're not." Dad picked up the platter of chicken and followed his sons into the dining room.

"He lied to us. He should be."

"I think Steve's learned his lesson. Right?" Dad nodded to Steve.

"Absolutely!"

"Fine." Josh proclaimed. "But that means I get a free pass if I conjure an ice guardian."

"I am willing to take that risk," Dad agreed.

Steve took the dish of string beans and dropped some on his plate.

EPILOGUE

Despite all the tubes and bags hanging off the IV pole, seeing Dr. Hicks in the hospital wasn't as upsetting as Steve thought it was going to be. The smell was the only thing Steve couldn't deal with. It was a false clean that barely hid the odor of bodily fluids underneath. Hicks had awoken out of his coma over the weekend. Doctors were monitoring his progress, but were confident he could be released by the end of the week. Since the immediate danger had passed, Steve had been allowed to visit with him.

"Sympathetic vibrations. I should have seen that." Dr. Hicks shook his head.

Steve shrugged. "I just got lucky."

"Hardly. That took a keen understanding of..." Dr. Hicks trailed off as he jotted something in his notebook. Steve had bought him a clean one on his way into the hospital. He knew that was all Dr. Hicks would be interested in.

"And they have returned to their dimensions?" Dr. Hicks asked as he finished writing and returned to this world.

"As far as I can tell. They're not here anymore."

A cloud passed over Dr. Hicks's face. "How can I be certain you are the Steve from this dimension?"

"My dad will vouch for me."

Leaning back on the pillows, Dr. Hicks closed his eyes. He was much better, but his energy had not yet returned. This was a lot of information to absorb. By now Steve was used to giving people some room to accept these new rules of the universe.

"I have a question." Steve took a breath. "What was Mom doing during the accident?"

Dr. Hicks squinted. "What do you mean?"

"It's important. Where exactly was she standing when you activated the device?"

"Well..." He thought for a second. "She had gone to her spot."

Steve leaned forward. "By the water fountain?"

Dr. Hicks nodded.

"Really?" Steve blurted before remembering where he was. "Really?" he asked again more softly.

"I'm certain."

Silently, Steve danced around the hospital room. Dr. Hicks had not seen Steve this happy in the entire time he'd known him. "What difference does any of that make?"

"She was touching the arch," Steve explained. "I don't think she died that day. I think she opened a rift and was sent to another dimension."

Steve smiled. "And I'm going to find her!"

TO BE CONTINUED...

ACKNOWLEDGEMENTS

Everything that I have ever written I have always sent to two people for their feedback. First, David Kazzie. He asks the tough questions. The ones about those plot holes that I hoped nobody would notice. His notes force me to get to the heart of what needs to be fixed. He can do that because he is an excellent writer. Also because I've known him since we were twelve. All decorum between us disappeared with our 1980s knit ties.

Go to David's website and check out all of his amazing books, available on Amazon, and follow him on Twitter.
www.davidkazzie.com
@DavidKazzie on Twitter

Second is Gino Patti. He has the uncanny ability to point out what doesn't work with what I thought worked great. It's infuriating. But he is always right, which is even more infuriating. Then I have to rewrite everything, which makes me furious. Then my book gets a thousand times better and I'm happy and grateful. He's exactly who you want giving you notes.

Check out his illustrations on his website and follow him on Instagram.
www.ginopattiillustration.com
@ginodraws on Instagram

Bethany Bryan brought an entirely new perspective to this book just when I thought I was finished. She pushed me to find a new depth to these characters. I am extremely grateful for her expert skill in shaping this book's final form.

Team of Steves

Steve Holding designed the cover for this book and its upcoming sequels. We've known each other since our college days and I've been following his work online for years. When it came time to figure out the cover, he was the first person I thought of to visualize the aqueduct and the rift. The end result was better than I imagined.

You can see more of his work on his website and follow him on Instagram.

www.stephenholding.com

@holdingstudios on Instagram

New Jersey Transit has a marvelous thing called "Quiet Cars." Most of this book was written in one of them on the way in and out of Manhattan. Also, I can't thank them enough for their endless delays that gave me even more time to write.

My wife Abby had to live through all of my emotional highs and lows while I was writing this book. That alone would be more than enough to ask of a spouse. Except Abby is beyond supportive. She actually takes this nonsense seriously and weighs her feedback with the same thoughtfulness and professionalism as any project she has in her day job. She will always be the very first person to read anything I write. Thank you for being an amazing wife, mother and creative partner. I love you!

ABOUT THE AUTHOR

The Scott Weinstein of this dimension is the Co-Producer of "Weekend Update" on *Saturday Night Live*, where he has worked for more than twenty years. His previous creative endeavors include the webcomic *After-School Agent*. He lives in New Jersey with his wife and their two children.
www.scottrweinstein.com
@WeinsteinScott on Twitter
@winestene on Instagram

The Scott Weinstein from Buck's dimension was an intern at *Late Night with Jon Blaze* when Everlast rose to power. He was detained along with the cast and writers for "seditious activities." After his release, Scott fled to Canada, where he eventually found work as a stage manager at Second City Toronto.

The Scott Weinstein from Stephanie's dimension worked as a personal assistant to Nicole Davies, until he was fired for bringing her a lukewarm chai tea. To get back at her, he signed a lucrative deal for a tell-all book. But the deal was scrapped when Nicole's lawyers sued him for violating a non-disclosure agreement. Now he works as a janitor at Tarp Scientific.

The Scott Weinstein from Stephen's dimension developed a linguistics AI program capable of accurately composing replies to text messages based on observations of its user. He later lost his job after the Science Board discovered that he had written a *fiction* book about interdimensional travel that utilized *made-up science*. Now he toils among the Dregs as an architect.

Made in the USA
Middletown, DE
03 July 2021